W9-AVN-875

www.crescentmoonpress.com

Rift Healer
Diane M. Haynes

ISBN: 978-1-937254-45-2
E-ISBN: 978-1-937254-46-9

© Copyright Diane M. Haynes 2012
All rights reserved
Cover Art: Tara Reed
Editor: Kathryn Steves
Layout/Typesetting: jimandzetta.com

Crescent Moon Press
1385 Highway 35
Box 269
Middletown, NJ 07748

Ebooks/Books are not transferable. They cannot be sold, shared or given away as it is an infringement on the copyright of this work.

All Rights Are Reserved. No part of this book may be used or reproduced in any manner whatsoever without written permission, except in the case of brief quotations embodied in critical articles and reviews.

This book is a work of fiction. The names, characters, places and incidents are products of the writer's imagination or have been used fictitiously and are not to be construed as real. Any resemblance to persons, living or dead, actual events, locale or organizations is entirely coincidental.

Crescent Moon Press electronic publication/print publication: March 2012 www.crescentmoonpress.com

Rift Healer

Diane M. Haynes

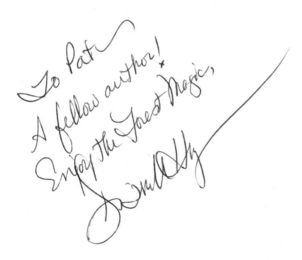

To Pat~
A fellow author!
Enjoy the Forest Magic,

FOR RICK

CHAPTER ONE

FEW VISITORS CROSSED Gisele Westerfield's threshold that snow-filled January in Bidwell, MA. So when she answered the soft knock at the front door, her emotions ranged from shock to pure delight. She was more than thrilled as her favorite relative sat down to tea in her cozy, herb-filled kitchen. Micah, her handsome sixteen-year-old grandnephew arrived bestowing gifts—tiny antique bottles for her essential oils, Belgian chocolate and her favorite guilty pleasure—family gossip.

They'd been laughing and chatting for five or ten minutes, certainly no more, when she noticed that his gaze was drawn to a framed photograph on the wall. Lacey and Haley Miller had posed beside their bikes with Lacey's boyfriend, Taylor, just last summer.

Micah studied the picture closely before he picked it up and his eyes narrowed. Gisele thought she heard him mutter, "That's her. It's really *her*..." He tapped the photo. "Who's *this*?" He pointed to the girl in the center, one of her friend Clara Miller's granddaughters, a pretty girl whose shoulder length, dirty-blond hair gleamed in the July sunshine.

"Don't stand so close, Micah. You're going to steam up that glass."

He moved the picture a fraction of an inch farther from his face. "Who is this again?" he asked as if he misunderstood her non-answer.

"It's nobody." Gisele tried to change the subject. "More tea? Cookies? How's your mother?"

"What are their names?" he asked again, his gaze locked on the one girl.

Gisele took a breath and exhaled. "The boy is Taylor, then Haley and La"

~ ☾ ~

"Haley?"

"Uh- huh." *Darn. It's Haley.* Definitely *Haley.*

"Beautiful name for a beautiful girl," he said, still riveted. "Is she—are *they* your students?"

"Yes," she acknowledged, with an unwilling nod. "I taught them herbal remedies and potions last summer. The cookies are chocolate chip?" His favorite.

"No thanks." He continued to study the photograph. "Will they be coming back?"

That did it. "She's only fourteen, Micah."

"And I'm only sixteen."

"You're a very old sixteen."

"A product of many lifetimes, I guess." He shrugged.

"That and being homeschooled by two highly educated parents," she added.

"Two years isn't such a big age difference." He hung the photo back on the wall. But while they talked during that brief visit, the picture served as a magnet, luring his gaze again and again back to the pretty girl.

Amazing, Gisele thought. *The two girls in the photo are identical twins, but he showed absolutely no interest in Lacey—just Haley, the twin whose intuition had recently kicked into overdrive.*

She sighed in frustration—the gods had been kind to Micah, giving him thick black hair, sculpted cheekbones and a devilish smile. When you added in his intelligence and charm with a self-effacing modesty, he presented a nearly irresistible combination. His prowess with the girls became the envy of his cousins and the talk of the family.

But Haley's grandmother was her best friend.

In one way, a match between her grandnephew and Clara's granddaughter would be a dream come true, creating family where strong bonds already existed. However, Micah's reputation as a heartbreaker wasn't one she wanted imposed on young Haley. She didn't want to risk Clara's friendship either. Gisele was determined to make sure their paths didn't cross.

~ ☾ ~

CHAPTER TWO

AWARE THAT SOMETHING major just took place during that late spring morning, a shift, a deviation, Haley stumbled across the hall to Lacey's room. *Had she felt it too?*

Haley shook her snoring twin, hoping for some kind of confirmation. "Hey, Lace, wake up. Did you feel that?"

"Wha-what's going on?" Lacey asked, voice thick with sleep, still in that fuzzy dreamtime.

Before Haley could answer, Lacey checked her bedside clock with bleary eyes and sat straight up in bed.

"What's wrong? It's two *in the morning!*"

"The earth moved—there was an earthquake. Did you feel it?" Haley whispered.

"Is that all? No, I didn't feel anything. I was *sleeping* like a normal person. Lacey stuck her head under the pillow. "Go away."

Throwing her sister's pillow to the floor, Haley hissed, "No, something important happened. *Listen* to me."

"Tomorrow. I'll listen tomorrow. Now go *away,*" Lacey whined, eyes closed.

"Fine, forget it then," Haley said. Puzzled and disappointed, she retrieved the pillow and threw it back on the bed.

She couldn't fathom how Lacey could sleep through such a thing. It was like two planets collided. The next morning, neither Lacey nor their mother understood her concern. Lacey, the brat, didn't even remember being awakened.

When the Boston news stations mentioned a small quake in the western part of the state, Haley paced the floors until seven before calling her father in Pittsfield. No reported injuries, but she still needed to hear her father's voice. After their parents' divorce last winter, her father moved to a new

~ ☾ ~

job and tiny studio apartment two hours away in Pittsfield, near their grandmother. She and Lacey spent one weekend a month and most of the summer at their Grandma Clara's house in Bidwell for their dad's court-ordered visitation. The other upside to the arrangement was the lessons they took from Gisele.

Her father answered on the first ring. As Berkshire County's Senior Structural Engineer, he oversaw inspections on local bridges and infrastructure. Even with a minor quake like this, she knew he had his work cut out for him. He reassured Haley that her grandmother only lost a few teacups. But he warned her that his work would keep him quite busy over the next few weeks, which probably meant no weekend visits to Bidwell until summer.

"I'm glad Grandma Clara's okay. Have you called Gisele?" she asked.

"No, I haven't," he said. "I'll check on both of them tonight. But right now, I've gotta run. Love you, Hayseed. Hug Lacey for me."

"Bye Dad," she said to dead air.

She called Gisele, but only reached the answering machine.

Online she discovered the epicenter of the quake, with a magnitude of 5.0 on the Richter scale, was located in the small New York town of Altamont. On the map, the concentric rings surrounding the tiny town eased out fifty miles, just touching Bidwell, MA. So, no big deal, right? Then why this huge, painful weight on her chest? And why this nagging feeling that she should *do* something? What could she do?

WHEN SHE FINALLY spoke to Gisele that afternoon, her normally warm and talkative herbal teacher sounded reserved, almost stand-offish, to Haley's repeated requests for information. By the time they hung up, Haley felt even more frustrated than before.

Although she worried and obsessed over it for a few days, soon life took over and the earthquake that no one but Haley

~ ☾ ~

cared about, lost its importance. Then the nightmares began. Two or three a week, which featured vague and changeable creatures emerging from dark, wet places. And often upon wakening, she experienced inexplicably itchy palms.

~ ☾ ~

CHAPTER THREE

ON A RARE Friday night when neither she nor Lacey had anything better to do, they walked to the carnival, set up in the Auburn Mall parking lot. They strolled around, chatted with friends, and shared a Belgian waffle. Bored by then, they almost left for home when Lacey spotted the sign, 'Madam Lola, Fortunes Told.'

"No," Haley said, as Lacey started pulling on her sleeve. "Absolutely not. I don't believe in fortune tellers."

"Really? But you believe in unicorns and fairies?"

"Unicorns and fairies are *real*, but fortune tellers–" Haley shrugged and shook her head.

"Oh, you're going," Lacey vowed, giving her a shove.

"Can't." Haley plastered a smug look on her face. "It costs twenty dollars and I only have fifteen."

"I'll give you five. Early birthday present," Lacey shot back, perfectly matching her twin's look in a way no one else on earth could. Haley glanced skyward in exasperation but allowed Lacey to push her into the small, exotically scented tent whose interior was draped in lavender flowing curtains. A small doily-covered table held a thick white candle, a deck of cards and a huge crystal ball. The girls sat down on metal folding chairs facing Madam Lola, whose jet-black hair and thick makeup did little to disguise her advancing age.

"Good evening," Madam Lola welcomed them. "You vish see future?" she asked with an accent reminiscent of Dracula. Lacey's mouth popped open. Haley swallowed hard.

Draculola began shuffling the worn cards, dozens of silver bracelets clanging halfway up her arms. "Tventy dollars, please."

Haley reached into her pocket and placed all her babysitting money, plus Lacey's five on the table as the reader

~ ☾ ~

reshuffled the deck with a practiced flair. "You haff question, or just vant a general reading?"

"Uh, just a general reading, I guess," Haley replied after finding her voice.

"Good, ve begin. Cut ze deck."

Lacey began to fidget, twisting in her seat, looking everywhere but at the reader. Haley poked her sister when it seemed like Draculola was reading their body language as well as the cards. After Haley cut the deck about halfway down, Lola revealed the first card.

"Ze Tower," she said. "You've had a bad time. A deevorce or separation recently. Much pain, many changes."

Mouths open, they exchanged astonished glances.

Madame Lola smiled. "Vas difficult, but better now."

The girls nodded, quiet for once.

And with a single card, she has us, Haley thought, frowning as she sat in the stuffy tent. Another card.

"Hmmm," Lola paused. "Next card....Knight of Swords. Good. A dark, handsome stranger comes. You afraid," her accented voice lowered as she looked at Haley. "But he vaits for you."

"*Vaits?*"

"*Waits*, dummy," Lacey said, shaking her head. "He *waits* for you. Keep up."

"Seven of Vands. A battle." She frowned. "A battle without end. You fight vith someone?"

"*Vands?*" Almost afraid to ask, Haley regarded her sister with a questioning look.

"*Wands!*" Lacey made a disgusted face. "Why are you being so difficult? No, we're not fighting with anyone." A pause. "Are we?"

"No." Haley sighed, her chin on her hand as she tried to devise a way to end this disaster. "Except each other."

"You vill," Lola insisted, nodding, "you vill." She turned over another card, then another. "Sun reversed, Moon upright." She frowned, lost in thought. "You are about to have ze most exciting and dangerous summer of your life." A quick intake of breath and Lola's eyes narrowed, as understanding seemed to dawn. She rubbed her hairy chin and looked down

~ ☾ ~

at the cards again before leaning forward. "Take every precaution. Accept all that is given you." She touched her temple. "In my head I keep hearing, 'One vill fall, one vill fall...'"

"When you say 'fall,' do you mean, like, die?" Haley said.

"Maybe. But maybe not."

"One of *us?*" Lacey asked, eyes wide.

"Not sure. Veddy unclear. Be veddy, veddy careful." She turned over another card. "Three of Swords...betrayal." She looked at Haley. "Not him," she continued, pointing to the Knight with a long red fingernail. "Another. A scary, dangerous betrayal." She sat back, "Is good you *both* came to see me tonight." Her pointer finger moved back and forth between the two wide-eyed girls.

"This reading... mostly for you," Lola continued to point her knobby finger at Haley. "But you are included as vell," she nodded at Lacey. "You come back next year. Tell Madame Lola what happens. She gives you new reading–haff price." The girls exchanged glances. "I never do this, haff price readings. You ask around."

What gives? Haley thought. *This doesn't seem normal.*

"Why? What's going to happen?" Lacey asked.

"Kids always easy." Madame Lola spoke as if she were daydreaming. "They vant know school, boyfriends, parents. Easy twenty bucks." She paused, then blinked, alert again. "But this—hard. Hard reading...make me vork. Like, you steal my money. But, yes, you come back next year. Don't forget. Haff price."

Still a bit confused, Haley indicated the cards on the table. "*All* of this will happen *this* summer?"

"Yes." Madam Lola scooped up the cards. The Knight of Swords popped out, as Tarot cards sometimes do, landing right-side up in front of Haley, startling her.

"Your soul-mate," Lola said, her voice low as she leaned forward, her finger pointing toward Haley. "Has seen you. He vaits for you." Held by the woman's gaze, she could only swallow.

Lacey thanked her as they nearly knocked each other over in their haste to exit the tent. They dashed away, as if being

~ ☾ ~

pursued by zombies or werewolves. From a safe distance, laughing and giggling, they looked for more greasy food to fortify themselves while they compared notes.

"I have goose bumps," Lacey panted, holding out her arms as proof as they stood in front of the fried dough kiosk.

"Quick, I have to know—how accurate could that even be?" Haley asked. "'Cause, you know, I'm a little freaked. And what did she mean—he's *seen* me already? Is it someone I know?" She looked around. "Is someone *watching* me?"

"He *vaits* for you." Lacey hunched over and pointed a crooked finger at Haley, who swatted her hand away.

~ ☾ ~

CHAPTER FOUR

BLIND WITH PANIC, Gisele Westerfield crashed through the underbrush of her enchanted forest with no way of outrunning the vile beings known as The Terrors, only seconds behind her. No one who knew the seventy-eight-year-old herbalist would recognize her as this frenzied creature fleeing for her life. *I may die here,* was her last thought before she stopped, hands on knees, chest heaving. As sweat poured from her temples, the casual observer might imagine she'd given up.

True, she could never outrun them. But if she remained calm...

She stood tall in the afternoon sun. With eyes closed, she took a long breath, pulled her pulsing crystal from her pocket and summoned the ancient techniques taught to her by her mother and grandmother. Standing on tiptoe at an angular plane, she locked her elbows and held the crystal straight in front of her. Eyes shut, chin to chest, she levitated six inches above the ground, which would allow her crystal to lead her south to the safety of her cabin. One hand protected her face, the other pointed her crystal as she leaned her body toward her toes and shot forward. Nearly upon her, The Terrors, an ugly collection of shrieking, screaming, flying monsters intent upon biting and slashing at every bit of exposed flesh, wailed their discontent at her narrow escape. She felt the wind from the creatures' wings buffeted her back and shoulders, while leaves and branches struck the front of her old body as she hurtled through the magical forest, her former refuge.

Sanctuary lay just beyond the bounds of the forest when, as she blasted through the last curtain of foliage, she was treated to one final heightened shriek of protest.

She'd never been so happy to see her tiny cabin with its lush herb and flower gardens. Settling lightly on the grass,

~ ☾ ~

Gisele braved a look over her shoulder. Swarms of screeching bats swooped through the trees and peppered the air over the forest, frustrated with their inability to follow her into the protected glade.

Bats?

Not The Terrors after all. Only now, from the safety of her clearing, she remembered. The Terrors come out strictly after dark. So it had been *bats,* hundreds, maybe thousands of them, that had emerged from the rift she'd been trying to heal.

"God help me," she prayed as she watched them mill about the forest. "I am *not* up to this." Nearly breathless, she made her wobbly way to her picnic table, sinking with a sigh onto the hard wooden bench. After a few minutes, with her strength mostly returned, she trudged to her cabin. *This will never do,* she thought. *It's time to make some phone calls. I have to get some experienced help out here. Now.*

While she prepared a pot of calming chamomile tea, Gisele thought about the night of the earthquake. She lost glassware and teacups, nothing irreplaceable. But when she'd checked the calendar, she realized it wasn't the first time a rift-causing earthquake occurred on this date. Fifty years ago, to the day, there'd been another.

Less damaging perhaps, but as it turned out, a killer.

During that quake, unusual serpentine mounds snaked through the trees of her beloved forest. On top of each five-foot mound, a crevasse opened from which various creatures crawled, flew or slithered. Fifty years ago the formations, which she'd dubbed 'rifts,' emitted great quantities of biting flies, beetles and snakes. It took her and a small crowd of magical friends weeks to close and heal all the rifts that developed. She shivered at the memory. This morning she thought history might be repeating itself and today she'd foolishly entered the forest alone, bent on healing any rifts she encountered.

She should've known better.

~ ☾ ~

CHAPTER FIVE

WHILE HER TEA brewed, Gisele located her witch hazel poultice and swabbed her cuts and scrapes, which almost kept her mind off the problem that sickened her heart.

Within the hour, she began calling family and friends. Another mistake. In retrospect, she should have waited a day or so to compose herself. Since she probably sounded like a hysterical old woman, her calls fell upon deaf ears. "Too busy," "too engaged in other activities," "no longer in that realm." All the excuses in the world couldn't disguise their uncaring attitudes. Although she tried frantically to communicate her need, she could tell they didn't believe her.

"What happened to you?" she wanted to scream. Because in the end, only two teenagers agreed to assist. For sport, probably.

They were trained, but so what? At sixteen, her grandnephew Micah and his distant cousin, fifteen-year-old Selena, should be observers, nothing more. Yet, after today's expulsion from the forest, she realized she had no choice but to accept their help. She certainly couldn't do it alone. At her age she should be taking it easy—knitting, reading and resting.

The earthquake made rest impossible.

As she stirred honey into yet another cup of tea, something else stirred in the back of her mind. Ah yes, the *other* issue— Micah and his obvious interest in her student, Haley. The girl's face and the earthquake phone call came to mind. Haley's psychic abilities were increasing as she grew into her Gifts. The girl *knew* things.

Gisele sighed. Unfortunately, at the very time Haley most needed her support and guidance, Gisele's own health issues and this rift problem forced her to pull back.

~ ☾ ~

Why do these infernal rifts have to appear now? She would have a devil of a time keeping Haley out of the forest and away from Micah, especially now that he was aware of her. *And, oh no.* If she remembered correctly, Selena fostered a major crush on Micah for years. Yet another reason to keep her students away from her helpers. Healing the forest would be hard enough without petty jealousies and teenage angst.

If Micah and Selena arrived early enough this summer and if the rifts weren't too numerous, maybe she could still rescue a portion of Haley and Lacey's summer herbal lessons. She sighed again. The situation was ridiculous, hopeless.

Gisele closed her eyes. She was so tired these days, certainly not up to the task at hand. Even with their parents' permission, did she have the right to expose these children to such danger? The perils would remain, no matter what happened. Did she have a choice?

And what would become of her beloved forest, her legacy, should they fail?

Well, at least she knew the answer to *that* question. Her gazing ball showed her that without intervention, the forest would gradually descend into an impenetrable darkness and every wonderful, magical being within would be lost forever.

And now, another one of her headaches. Last year she'd been diagnosed with a slow-growing, inoperable brain tumor. No one else knew, not even Clara. The tumor slowed her down a bit, caused some weight loss, but still, she was coping. She walked to the cabinet which housed her prescriptions, wondering how long she would last under these conditions and with all this stress

~ ☾ ~

CHAPTER SIX

"FIRST DAY OF vacation! Yay!" Haley shoved her sister's shoulder. Riding with their mother, they arrived at Grandma Clara's around noon. Lacey was out of the car, wrapped in Taylor's bear hug almost before the vehicle stopped.

"I've missed you so much," he said as he looked down at her, his deep copper hair gleaming in the July sun. "Did you realize we've been a couple for almost a year now?"

"What a great year," Lacey smiled.

"I've been here for nearly an hour, just waiting to see you. I think your grandmother's going charge me rent. But whatever she wants, it'll be worth it. You know,"—he tilted his head to the side—"you're even prettier than the last time I saw you."

Grinning happily, Lacey stepped back to fully appreciate his new height. "Wow, you've gotten so tall," she said.

"Six inches this year." Taylor smiled as he lifted her chin to kiss Lacey softly on the lips.

"Keep it down, you two." Haley leaned against the car, her arms loaded with their possessions. She closed her eyes and breathed in the smells of Bidwell, home to Gisele's enchanted forest where last year she and Lacey encountered fairies, dragons and unicorns while searching for herbs. She couldn't wait to visit the forest again, harvest some herbs and maybe meet a few supernaturals. "Hi, Taylor."

"Mmmm...hi," he replied while he pulled Lacey into another tight embrace.

"Hello, Taylor." Her mother's icy tone clearly stated, *Hands* off *the merchandise.* Haley smirked at her mother's intrusion.

"Hello, Mrs. Miller," Taylor answered in a way that meant, *we can't* wait *'til you're gone.*

~ ☾ ~

He never even looked up, Haley thought with a sigh. *He's completely devoted to Lacey. Someday, maybe I'll find someone like that.*

The girls wasted not a single moment dragging suitcases up the stairs and changing into swimsuits. Racing back down, they kissed their grandmother hello and their mother goodbye. Their mother's traditional 'words of warning' flew over their heads as they mounted their bikes and together with Taylor, rode down the street.

Next stop: Spot Pond.

TAYLOR AND LACEY sat on the beach gazing into each other's eyes. To keep from gagging, Haley walked around the small beach–ever alert for that dark, handsome stranger.

Too old, way too young, really not handsome, she looked around. *Obviously, it's probably not gonna happen on the first day.*

Glimpsing her mother pulling into the parking lot, Haley turned back and smiled at Lacey and Taylor engaged in a serious lip lock on the blanket. *Might be fun to watch this,* she thought. But then self-preservation kicked in—*she'll drag us back home, two hours into our vacation.* Shaking her head, Haley hurried back to the lovebirds.

"Mom's coming. Get up," she hissed, grabbing a book, while the other two sat up and pretended to be talking. "You owe me," she whispered just before her mother got to the sand.

"Mom!" She waved as her mother scanned the beach. "Did you forget something?"

"Why'd you take off like that?" her mother called as she strode to the trio, one hand on her hip.

"Because we've been waiting all year to come here," Lacey laughed. "What's the problem?"

"I just wanted to tell you to be careful, be good for your grandmother and"–she looked at Taylor–"behave."

"You came all this way to give us a lecture?" Lacey shook her head in disbelief.

The smirk won't help, Haley thought, as she elbowed her

~ ☾ ~

sister.

"I'm a mother, that's what we do." Her mother glared at Lacey and folded her arms over her chest.

"We'll be good, okay? Don't worry," Haley said. "It's *Bidwell*. How much trouble can we get into?"

"Yeah, that's true," her mother agreed. "Are you going to Gisele's?"

"Yep," Haley said. "We'll call her when we get back to Grandma's."

"Go easy on her," their mother warned. "She's getting older, you know. Your grandmother doesn't think she's feeling well."

"We'll help her out. Promise," Lacey said.

"Good. Well, have fun and behave yourselves," she repeated, as mothers do, then hugged her daughters. "You too, Taylor."

She walked away, followed by three eye rolls.

"Taylor, have you heard anything about Gisele?" Lacey said.

"No. When I saw her a few weeks ago, she seemed fine." He shrugged his shoulders. "She's gotten a little thinner, but otherwise, no change that I could see."

"Hope so," Haley said. "I can't wait to see her."

"And I can't wait to go back into the forest." Lacey grinned.

Later at Grandma Clara's, Haley called Gisele, who seemed somewhat distracted and ambivalent about their classes, but in the end, agreed to see them at nine o'clock on Monday morning. Haley tried to convey her concerns to her sister, but–

"Yay!" Lacey exclaimed, hugging a blushing Taylor. "We have all day tomorrow to be together."

Haley and her grandmother exchanged looks.

THE NEXT DAY, with Lacey and Taylor off 'to pick strawberries,' or something, Haley set out on a mini soul-mate hunt. First, she headed to the Bread & Bud for a soda.

Zero.

No candidates.

~ ☾ ~

Likewise for the fifteen minutes she stood outside, fiddling with her bike. Then, off to the hardware store, surely a place where men and boys would gather. No one, other than the oldest, baldest clerk in the universe, appeared on the scene. She bought a keychain.

Finally, she returned to Spot Pond with her book, hoping for better luck.

Nada.

Zilch.

Zippidy-do-dah.

Where is *he? Where is my dark stranger?* She wondered from behind her book, watching the families, the older thirty-somethings and the unsuitables interact. She and Lacey led their lives in quiet competition, which, Haley thought with some pleasure, she usually managed to win—until now. Lacey's long-distance relationship with the ever-attentive Taylor was both sweet and exciting. Everything Haley always wanted. But Lacey saw him first.

Maybe she'd heard Draculola wrong.

Maybe the woman was mistaken.

Maybe *she'd* die an old maid...

Whatever. Somewhat dejected, Haley gathered her things and rode her bike back to her grandmother's house.

Maybe the 'hunting' would be better tomorrow.

~ ☾ ~

CHAPTER SEVEN

THE FOLLOWING MONDAY morning, Taylor arrived earlier than planned. "I haven't been so happy in months," he said, accepting a glass of orange juice from Grandma Clara. He held it up and proposed a toast. "The best summer ever." He stared at Lacey.

Already tired of rolling her eyes, Haley let her chin fall to her chest.

"Please say hello to Gisele for me, girls," her grandmother said. "And behave yourselves, now."

"We will, Grandma," Lacey assured her.

"My palms are itchy," Haley complained as she rubbed her hands on her jeans.

"It means you're coming into money," Taylor said. "At least that's what my mom always says."

"Good. I don't have much of an allowance this year. Maybe I'll do something wonderful, like find a lost dog and get a reward for it." She looked from her hand to Lacey. "Still itchy...are yours?"

"Nope, no reward for me, I guess." She eyed Taylor. "I'm going to be too busy to look for strays."

Haley put an old paper bag on the counter. "Look what I found in Dad's closet. Water guns!" She rinsed off a dusty pink plastic Luger before filling it. "Want one? It's gonna be hot today and I think we should bring them."

"You want to play with water guns?" Taylor looked surprised, but nodded his head. "I'll take one, but it might be the two of us against you. Are you sure you want to do this?"

"What makes you think it won't be us against you?" Haley said with a smile, glancing at her sister.

"Okay, I'm in," Lacey said, filling her poison green Derringer.

~ ☾ ~

"You two will be sorry. I'm a very good shot." Taylor grinned as he held his blue six-shooter under running water.

"Don't cause too much trouble," Grandma Clara called after them as they ran down the stairs. Taylor aimed his water gun at Haley when Lacey knocked his arm away. "Don't get her wet now. It's too cold." She smiled at her sister. "Later."

THEY WHEELED INTO Gisele's secluded driveway at precisely nine o'clock, chattering about another fun summer with their herbal teacher.

Gisele met them with a smile from the tiny front porch of her flower-bedecked cottage, her long silver hair pulled in an untidy bun on the nape of her neck. Stray silver tendrils softened the area around her face, wrinkled by a lifetime of smiles.

"You've lost weight," Haley said. "You look fantastic."

"Yeah, I suppose I have," Gisele's smile wavered a bit as she brushed aside the compliment. "Come in, come in. I've missed you. Welcome back, Taylor."

They took a seat at Gisele's table, set for four. While inhaling the delicious aromas swirling from the oven, Haley studied the wall of jars filled with herbs and potions, a few of which she'd helped gather last year. Against the far wall, Gisele's neatly made brass bed, a riot of color from her handmade patchwork quilt, reflected her personality. But a newly placed room divider cut the room in half while the jumble of pillows and blankets piled on her overstuffed couch, seemed at odds in Gisele's normally everything-in-its-place cottage.

"So tell me about your winter." Gisele pulled a tray of hot, golden honey cakes from the oven. "Was it as bad out your way as it was here? We got six *feet* of snow."

As Haley and Lacey began their story about the previous December's devastating ice storm, a car rolled into the driveway, accompanied by two short beeps. Gisele heard and felt the bass reverberating from Micah's speakers as his favorite Heavy Metal group, Blakk Tarr, wailed in the quiet

~ ☾ ~

dooryard.

Gisele sighed. *Oh, no. How did this happen? I specifically told him to come tomorrow.* He and Haley shouldn't meet. Things would get too complicated, and she didn't have time to referee. It was her own fault, she supposed. She should have told Haley not to come at all. The thing was, she missed the two girls far more than she would have thought possible.

Her problem arrived with the other two—Micah and Selena.

No. The *real* problem, as always, was Micah.

She hurried to the door. Maybe she could put them off, divert them until she could dismiss her students, so that with Micah and Selena, she could attend to the difficult task of healing the rifts. "You weren't supposed to be here 'til *tomorrow*," she told them, sounding ungrateful even to her own ears.

"They let me out of work a day early." Her grandnephew hoisted a duffel bag over his shoulder. Then he grinned. "And Selena didn't keep me waiting, for once."

"You're the one who's always late," the angel-faced blond teased, slapping his arm affectionately.

Gisele glanced back into her cabin and noticed her students' interest in the newcomers. "More students?" she heard Lacey ask Haley, who shrugged. Taylor peered out the door.

"I'm busy at the moment," Gisele said, somewhat ungraciously while trying to close her front door. "I have company. Can you come back in an hour?"

"Don't worry. We'll stay out of your way," Micah assured her. "I'll just toss my gear on the couch."

She watched him glance pointedly at the bikes and grin with recognition. When he looked back at her, Gisele swallowed hard. In that instant, she knew there was nothing, *not one thing*, she could do to keep him from Haley.

"Yeah, we can find something to do." Selena giggled, still flirting with Micah, completely unaware that in one moment, everything had changed. Ignoring her, Micah walked up the stairs.

~ ☾ ~

CHAPTER EIGHT

HALEY STARED AT the dark, handsome stranger in the doorway, completely missing the introductions. *The Tarot reader was right.*

"Close your mouth," Lacey hissed in her ear.

Haley's jaw snapped shut as she realized that she hadn't heard his name. With a quick movement, he was at her side, smiling down at her.

Out of the corner of her eye, Haley saw a flash as Taylor's arm wrapped protectively around Lacey's shoulders. *He needn't have worried,* she thought. *The new guy's interested in me, not her.*

"Sorry I missed your name. What was it again?" he asked.

"Haley." Her face felt hot as he shook her hand, not even bothering to set his bag on the floor. "Um, and yours?"

"Micah." He smiled. His teeth were straight, white and perfect, just like his high, tanned cheekbones, his astonishingly light blue eyes and his thick, black hair. Perfect, all perfect.

They were still shaking hands.

"You gonna to put your stuff down somewhere?" came an annoyed voice, breaking the spell. A short blonde girl stared at Micah, before zeroing in on Haley. "I'm Selena, in case you missed *that* too." She shot a nasty toward them clearly meant to warn away potential adversaries.

"Haley." She released his hand. Uncomfortable looking at either of the newcomers, she stared down at her teacup until her breathing slowed.

"I heard it the first time. Once was enough, I think," Selena said, pulling her china doll face into an unflattering sneer when Haley glanced at her. Lacey cleared her throat, an obvious warning.

~ ☾ ~

"Micah is my grandnephew and Selena is a fourth or fifth cousin once removed, on my mother's side," Gisele explained, winding up the introductions. "Micah, I left fresh pillows and bedding on the couch. You can bunk over there." She waved toward the living room. Nodding at Haley, Micah shouldered his duffle bag and sauntered away. "Thank you both for coming," Gisele continued. "I really can't take care of this mess by myself."

"You're welcome," Selena answered, charming once again. "It's our pleasure to help out. Sorry no one else could make it. They're all so busy, you know."

"Make it? For what?" As usual, Lacey asked the question on everyone's mind.

"Here's the thing." Gisele sighed before addressing her students. "You know, of course, about the big quake." They watched her, nodding their heads, all eyes questioning.

Actually, *two* of them watched Gisele. After a moment, Haley's eyes were drawn elsewhere.

She drank in Micah's form as he bent and stretched over the couch.

"Haley, I'm only going over this once," Gisele said. Before she could tear her gaze away, Micah glanced over his shoulder at her, smiling.

Caught, by *everyone,* Haley realized to her chagrin as she found herself being treated to another sneer from Selena. Blushing, Haley attempted to give Gisele her full attention, even as she heard Micah's low chuckle from the direction of the living room. Could her face get any hotter?

Staring at Haley, Gisele began again. "After the quake, our forest developed rifts, mounds with openings that began releasing dangerous and unwelcome creatures."

Haley's mutinous eyes glanced toward the couch again. *It's like I can't control them.*

"These evil beings must either be destroyed"–when Gisele stopped speaking, Haley dragged her wandering eyes and mind back where they belonged–"or returned to the earth. The rifts must be closed and...healed, for lack of a better word." Gisele's gaze held Haley's as she spoke.

"But where did the evil come from?" Haley asked, anxious

~ ☾ ~

to be part of the discussion and back in Gisele's good graces.

Gisele sighed. "When my ancestors invited magical creatures to our forest, they were followed on the slipstream by various creatures of the night, dangerous wastrels, who continue to inhabit our realm. Occasionally, they resurface–"

"Um, what are wastrels?" Lacey asked.

"And what's a slipstream?" Taylor added.

"Wastrels are evil creatures of various sizes, intent upon wreaking havoc in our world. They're also known as The Terrors. You remember The Terrors, right?" Haley nodded, exchanging nervous glances with Lacey and Taylor, remembering a frightening encounter with those things last year, during a Solar Eclipse. Haley noticed this portion of the conversation seemed to interest Selena and Micah.

"The Terrors," Gisele began again, "only come out at night, which is why we leave the forest well before dusk."

"They chase you," Lacey said, "shrieking and screaming. And if they catch up to you, they'll bite and claw at you and beat you with their wings. There are tons of them and they only stop at the edge of the forest."

"They can kill?" Selena's eyes were round with fear? Or was that excitement?

"It's entirely possible," Gisele answered as Taylor looked away. "The slipstream is a positive flow of glowing energy created by my ancestors, which encouraged magical creatures to travel through the ether and eventually settle here. Unfortunately, its luminescence attracted the wastrels as well." Gisele sighed. "Back to our current problem–*maybe* I can heal the rifts, but I can't do it alone. I could've once, but I'm too...old now, so I need reinforcements. I called family and friends, anyone who might help, but they're all unavailable or uninterested in assisting right now and the rifts grow daily. I can't wait." Her voice held pain, concern and distress that none of her contemporaries would assist in her time of need. "Micah and Selena were the only ones kind enough to lend a hand."

"But why? Why did this have to happen?" Lacey wondered aloud.

"Why does anything happen? Why do good people have

~ ☾ ~

accidents or get cancer? Because life isn't fair," Gisele said with a sad shake of her head. "It just...happened, I guess. Right now there's no other explanation."

In spite of herself, Haley's gaze wandered back to the couch, where she got caught again, this time by Micah. With his long legs stretched in front of him and fingers laced behind his head, he stared back at her, a small smile playing on his full lips.

A peacock would be less obvious. Blushing yet again, she turned in her chair so she couldn't see him without attracting unwanted attention from the others. She bit her lower lip after hearing a low chuckle from the direction of the living room.

"Actually, some of the people you called think you're exaggerating. They said when it occurred before, they fixed the problem and it couldn't ever happen again." Selena's tone was apologetic.

"They're wrong." Gisele swallowed, disappointment showing.

In spite of herself, Haley leaned back and stole a peek at Micah. He sat with his lips pressed together in what she took to be anger, annoyance at least. *You know something and it's making you mad. Wonder what it is.* This time when he caught her looking, he turned away.

"*We'll* help you, Gisele." Taylor was on his feet.

"Tell us what we have to do." Haley knew with all her heart that Gisele couldn't manage this task without them, but she could also read the smug look on Selena's face.

"No. Absolutely not," Gisele insisted. "It's too risky for you to go into the forest without training. I can't take chances with your lives."

With narrowed eyes, Haley cocked a thumb at the tiny gloating Selena. "*She's* helping?" The girl was a runt, a shrimp, a hobbit.

"Yes," Gisele said. "Born into a distinguished magical family, Selena's spent years training in the magical arts. At fifteen, she's still too young, but I am out of options."

"And Micah?" Haley turned, her eyes once again meeting his ice-blue gaze.

~ ☾ ~

"Micah is an Adept, born with strong magical abilities and has been in training with master teachers all his life. Although he's capable of assisting, I'm not happy exposing my grandnephew to the dangers of this forest. Even *with* his parents' permission." Gisele looked at her students. "That brings us to you three. Obviously, I can't bring you into the forest, it's far too dangerous. And I'll be much too busy and exhausted to teach. So, I guess this is it for the summer." She inclined her head toward Micah and Selena. "If the three of us are successful, maybe I'll be able to work with you next year."

"This is going to take *all summer*?" Lacey asked.

"If I remember correctly, that's about how long it took last time," Gisele answered.

Taylor sighed. "I guess if you don't want our help–"

"No," Haley interrupted. "We can help. I know we can, Gisele. You *need* us."

"I'd love to take you up on your offer. Truly, I would. But I can't." Gisele let out a long, tired breath. "Look, we have a lot of work ahead of us. It's time for the three of you to go."

"Gisele," Lacey pleaded.

"I'll call you at your grandmother's and keep you informed," Gisele promised.

Micah moved instantly to Haley's side, again offering his hand. "It was very nice meeting you. I'm sure we'll cross paths again soon." He covered her small hand with his. His light touch thrilled her.

"I hope so." Haley released his hand with reluctance.

~ ☾ ~

CHAPTER NINE

THEY RODE THEIR bikes slowly down the driveway. "We had so much fun hanging out with Gisele in the forest last year," Lacey said. "What will we do with our time now?"

Taylor shrugged. "We could go swimming, or have a water gun fight."

"This sucks," Haley muttered as they meandered down Gisele's street. There was no hurry to get anywhere now. "My hands are itchy again," she frowned as she looked first at one hand, then the other. "You know, I still think we could have helped, somehow."

Taylor nodded. "I feel bad she's going in without us."

"Yeah, maybe we can talk, hey, look at *that*," Lacey whispered, staring into the woods. Haley and Taylor followed her gaze and saw on the edge of the forest, the unicorn stallion. Surrounded by deep green hemlock trees and illuminated by a misty shaft of golden sunlight, he shimmered and glowed in the most magical scene ever. At that moment, the unicorn lifted his muzzle, caught a look at the kids and disappeared, dissolving in a thick curtain of glitter. As the sparkles faded in the sunshine, the three exchanged wide-eyed looks.

"What's he doing out *here*, where anyone driving by could see?" Haley asked, looking up and down the empty street. She knew the unicorns were only found deep in the forest, rarely venturing anywhere humans would catch the slightest glimpse. Last summer, they hiked in the forest many times and saw the unicorns only once. "Let's go in," she said, pedaling her bike over the roots and rocks to where the unicorn first caught their attention. Kneeling down, she spied a trace of glitter still shimmering on the pine needles.

"Is this a good idea?" Taylor asked, astride his bike in the

~ ☾ ~

middle of the road. "We're not carrying crystals, you know." Last year they learned it was unsafe and unwise to venture into the forest without the protection of at least one magical gem from the Crystal Cave.

Haley glanced over her shoulder and motioned them in. Lacey followed her. Haley pointed to a strange mound of earth, a few yards deeper into the sun-dappled forest.

"What *is* that?" Lacey said.

"Not too smart, you guys," Taylor called. "Come back."

"I don't know. I don't remember seeing this before." Haley looked around. Shielded from the road by the stand of hemlocks, the unusual formation stood nearly as tall as a man and about eight feet wide. Somewhat flattened at its apex, it formed a long serpentine line, which eventually disappeared into the forest. Despite its size and length, she thought if it hadn't been for the unicorn, they never would have seen it from the road.

Taylor dropped his bike on the ground and followed them in, huffing with annoyance.

"What are you doing here, nosey?" Lacey asked with a smirk.

"I'm tired of being ignored and—whoa! That's *it*. That's part of the *rift*," he whispered as he gazed at the mound. "This is bad. We should leave. Right now."

"Why should we leave?" Lacey said. "And why are you whispering?"

"Didn't you hear Gisele? *Monsters* come out of these things. Let's go." He reached for Lacey's hand.

"Wait a minute." Haley grabbed the water guns from their bikes and tucked hers into her back pocket. "Here, take yours. My palms are tingling and itchy all the way up to my elbows. Maybe I can do something here."

Taylor snorted. "With a water gun? Are you crazy? What are we going to do—make mud pies?"

"I don't know, Taylor," Lacey shot back. "*My* hands are tingling too. I think we should give it a try." She aimed her water gun at the mound, holding the toy weapon straight out from her shoulders like it carried silver bullets, rather than clear, harmless tap water.

~ ☾ ~

Sighing and shaking his head, Taylor grabbed his blue plastic six-shooter. "This is so stupid. We're going to get eaten and all they'll find is melted, plastic water guns."

Standing to the side, Haley cocked her head as she studied the long earthen line. Taylor was partially right, they'd found the rift. Here was the perfect chance to prove herself. There were no monsters leaking out, none that she could see anyway. Maybe this part of the rift was long dead, abandoned. A good place to practice. Her hands burned now, itching to get on with it.

But get on with what? *What am I supposed to do?* She heard Lacey and Taylor approach from behind. When they stopped a few yards away, the forest fell into an absolute and profound silence, and she realized no birds or crickets sang. With a sudden, unexplainable feeling of knowing, Haley took a deep breath, closed her eyes and stood palms down in front of the rift. She heard and felt a buzzing in her head that got louder and more piercing with every second that passed, until she felt and heard nothing...

WHAT HAPPENED NEXT occurred at lightning speed. Lacey felt a low angry vibration that seemed to originate from deep underground. It sounded to her like huge pieces of metal folding, cracking and splitting. Surrounding the immediate area, dozens of birds shrieked and took flight. From a ragged slash that split the top of the mound, burst hundreds of gigantic, green-black pincer beetles, which began climbing out of the earth and engulfed Haley's legs, attacking and biting her where she stood.

Horrified, and armed with only her water pistol, a screaming Lacey began squirting the vile bugs, with absolutely no hope of helping her sister.

But it was all she could do.

And as it happened, all she would *need* to do.

A violent acidic bubbling on the shells of the attacking insects, caused by the squirted water droplets, destroyed dozens with Lacey's first shot. Taylor quickly jumped in, shooting as fast as he could and soon exploding beetles

~ ☾ ~

littered the forest floor.

Lacey couldn't believe the way Haley somehow ignored the beetle pieces and guts and while using only the energy that flowed from her hands, healed the rift. Then, without warning, the few surviving beetles skittered to the top of the mound and jumped into the crevasse just as it closed and flattened in on itself. As Lacey watched, the rest of the long line of the rift followed suit, leveling out as far as they could see and leaving no trace of a mound or rift. The momentous event must have taken less than ten minutes.

This rift, at least, was healed.

As Lacey moved to her sister, she watched in horror as Haley's eyes closed and she collapsed, falling on dozens of dead beetles.

"Haley!" Lacey screamed.

~ ☾ ~

CHAPTER TEN

TEN MINUTES AFTER her young students meandered out her driveway, Gisele, Micah and Selena finished packing their provisions for a morning hike to search for rifts. After consulting her gazing ball last evening, she already knew there were impassable areas that she was anxious to examine. If she were able, she'd like to try closing a couple of rifts this morning. *I think we should skip the 'bat rift' until we have a little more experience.* She watched as, armed with a compass and a sextant, Micah prepared to map the extent of the damage within the forest. With Haley gone, Selena's mood quickly improved and she became a lot more cooperative. *Still,* Gisele thought, *I'll miss those three. They're good kids and good students.*

As they moved their gear toward the door, the photo of Gisele's three favorite students fell to the floor with a clatter. She and Micah exchanged glances as she walked across the room to pick it up, studying it a moment before she returned it to the nail on the wall. "Do you think something's happened?" she asked him.

"I'm not sure," Micah said. "I can feel something's wrong, but I don't know if—"

"Oh, for crying out loud—a picture fell off the wall. Let's not make a huge deal out of it," Selena complained. "Let's just go. I'm dying to see one of these famous rifts, so I can knock the crap out of it." She shrugged into her backpack and strode toward the door. Micah glanced again at Haley's picture, grabbed his gear and with his head down, followed his cranky cousin.

Shaking her head, Gisele walked out the door. *Maybe she's right. Maybe I worry too much.*

After hiking about forty-five minutes Gisele heard, "Rift

~ ☾ ~

ahead." Selena's announcement took them all by surprise, including Selena by the look on her face, though she quickly recovered.

There wasn't a rift in sight.

"I wondered if this would happen. The forest is sharing its magic with us," Gisele said.

"Oh, I don't know." Selena said, "I've always been able to detect evil."

Micah smirked, glanced toward the sky and turned away. Five minutes later, they found their first rift.

"Let's get to work," Gisele commanded as they approached the mound, armed only with three wands, a crystal and a prayer.

~ ☾ ~

CHAPTER ELEVEN

HALEY RETURNED TO awareness as she felt Lacey and Taylor tow her limp body from the forest. Her eyes opened briefly and she watched her heels make twin tracks through pine needles and beetle bodies. *Am I drugged? Why can't I move my legs?* She wondered, closing her eyes. *And what's that noise?*

While lying on the rocky ground by the side of the road, Haley felt Lacey use a t-shirt to briskly wash her face, arms and legs with the apparently magic tap water from their squirt guns. She mumbled and pulled away in protest when droplets of water splashed on her cheek.

"Oh my goodness," Lacey muttered. "Look at these welts."

Everything hurts, she thought when she tried to clench and unclench her fingers and toes. "Water, please," Haley mumbled, her eyes still closed.

"Haley?" Taylor patted her face as she lay on her back next to the road. "Are you all right?"

"Yeah, I think so. Stop hitting me," she grumbled. She heard something else. Was someone calling her name? She waited a moment. Maybe not. "The water?"

"All we have are the water guns, Hayseed."

Still listening for that shadowy voice, she heard a swish of material as Lacey pulled her green Luger from her pocket and placed it into Haley's waiting hand.

"'S'okay." Haley squeezed the trigger of the squirt gun, emptying the warm water into her parched mouth. "Tastes like plastic. Mine?" she murmured, lifting her hip so Lacey could reach her hot pink Derringer. After she drank for a while, Haley pulled herself into a sitting position and groaned. "Where's Taylor?"

"He went back into the forest to get our bikes. Are you all

~ ☾ ~

right?"

"I think so. Tell me, what happened in there?" Haley asked while checking her arms and legs for bites. She looked up in time to see Taylor standing next to her bike with his mouth open.

"I was going to ask you the same question...what in the world did you just do?" he demanded.

Haley squirted water into her mouth. *This Super-Hero business is thirsty work.* "I think I healed a rift, but, well...can you tell me what happened after I raised my hands?"

"After you raised your hands?" Lacey's eyebrows shot up in surprise. "You mean you don't know?"

Haley shook her head.

"It was intense—so much noise! The mound opened up and big green beetles came out, *gross* beetles. We killed as many as we could with our water guns. Then, all at once, the mound sort of folded in on itself. Oh, and the beetles we missed, they jumped back into the opening and the whole thing sank below the ground." She looked at Taylor as if for confirmation.

He nodded before adding, "And the earth seemed to push the two halves of the split together, so you can't even tell the rift was there. If anything else happened while we were dragging you away, I missed it. When I went back to get the bikes, I looked for evidence of the rift and all I could see was a narrow path snaking through the woods." He grinned. "Good job, Haley. Didn't know you had it in ya."

"You killed beetles with *water*?" Haley's brow furrowed in disbelief.

"Yeah, we had nothing else to fight with and they were attacking you, so I squirted them and they exploded. Like magic." Lacey rocked back on her heels. "But, you! You were amazing. You stretched your arms out and all hell broke loose. It was like watching a magician on stage. And when the bugs started coming out, you never moved...even when they *crawled up your legs.*" She shook her head in wonder.

"Thanks, but I don't remember any of it. Listen, I think we have to get to Gisele and...the others." Haley cocked her head

~ ☾ ~

to the side. *There it was again.* She could almost hear something. "They need help. I can feel it."

"Yeah, but how do *you* feel?" Taylor asked, trading worried glances with Lacey as he helped Haley to her feet.

"A little dizzy, but I'm okay," Haley responded. "As long as you guys are backing me up with your water guns, I could do this again."

"Seriously?" Lacey looked her over. "You're a mess, Hayseed. Maybe you should take a nap."

"No. Right now I feel like I have a purpose. Like healing the earth is what I'm supposed to do. We should go."

"But you fainted," Lacey reminded her.

"No, I didn't, and I'm much better now."

"How did it feel when you did that...that...healing the rift stuff?" Taylor asked.

"I was vibrating all over with this weird humming sound in my head, as if I was in the center of a beehive." She looked at them. "But I wasn't scared. More...exhilarated, I think."

Taylor and Lacey just stared at her.

Her mouth fixed in a hard line, Haley squared her shoulders. "Gisele needs us. Let's go—now." She mounted her bike and began riding as the other two watched. Under her control, the handlebars wobbled a bit, but not too bad. "See? I'm fine. Let's go to Gisele's cabin. I need to splash some water on my face, we can refill the water guns and get some tools," she pedaled harder, gaining speed and strength with every push.

"Tools?" Lacey struggled to keep up with her sister.

"Yeah. Remember that Altar Stone from last year?"

"Yeah," Taylor huffed behind her.

"I think there will be something there to help us."

They raced back to the cabin and with every passing second, Haley's strength of purpose increased. She rode so fast she left the others straining to keep up.

~ ☾ ~

CHAPTER TWELVE

TAYLOR LOCATED GISELE'S hidden key under the shingle right where she'd shown them. While Haley washed up, Lacey refilled their water guns. "I just hope they won't be needed again for a while."

In the woods just behind the cabin, they found the tall, flat-topped rock Gisele called the Altar Stone. On it rested two crystals from the Crystal Cave, a bag of sharp black stones, a tin of matches, a slingshot, a leather pouch with the word 'Mandrake' stamped on it in gold, a large walking stick and a—

"*Cherry bomb*? We're taking *fireworks* into the forest?" Taylor was incredulous.

"You first." Lacey said to her sister and hung back.

Haley held her hand over the leather pouch, the walking stick and the rest of the tools.

Nothing.

When she put her hand over the crystals, they glowed as if they had never left the Crystal Cave. Smiling, she put them in her pocket. "*Two* crystals. They can't keep us out now."

"That's funny. Last year we only got one crystal each. Are you sure one of those isn't for me?" Lacey said.

Haley shrugged and placed them back on the Altar. "Go ahead and try."

Lacey held her hand over the crystals. "Not even a flicker of light. Definitely yours."

With exaggerated annoyance, Haley retrieved her glowing crystals. "Told ya."

Lacey held her hand over the pouch of Mandrake, which radiated a golden light. The bag of stones and the matches also shimmered at her touch. "Guess these are for me," she said. "Wonder what I do with them?"

~ ☾ ~

"Whatever it is, I hope you guess right," Taylor said, the new owner of a glowing walking stick and the slingshot. He nervously picked up the cherry bomb by its wick. "What am I supposed to do with this?"

"Whatever it is, I hope you guess right," Lacey teased, as she placed her new tools into her bag.

"Here's an extra pouch, Taylor," Haley said. "I think we should keep it separate."

"Thanks. Now we just have to find them. Where should we go?" he asked, as they stood knee deep in ferns at the edge of the forest.

Haley held up one of her crystals, which glowed most strongly when she pointed it straight ahead. "That's North, right?"

Taylor nodded his head.

"Then that's where we go. I only hope we're in time."

They walked for about twenty minutes when she noticed the crystal pulsing in her hand. "Hey, guys, what do you think this means?"

"Maybe we found them?" Lacey said, looking around the trees and ferns.

"I don't hear anything but birds," Taylor said. "If they were nearby, we'd hear fighting or talking, *something*..."

"Unless," Lacey swallowed. "Unless it's over and they're..."

"Don't say that!" Haley said. "Let's keep walking. They must be somewhere around here." The pulse of the crystal sped up.

"Turn it around," Taylor suggested. "Aim it at something."

Haley pointed the crystal at the South, the direction from where they'd travelled and pulsing stopped. She turned to the East with the same result. As she turned in a circle, the pulsing resumed, growing stronger and faster until when she pointed it toward the West, it started to vibrate. "This is where they are. Let's hurry." She strode through a bank of trees and came face to face with a--

"Rift!" When she stopped short, an inattentive Lacey plowed into her, nearly pushing her onto the mound. "Be careful!" she hissed, checking the area for Gisele, Micah or even Selena.

~ ☾ ~

Taylor poked his head over their shoulders. "So, where are they?"

"I don't know. All we have is this dumb rift," Lacey said.

As a group, they walked closer to it, still on the lookout for the others.

"This crystal is vibrating like crazy, so I guess we should get started." Haley stepped to one side of the rift where the ground opened up to a small clearing.

"Really?" Lacey interjected. "We're not going to help *Micah?*"

"We're looking for *Gisele*, but the crystal really wants me to take care of his rift, so let's move," Haley snarled and gave Lacey a little shove. Lacey dropped her bag onto the ground and turned to yell at her sister when the bag burst open. Furious, Lacey grabbed the match tin and accidentally turned the bag of black stones upside down, spilling them. Before she could retrieve them, the stones skittered away, forming a fifteen-foot circle around the three of them.

While they watched this phenomenon, the tin of matches burned Lacey's hand, causing her to drop it. One of the matches fell out of the tin and onto the stones, which burst into three-foot high blue flames, trapping them within the circle.

Haley screamed and jumped away from the edge. Taylor pulled both girls into the center of the circle. "What should we do?" Haley yelled above the noise of crackling fire, which quickly rose to a height of about six feet, blocking their vision of the rest of the forest.

"Heal the rift," Taylor shouted. "Maybe that will put the fire out. What else can we do?"

With a pounding heart, Haley hugged her trembling sister. "Sorry I pushed you. I didn't mean to start all this."

Taylor called from the edge of the circle, "Look at this." Haley gasped when he put his hand into the flames, seemingly without pain.

"Get away from there," Lacey said. "Are you crazy?"

"Don't worry. It doesn't hurt," he said. "I think it's here to protect us."

Haley's crystal began vibrating so hard, it almost fell out of

~ ☾ ~

her hand. "It's time. Let's get ready."

"Wait. How the heck are we supposed to defend you?'" Lacey said. "All we have are a walking stick, a bag of Mandrake, a slingshot and a cherry bomb."

Haley closed her eyes and took a deep breath. "Trust." And she raised her hands.

SUDDENLY, FROM A crease on the top of the mound, hundreds of black, jagged shapes thrust themselves, squeaking and squealing into the sky above.

When they wheeled around, Lacey thought they would attack and stood ready to meet death.

"Help me!" Taylor fumbled with his slingshot. "There isn't much time!"

"What should I do?" The grinding, metallic sounds of the opening earth filled the air and seemed to excite the twitching black shapes into a frenzy. Startled birds filled the sky.

"Light the cherry bomb. Quick!" With trembling hands, Taylor inserted the firecracker, their one chance, into the pouch of the slingshot and pulled it back. "Now."

Lacey retrieved the tin of matches from the ground, struck one and touched it to the protruding wick as the first of the shapes, which she now realized were bats, began to dive bomb them.

Taylor aimed his precious missile into the air and pulled back. Just before he released the shot, a cartwheeling bat dealt his forehead a glancing blow, causing the cherry bomb to barely clear the wall of flames and land, ineffectively, on the ground. A second later—

KA—BOOM! A hole big enough to drive a car into, threw dirt, rocks and roots up in the air. Taylor's hands fell loosely to his sides in a gesture of defeat and loss as debris rained down on them.

Shaking off her shock and the ringing in her ears from the blast, Lacey pointed at Taylor's slingshot. His eyes widened as he saw another cherry bomb resting in its pouch. "Light it!"

Lacey produced another match. On his knees to protect his

~ ☾ ~

aim and with blood flowing from his forehead, Taylor pointed his slingshot to the heavens and let fly. They blocked their ears. Another KA—BOOM! and tiny bat bodies rained down on them. Ignoring her instinct to vomit, Lacey lit another. Taylor's missile soared, exploded and more swooping bats fell to earth.

While Taylor continued to fire rounds into the sky, Lacey noticed a change in their opponents' patterns. "They've stopped attacking. They're racing back to the rift," she said, as a long, black twitching line spiraled like a tornado into the fissure. The rift's deafening collapse followed a long row as far as she could see. She sighed, "I think it's over."

"Good, I can barely hear anymore."

"Me, too." They looked at Haley who wobbled a bit before falling to one knee. Lacey reached her in time to cushion her fall.

"WATER. THAT'S ALL I need." Haley felt a water gun being pressed into her hand and heaved a sigh of pure relief as she squirted the cool water down her throat. "That's better." She opened her eyes. "Hey, where's the fire?"

Lacey and Taylor looked up at her question and from their shocked expressions, she realized Taylor was right—it had been there to protect them. "And what were these?" She poked at a tangle of severed wings, lying next to her.

"Bats." Lacey's mouth twisted into an odd expression, which Haley knew meant, 'let's get out of here before I'm sick.'

"Help me up and we can leave." Haley grabbed Taylor's arm. "What happened to you?"

He grinned. "Bat scratch."

"Eww. Let's sit over there." She nodded to the right.

After settling on a flat boulder, Lacey dug into her backpack and produced a damp t-shirt to wipe the blood off Taylor's face. "I don't have any bandages."

"That's okay. It's almost stopped."

Lacey returned to the circle, found her bag of Mandrake and match tin and tucked them into her pocket. She turned to

~ ☾ ~

Haley. "Are you ready to go?"

"Yeah, I'm getting more nervous for them by the second."

"For *Micah*, you mean?" Lacey teased.

"Go formica yourself," Haley muttered and pointed her crystal to the left. "Should we go west?"

No response.

"North?" Same thing.

"Maybe you should use the other crystal?"

"Sure, I'll try that," she pulled the new crystal from her pocket and handed the other to Lacey. "Hold this for me, please."

Haley held her new crystal in front of her. "Straight into the forest?"

A weak glow.

"Far right?" The crystal pulsed and thrummed in her hand. "East. We go east," Haley said.

"You don't think it's trying to return to the Crystal Cave, do you?" Lacey asked in a small voice. "That's northeast."

"Hope not." Haley paused, biting her lower lip.

"I agree with Haley. I think this is the best plan." Taylor took the lead, stamping the ground ahead of him, checking for rifts, snakes and things that usually only appear in nightmares. The forest was beautiful, sun splashed and lush with ferns, saplings and mature, old growth conifers and deciduous trees. *Much too peaceful to be the center of evil,* Haley thought, as she followed the glow of her crystal. They walked for some time, checking the ground, watching her crystal, not speaking. Finally, Taylor signaled for them to stop so they could listen.

At last. The sounds of fighting-shouting, thumping and brawling could be heard not far off. "You'll need your water guns," Haley looked at Taylor. "Should we approach quietly or should we go in fast?"

"I think we need to hurry," Taylor urged.

They ran.

Less than two minutes later, armed with water guns and their special tools, they joined the others to confront their third rift in under an hour.

Streaming out of this rift crawled thousands of tiny pink

~ ☾ ~

worms fortified, Haley soon learned, with a bite like a hot matchstick. "Ouch!" She slapped at her ankle. "It stung me." A slimy pink trail oozed down her foot.

A few dozen would be no problem, but the sheer numbers overwhelmed Gisele, Micah and Selena, whose wands proved ineffective against the tiny marauders and their nasty bites.

They found Gisele attempting to eradicate the worms with incantations, while Selena and Micah were reduced to stamping out the noxious pests with their feet. Taylor and Lacey stepped forward, spraying the little worms with their tap water, paying special attention to the area at Gisele's feet.

The water worked its magic and before long, hundreds of tiny exploding worms covered the forest floor with sticky pink goo.

With Lacey and Taylor wetting down the area surrounding a frustrated Micah and his surly cousin, Haley turned to the rift–itchy, tingling palms down, holding her new crystal between both hands.

LACEY HEARD THE now welcome crunching, grinding, metallic sounds filling the forest, once again sending scores of startled birds into flight. As the area around the rift weakened and buckled, a swishing noise emanated from the hundreds of surviving pink worms as they fled, intent upon returning to the rift before it closed. Within seconds, the mound crumpled in on itself, following the rift's line toward the center of the forest. Caught away from the crevasse, any remaining worms withered and died with the noisy collapse of the rift. She looked to Haley whose arms hung by her side. "She's going to fall."

Micah strode to where Haley wobbled on her feet.

"Catch her," Taylor called from a few yards away.

Micah put his hands out to catch her. When her knees buckled, Lacey watched the care he took as he gently lowered her to the ground.

~ ☾ ~

CHAPTER THIRTEEN

"I HAVE A WET cloth for her face," Lacey offered from a few feet away.

"I'll do it," Micah insisted.

Haley felt the cool cloth gently wiping her cheek. "Water, please," she asked, eyes still closed. A bottle pressed against her hand, she took a small sip and sighed. "Thank you."

"Can you sit up?" he asked when she finally opened her eyes.

"I think so." When she moved to sit on a stump, she noticed him eyeing the dozens of raised welts and bruises on her legs and ankles.

"What the heck happened to you?"

"Beetles?" Gisele guessed as she applied her healing wand to Taylor's forehead.

"Yeah," Taylor said. "And bats."

"Both in the same rift?"

"No, we took care of two rifts before this one." Lacey said.

Micah turned to Haley. "This is your *third* rift today?"

"Yes, and I have to say, this was the easiest."

Taylor nodded in agreement.

Gisele's mouth fell open. "You healed three rifts in one day?"

"Yeah," Lacey replied. "Pretty good, huh?"

"Amazing." Micah looked into Haley's eyes and she felt herself blush.

"We heard cannons or something from the west," Gisele said.

"Yeah, sorry. That was me," Taylor chimed in. "I sent off a few cherry bombs—"

"You set off *fireworks* in my forest?" Gisele dropped her crystal and leaned away from him, eyes filled indignation.

~ ☾ ~

"Gisele, it was left for him on the Altar Stone." Lacey handed her the crystal. "I was given the matches to light them."

Gisele crossed her arms over her chest, still glaring at Taylor. "Why don't you tell us about it."

Taylor swallowed and began the story by talking about the unicorn.

"Where was the unicorn?" Gisele demanded. "On the side of the road? Surely, Taylor, you're mistaken. In over fifty years, *no one* other than myself and a small group of trusted friends has ever seen them. Our unicorns value their privacy, above all. And my *stallion*?" She shook her head with emphasis. "Never."

Haley rubbed the back of her neck and lightly touched a bruise on her knee. She was about to comment when Lacey rushed to Taylor's defense.

"I saw him too, not ten minutes from your cabin," Lacey said. "We *all* did. That's why we left the road and entered the forest. That's how we found the rift. Hidden behind some evergreens."

The picture of disbelief, Gisele's face took on a pinched appearance as she ran her healing crystal up and down Selena's legs, which were riddled with bites.

"They're right." Haley reached for and held Micah's hand while she rubbed her crystal slowly up the length of his arm. As the bite marks disappeared, his expression softened.

After healing his bites, Haley smiled and turned the crystal on herself. Micah gently removed the stone from her hand to return the favor and began healing her. "Take a breath and relax," he said.

The crystal's warm glow created a soft electric current on her skin that awakened an intense feeling like nothing she'd ever experienced. She closed her eyes and sighed with pleasure. *Were the others having this reaction?* She wondered, looking around surreptitiously. No one else seemed to be having a similar response.

No one that is, but—Micah, who returned her look as if he read her mind. She trembled when her startled gaze met his, inviting and warm.

~ ☽ ~

"Are you all right?" he asked like they shared a secret.

She nodded and refocused her gaze past his shoulder at the ever-annoyed Selena, who turned away in disgust. Haley closed her eyes. "Yes," she said, thinking that even with all this craziness, she'd never felt more 'all right' in her life. The crystal performed its healing magic. When her pain eased, she relaxed her shoulders and sighed with relief. "Ahh," she said as the stinging began to fade. "That's better."

Micah traced the healing crystal over her throat, cheeks and forehead, spending a bit more time than she thought necessary, though she was well past complaint. "Can you walk or do you need to be carried back to Gisele's?" he asked with a teasing grin.

"No, that's o–"

"Aren't you done yet?" Selena's sharp voice chopped through their quiet interaction. "I think others could use that crystal too, don't you?"

Haley blinked and sat up. "Yeah. Hey, Lace come get this," she said, feeling as if awakened from a dream.

Micah surrendered her crystal to Lacey, but not before his hand lightly brushed Haley's. As she looked into his eyes, her lips parted and her heart leapt. "Thanks, again," she said, lowering her eyes.

"My pleasure."

"Am I back to normal?" she asked him, touching her face and throat.

"You're back to beautiful." He smiled. "I don't think you could ever be just normal."

Shaking her head, Gisele sighed loudly and Haley heard her mutter, "By the gods, I hate being right all the time."

Before Haley could figure out the meaning of that statement, Gisele ordered, "Everyone, drink some water. Whether for good or for evil, magic will sap your strength. We'll have to share, but we all need it. Then we're leaving. I think we've experienced more than enough adventures for one day and we still have a lot to talk about." Her stony glance took in Haley, her sister and Taylor.

~ ☾ ~

GISELE LOOKED AT Haley, as the somewhat dazed group found seats in her tiny kitchen. "Here's a pouch for your crystal. Remember they lose some of their power when exposed to sunlight."

"I have two."

"Oh, yeah," Lacey pulled the original stone out of her bag and placed it on the table.

"*Two* crystals? Where did you get *two* of them?"

Gisele looked so fierce, Haley stammered a bit trying to answer. "Well, um...I—"

Lacey rescued her. "They were left for her on the Altar Stone. Where else would she get them?"

"This is unheard of," Gisele grumbled, rummaging in her bag. "No one and I mean, *no one* has ever been gifted with two crystals at once. *Never.*" She produced a larger pouch and stuffed the first one back in her bag. Micah cleared his throat and Haley watched while he and Gisele seemed to be having a silent argument.

She grabbed the pouch and the rest watched as she put the stones in the bag, and then tucked it into her pocket. Gisele folded her arms and leaned against her kitchen counter.

"So. How did you heal the rift?"

~ ☾ ~

CHAPTER FOURTEEN

"YEAH," MICAH POSITIONED himself in the seat opposite Haley and leaned forward intently. "How *did* you know?" His eyes appraised her in a way that made her feel both very special and uncomfortably shy at the same time.

"When we were in the forest and I saw the rift," she began, "my hands started to tingle and itch—"

"Mine did too." Haley smiled to herself when Lacey showed her hands to the others, as if that would prove anything.

"They itched all morning and it was somewhat annoying. But once I saw the rift, they started to *tingle* too." Haley smiled. "Suddenly I knew I could fix this. The only problem was, I couldn't defend myself while I was healing it. I had to rely on Lacey and Taylor." She looked at her sister and Taylor. "They didn't know what to do at first and that's how I got all the bites. Thank goodness they figured it out in time."

"The *only* problem?" Gisele said more to herself than to anyone else.

Haley shrugged her thin shoulders. "Also, I zone out and I'm not aware of my surroundings when I'm healing. After it's over and the rift is healed, my legs just give out."

"How long did it take you to heal the first rift?" she asked.

Haley wondered how Gisele could talk with her lips pressed together so tightly and barely managed to stifle a giggle. "I'm not sure—" she looked to Lacey for help. Micah continued to watch her every move, while Selena sighed loudly in boredom.

"Ten minutes or so," Lacey jumped in. "About the same amount of time it took with yours."

"*Ten* minutes?" Leaning forward to catch every word, Gisele slumped against the counter as if in surrender. She

~ ☾ ~

looked down and shook her head in disbelief. "What about the fainting?"

"I didn't actually faint. Like I said, I just got really weak and my knees gave out on me. I think I recovered a little faster this time." After an involuntary glance at Micah, she looked down at her hands.

"The second rift?"

"About the same, I think," Lacey looked at Taylor, who nodded.

"And the water guns?" Gisele asked, squeezing the bridge of her nose.

"Haley's idea." Lacey cocked a thumb in her direction.

All heads but one swiveled back to Haley. Selena was busy examining her manicure. Haley wondered if the urchin would remove her shoes to check her pedicure, just to get Micah's attention.

"So, why did you bring water guns?" After moving to the table, Gisele sat with her hand propping up her chin, reminding Haley of the semester she failed three classes. Dejection City.

Tired of the spotlight, Haley shrugged. "I don't know. Intuition? Beginner's luck?"

"She's always doing that," Lacey said with a casual wave of her hand. Haley glared at her. She didn't need, or want, all this attention. Looking around the room, various emotions were easily detected: Selena's anger, Gisele's desolation, Lacey and Taylor's misplaced admiration, Micah's—what? Interest? And was this interest mere curiosity or romantic? She sighed.

"When did you get the crystals?"

"After the first rift, we came here, got some water and stopped at the Altar Stone." *Shouldn't Gisele be happier? After all, here are three new helpers, ready, willing and able to assist. We did it. We healed three rifts and no one got hurt, so why does Gisele's questioning feel more like an interview with Taylor's father, the Police Chief?*

"So you healed the first rift without training and without a crystal," Micah said as, arms crossed, he leaned back in his chair with that speculative look on his face again. He tapped

~ ☾ ~

his lower lip with his right index finger and glanced sideways at his great-aunt.

Haley nodded, keenly aware of decisions being made without her input. After what she, Lacey and Taylor just accomplished, how could they *not* be a part of this? What more could they have done? Her eyes went from Micah to Gisele and back again.

"And you've never done anything like this before?" he said.

"No."

"Three rifts in one day," he said, but not to her.

Gisele bristled and looked away. "I'm still angry you entered the forest without a crystal, or the slightest idea of what needed to be done," she said. "You could have been seriously injured, maimed or even killed."

Taylor jumped in. "We know what we're doing now and we'd like to help. You know, *officially.*"

Selena snorted her displeasure. "We don't need little kids in the forest."

Micah bit his lip.

"Excuse me, but how old are *you*?" Taylor asked her.

"I'm almost sixteen, if you must know, but–"

"So am I, and you are half my size."

"We have skills, talent and training. You have, what? Water guns? You'd be a liability out there and I'm not here to babysit." Selena plunked herself down on a chair.

"How many rifts did *you* heal today?" Haley asked in a quiet voice.

Micah raised an eyebrow and his lips quirked in a smile.

Selena tossed her blonde hair. "Gisele is more than qualified and we don't need *you*." She stood up. "That's it, we're leaving. C'mon, Micah. We'll come back when they're gone." She flung open the screen door and clattered down the steps. Micah scratched the back of his head in the ensuing silence.

A car door slammed. "Micah!"

"So Gisele, will you accept our help?" Taylor asked.

Micah looked back at Gisele, an obvious vote in favor.

"Mi-cahhh!"

"Let me think about it." Again, Micah raised an eyebrow, a

~ ☾ ~

silent but not subtle challenge.

"We saved you today," Lacey said.

"I am aware of what the three of you did in the forest. It was a brave and dangerous thing to do and we appreciate it. But there are far more fearsome things out there than bats, beetles and worms and I have to consider your safety above my own."

"When can we come back?" Taylor pressed.

Outside, the car horn beeped. At the table, no one moved.

"How about Thursday? That's the earliest I can go back in. I'll let you know then," she said. Looking at their hopeful faces, she rose from the table and sighed. "Best I can do."

Recognizing this as a dismissal, Haley looked at Gisele as she stood up. "Just one question: How'd *you* do? How much of the rift did you heal?"

"I only closed ten feet or so," Gisele admitted.

Haley blinked. "Ten feet? Even with your crystal?"

Gisele nodded, her eyes reflecting her misery.

Another beep. "Let's go!"

"You need us." In a mock show of bravery, Haley jutted out her chin and crossed her arms over her chest, though the effect was somewhat spoiled when she noticed Micah stifling a smile.

"Thursday. We'll talk then," Gisele promised.

OUTSIDE THEY WERE treated to the back of Selena's head as she sat in Micah's car. Next to the bikes, Lacey pulled a small leather pouch out of her back pocket. "The Mandrake," she whispered. "I never used it."

As they huddled together a small smile spread over Taylor's face. "We're going back in."

"How do you know that?" Haley asked. *I'm going back in, no matter what happens.*

"Since we didn't use the Mandrake today, isn't it possible we may need it the next time we go into the forest?" Taylor said.

"I think you're right." Lacey turned to her sister. "I wouldn't have gotten it unless it will be used at some point,

~ ☾ ~

don't you think?"

"We're going be part of this, no matter what," Haley vowed as she patted the crystals in her back pocket. "Let's go swimming."

Riding past the area where they saw the unicorn jogged Haley's memory. "Hey Lace, your palms were itchy when we saw the first rift, right?"

"Yeah."

"Were they itchy when we battled the second? Or the third?"

Lacey paused to consider. "No, I don't think so. But, why not?"

"I don't know. Maybe things happened too fast? Maybe you don't remember?"

Lacey's brow furrowed in concentration.

"Here's a thought." Taylor turned to Haley. "If *both* of us doubted you, would you have tried to heal the rift, or would you have ignored your feelings and gone swimming?"

She paused to consider the question. "I'd like to think I would've taken a stab at it anyway, but I can't say for sure. Knowing that Lacey's palms itched and burned like mine gave me the courage to try."

Taylor smiled. "I'm glad you didn't listen to me."

Grinning, Lacey changed the subject. "So, I guess you finally met your dark, handsome stranger, huh, Hayseed? And is he *cute.*"

"Do you think so?" Haley asked, like she hadn't noticed, and like she could get those beautiful blue eyes out of her head.

"Well, yeah. He's gorgeous and–"

"I'm right here you know," Taylor said, looking at Lacey. "You might want to drool a little less in front of your own boyfriend."

"–and he kept watching you like...like, he knew you from a long time ago," Lacey continued, eyebrows raised. "With those eyes, those spooky light blue eyes..."

Haley noticed that too, and it thrilled her that Lacey's observation proved her imagination wasn't working overtime. "Have you ever seen a straighter, more elegant nose? He

~ ☾ ~

looks like royalty."

"Never," Lacey said. "And listen, you have *got* to tell me if that silky black hair is as soft as it looks."

"I'm not even here, am I?" Taylor muttered, half to himself.

"I never thought I would admire a jaw line, but oh my," Lacey gushed. "I think he shaves–"

"*I* shave." Taylor's exasperated outburst caused both girls to burst into laughter.

"Watch out for that Selena, though," Lacey warned between giggles. "If she owned a gun, she would've shot you today.

"I saw that. I think she'd rather die than give us credit for saving her skinny butt," Haley said.

"She's really beautiful, huh?" Taylor's observation stopped all conversation.

"What? You think she's prettier than me?" Lacey's face puckered, while the expression on Taylor's face went from teasing to surprise to total mortification in mere seconds.

"No, of course not," he blurted out.

"Why would you say that?"

"I'm sorry. I won't ever say it again." Taylor looked to Haley, his eyes round with dismay.

With raised eyebrows, she gave him a smile and a tiny shrug.

Glaring at a bewildered Taylor, Lacey said, "I guess she's got a thing for Micah. 'Course, who wouldn't?"

Taylor heaved a huge frustrated sigh.

"Oh, for heaven's *sake*," Haley turned to him. "Lacey adores you. You know that. But this is big. I've never had a boyfriend before, not even close. If he likes me, and we don't even know if he does, it would be like..." She tried for a comparison even a *boy* would understand. "Like, hitting a grand-slam out of Fenway Park, during your first time at bat. Do you get it now?"

"Okay, I get that. Go ahead and be girls. Let me know when you want to talk about something interesting."

~ ☾ ~

CHAPTER FIFTEEN

ARMS CROSSED, MICAH stood inside Gisele's front door watching the three friends mount their bikes and ride away. Having made her point, Selena stalked up the stairs with her head held high and brushed by him as she re-entered the kitchen.

"I should get you back to Aunt Marie's." Micah glanced once more at Haley's retreating figure and smiled to himself.

"Already? But it's not even three o'clock," she protested.

"You said you wanted to go."

"That was before. Shouldn't we be making plans, mapping out strategies?"

Gisele stifled a yawn. "Actually, Micah, that's not a bad idea. If you two get out of here, I can take a nap."

"I'll be back in a few hours. Go ahead and take your nap." He kissed her cheek. "Good job today, Auntie G."

"Hmph," she muttered. "Would've been a lost cause without Haley."

"That's possible." Micah said.

"Or maybe we were just hitting our stride when they showed up," Selena said.

"Nothing worked for me." Gisele looked at her hands. "None of my tools or spells. I didn't have the foggiest idea what to do next. Those kids saved us."

"We would've been fine and we will be fine," Selena assured her. "The forest is helping us–sending us what we need."

"And what we *need*, is Haley," Micah interjected. "If she has this much raw power, there may be no one else who can do this. And if it's just coming out now, I'll bet she has more abilities that haven't surfaced yet."

"We'll be fine," Selena repeated, scowling. "We can do this without having children in the forest."

~ ☾ ~

"The twins are only a year or so younger than you," Micah said. "And their water guns saved us today."

"Let's go," Selena growled, grabbing her purse. "See you on Thursday, Gisele?"

"I'll be here," Gisele said with a sigh.

THE DRIVE TO Pittsfield strained their already uncomfortable relationship. "Want to go out for dinner?" Selena asked. "It's a little early but we could—"

"No thanks, I've got to get back."

"To what, or should I say, to *who*?" she sneered.

"Shouldn't be your concern." He frowned.

"But it is. I thought we—"

"We've talked about this," he reminded her. "You and I are distant relatives and friends, nothing more."

"Can't we-?"

"We have nothing more to talk about."

The rest of their tense ride passed silently, punctuated only by Selena's angry sighs. He pulled up to a small white Victorian, one of several on the block. "We're here. I'll pick you up at eight thirty on Thursday."

"You're not coming back tomorrow *or* Wednesday?" Selena's voice rose with every word, almost reaching into that select range only dogs could hear.

Careful, this could get ugly fast. "I have lots of things to do." He looked away, anxious to be gone.

"I'll just bet." She got out and slammed the door, rattling the window.

"Selena," he said, annoyed now.

She walked up two stairs, then turned around.

"Maybe I won't be here on Thursday. Maybe you'll be stuck with that stupid, little, *Hay-lee!*" she shrieked. Dogs up and down the street began to bark.

"See you Thursday."

Without another word, she ran up the stairs and into the house.

Shaking his head in exasperation, Micah turned his car around and drove back to Bidwell.

~ ☾ ~

CHAPTER SIXTEEN

THE MILLER GIRLS, Haley, Lacey and Grandma Clara were chatting in the kitchen after an early supper when a knock sounded on the front door. Haley answered it and nearly gasped, Micah stood there, cool, irresistible and smiling down at her. *Calm down,* she willed herself. *He probably just wants to talk about what happened today.*

"Hi," she said.

"Hi. Can I come in?"

"Of course. We're just cleaning up from supper." She led the way to the kitchen, willing her racing heart to slow down. "Grandma, I'd like you to meet Micah," she said when he entered the room. "He's Gisele's great-nephew."

"Hello, Micah. Nice to see you again," Clara greeted him warmly. "You've gotten tall and quite handsome since I last saw you."

"Thank you." He smiled. "I think I was about nine years old the last time we met."

"So what brings you here this time?" she asked, trading glances with Lacey.

"I'd like to take Haley for an ice cream, if that's okay?" Though the question was directed at her grandmother, his eyes were on Haley. He smiled when she grabbed her purse.

"Well...I..."

"Don't worry, Grandma. I won't be late." Haley kissed her grandmother's soft cheek.

"Um, I'm not sure about this. Your parents didn't mention anything about dating."

"It's not a date—just ice cream. Don't worry. I'll have her back by nine." Micah rested his hand at Haley's waist, guiding her to the door. She stiffened at his unexpected touch. Grinning, she glanced back and was delighted to witness their

~ ☾ ~

stunned expressions.

"This is a surprise," Haley said as they walked down the stairs. "I didn't expect to see you 'til Thursday."

"I couldn't wait that long."

"Really?" she half smiled and felt warmth on her cheeks. *He is so cute.*

"Yes, my aunt doesn't really want you to come into the forest with us again, but I disagree. I'd like to see what else you can do to bolster my case," he said, opening the car door for her.

"Oh." Haley's face fell.

"Of course, I'm pretty sure it'll be fun hanging out with you, too," he added, to her relief.

"Really?" She looked out the window in an effort to hide her smile.

"Yes. How old are you, Haley?"

"I'm almost fifteen," she replied, loving the way he said her name. "You?"

"Sixteen–"

"That's okay, then." Happy she'd been mistaken; she'd assumed he was much older.

"–and three quarters," he added.

"Hmmm." She twisted the handle on her purse.

"Here we are," he said, pulling into a Freddie's restaurant.

They were seated right away. "I'm starving," he said looking at the menu.

"I thought we were here for ice cream."

"Have whatever you want, but I need real food."

They spent the next five minutes perusing the menu. "Where *is* the waitress?" he asked, looking around.

She shrugged. "Freddie's isn't known for fast food."

"No." He smiled. "Their service is about as fast as a glacier and almost as warm."

Her brow furrowed slightly. "You don't talk like a sixteen-year-old."

"Blame my parents. They're brilliant and surround themselves with friends who are geniuses and leaders in their field. Conversations at dinner centered around physics, scientific breakthroughs, magic and Nietzsche. My father

~ ☾ ~

could have worked anywhere in the scientific community, but he chose to teach." He looked away. "We don't have conversations. He lectures."

"Oh, sorry."

"It's not so bad. They're good people but I never knew what it was like to be a kid. You know that I'm an Adept. I demonstrated magical tendencies when I was only two years old. My parents trained me in the magical arts and home schooled me until I could control my magic and my impulses. The only time I got together with other kids was during the holidays and family barbeques. Being home schooled was fun, but I felt like I was missing so much and when the time came, I demanded to go to a regular high school."

"Are you happy there?"

"Very. Most of my classes are in Advanced Placement with the brainiacs, but that's fine. It's what I'm used to. It was the social part I missed most, being with people my own age. It took me months to work up the courage to talk to a girl."

"You seem to have passed that hurdle with flying colors."

The waitress eventually sauntered over and took his order for a double cheeseburger and fries while Haley ordered a small hot fudge sundae.

"So Haley, about your Gift..." he began.

"My *Gift*?"

"Yeah, your little Gift. You know, the one where you heal the earth?" he prompted. "How long have you been doing that?" He looked directly into her eyes. She blinked and looked away.

"I don't know," she said. "Since maybe...ten o'clock this morning?"

He shook his head. "And you've never done anything like this before?"

"Never." She looked down at her hands.

"Amazing. Talents and abilities usually show up much earlier than this. So, I'm thinking maybe you have more," he said, raising his eyebrows.

"Sometimes, I *guess* correctly. I get a feeling that I need to take specific action or carry a certain item—and later it turns out, well, I was right." Still looking down, she folded and

~ ☾ ~

refolded her napkin. Anything to avoid his relentless gaze. "Is it getting warm in here?"

"I don't think so. Are you talking about the water guns?"

"Yes, and a snorkel last year, and there were other times, too."

"Pre-cog," he mused.

"What?" Now she looked up. *There was a name for this?*

"Precognition."

"I've heard that term. Is it seeing something before it happens?"

"Something like that," he said, lightly tapping the table. "I'm *starving*."

Resisting the urge to say, "I told you so," she raised her eyebrows and shrugged. A few minutes later the waitress finally showed up with their food and they dug in.

"But I don't see things. I just need to do something specific. It's like a nagging feeling." She frowned while she tried to explain. "Doesn't happen very often. Great ice cream, by the way," she said, licking the spoon. "Worth the wait."

"I agree," he said, watching her with those eyes again. "Definitely worth the wait," he stared at her so intently she began to feel a little self-conscious. "Maybe I'll get an ice cream, too."

"Sure, I've got two more hours to waste." She laughed.

He smiled before turning thoughtful. "Maybe we could train you to embrace and enhance your Gifts."

"Sounds good to me. So what are your Gifts?"

He smiled. "What are you asking about, really? My magical Gifts, Talents or Skills?

She shrugged. "Umm..."

"Let me explain. Skills are something you acquire. I was interested in sword-work, wand-training and a few other things. Skills don't generally come naturally, so I've had to practice, like you would riding a bike. Hours a day until I got it right." He shrugged. "And now I'm pretty good with those tools. But there are a few more Skills I'd like to master. Which brings us to Talents," he continued. "Something you're born with, but with and schooling and practice can be refined and mastered. Do you have any Talents, by the way?"

~ ☾ ~

"Like what?"

"Can you sing, play an instrument or paint?"

"Oh, that kind of Talent. I draw and I can write," she said, hoping she sounded modest enough. The truth was she was widely considered the best artist in her class and often received 'A's' for her writing skills.

"You write? Like poetry?" he asked.

"No. I write short stories," she shook her head smiling. "I don't get poetry."

"Me neither." He laughed. "I play the guitar a little and I can sing, but my magical Talents are, well, they're unique." He took a deep breath as he leaned toward her for privacy. "As my aunt explained, I'm an Adept, a child of a magical family and I've been in training all my life. My Talents..." he paused, then looked into her eyes. "One is that I can, well, sometimes...see ghosts–"

"Really? Like a ghost whisperer or something?" Haley said, her eyes wide.

"Yeah, it's my least favorite Talent. I'm not completely comfortable with it yet, but Aunt Gisele says with practice, it won't bother me so much," he said. "And for some reason, she's pretty adamant that I learn to refine it. Right now I can see them sometimes, but she wants me to be able to see them *all* the time and *hear* them too."

She looked away and tried not to let on how awful she thought it would be to have that Talent. Her nose wrinkled in distaste.

"It's....creepy. Some of the ghosts have been dead over a hundred years." he said with a soft sigh. "And they're floating around, moaning. It's disturbing."

"Are there any here?" she asked, looking toward the ceiling.

"Not now."

"What do you mean, not *now*?"

"Well, earlier there was a guy who died of food poisoning after he ate here—"

She pushed her dish away in horror.

"I think your ice cream is fine," he laughed. "And I'll let you know if any others show up."

~ ☾ ~

Surprised at how far forward she'd crept in her seat, Haley pushed her butt against the backrest. "What else can you do?" she asked, not at all sure she wanted to know.

He swallowed. "Right. That brings us to my Gifts. As opposed to Talents or Skills, Gifts are thrust on you like a moldy fruitcake no one else wanted and you have to learn to make the best of them. People are born with their Gifts, which can appear at any point, but for most of us, they emerge during puberty—as if we don't have enough to think about at that time." He looked up at the ceiling, remembering. "Well, they're not *all* bad."

"Tell me about yours," she whispered.

He tore his eyes from the ceiling, caught and held her gaze. "I can make people do *anything* on command."

"Like, hypnosis?" she asked, blinking under the over-bright fluorescent lights, her spoon halfway to her mouth.

"Almost," he said. "Except, a hypnotist is unable to persuade his clients to do anything they wouldn't ordinarily do. And I can." He shrugged his shoulders, almost as if he were apologizing.

Haley frowned as she sorted through this weird information. "So, let me get this straight. You think you could tell me to do something—anything—and I'd do it?" Her brows knitted together and she shook her head in disbelief.

"I don't just *think*. I...*know*." He lowered his voice as he leaned forward. "I could make you run around doing cartwheels in the parking lot if I wanted to. You would be unable to refuse."

At that, she sat straight up, staring at him. She didn't believe it—not quite, but she was too afraid to *dis*believe.

"It's true." He nodded. "Fortunately, I have a strong code of honor that I adhere to and I do not abuse my Gift. But I *could* make you do whatever I want."

She shook her head. "I don't believe you," she said in a low voice.

"I guess I'll have to prove it to you. Put that spoon down," he ordered.

She looked at it, all but forgotten until now. Realizing she *wanted* to let go of the spoon, she frowned. "No," she said

~ ☾ ~

between clenched teeth as she fought the urge to comply.

"Haley," he took a deep breath. "Put the spoon *down*."

The fingers holding her spoon twitched as she looked into his eyes and said, "No," in a voice she almost couldn't hear herself. Her mouth went dry with the effort.

"Put-the-spoon-down-*now*." His glacial blue eyes bored into hers. Her right hand trembled with the effort of resisting his will. Then she watched, wide-eyed, as her traitorous thumb lifted on its own, causing her spoon to waver and fall to the table with a clatter in the quiet restaurant, spilling its load of ice cream.

She swallowed. "How did you do that?" she asked, now truly frightened.

"I told you, it's my Gift," he said, using his napkin to wipe up the mess. "It's not one I use often and never on my friends. Never, ever."

Haley swallowed once or twice while wondering how fast she could get away from this beautiful, fascinating, irresistible boy with his dangerous Gift. Terrified, yet inexplicably still drawn to him, she slapped her palms down on the table and leaned forward, ready to shove away, to flee at any moment. His eyes softened as he saw the movement and he covered her small hands with his. Her breath caught. *What's he going to do to me?*

"Don't be afraid," he pleaded. "I would never, ever, take advantage of you. Please believe me."

"Are you doing it again?" she asked, because all of a sudden she did believe him. And she knew she would always believe him. Could she ever trust her own feelings around him?

"No, I'm not doing it again, but I *am* telling the truth. And now, let me tell you about another Gift I have." He never blinked as he readied himself.

"I don't think I want to know–"

"You do. I promise you do," he said, holding her there with his eyes.

She drew in a breath, steeling herself against whatever was about to come.

He touched a spot in the center of his forehead. "In my

~ ☾ ~

mind's eye, I see people who will be important to me in my future."

She frowned and shook her head slightly, not understanding. "And–"

"And you are *all over* my future." He smiled as if that should explain everything.

Flattering, but– "How do you know it's not my twin?" she said.

He sighed. "It's going to sound quite vain, but 'normal' people," he made air quotes, "no longer hold any interest for me."

"Lacey's not normal." She laughed, her voice wavering with nervousness.

"Even so," he said. "I'm looking at the only twin who'll ever keep my attention." He paused. "So, tell me. Are you still scared?"

Haley paused to consider. Her heart had stopped racing. She felt calmer, almost peaceful. "No." It was only half a lie. "But I think I'll feel better when I finish my ice cream."

He chuckled. "I'll show you how to resist," he said. "Very few people can, but I want you to be comfortable with me, always."

Haley sighed. "That would be good." *What have I gotten myself into?*

"You're very strong, you know." He sat with his chin propped on one hand.

She looked up, surprised. "Really?"

He nodded. "Most people cave at my first Suggestion."

"I guess I'm not like most people."

"Definitely not."

"WELL, I SUPPOSE I should be getting you back," he said after she finished.

"Already?" she asked. "But you didn't have any ice cream."

"Next time. For tonight, let's not worry Grandma Clara, okay?"

Walking back to his car, she thought of another issue. "So, Selena? What gives with her anyway?"

~ ☾ ~

"Ahh, Selena...we've known each other all our lives and unbeknownst to me, she decided years ago that we'd be married to each other one day." He rolled his eyes. "Not gonna happen." He held the door for her. "I believe she and I had our last conversation on the matter this afternoon."

"Will she be coming back on Thursday?"

"She said she would. We need her strength, you know," he said, starting the car.

"Her strength?"

"She's fought demons and won," Micah said.

"That little girl?" Haley asked, shaking her head.

"She's a tiger," he warned. "Don't underestimate her and don't cross her."

"That may be difficult. She doesn't like me at all," Haley said.

He shrugged as if Selena's likes and dislikes were of little importance. "She'll get over it. All she really needs is a boyfriend."

They drove in silence for a time while Haley mulled over the extraordinary evening. Her feelings ran the gamut from intrigue to panic and back again.

Micah turned onto Clara's street, pulled over and turned off the car.

Haley's brow furrowed. "You stopped too soon. She lives–" She pointed toward her grandmother's house, illuminated as always by the yellow bug light.

"I know where she lives." He faced her. "We'll be there in a moment. Right now, I'd like to ask you something."

She turned to him. "What is it?"

"I'd like to kiss you goodnight and I'd rather not have an audience. Would that be all right?" he asked, shifting his body closer to her.

Okay, so this was a question, not a demand, she thought. *So he's not manipulating me.* It saddened her that his every statement must be scrutinized in this way, but apparently that was her reality now. Her decision made, she turned to him. "No."

~ ☾ ~

CHAPTER SEVENTEEN

Leaning toward her, his eyes half-closed with expectation. "No?" They snapped open in disbelief. After a moment, he smirked. "So, what's the punch line?"

"No, I won't kiss you," she repeated. "I don't know you."

"Kissing's a great way to get to know a person," he said, a half smile playing on his lips as he moved in closer.

"*No,*" she said for the third time, thinking she could probably make it to her grandmother's house if she had to make a run for it. She grabbed the door handle.

Sighing, he moved back to his own seat. "Ooo-kay." He reached for the ignition.

"Um, I have a question," she said to fill the uncomfortable silence.

He turned to look at her, his raised eyebrows just visible in the dim light of a distant streetlight.

"Today after you healed me with my crystal..."

"Uh huh..." he said when she paused.

"And you said I was '*back* to beautiful...'" She swallowed.

"Yes?"

"Did you mean that? Or, were you just trying to, well..."

"I meant every word, I assure you," he said, the hint of a smile pulling at the corner of his mouth.

"Oh, well, thank you. Outside of my father, I think you're the first person to call me beautiful. 'Course there was Bobby Blair in second grade, oh and Grandma Clara..." she babbled through her nervousness, feeling her color rise. *Good thing it's pitch black in the car. He can't tell I'm blushing*—unless, *with one of his stupid talents he can see in the dark or sense temperature changes, or...God, what if he has x-ray vision?*

"I'm sure I won't be the last." He paused. "Listen, I've really enjoyed being with you tonight. Would you like to

~ ☾ ~

spend the day with me tomorrow?"

Okay. Another question. Her breath caught. "*Alone* with you?"

"Well, yes. I thought we might go to Spot Pond."

She looked out the window, debating.

"What are you afraid of?" he asked.

There it was, the question she always dreaded. "Nothing." She couldn't meet his eyes. "You don't scare me." In truth, she was terrified.

"This is about my Gift, right? You're afraid I'll make you do something embarrassing? I only showed it to you to prove I could actually do it. I would *never* use it on you. I promise." He took her hand. "Would you please look at me?"

She looked up, her stupid eyes filled with tears. And why that happened, she couldn't imagine. Swallowing was hard, but she tried anyway.

"Haley, I think—no, I *know* we have a magical connection. I'd like to explore it, but"—a soft chuckle—"I can't do it alone."

She bit her lower lip. *He's so beautiful and kind, so why am I afraid of him? Is it his Gift? I don't think he would hurt me...*

He tried again. "Are you still interested in helping us?"

"Yes." She nodded the second the words left his mouth.

"In the forest?"

"Uh huh." She nodded vigorously, her fear momentarily forgotten.

"Well, *that* was quick." He sighed. "In that case, I'm going to need to see what else you can do and maybe I can help you to more fully develop your Gifts."

"Oh, *that's* all right then," she agreed.

"So, is Spot Pond okay?"

"What about the Library?" she countered, thinking, *It's more public and the librarian would be watching. Just in case.*

"I'd rather be able to talk above a whisper, if you don't mind." In the darkness, his voice sounded almost cold. "The Common?"

"Okay, what time?"

"Noon?" From the raised timbre of his voice, his surprise

~ ☾ ~

was unmistakable.

"Sure." *Slow the breathing,* she mentally slapped herself in the head.

Shaking his head, he started the car. "Great. Let's get you back before I'm banned from your grandmother's forever." He drove the short distance to Clara's. At the front door, he lifted her hand to his lips and kissed it while he looked into her eyes.

"Got your kiss after all, didn't you?" She tipped her head and smiled, but her bravery was all an act. Inside she quaked with excitement and a nameless panic. She prayed he would leave before she embarrassed herself somehow, like throwing up on his shoes.

"Good night, Haley. This was fun." By the porch's amber light, Micah turned his devastating smile on her. "I'll pick you up at noon." He gave her a nod as he released her hand.

"S-s-sounds great," she stammered. *Ahh, the real Haley returns.* Trying not to show how awkward she felt in this situation, she lunged for the door and shoved, knocking her nosey sister on her butt.

Haley helped Lacey to her feet as she shut the door. "What were you doing?" she demanded.

"Eavesdropping. What d'ya think?" Lacey wiped invisible dust off her shorts. "So what happened? Out with it."

Grandma Clara's reedy voice spilled down the hall. "Haley, is that you?"

"Later," she whispered. To her grandmother she called, "Yeah, I'm back, Grandma."

"So...did you have a nice time?" Her grandmother approached, a pinched expression on her face.

"Yeah, I did. What's the matter, Grandma?" she asked. "You look a little worried."

"No, I'm fine. I wasn't instructed how to handle the dating thing, that's all. Of course, all you did was go for ice cream with Gisele's nephew. So how dangerous could *that* be?" She glanced at the clock. "I just thought you'd be home earlier than this."

"We went to Freddie's," Haley sighed, hands in the air.

"Ooh," Lacey and Grandma Clara said at once.

~ ☾ ~

Haley knew that would explain everything. Great food, but the service was a bit...unhurried...

"Why'd you go *there*?" Lacey asked. "They're so slow."

"He likes their food and the ice cream was great. We had fun." She yawned. "It wasn't a date though, Grandma, so I think you're fine."

"He picked you up, right?" Grandma Clara asked.

"Yeah."

"And took you out. Did he pay your way?"

"Uh, yeah, but–"

"And he walked you to the door?"

Haley nodded.

"Where I come from, *that's* a date."

Haley's eyebrows rose. "Hmm. Well, it was fun, but now I'm tired. I think I'll turn in early."

"It's not even nine thirty yet," her grandmother protested.

"Really?" Haley replied. "Maybe I'll take a bath and read for a while. Night, Grandma."

"Yeah, me too. Night!" Lacey called, running up the stairs.

Clara just shook her head. "I know a brush off when I see one. Goodnight."

IN THEIR ROOM, Lacey shoved her onto the bed. "So, what happened? Details, I want details."

Haley smiled and took a breath. "He is amazing."

"And *so* cute," Lacey said. "Did he kiss you?"

"No," Haley said, biting her lip.

"Too bad, but maybe next time."

Haley sat up and studied her reflection in the large oval mirror over the bureau. "Do you think we're beautiful?"

"I think we're attractive and sometimes even pretty when our hair is fixed up. But I don't think I'd go as far as beautiful," Lacey said, with a wistful smile. "I wish."

"*Dad* says we're beautiful." Haley tried smoothing her streaky, dirty-blonde hair.

"Dad loves us."

"So you're saying, in order for someone to think we're beautiful–"

~ ☾ ~

"They'd have to love us, yes," Lacey smiled and color flared on her cheeks. "Taylor says *I'm* beautiful."

"Do you think he loves you?"

"He says he does." More blushing.

Haley remembered how he looked at Lacey their first day back here. "I believe him." Though Haley realized she'd accidentally ferreted out one of her twin's most closely guarded secrets, she wasn't ready to share her own. "You *are* beautiful," she said, hugging her sister as they gazed side by side at their reflections. "Inside and out."

"So, what else did you talk about?" Lacey asked.

"Mostly the rift. He's interested in what else I can do besides healing."

"Why? What else can you do?"

"Well, the intuition stuff, I guess. He thinks I might be able to do other things as well."

"What's his last name?" Lacey asked. "Is it Westerfield, like Gisele's?"

"Uh, I don't know."

"Haley Westerfield," Lacey tried it out. "It's got a nice ring to it, don'tcha think?"

"Like Lacey Plante?"

"Yeah, that's good too. So, when's his birthday and what's his sign?"

"Didn't ask."

"Where's he live?"

"Um..."

"What *did* you talk about?"

"I don't really remember." Her gaze flashed on her sister before finding something interesting on her knuckle.

"Maybe he hypnotized you," Lacey joked.

Caught by surprise, Haley blinked at her twin. "Maybe he did.

MORE CONFUSED THAN upset, Micah ticked off the possible reasons for Haley's snub as he put the car in drive. Was she afraid of him because of his Gift? That was the most likely, since she seemed interested until he decided to show

~ ☾ ~

off. He'd honestly tried to mind his manners, but in hindsight, was forced to conclude he'd been far too aggressive with someone who wasn't ready for such a display.

But if that weren't the reason, could it be he wasn't her type? Or, not...handsome enough? He tightened his grip on the wheel as he drove.

Being unaccustomed to rejection left him unsure how to proceed. Should he try to talk it out with her? Or ignore the snub and continue to pursue her? Had she completely spurned him or just put him off? Curiosity burned as he drove to his aunt's cabin. Maybe a chat with Jake would help. His best friend had been sent packing more times than either could count, yet he maintained such a positive attitude while in pursuit, the girl often found herself surrendering to his charm, wit and persistence.

Observing Haley's Gift in the forest that morning reassured him that he was correct in fighting for her to assist. Though he knew Gisele would strongly disagree with him on this, tonight he'd gotten enough of a glimpse into Haley's mind to know he'd been right. He would fight hard for her to help in the forest. There was simply no other way. Even as an untapped, unschooled talent, it appeared to him she could be every bit as gifted as he.

Well...almost.

Micah hoped he hadn't scared her too badly with his spur of the moment demonstration during their non-date. He chuckled to himself. Haley's reactions to his Gift proved to be as atypical as she herself. The few girls he told--it was hard to keep the secret at first--were intrigued, fascinated. One even offered to submit herself as a guinea pig. But not Haley. Though she didn't yet realize it, she was stronger than most. He would do whatever it took to ease her fears. He would never, *could* never harm her.

Last January after seeing her picture on Aunt Gisele's wall, he decided that but for her, he would have no other. No other girls, no flings. Of course it hadn't been easy—the world is filled with beautiful girls, but Micah remained honor-bound to wait for her.

A girl he had yet to meet.

~ ☾ ~

To forestall the inevitable questions from his friends and female admirers, *"Are you a monk, a priest or gay?"* he took Selena to his prom, fueling a different—and possibly hotter—fire. At the time, the implications to her hadn't even crossed his mind. He shook his head at his own stupidity.

In saving himself for Haley, he'd made mistake after mistake with Selena this year and now he would pay for it. Hopefully, Selena took today's conversation seriously and would look elsewhere for her romantic entanglements.

He spent an hour or so that warm night cruising the streets in and around the small town of Bidwell, several times finding himself rolling slowly past Clara Miller's old Victorian.

Haley, he called out with his mind. Unsurprised when she failed to show up on the porch—telepathy did not appear to be one of her Gifts—he vowed to himself when it came to Haley, he would always keep trying. In every sense of the word.

Besides, he really enjoyed the way her full lips framed her words, the way she said his name and the way her soft hair waved in just the right places—*Haley*.

WRAPPED IN A fluffy robe and fresh from her bath, Haley stepped into the bedroom she shared with her sister. "What do you want?"

Her nose in a book, Lacey didn't even look up. "Nothing, why?"

"You called my name."

Lacey's brow furrowed in perfect imitation of her twin's. "You're hearing things."

Haley walked to the window and twitched the curtain aside just as a set of taillights winked behind a grove of trees.

~ ☾ ~

CHAPTER EIGHTEEN

"WE'LL HAVE THIS out now," Gisele muttered to herself as Micah's favorite band, Blakk Tarr, abruptly cut off in mid-shriek from her driveway. "I don't care how much talent they supposedly have, I cannot expose those children to such danger. They can't be allowed into the forest."

"How was your nap? Feeling better?" Micah strolled through her door like he owned the place.

"Yes, thanks I am." She noticed the rosy glow of his aura, a sign of love and high excitement. "What have you been up to?" *As if I didn't know.*

"I took Haley out for ice cream," he said with a grin.

"So, you're dating Selena *and* Haley?" she glared at him. This situation couldn't get much worse.

"No. Selena and I are just friends—"

"Does Selena know that?" Gisele asked, her lips pressed together.

"I've never made a secret of it, but yes, we talked about it and we're *just* friends," he said. "Really."

"I thought you two were an item—"

"Only in her mind."

"Haley's just fourteen," Gisele spat out. "And my best friend's granddaughter. If you—"

"Aunt Gisele," Micah held up his hands. "First of all, she'll be fifteen next month, second, I would never hurt her and third," his shoulders slumped, "I don't even think she likes me."

Gisele let his last comment slide. She knew better. "You have a reputation, young man—"

He acknowledged her remark with a slight tilt of his head as he looked away. "Honestly, I don't think you have a thing to worry about this time."

~ ☾ ~

"Those kids can't be allowed to enter the forest," Gisele stated.

"They'll go in anyway and I'm shocked you didn't realize that."

"They can't. It's just too dangerous."

"Haley has *two* crystals," he reminded her. "It's unprecedented. You won't be able to keep her out, I promise you." They stared at each other, her eyes meeting his, so clear and determined. The two of them were the best and strongest of their respective generations. "She healed the first rift without training or tools. You know we can't do it without her," he bit his lip and looked away before delivering the bombshell. "And I'm sorry, but I won't even try."

"That's it, then." Gisele closed her eyes and sighed, forced to accept the unacceptable. "I don't know what I'll say to Clara if anything happens to them—"

"Nothing will happen to them."

"There must be another way."

"There really isn't. You saw what she can do," he said.

"Have you seen the new...creatures?"

He matched her sigh with one of his own. "In my nightmares."

"Beetles and pink worms are nothing compared to—"

"I know, I know. But there are six of us...well, *four* of us," he said. "But Lacey and Taylor are quite experienced with water guns." He laughed.

He can afford to be cheerful, Gisele thought with dismay. *The battle's over. He fought for her and won.* She shook her head. Though she recognized the validity of his argument, it didn't make her feel any better. "What are your plans for tomorrow?"

"I'm going to the Town Common with Haley," he said. "We'll start working to identify her Gifts. I'd like to see what else she can do."

"So, is *that* the attraction? Her Gifts?" Gisele asked. His obvious fascination with the girl seemed a bit over the top.

"Not by a long shot. I was intrigued the first time I saw her picture..." His voice trailed away as he spotted the photo that lured him back to Bidwell, even more than Gisele's phone

~ ☾ ~

call. "By the way, she did really well against my *Suggestions*."

Gisele whirled, "What did you do?"

He held his hands up as if to ward off blows. "Relax. Give me some credit, please." He smiled. "She's very strong, you'll be happy to know. Took me three tries."

"Three?" Gisele's eyes widened as she caught her breath. "Same as me."

"I told you. We may just have something here," he said before looking away.

"Huh, we may have a chance, after all," Gisele followed his glance to the picture on the wall. "I'll call the parents tomorrow."

THE NEXT MORNING, Gisele sat before her large gazing ball after Micah left, intent upon getting some guidance for the next day's walk in the forest. She had just removed the velvet covering and lit her candle when clouds within the eight-inch crystal ball began forming and reforming. She saw trees, a full moon, and *smelled* the ferns, moss and pines. She gasped in shock, then the glass went black and she distinctly heard the words, "one will fall, one will fall, one will fall..."

She sat back in her chair, stunned. She'd seen many things in her ball over the years, but had never heard a voice through it or actually experienced the sensation of smell while using it. Covering her mouth with her fingers, she leaned forward once more, looking into its depths. Nothing else appeared and the ball sat, beautiful but silent.

~ ☾ ~

CHAPTER NINETEEN

AT BREAKFAST, AS Haley's fork chased her fruit salad around the plate—she was *way* too nervous to eat—Grandma Clara asked about their plans for the day.

"Taylor and I are riding our bikes up Route 30 to pick blueberries," Lacey said. "Can we make blueberry muffins or a pie or something afterwards?"

"Oh yes, that would be fun," Grandma Clara agreed. "I have some great recipes you can try." From a low shelf she pulled out an ancient cookbook and together she and Lacey perused its yellowed, well-worn pages.

While they were engrossed with their project, Haley threw most of her breakfast into the trash before leisurely sipping her stomach-soothing chamomile tea.

"I think I can make this...Blueberry Buckle. It seems easy enough," Lacey turned to her. "Want to come with us?"

"No, that's okay." Haley said and was rewarded with a smile. "I think I'll go to the...Common and hang around, maybe read a book."

Lacey's eyes narrowed, instantly suspicious. "Alone?"

"Course not. There'll be plenty of people there, silly. You have fun picking blueberries though." Haley sighed and looked away, her foot tapping nervously.

That's all it took. "I've got to get some stuff from upstairs. Why don't you come and help me?"

Haley recognized the request for what it was—blackmail, pure and simple. "Sure." She downed the rest of the tea and put her cup into the sink. "I'll do these later, Grandma," she said.

"That's okay, I'll take care of them. Go ahead and help your sister."

~ ☾ ~

"OUT WITH IT," Lacey said as she closed the bedroom door.

"With what?" Haley played innocent, but she knew it was only a matter of time. There are few secrets between twins.

"Are you meeting him there? You'd never go to the *Common* alone," Lacey said with barely disguised scorn.

"Nope, he's picking me up here."

Lacey smacked her sister's arm. "Why didn't you tell me?"

"Thought you heard our plans at the door last night, you little sneak."

Lacey scratched her chin. "Must have missed that. Damn. What else are you going to do?"

"That's the whole plan." Haley smiled. "I can't wait."

"You have to tell me *everything* when you get home." Lacey cracked open the bedroom door and voices floated upstairs. "Taylor's here. I'll see you later. *Everything,*" she repeated, pointing her finger for emphasis.

"Where's all the stuff you were helping with?" Grandma Clara asked when they appeared downstairs empty-handed.

"Must've left it all down here." Lacey shrugged. She and Taylor grabbed hats, berry buckets and sunscreen from the sofa. Lacey glared over her shoulder at her twin as she left. Haley bit back a giggle.

Her grandmother followed shortly after with her shopping list, leaving Haley alone with her thoughts and racing heartbeat. She ran upstairs to change into something suitable for a non-date with the cutest guy she ever met. As she looked at her reflection in the door mirror of her father's old bedroom, she wondered how someone like Micah could actually be interested in a girl as boring as she. *He seems to be*, she thought, then proceeded to change her clothes three times. *This is getting me nowhere.* "That's it," she decided. *Denim shorts, pink tank top. Done. He'd like it or he wouldn't. Hmmm, maybe the blue?*

"No."

A knock on the door and she nearly lost what little breakfast she'd eaten. *Why am I so nervous? I need to relax.* She ran down the stairs while yanking a shirt on over her

~ ☾ ~

tank top. *He already seems to like me. The hard part's over.*
She opened the door and there he stood.
A vision.
He, too, wore denim shorts, as well as a short-sleeved shirt, unbuttoned to reveal nicely tanned pecks, abs and all kinds of girl-attracting muscles.
Yikes, breathe, she reminded herself, tearing her eyes away from his amazing torso before getting lost in his eyes, his smile. Whatever. He was a minefield and here she stood, defenseless. Add his dangerous Gift and any other supernatural powers of his she had yet to discover, and no wonder she was practically hyperventilating. *I don't know whether to be excited or terrified, she thought. It's a good thing we'll be out in public.*
But wait. His eyes were checking her out too.
Well, well. Both she and Lacey had gotten curvier over the last year. Her face lost its baby fat and her cheekbones became more prominent. And just yesterday, he called her beautiful. What did she have to worry about?
"Hello," she said.
"Hello gorgeous." He smiled. "Ready to go?"
"Absolutely." She grabbed her shoulder bag and followed him out to his car.
Haley was silent during the trip, trying to tame her runaway heart, which threatened to burst from her chest. She took a few slow, deep breaths to get herself under control.

BIDWELL'S TOWN COMMON sprawled over an acre in the center of town. The white Victorian era bandstand graced the middle of the Common, surrounded by a well-tended lawn. Two dozen one-hundred-year-old oak trees shaded and cooled the citizens who sat on various park benches as well as those jogging on the sidewalk. Micah spread his blanket under the largest tree, the one farthest from the bandstand and any other people. *Private, yet still public,* she smiled.
"Hungry?" he asked.
"A little." *Not really.*
"I brought an Italian grinder. Here, take half," he offered.

~ ☾ ~

"Oh, I couldn't eat all that," she protested, laughing.

"Just eat what you want. I'll finish it off. I'm starving," he said between mouthfuls.

"You'll get my germs," she teased.

"Here's hoping." He grinned, biting into his half.

"You're always hungry," she shook her head.

He stopped chewing as he looked at her. Finally he swallowed. "Yes, I am."

She had a feeling he wasn't thinking about food.

After lunch, which Haley hardly touched, they got down to business. "With some reluctance, Aunt Gisele's agreed to allow you, Lacey and Taylor to assist us in the forest this summer," he said.

"Really? This is so exciting. We'll do a great job, I know we will."

"I'm not so sure about the other two, but I know we need you."

"They'll be fine. They're really helpful and those beetles might've killed me if they hadn't figured out how to defend me."

"Based on *your* clues," he said.

She shrugged off the compliment.

"How do you feel about being a magical person?"

"Am I?"

"Without a doubt."

"I'm so different from you." She sighed. "You decide to do something and it just happens. I'm not...quite...conscious when everything goes crazy, so I don't feel particularly magical. I feel special, but not magical. I suppose if I could actually witness a magical moment that I've created, it would be different..." She smiled. "It's pretty cool watching yours at work, though."

"You're excited about doing this?"

"Absolutely. We're very excited to be helping," she said. "It felt wrong to leave Gisele when we just knew there was something we could do."

"At some point, I'm going to show you how to resist my Suggestions. I want you to be comfortable with me, always. Unfortunately, we don't have time for that today." He paused

~ ☾ ~

before asking, "But can I assume you're open to becoming more psychic? Learning new skills that will help you use your Gifts?"

"Yes, of course."

"Good," he said. "Let's begin. Are you comfortable?"

She nodded.

"Good. Close your eyes and imagine an orange ball..."

For the next two hours, Micah introduced Haley to creative visualization, meditation techniques and other exercises used to strengthen her psychic abilities. A willing student, she soaked it up like water in a desert.

"Gisele would like to break the news to the three of you, so please don't tell Lacey or Taylor about going into the forest, okay?" he asked when they were packing their belongings. "It's supposed to be a surprise."

"I think I can manage to keep a secret for eighteen hours." She laughed.

"*Can* you?" he asked.

"You'd be surprised what I can keep from her," She raised an eyebrow. "*I* can be pretty close-mouthed, but *her* stories know no end. She tells me everything. Ugh."

On the way back Micah said, "Gisele was really against this you know, but I told her I wouldn't do it without you. I hated going against her, but you are so much stronger than she is. I'm convinced it would've killed her."

Haley's cheeks flushed. "Do you really think I'm stronger than Gisele?" Of all the things he'd told her, this piece of information felt the most complimentary.

"She's be the first to admit she's well past her prime, but even in her heyday I'll bet you'd probably be better at this than she was." He paused. "You're a natural healer. One of a kind."

Wow, she thought. *He thinks I'm beautiful, powerful and talented. Can this possibly get any better?* "Thank you for the vote of confidence. I promise to do my very best," Haley said as he walked her up the stairs. She tried to sound adult and mature while her heart beat itself nearly to death in her chest. "Oh, and thanks for an amazing day. You're a great teacher and I learned a lot. See you tomorrow."

~ ☾ ~

She glanced over her shoulder at him as he stood just inches behind her on the porch. She wasn't ready to be kissed just yet and his closeness made her nervous.

His eyes grabbed and held hers. "I can't wait," he answered with a quiet intensity that caught her off guard and left her stomach doing flip-flops.

~ ☾ ~

CHAPTER TWENTY

HALEY FLOATED INTO the living room where Lacey sat, arms crossed over her chest. "Did you have a good day?" Haley asked, not really caring.

"It was great." Lacey practically exploded off the couch. "We got blueberries. What'd you get?"

"Heaven," Haley whispered, eyes closed, picturing Micah's face in her mind.

"On the *Town Common?* Do not think for one minute that you're not telling me what you did today," Lacey hissed. "I tell you *everything!*"

"And haven't I begged you not to?" Haley said. "Lacewing, I just had a wonderful day. I'm going upstairs to think about it *alone* for a little while. Maybe we can talk after supper."

"What a freakin' gyp!" Lacey stalked to the porch glider and began rocking furiously. Open-mouthed, Haley watched her sister's tantrum for a moment before running upstairs, smiling, humming and thinking of Madame Lola's tall handsome stranger.

THE NEXT MORNING after a day in which Haley revealed absolutely nothing, Lacey ate her breakfast in stony silence. Her foul mood permeated the kitchen until finally Grandma Clara asked, "Is there anything wrong? You girls are so quiet this morning."

"Everything is fine." Haley's feelings of happiness and serenity were undisturbed by her sister's barely unvoiced snit.

"Great. Wonderful." Lacey stabbed a fork into her eggs.

Taylor showed up around eight forty-five and waited for the girls on the porch.

"Got your crystal?" he asked Haley, who nodded. He

~ ☾ ~

looked at Lacey. "The Mandrake? Squirt gun?"

"Yup."

He patted his pocket. "Got mine."

"You won't need the water guns." Haley said with quiet authority.

"What?" Lacey asked.

"We're not going in?" Taylor said, his eyes round with disbelief.

"I don't know. I just know we won't need the water guns today, but you can take yours if you want," Haley said. "Mine's upstairs."

Lacey and Taylor exchanged glances and Taylor made up his mind. "I'm keeping it."

"Me too," Lacey said.

"Whatever." Haley mounted her bike. She rode to Gisele's in silence as the other two chattered away, each offering up possibilities for the day ahead. Micah's car parked next to Gisele's yellow Toyota caused a quick lurch in Haley's heartbeat. She smiled at the thought of him waiting inside the cabin for her.

"Get that look off your face," Lacey growled.

Taylor's brow furrowed. "What's the matter with you?"

"Nothing, nothing at all." She stomped up the steps.

"Are you two fighting?" he asked Haley.

She shrugged. "She'll get over it." They followed Lacey into the cabin, where the kitchen table was piled high with enough supplies for a six-day hike.

Taylor grinned with excitement.

Haley looked across the room and locked eyes on Micah. "Well, hello." He smiled.

"Hi," she said, quickly looking away.

"Okay." Gisele's tone was all business. "Are you three still interested in this fool's errand?"

They stared at her.

"Do you still want to come into the forest with us?" she elaborated.

"Yes," they said as one.

Gisele shook her head. "This is so dangerous, but I'm convinced that the three of us"—she glanced at an obviously

~ ☾ ~

angry Selena, then at Micah, who held her gaze—"cannot do it alone. If you come into the forest, you must do as I say, when I say it. Do you understand?"

Three heads nodded.

"This morning I called your mother, Taylor." Gisele looked at the Haley and her sister. "And your father. I told them a story about doing some research in the forest, and that you'd agreed to help. So, I got specific permission for you to be here as much as we need you over the next month."

"What did you say we'd be doing?" Lacey asked.

"Cataloguing poisonous native plants and mushrooms for a possible book. I wanted to impress upon them that it could be dangerous, but I would never leave your side and you'd be learning a little Botany at the same time."

Taylor looked nervous. "How did she take it?"

"Better than I thought she would," Gisele chuckled. "But I'd begin a folder of rough drawings in case she wants to see proof of what we're doing. And I will point out a few, so I don't feel like a complete liar." She looked at Haley. "Your father had no problem at all. He trusts that I'd never subject you or Lacey to any danger. First time I've ever lied to him, I think." She looked away, shaking her head. "Back to business and these are the rules: always keep the others in sight. No one walks alone, ever. I will lead and Micah will be last." She paused. "Should something happen to any one of you, your families will have my sorry head on a stick. If you cannot follow directions, you will not enter the forest again, I don't care how helpful you are. Is that understood?"

More head nodding.

Gisele shook her head. "I hate that I have to resign myself to this bad idea. Anyway, our goal today is to carry my crystal and Haley's *two* back to the Crystal Cave to heal and reinvigorate them. They are seriously depleted from neutralizing the rifts and must be returned to their Source for reenergizing. Hopefully, we will find their replacements on the Stone Altar. But these"—she held hers up to be viewed—"must go back today. Selena indicated to me where she believes the rifts have occurred and I have chosen a trail where, with any luck, we will encounter only one."

~ ☾ ~

She took a breath and continued. "Last night, my gazing ball alerted me to several new concerns. The first is a Terratress, the Treasure Keeper. She will hold no attraction for the females of our group, but she will attempt to lure the boys into her tree, where they will be killed and robbed of their gold, gems, coin or anything of value, similar to what mermaids do to sailors."

As one, the girls' faces went white, even as Taylor's mouth fell open.

"How?" Lacey whispered, staring at Taylor.

"The Terratress is a beautiful apparition, ghostly white, with waist-length silver white hair. Like a mermaid, she has no legs but her body ends in a long serpent-like tail, which she wraps around pine tree branches. Legend has it, her scales actually sparkle in the sunlight. From high above the forest floor, it is said she plays a silver lute, irresistible to the opposite sex. When a man hears the enchanting music, he becomes impossibly drawn to her. Just as he is about to reach her, she lets out a murderous shriek, turns into the monster she is, curls her tail around his body, crushes then drops him. The Terratress then slinks down the tree and robs the body of any gold or valuables. After collecting her treasure, she slithers back up and awaits her next victim. She prefers to make her home in very tall, very old pine trees."

"So you're saying mermaids are real too?" Haley asked.

"Of course. We have a few in our lake," Gisele said.

"Terrific." Lacey turned to Taylor. "Still want to go?"

Taylor licked his lips. "Of course. I'm not afraid."

"You should be," Gisele said.

"Um, how is a Terratress eliminated?" Haley asked, her heart pumping so hard she almost felt sick. She tried not to stare at Micah, though that appeared to be a losing battle. Out of the corner of her eye she watched him, seemingly unconcerned, as he packed his gear for their hike. *One vill fall, one vill fall*, Draculola's words returned to her.

"I'm not sure," Gisele said. "Hopefully, the tools we find on the Stone Altar will help us."

"I still have the Mandrake from last time. How should I use it?" Lacey asked.

~ ☾ ~

"Maybe as an alternative to the water guns?" Micah finally spoke. "Or maybe you'll need it today for something else..."

"You'll know when the time comes. Let's split up the assignments," Gisele told them. "Haley will heal the rifts. We're all available for her protection. However, Selena, Haley is *your* primary responsibility."

You could search for years and never find two people who would disagree with a decision more than Micah and Selena did just then. Haley watched Micah look down, biting his lower lip. Selena turned away without bothering to hide her disgust. *Sure, like* she *wants to babysit* me. Haley's eyes flicked to Gisele. *Can't she see how badly this could turn out?*

"Selena will also inform us where new rifts are forming. Micah will assist in the calling and directing of The Elementals in battle—"

"Elementals?" Lacey asked. "Who are they?"

Gisele smiled. "You've met them all, at one time or another. The Tinky-tinks are Earth Dwellers, and my dragons, Pat and Mike, are Fire Elementals, for obvious reasons. The Sylphs, or Water Sprites are available for water magic and the Fairies are the Elementals of the Air."

"Can't you call them?"

"Yes, but it's Micah's Gift," Gisele looked to Micah who shrugged. "It's so fortunate we have you. I've never known anyone who can call them like you do. I've tried, but the only time they appear to me is when I bring offerings and gifts." She put her hand up to her face as if she were sharing a well-known secret. "Bribes."

"What are Tinky-tinks?" Selena frowned.

Gisele looked up. "That's right, you've never met them. Tinky-tinks, or Tinks, as I call them are forest dwellers, about a foot tall, who move through the forest by tunneling under the duff. When they are about to surface, a plume of leaves, needles and dust flies into the air, announcing their arrival. Brown fur and leaves cover their little brownish-green bodies."

"They have huge pointed ears and what looks like cotton-candy tufts of fur sticking out of them." Lacey smirked.

Haley knew her sister didn't care about explaining to

~ ☾ ~

Selena—she just wanted to show off her knowledge. She flashed Lacey a warning look to no avail.

"And they have big eyes and pointy chins." Lacey raised her eyebrows in mock innocence. "An-n-n-d, they announce themselves by saying, 'Tink, tink, tink.'"

Selena turned and sneered. "Who asked *you*?"

"You're pretty scary for a midget," Lacey said, grinning.

"Lacey," Gisele said.

"How dare you?" Selena took a threatening step toward her.

"I was just kidding. Don't go all postal on me."

A nervous laugh escaped Haley's lips and Selena's lip curled as she pointed at her, her loathing obvious. "When I snap, *you'll* be the first to know."

"That's enough, all of you!" Gisele ordered. "There'll be no snapping and no going postal. When we enter the forest, we go as a team or not at all. Is that understood?"

Haley and her sister nodded their heads. Selena gave a half shrug.

"Thank you. Now, back to the assignments. In addition to calling The Elementals, Micah will, of course, also be invaluable during the fights with his wand and his sword."

"If we ever fight creatures larger than bugs and worms," he said with distaste.

"I wouldn't mind if all the rifts were filled with bugs and worms," Gisele said, holding a roll of parchment. "Taylor, here's a map of the forest. Can you keep track of the rifts' locations and note on the map when we've closed and healed them?"

Taylor brightened. "Of course."

"You will also test the ground with your staff—more on that in a minute—and assist in destroying any entities that exit the rift, especially if they get too close to Haley. We expect you to do this to the best of your ability, but do not take chances with your life. Again, we're a team, okay?"

Taylor nodded.

"Lacey, your job is similar to Taylor's in that you will assist in destroying entities as they emerge. You will also help me, especially in battle. I'm not as quick as I used to be and I

~ ☾ ~

could use the backup. There will be something else for you to do, but I'm not at all sure what's coming." Lacey smiled, and Haley knew it pleased her bratty sister to be included, *considering she nearly got us kicked out before we even started.*

"I will place and direct all of you to our maximum benefit in battle, but understand this fight may take a while."

A battle that seems without end. Are you fighting with anyone? Madam Lola's words returned to Haley in a rush. She glanced at Lacey, who seemed unaffected. Haley couldn't wait to tell the old fortune-teller how right she was.

"I will provide you with as much information as I can so you can perform to the best of your ability. Is everyone clear on their duties?" Her team nodded their heads, while neither Selena nor Micah attempted to mask their displeasure. Haley began to feel uneasy. Gisele said the danger would be greater if members of the team didn't work together.

"What about testing the ground with my staff?" Taylor asked.

"Yes, about that." Gisele rubbed her temple. "My gazing ball showed me that there are now fissures in the forest filled with quicksand–"

"What?" Taylor sputtered. "That can't be right. There's no quicksand around here–at least that's what my father told me."

"You're right. Massachusetts doesn't have the right conditions for regular quicksand, but *this* quicksand is unlike any other. The new formations follow narrow lines, maybe a foot wide, crisscrossing the forest, and are filled with quicksand. They are very dangerous so we will be testing the ground for stability wherever we go."

Lacey sighed. "Remember last year? It was great. We saw the unicorns, the fairies, the Tinky-tinks."

"Who shot at me," Taylor muttered.

"We met the dragons," Haley said.

"Stupid giant carnivorous frogs tried to eat me," Taylor said.

"We played with the Water Sprites," Lacey smiled.

"The Terrors tried to kill us," Taylor shook his head.

~ ☾ ~

Micah sat with his mouth open. "Sounds like you had quite the summer." He turned to Haley. "You've seen The Terrors? You've been in the forest at night? What happened?"

"Later," Gisele said. "Let's concentrate on what we're doing today."

"Okay, so we have rifts, things coming out of the rifts, strange quicksand, a shrieking Terratress…is there anything *good* out there?" Taylor asked, his exasperation showing.

"Besides The Elementals?" Gisele said. "Actually, yes."

Shock registered on Taylor's face. Haley noted that Selena still looked bored, obviously she had been briefed on all this. Probably Micah too, but he at least paid attention to Gisele's directions and explanations. "Really? What is it?"

"There's something new in the forest that I call Dwarf Closets. It works like this: if you're being pursued through the forest, look for a group of stones—boulders, with an obvious opening. Jump through that opening while hitting the side and the stones will close around you. This will create a circular stonewalled sanctuary, complete with a roof. You'll be protected from anything on the outside. Well, except for earthquakes," Gisele said. "I will be consulting my gazing ball often and I'll keep you apprised of any new information." She pulled out a small black velvet bag.

"You still have your magic bag?" Haley said. "I haven't seen it since last year."

"Of course. I never go into the forest without it."

"What's so special about a black bag?" Selena asked.

"No matter what Gisele puts into it, the magic bag doesn't get bigger or heavier," Haley said, secretly proud she knew more than Selena. "I'm surprised you didn't know that."

Selena's lip lifted in a sneer and Haley instantly regretted baiting her.

"That about covers everything, right?" Micah said with a smirk. "We should probably get started."

Gisele nodded as she passed out sandwiches. "Everyone brought water?" she asked, checking and rechecking. Quiet now, the members of her upstart team nodded in agreement, strapping on their backpacks and their game faces.

Upon arrival at the Altar Stone, they found it loaded with

~ ☾ ~

tools: another ash staff, an ultra-thin silver rope, a bag of Mandrake, a beautiful flowered crown, a four-inch round mirror and two large crystals. The Altar Stone also held a blue pouch filled with large white faceted stones—"Salt?" Gisele chuckled, while stowing it in her magic bag—and lastly, three wands awaited their new owners.

Gisele and Haley claimed the crystals.

Lacey walked away with the silver rope, shrugging her shoulders. Taylor snagged the Mandrake. Selena pocketed the mirror, while Gisele took the staff. She then explained the magical significance of each wood as her students held their hands over the glowing wands. Guided to the chocolate brown wand, Lacey received Walnut, "for motivation and focused energy," while Taylor accepted Oak, "for protection, good luck and strength." Haley's Cherry wand rolled into her outstretched hand, accompanied by a sigh from Gisele. "For love, renewal and confidence," she said, handing each of them a wand case, which they attached to their belts.

"How do all these things find their way onto the Stone Altar?" Lacey asked, tracing the knots and burls on her wand.

"It's magic, child. The forest provides. That's the only explanation I have," Gisele said, then directed her next comments to her three students. "Understand, with no wand experience, all you can manage is touch and disable. This Thursday, we'll have a wand-training class. Now, who gets the lovely circlet, I wonder?"

Selena strode to the Altar, pushed her arm in front of Lacey and, while ignoring her icy glare, held her hand over the flowered crown. Nothing happened. Gisele and Lacey did the same, receiving similar results. Haley sighed and placed her hand over the crown, causing it to glow with an inner, unworldly light. Picking it up, she closed her eyes and held it flat. Without knowing why, she adjusted it a quarter turn to the right and placed it on her head. She glanced at Micah. His mouth had fallen open and his eyes smoldered at the sight of her. She watched as he swallowed and turned away.

Gisele entered the forest followed by Taylor, then Lacey, Serena, Haley and Micah. Lacey turned around. "I feel bad for Micah—he didn't get anything from the Altar Stone," she

~ ☾ ~

said. Haley glanced over her shoulder to gauge his reaction.

"Don't worry." He flashed his trademark grin. "I have everything I need right here." He patted the scabbard which housed his sword and winked at Haley, who had slowed to walk next to him.

"Pay attention." Gisele turned around, making the briefest eye contact with Micah.

"I'm all over it, Aunt Gisele."

"I can see that," Gisele hissed. "Pay attention."

"She worries too much," he whispered loudly. After a quick look at Gisele, his eyes never left Haley.

She wondered if Gisele might be right to worry.

~ ☾ ~

CHAPTER TWENTY-ONE

LESS THAN FIFTEEN minutes later, Haley accidentally kicked a small rock, which rolled a few feet then fell into the earth without a sound. She blinked, called the others over, then dropped a stick and they watched as it quickly receded into a small area of leaves and sand.

As a result, Gisele identified a long line of quicksand. "Can we do something about this?" she said, evaluating the danger as her team stood near its edge. "Taylor, please note this manifestation on our map and check with your staff to see how far it goes. But don't leave our sight."

Touching the edge of quicksand with his walking stick, Taylor followed the line east about twenty feet and marked it. Standing well away, Haley saw the difference in color and texture from the surrounding ground was minimal. This could fool anyone. "But it's only a foot wide," she said. "You could get out of it like regular quicksand, right?"

"No. Line quicksand is much more dangerous than the regular kind," Gisele said. "It actually pulls you down. Unlike common quicksand, there's nothing passive about it."

"So how can we disarm this?" Haley asked.

"Let's try the easiest solutions first. Squirt guns?" Gisele said.

Both Taylor and Lacey began squirting a small area. After a few minutes with no change, Gisele turned to Selena. "How about the mirror? Aim the sun's reflection on the quicksand."

Two minutes of concentrated sun and heat on one spot produced no helpful results.

"Wait a minute." Gisele pulled a blue pouch from her magic bag. "Let's try our salt."

She dropped a golf ball-sized, faceted salt crystal on the line. Immediately the quicksand began to bubble and froth

~ ☾ ~

and as they watched, that section of the line solidified. Then, while Gisele salted the rest of the line, Taylor made a note on the map of this, their most recent healing.

"Note this in red on the map, Taylor. I still don't trust it," Gisele said, even after both she and Taylor tested it with their staffs. "Hikes through the forest will never be the same."

They proceeded to double-check the entire line. Satisfied, they moved on, the small troupe on hyper-alert, watching and listening for any signs of danger on their way to the Crystal Cave.

Haley sighed. The trip to the cave, one of her favorite places in the forest, normally took about an hour and a half. *At this rate, we might make it by nightfall.* So much had changed since last year, and yet when she looked at Micah's radiant, excited face, she felt just a little grateful. She probably would not have met him without this crisis. *Way to go, rift.*

They stopped twice more, salting, healing and re-integrating new lines of quicksand. The group became more efficient, taking less than five minutes to dispatch each line. Walking however, continued to be much slower than usual, as each step had to be tested for safety.

Around noon they stopped outside their favorite lunch spot, a shady, log-strewn clearing, surrounded by towering pine trees. Obviously intent on his sandwich, Taylor strode forward, only to be grabbed by his backpack. "Wait a minute. This could be a Tree-Trap," Gisele said, halting him mid-step.

"A what?" Still leaning forward, Taylor awkwardly twisted to see her face.

With an apologetic smile, she released him. "A Tree Trap. Something I just remembered seeing in the gazing ball. It's a clearing totally surrounded by pine trees, like this one." Her sweeping hand indicated the ancient conifers. "Once you get inside, the trees creep toward you, slowly at first, but then they hedge you in and crush you."

"You didn't mention this before," Lacey said.

"I'm old. I forget things. Shoot me." Gisele's response caused Haley to giggle silently behind her.

"But we've eaten here before," Taylor protested.

~ ☾ ~

"Everything's changed," Gisele said. "Let's test it." She tossed a branch into the center of the clearing.

Other than the soft swishing of pine needles, there was no accompanying sound, but Haley detected gradual movement as the trees began to lean forward into the circle, seemingly concentrating on the area around the branch. "They move so slowly. Couldn't you get out before they crushed you?" she whispered while watching their measured progress.

"No, the trees themselves are slow, but–" Gisele tossed another branch between two of the advancing pine trees. "See what happens?" Instantly, branches on either side of the trees interlocked, creating a deadly wooden cage.

"How should we neutralize this?" Micah asked.

"I'm thinking a wand or a sword," Gisele said, her eyes dancing. Haley noticed for the first time since entering the forest, her teacher looked almost hopeful.

"Let's try the sword," Micah suggested, pure joy on his face. He pulled his beautiful, glowing sword from its sheath. White sparks flew as the others drew back in awe.

"Would you test the ground around the outside first?" he asked while deftly tracing deep blue figure eights through the air in front of him.

"Of course." Gisele nudged a reluctant Taylor forward. "Use your staff." Over her shoulder she said, "Don't get too flashy, Micah. We don't want to attract anything else if we can help it."

Micah just smiled, sweeping wide arcs with his sword. "Nothing flashy."

From within the clearing, violent noises could be heard as brittle branches crashed and broke against each other. The air filled with the scent of pine as a flurry of sticky pine needles rained down on them.

"It's safe," Gisele said over the din. "Counterclockwise, I think."

Micah pointed his sword toward the earth, close to the base of the trees, causing ice blue fire to erupt from its tip as he walked the perimeter. His light show dazzled Haley, who stood apart from the others with her hand over her mouth. Watching the blue flames rise to almost Micah's height, she

~ ☾ ~

was reminded of the terror she felt just before healing the second rift. The others were impressed as well, especially Selena whose fawning, over-the-top hero-worship of Micah fooled no one. Once the flames encircled the trees, they began to straighten, then arc backwards. So slowly she almost missed it, Haley watched as the pines drew back to their original spot on the forest floor. The blue fire made its way inside the clearing and burned for a minute before dying out. "It's safe now," Micah said, re-sheathing his sword with a *zing*.

"Thank you," Gisele said. "Everyone, please wait here while Taylor and I check the clearing for line quicksand." After swallowing several times, a wide-eyed Taylor accompanied Gisele inside the former Tree-Trap to confirm its safety for the rest of the group.

"Oh Micah, you're incredible! That was awesome!" Selena, all wide-eyed reverence, stroked Micah's arm and shoulder, positioning her body against his. "How did you ever learn to do that? My parents never taught me to work with a sword. Can you teach me? Please, *please?*"

"That was amazing." Haley's quiet comment captured Micah's attention away from Selena and her ridiculous display. "Where did you get that sword?"

Micah turned to Haley, ignoring Selena's cloying spectacle and patted the hilt of the sword. "Isn't it beautiful? This sword's been handed down to the oldest son in my family for many generations," he said with pride.

She thought she'd never seen him so happy.

"Oh, Micah, Micah that was *just*—" Selena's loud gushing was accompanied by childish clapping and not-so-childish poses.

"You liked it. We got that. Now calm yourself," Lacey said. Though Haley knew her sister was still a bit annoyed with her, Selena's nonsense seemed to utterly infuriate her.

"I'm not talking to *you*," Selena shot back. "If Micah doesn't like it, then I'll stop, but—"

"That's all I have to say? Good. Stop, you're being ridiculous." Micah glanced briefly skyward. Haley turned away to hide her amusement from Selena.

~ ☾ ~

"All set," Gisele called as she settled on one of the logs.

Muttering, Selena stomped into the clearing and flung herself on a stump far from the others. Lacey strode in the opposite direction with Taylor in tow.

"So is this place cured now?" Haley asked, looking up at the big trees to avoid Selena's angry, accusing glare.

"Yes, it is. *Finally*, one place we don't have to worry about." Gisele smiled as they claimed seats on logs and dug into their lunches. "Eat up, everyone. We don't have much time."

"So, tell me what happened when you saw The Terrors," Micah said, biting into his sandwich.

"I'll be happy to tell you about my part, which wasn't too bad, but Lacey and Taylor have one heck of a story," Haley said with a grin. "It happened during the Eclipse last year. We were supposed to remind Gisele about it, because she doesn't have a TV, but of course we forgot. Crazy nervous all day, Gisele hurried us from one part of the forest to another, looking at the sky, muttering to herself..." She rolled her eyes, somewhat amused by Gisele's actions. "So on our way back, with Gisele speed-walking her way out, *those* two"–Haley jutted her chin at her sister and Taylor–"got separated from us. When we realized they weren't behind us, it was already too dark to go looking for them, so Gisele levitated with me to the cabin. What a terrifying trip! Weird screaming and biting things all over us." Haley rubbed away the goose bumps from her upper arms.

"I stood in the yard," she continued, "waiting while Gisele returned with them. When I heard her say, *now!* I pointed my crystal toward the place she entered and a blue line appeared from deep in the forest, joining mine with hers. Gisele's crystal followed the line and that's how they found their way out."

"You heard her from all the way in the forest?" he asked, frowning thoughtfully.

"Yep. Just like she was standing right next to me."

Micah tipped his head and smiled at Haley. She realized she'd surprised him once again. He crossed his arms over his chest and gave her a crooked smile. "We are so well matched.

~ ☾ ~

Someday you'll realize that."

They ate in silence for a short time. "So, what's with Lacey?" Micah asked in a low voice, after glancing at her and Taylor, yards away.

"Oh, she's mad because I wouldn't talk about what went on between us yesterday."

"It's none of her business." He shrugged.

"We're twins." She bravely strayed into his personal space to pat his knee. He couldn't possibly understand the twin-thing. "We tell each other everything."

"Everything?" Micah said, swallowing hard.

"Yup." She smiled and bit into her sandwich. "Though I must admit I'm getting kind of tired of all that sharing."

They ate in silence for a while.

"So, just for the record, what *did* go on between us yesterday?"

"Break's over." Gisele stood up and passed around a small trash bag.

"Oh, too bad. Maybe another time," she smiled at his mock frown.

Resuming their trek, they encountered one more vein of line quicksand, which they quickly dispatched. Their progress through the forest had been painfully slow, so Haley was overjoyed to finally hear the sounds of tumbling water in the distance. They followed a fern-lined path until they reached a dazzling waterfall, cascading like a sheet onto a pile of white quartz boulders, before ending in a small pool. The area thrummed with dragonflies and the sounds of birdsong.

Haley sighed. Already a long day, and it wasn't even half over. She followed Gisele up the mossy steps next to the waterfall, before ducking under the falls, leaving the others to enjoy the soothing sounds of splashing water and watch the golden carp frolicking in the pool. After depositing the three spent crystals in the shallow crystal Blessing Bowl in the Crystal Cave's tiny stone alcove, Gisele whispered her thanks. "Return to Source and regain your power." They quickly descended the steps only to find a commotion at the pool. On her knees, Lacey made repeated attempts to retrieve a beautiful palm-sized, fire colored stone. Though able to grasp

~ ☾ ~

the rock, when she tried to bring it to the surface, the magnificent gem mysteriously melted through the crevices of her fingers and sank to the bottom of the pool.

After twice witnessing Lacey's futile attempts to secure the stone, Gisele gently informed her that the rock could not be meant for her. Haley smiled at her sister's stubbornness when Lacey resolutely refused to give up and continued in her attempts to capture it, this time using both hands. The exquisite stone simply found new crevices through which to disappear.

"Let me try." Selena stepped forward, but she too was unable to corral the stone after repeated attempts. Haley watched as each member of the group found their best efforts to possess it were stymied by the glowing, fiery stone.

"Your turn," Micah said to Haley as Gisele shook off her wet hands after her own unsuccessful attempt.

"Not sure I want to," Haley murmured. "It's so beautiful. What would I do with it if it came to me?"

"You'll know when the time comes," Gisele said. "Try."

Haley knelt down on the soft moss and put one hand just under the surface of the pool and watched in wonder as the stone floated into her hand and stayed there when she lifted it, flashing and sparkling, out of the water and into the sunlight. "Wow."

"Figures," Selena snarled and sulked away.

"It looks like a fire opal," Gisele said, astonished. "If that's true, this piece would be beyond price, with its enormous size and fiery color. And it jumped right into your hand."

"I saw it first," Lacey said. "Can I keep...uh, can *we* keep it?"

"You mean, like take it home?" Gisele asked over her glasses.

"Yeah, we found it." Lacey's eyes flickered greedily over every surface, searching out each flashing facet. The others seemed just as fascinated. The glittering gemstone held little allure for Haley. She allowed the others to hold it.

"Nothing in the forest is ours to keep," Gisele said. "The opal chose Haley, and she will know what to do with it when the time comes." Amid protests, she pried the stone out of

~ ☾ ~

Lacey's hand and quickly inserted it into a small silk pouch. She then pulled on the long drawstring, creating a necklace.

"Wear this," she instructed, handing it to Haley.

Micah leaned toward Haley. "How does that stone make you feel?"

"Scared," she said. "Why? How does it make *you* feel?"

"Nervous." He took a long, ragged breath. "Very nervous."

"Let's go," Gisele beckoned to Taylor who reluctantly tore his eyes away from the pouch now resting on Haley's chest.

~ ☾ ~

CHAPTER TWENTY-TWO

HEADING SOUTH, THEY followed a different path in hopes of finding and healing a rift. They neutralized two lines of quicksand, which Taylor dutifully noted on his map. Rather than watching for signs of danger, Micah walked behind Haley admiring her butt.

Gisele interrupted his daydreams, "I think you should wear these now." She handed each of the boys a pair of earplugs.

"The Terratress?" Micah tilted his head back to scan the huge pine trees surrounding them, any of which could be home to the monster.

"Yes, I feel she's quite close." Gisele's glance took in the upper branches of several huge pine trees. They made their way around a thick stand of birch trees and nearly walked into a—

"Rift," Selena said.

As he removed his earplugs, Micah whispered to Taylor. "She's wrong. The danger's here at the rift, not in the trees. Besides, I really like Haley and I'm not afraid of being lured away from her by a snake."

Following his lead, Taylor did the same.

Haley made her way to the rift, somewhat larger than the previous three. Just as she raised her hands to begin the healing process, the first haunting notes of a magical lute drifted down from directly above them. Micah's eyes opened wide and he trembled in response to the unearthly sound. His hands fell to his side as he looked up into the tallest pine and beheld his queen in all her glory, beckoning to him and only him.

Fifty feet above, Micah saw a long, scale-covered silver tail coiled around a thick branch. There, a vision of startling and

~ ☾ ~

terrible beauty played her lute. Gisele's generous description of the monster never even came close and he discovered, portions of her incredible form hidden from his view were magically recreated by his eager imagination. The Terratress' silken, silver-white hair trailed down in rippling sheets at least four feet long, barely covering her naked breasts. Her eyes were huge, luminous and dark, her full, red lips beckoned. The scales on her body glittered in the dappled sunlight with her every movement. The haunting melody of her lute caressed his ears, offering wanton pleasures he desired but could scarcely imagine.

"Beloved," he whispered. "I'm coming for you."

Hate surged as he glared at Taylor. They began a mad dash for the towering pine tree. Near the bottom of the tree, he and Taylor viciously fought each other, both searching for the quickest and easiest way up. Using his height advantage, Micah won, easily knocking his unworthy rival aside. Unwilling and powerless to give up his fight, Taylor began his climb from the other side of the tree, supporting his own efforts by thrusting broken branches into Micah's legs.

Micah howled in pain and aimed his wand at his contemptible opponent. A branch shattered over the bastard, raining splinters on his ugly head. Taylor returned fire, hitting the tree, causing huge branches to crash to the ground. Micah easily dodged Taylor's return fire. As he climbed higher, Micah fired over his shoulder and heard a huge crack. He watched as a large portion of the trunk split away from the main. Taylor leaped from his sagging perch to the part of the trunk which remained upright. Micah didn't spare him another glance as he scrambled toward his queen.

HALEY, LACEY AND Selena stood at the bottom of the tree, screaming.

"Quiet, you foolish girls." Gisele fired her wand at the harpy to no effect, as the monster simply diverted the wand's blue streak toward Taylor, shattering a large branch close to his head. "So much for shooting her out of the tree. Come here," Gisele called to the girls. Mercifully, the girls fell silent.

~ ☾ ~

"I have a plan. It's dangerous and risky, of course. On top of that, we have only one chance of success. We work as a team, or we'll lose them both." She looked up when Haley gasped. Nearly a quarter of the way to their goal, Micah and Taylor fought each other fiercely as they came together to ascend the side of the tree with lots of branches.

"Quick, what's the plan?" Haley asked. "What should we do?"

"We wait for the perfect moment and that will be the hardest part, because we have to sit tight until the boys are almost in the harpy's grasp."

"Why?" Lacey asked, still looking upward.

"The harpy uncoils her tail and fills her lungs with air just before releasing a terrifying scream. It's the only time she's vulnerable. Otherwise, she's too strong for us to pull her out of the tree. When I signal Haley, show her your opal. Then Lacey, toss your rope at her and Selena, throw your mirror into the air. I can only pray this will work."

From the ground they watched in horror, terrified that one boy or the other would be thrown to the ground. The Terratress slowly uncoiled her long silver tail in preparation of loosing her bloodcurdling scream upon the boys. Gisele knew that if the monster waited long enough, she might manage to take them both. The harpy smiled at her prey and took a deep breath. *This is it, we can't wait any longer.*

"Haley, show her your opal, *now!*"

At Gisele's command, Haley's massive opal flashed, catching the monster's eye. The Terratress was a Keeper of Treasure and there was no question her gemstone was bona-fide treasure. With that, the harpy turned, ignoring the insignificant boys with their minor booty, in favor of the glittering beacon of wealth that waited below. She slithered rapidly down the tree, disregarding the sudden protests of her former quarry.

"Ready, Lacey? Don't worry about your aim. Throw it...*now,*" Gisele said. An ultra-thin silver rope hissed through the air, finding its mark with uncanny accuracy. The tip of the rope sailed two yards past the monster's beautiful head, looped back and began twirling tighter and tighter around its

~ ☾ ~

throat.

The fight may still have been lost there, for the Terratress was known not only for her terrible beauty, but also for her immense strength. "Selena. *Now!*" A tiny round mirror from below caught the summer sun's reflection. The sudden glare blinded and confused the harpy just long enough for Lacey's frantic pull on the rope to unbalance the creature, causing her to plummet through the branches to her own hideous death.

Gisele dove at the last second and just barely managed to shove the mesmerized girls out of the way before the harpy slammed into the ground.

AWAKE AND AWARE near the top of what appeared to be the tallest tree in the forest, Micah looked at Taylor in confusion, until it slowly dawned on him. "Terratress," he said as they began their descent. *Who else would make a nest this high in the air?* He pointed at an opening below them. The crotch of the pine tree had been hollowed out and lined with fur, feathers and...plaid *flannel*, by the look of it.

"Can you believe that!" Taylor exclaimed. "Think there's any treasure in there? Want to look?"

"No, I think it's probably booby-trapped," Micah said. "See how well it's hidden? From the ground, you'd never know it was here. He looked at Taylor's scratched and bloody arms, the welts on his cheek and forehead, torn shirt and shook his head. "Wow, did I do all that? Sorry, man."

"Looks like I gave as good as I got." Taylor laughed at Micah's shredded jeans. "Do you remember anything?"

Micah thought for a moment and shook his head. "Music, just...music."

"I don't remember much more than that, myself."

When they looked down at the four angry females waiting for them, Taylor said, "I think I'd rather face the Terratress."

"If we fall, do you think it'll play on their sympathies at all?" Micah asked with a nervous laugh.

"I think they'll leave us on the ground," Taylor said with a chuckle, as he scanned their surroundings. Their height afforded them a spectacular overview of the forest, especially

~ ☾ ~

the area where the rifts joined. "Hey, wait a minute. Look at the rift...see how it joins the other one at an angle?"

Micah strained to see around the pine-needled branches. He pointed toward the north. "And there's the center. It looks," he paused. "It looks like a brain."

"And the brain is the center of a wagon wheel and the rifts are the spokes," Taylor said, one arm clutching the sticky, pine-sapped branch as he leaned away for a better view. "Look at them all. We'll be here for months. Maybe we should try to kill the brain first. But–"

"No, if we do that, I think everything will come for us at once, don't you?" Micah said. "We should stick to Gisele's original plan. Heal each rift we find. Now that we know there's a brain, we should save that for last."

"We don't have enough people to fight everything that'll come out of all those rifts," Taylor said. "Until now, I still had a hope of winning this fight."

"Don't give up. We have The Elementals on our side," Micah said. "That's a huge advantage. Can you map what you've seen here?"

"I think so."

"Good. I can help if you need it. Guess we'd better get down there and face the music," Micah said. "Ahh, bad choice of words."

Taylor chuckled. "Race you down."

"ARE YOU ALRIGHT?" Lacey ran to meet Taylor.

"Yeah, I think so." He picked splinters from his hair before she began smacking his shoulders and back. "Hey! What are you doing?"

"What were you doing up there? I was so worried!" Each word was punctuated by an ineffective slap. "You could have been killed."

He lifted an elbow to ward off the blows. "I'm sorry. We couldn't help it. We were bewitched. The last thing I heard was some incredible music. I don't even remember climbing the tree. Stop hitting me."

"Lacey, that's enough." Gisele stepped in to defend Taylor

~ ☾ ~

who looked more traumatized than before. "They're not responsible for their actions." She glared at both of them. "Foolish as they were to ignore my warnings, humans are no match for magical beings." Gisele showed them what was left of the harpy, the fine silver scales had turned to dust, the beautiful hair had all but disappeared. Bones, teeth, lute–all gone.

Micah shook his head to clear the image from his mind. *What got into me? What must Haley think?* He looked at her but she avoided his eyes. He took a deep breath and got down to the business at hand. "We discovered a few things while we were in the tree." He went on to describe the rift's configuration and their new knowledge of the brain as seen from the top of the tree while Taylor worked to update his map. After a short discussion, Micah looked down at his ripped jeans.

"Damn it Taylor, my leg's bleeding."

The girls just glared.

GISELE TURNED HER attention and speculation to the newest rift. What sort of beasts would it contain? "I'm guessing it's not full of worms or beetles," she said, removing her new crystal from its pouch.

"Why not?" Lacey asked.

"The larger the rift, the larger the creatures, is what I'm seeing in my gazing ball. We have a lot to look forward to and we should regard the smaller rifts as practice."

"Practice?" Taylor said.

Gisele raised her head. "For what's coming. That's why we need discipline now. Everyone doing their assigned jobs. We must tighten up. Soon there will be no room for error. For instance, Haley is at the front and center. She should emerge from each battle unscathed. No bites. At some point, the bites may be venomous and just one could be fatal. If we were to lose her"–Haley's eyebrows shot up and she swallowed–"then we have lost everything. I can't heal the rift with her speed."

"What's in this one, do you think?" Lacey asked, looking at the innocent-looking mound.

~ ☾ ~

"I have no idea. But I've been given a heads up on some of the creatures. If I can, when they emerge, I'll identify them and how much tolerance we have to their bites or stings. But remember, none of us can do what Haley does, at least not with her speed. Eventually the Entity is going to figure that out. We must protect Haley.

"Is everyone ready?" she asked. "When attacked, go through your tools to figure out what works. If something is ineffective, discard it. Keep everyone informed as to what eliminates them and what does not. Ready, Haley?"

Haley nodded.

"Go."

Gisele watched as Haley held her crystal between shaking hands. Immediately the noises began. In place of birdsong and cicadas, crackling, ripping, groaning sounds emanated from deep within the earth. In the blink of an eye, the top of the rift came alive with black and red movement. Long, slender crested salamanders flowed like molten lava from the rift's widening crevice.

"Fire lizards," Gisele announced as dozens of the two-foot lizards spilled onto the forest floor. "Ten or more bites are fatal."

"Wand is working," Micah called from the far left, tapping the lizards with a cool blue light as they neared Haley.

"Not the water guns." Taylor tossed his to the ground.

"The mirror works," Selena said with some enthusiasm as the mirror's reflected light caused the two-foot-long lizards to wither and die. "Ouch! One tagged me from behind. "

"The Mandrake works great," Lacey said with a broad smile as she created a wide swath around Haley. "It bothers them to touch it." She scattered the area behind Selena with her Mandrake when several threatened.

"Thanks." Selena wiped the sweat from her forehead before plunging back into the fray. Lacey nodded in acknowledgement.

"Keep up the good work, everyone. The rift is almost healed." Gisele smiled as she witnessed Taylor cheerfully pelting the strays with Mandrake. She turned to watch Haley and when she glanced back, she saw to her surprise that

~ ☾ ~

several of the beasts had made it past Taylor who was digging in his pouch for more ammunition. She heard a noise overhead and looked up in time to wonder, *How did a fire lizard get into that tree?* when it flung itself to her shoulders. With a strangled scream, Gisele fell to her knees and the stragglers attacked, seizing her by her belt and dragging her to the rift. She was bitten several times before being helped to her feet amid screams and cries, some of which were her own. Micah and Taylor made quick work of the pair who had managed to haul her to the base of the rift, as well as the half dozen who showed up to help.

With a crack and a shudder, the rift began to collapse. The few remaining lizards scurried back. Before reaching safety, most were deftly picked off by showers of strewn Mandrake or an expertly handled wand. Sitting up with Taylor's help, Gisele saw Haley as she wobbled on her feet and rasped, "Get her." When she saw Micah catch Haley, she asked Taylor who needed healing.

"You do," he said, a stern look on his young face.

"But-"

"No buts. Today, you're first," Taylor took her crystal to begin the healing process on her feet, back, shoulders and arms, everywhere she'd been bitten or dragged.

"Looks like I'm the winner today," she said. "I count seven bites."

"I'm so sorry we didn't get to you faster," Selena said as she knelt by her side.

"Me, too," Taylor and Lacey said together.

"I'm okay," Gisele held out her crystal. "Selena, take this and help the others, please." I need to get up." Amid protests, she stood and stretched. "See? Good as new."

MICAH SUPPORTED HALEY'S head and shoulders, checking her for injuries as he offered his bottle of water. "Water please," Haley whispered. She drained nearly half the bottle before opening her eyes.

"You did great," Micah said before she could ask. "Only got a few bites and we killed most of them." He nodded toward

~ ☾ ~

the lizard-littered forest floor.

"*Eww!*" she said taking in the carnage around her.

"Let's get you out of here." Micah easily carried her to an area of soft moss across the clearing. "Can you sit up, or would you rather lie down?"

"I'll sit, thanks." Though she wavered when he let her go.

"I'll stay right here for a minute, I think," he said and felt her sigh when she leaned her head on his shoulder.

"How are we doing over here?" Gisele asked, limping to where they sat.

"Never better," Micah said. "But why are you up?"

"Why are you limping? And why are you all dirty?" Haley frowned. "What happened?"

"An altercation with a couple of lizards," Gisele said. "I'll tell you all about it when we get back. We should leave shortly, as soon as you feel up to traveling. Will you be able to leave soon, Haley?"

Haley nodded. "I'm getting better every second." With another drink, she gave a start and suddenly seemed very aware of her proximity to Micah.

When she shivered and drew away from him, he was sure she saw his confusion. "Thanks for catching me," she said over her shoulder as she jumped to her feet and walked away.

Gisele stared at Micah after her abrupt departure. "What did you say to her?"

"Nothing, but for some reason, I seem to be making her very uncomfortable." He watched her talking to Lacey. "I don't know what I did."

"I'm sure she'll tell you eventually. Here's a fresh bottle of water, Micah. We don't leave until it's gone." Gisele left him to sit there, wondering how he could possibly win Haley's love, if she couldn't bear to be near him. Out of the corner of his eye, he watched as she stood with her lively sister who appeared to be acting out her version of the battle. But he noticed Haley's eyes occasionally wandering back to him, sitting alone across the clearing. *Is she mad at me because of the Terratress? She should know I couldn't help what happened. Not really.* He closed his eyes, trying to feel something, *anything* but his own yearning for her.

~ ☾ ~

"Has everyone had water? Drink up. We still have an hour's hike at least."

When the group was fit to travel, they set out, tired but exhilarated. They encountered two more lines of quicksand, which they healed and noted on Taylor's map. They were nearly out of the forest when Gisele halted, staring open-mouthed in front of a bank of trees, saplings and brush. Not even Micah with his sharp eyes could see what stopped Gisele in front of this ordinary copse of trees. Until the foliage began to move.

~ ☾ ~

CHAPTER TWENTY-THREE

HALEY DREW IN a breath. Before her stood a tall man cloaked in leaves and twigs who appeared to have oak leaves and ivy growing from his olive green face. Haley's mouth fell open. Until he blinked, he was all but invisible. He stepped forward, spreading his arms wide. Startled, she stumbled back and pointed her wand at his feet. From around her came the swish of sliding material and though no one spoke, she knew the team had readied themselves for yet another challenge.

"Thank you," the creature rasped in a graveled voice. "The citizens of the forest and I wish to thank you for your help during this crisis." Haley watched his movements. Although his features were clearly visible while he spoke, he instantly blended with his surroundings when he stood still.

"You're very welcome." Gisele appeared genuinely astounded for the first time since Haley knew her. This was *big*. Gisele turned to them and said, "May I present The Greenman, The Lord of the Forest, the Deity charged with the care and well-being of the woodlands." Haley breathed a sigh of relief and smiled as all wands lowered.

"We of the forest are honored to share our fields and woodlands with you and your young friends. Please know you will always have safe passage for as long as we can provide it," The Greenman said.

"Thank you, Lord," Gisele said. "But we are not yet finished."

"Indeed, you are not. You have but scratched the surface in eliminating the scourge. But you have done well thus far. I am here to assure you that, although we cannot interfere with your challenge, when you need our assistance, we will be quick to offer it."

~ ☾ ~

"How shall we call you?" she asked.

"We are always watching," he assured her. "But this may help." He proffered a silver maple leaf medallion on a thin sterling chain. "Simply warm the pendant in the palm of your hand while describing your need."

"I always knew you were here, but it's an honor to finally meet you," Gisele said.

He bowed his leaf-covered head. "The honor is mine. I've watched you care for my land, forest and trees as well as share your extensive and benevolent knowledge over the years. Our forest has never seen a better caretaker."

Gisele swallowed and looked like she might cry.

"Excuse me, um, Mr. Greenman, Sir? Gisele was hurt today," Haley said, "She won't admit it, but she's still in pain. Can you help her?"

"Haley, I don't think..." Gisele said, shaking her head.

"The very reason I appeared to you today." He stepped forward and placed a leafy hand on Gisele's forehead for a moment then stood back. "Better?"

She visibly relaxed and sighed. "Much. Thank you, Lord. My crystal wasn't up to healing this old body."

"Excuse me, Sir, but who's been leaving tools on the Stone Altar for us?" Lacey asked in a small voice. "And why don't they come with instructions?"

The Greenman smiled. "That, sweet child, is the result of Forest Magic, just as Gisele told you. The tools were manifested by forest spirits for your use in order to eliminate the evil that threatens our sanctuary. They rely on intuition for their correct use. You must train yourselves to listen to your subconscious perceptions for the answers. Each one of you has an important part to play in this difficult task and we have faith in your ability to succeed." He paused, his noble head tilted as if listening to voices far away. "Alas, I am needed elsewhere. For now, I must bid you farewell. We will meet again." Stepping back, he closed his eyes and disappeared from sight. A soft "Be well," floated in the air around them.

Taylor broke the shocked silence. "Whoa. He's *always* here?"

~ ☾ ~

"That's right," Gisele dabbed her eyes. "But you'll never see him unless he wants you to," she said over her shoulder as they headed home.

"ABOUT THIS THURSDAY," Gisele said, once they were seated in her cabin. "Although, I'd like to go back into the forest, I don't think I'll have the energy and I'm sure I'll need a little recovery time after getting close up and personal with the lizards." She rubbed a painful shoulder.

"Didn't The Greenman's healing work?"

"Oh, yes. I'm so much better off with his assistance. But I think you forget how old I am," Gisele smiled. "I need my rest."

"We could do it," Micah offered.

"No. And not because you're incapable," she held up her hand to forestall his protests. "We're a team. We go in as a group. So we'll stay here and do some wand training. Selena, you and Micah are excused for the day, if you wish."

"Yeah, I'll pass," Selena said, eyes skyward.

"Micah?" Gisele asked.

"I'd love to come." He slid a sideways glance at Haley. "I can always learn something new."

Haley watched Selena sneer. *Probably wishes she could change her mind.*

"If there's nothing else, you're all free to leave," Gisele said. "I need a nap. These little walks of ours are exhausting. Great job today, everyone."

Tired but satisfied with their accomplishments, Haley and her friends hugged Gisele and departed. Taylor, Lacey and Haley walked to their bikes as Micah and Selena got into his car.

"Bye, beautiful," Micah said to Haley as she lashed her belongings to her bike. He smiled as she blushed and refused to respond.

SELENA SNORTED HER displeasure.

"What?" he asked. *If I can make her blush, maybe there's*

~ ☾ ~

hope for me yet.

"Can't you control yourself, in front of me, at least?" she said.

"Why?" he asked, "I really like Haley. Why shouldn't I be able to show it?"

"She doesn't like *you*. She's ignoring you, like you're ignoring me." Selena's bitterness pierced her every word. "You know, I thought *we* had something. Something real. And now–" She stopped, barely holding back tears.

"When was that?" he asked.

"We went out and you kissed me. It was wonderful," she said.

He sighed. She was talking about things that happened over two years ago. And it wasn't even long enough to call a summer romance. Of course, at this point, he'd only known Haley a few weeks and for all intents and purposes, he'd decided that she was The One.

What he would have with Haley was different, though. Glorious. Fated.

Of course, I'd feel a lot more confident if she would act as if she didn't hate *me all the time...* "Selena, you were thirteen and I was fourteen. Just children having a little flirtation. Please tell me that's not what this is about."

"You said, when we had kids, they'd be special–beautiful and magical–just like us," she shot back.

"At thirteen and fourteen, we talked about having kids? I think the conversation would have gone, *If* we had kids..." He sighed. *She's unbalanced. That side of the family always had...issues. I can't possibly trust her to protect Haley out there.* "My future is with Haley, not with you. At least not in the same way. The things I see don't change. You need to accept this." *Why isn't she getting this?*

"I thought *she* was the fling," her voice trembled.

"Selena, in two years I have made no effort to get in touch with you. None."

"Yes, but, when we saw each other at family functions, you always had an excuse why you didn't call or..."

"Oh, be real. If a guy is in love, nothing, *nothing* will keep him from the object of his desire." She was still in denial,

~ ☾ ~

anyone could see that. He didn't want to be brutal, but the truth wasn't sinking in. "Listen, if I didn't have to take you to your aunt's house, Haley's bike would be in my backseat right now," he said with unfounded confidence. "From now on, I will be spending every second with her...that she will allow."

"After *three weeks*?" Bitter resentment dripped from her mouth. "I don't believe it."

"I fell in love during our first handshake. I couldn't let her go," he said. "When it's fated, there's nothing you can do to stop it, and you don't even want to."

He glanced over at her, knees crossed, arms folded over her chest, bottom lip sticking out. "I'm sorry. Truly I am," he said. "But I want her, not you."

"Fine." No longer pleading and sad, her slitted eyes grew cold and spiteful. "I'll back off."

That'll be the day. "Thank you."

"You took me to your *prom*."

"Yes, and I'm sorry if that gave you the wrong idea."

"What other idea could I have? You don't take just *anybody* to your Junior Prom," Selena pouted. "She's not like *us,* you know."

"You're right," he acknowledged. "She may be much more powerful."

"She—is—not."

"Please don't forget who you're talking to. I know what she is. Haley healed three rifts today. She was gifted with two crystals—that's *never* happened before and I think she may possess abilities she hasn't even discovered yet."

"Stupid little girl."

That was funny—Selena was shorter than Haley by at least six inches. Best not to point that out. "Please don't be jealous. You're so beautiful. You can have anyone you want."

"*Almost* anyone." She crossed her legs and lapsed into an angry silence. "Just don't have sex with her in front of me, okay?"

"We're not having sex, *okay*? Like you said, she hardly even speaks to me." *And what am I going to do about that?*

"Well, it's only been a few weeks," she pointed out.

"Nothing like that will happen this summer and probably

~ ☾ ~

not next summer either." *How do I know this? And why am I telling her?*

"Good." She looked out the window as they drew up in front of her aunt's house.

Micah sighed. He regretted that he had to hurt her but ignoring her hadn't helped, flimsy excuses didn't work and Haley was the only one he'd ever want.

"I'll be here at eight thirty," he said, cheerful now that this conversation was behind them. But when he glanced at her and saw an evil smile on her face, he wondered how badly he might have misjudged her.

~ ☾ ~

CHAPTER TWENTY-FOUR

"WELCOME TO WAND-TRAINING, my friends." Gisele beckoned to them. "Sit down and try some Psychic Development Tea. Drink up and we'll get our wand class started. Today, I'll instruct the girls. Micah, you're with Taylor."

"Oh. Okay." He smiled at Haley and sighed before turning to face Taylor. She could tell would rather have partnered with her, but she was a little relieved at how things turned out. Although she was seriously attracted to him, his Gifts terrified her and after that incident with the Terratress—well, spellbound or not, maybe he wasn't as interested as he first implied.

After finishing their tea, the class began. "First, stand up, holding your wand," Gisele instructed. "Now ground and center. I'll walk you through it.

"Close your eyes and breathe in deeply through your nose and out your mouth. Slow down your breathing. Do it a few more times. Now, imagine you're a tree and your roots extend from the bottoms of your feet through the floor into the cellar and down, down to the center of the earth. Your roots are holding you, anchoring you in place."

Haley took a deep breath in.

"Breathe slowly."

She exhaled and felt herself calming.

"Now we'll open up your energy centers, your chakras. Envision a silvery white light flowing from the heavens through the roof down to the top of your head. Breathe in and out slowly several times. This will open up your Crown Chakra," Gisele explained.

"At this point, the light travels to the center of your forehead, opening up your Third Eye Chakra, then to your

~ ☾ ~

throat, energizing that chakra and finally lands in your Heart Chakra. Feel the love? The warmth? That's Spirit, strengthening your Heart Chakra."

Haley became aware of her body vibrating with energy and warmth spreading deep to her core.

"Now, when you feel the power in your heart is as strong as it will ever be, direct it out and down your arm to the hand holding the wand. Feel the tingle? That's energy. Focus and follow through. Don't expect to get this the first time. Concentrate on the energy and watch your breathing."

Haley smiled when she experienced a tingling down her arm similar to what she experienced when healing a rift.

Gisele put a plastic cup on the table. "Focus your energy on the cup. See if anything comes of it."

Haley aimed her wand, focused and...nothing happened. She tried again and grimaced in frustration.

Pfft! The tiniest blue spark erupted from Taylor's wand. Of course, since his eyes were screwed shut in concentration, he missed it. With eyebrows raised, Micah and Gisele exchanged glances, clearly impressed. A little jealous at Taylor's success, Haley resumed her concentration with nearly the same sad result as before.

"C'mon, girls, you can do it. Especially you, Haley," Gisele said. "You're already doing this with your crystal."

"Not consciously," she muttered after another futile attempt.

They struggled for the next half hour without much progress. Discouragement filled the little cabin.

"Practice one hour a day."

Homework?

"But it's not working," Lacey complained.

"If you don't practice, I'll guarantee it'll *never* work. Oh, and I'll know whether you've practiced or not," Gisele said.

"It's only eleven o'clock. Are we finished already?" Haley asked.

"No, last night I saw something in the gazing ball which we need to discuss," Gisele said. "Snow."

"Snow, in August?" Haley said.

"I must admit I was a little surprised, myself." Gisele said,

~ ☾ ~

"But that's what I saw. Anyway, I thought you'd like to know in advance. I can't figure it out, but maybe you can."

"Forearmed is forewarned," Micah said.

"Maybe," she mused. "Another half hour of wand practice and you're free to go."

They practiced in Gisele's sunny yard with varying degrees of success before calling out their good-byes as they left.

"An hour a day!" echoed behind them.

AROUND SEVEN O'CLOCK that evening, Micah showed up on Mrs. Miller's porch, carrying a grocery bag, which he presented to Haley. He watched her face fill with delight as she found a half gallon of mint chocolate chip ice cream. "Wow." She pulled out a jar of hot fudge sauce, walnuts, rainbow sprinkles, a jar of cherries and a can of whipped cream. "All my favorites." She laughed.

"Sundaes for everyone," he announced. Four super-large, totally unfinishable sundaes were constructed, accompanied by giggles and shrieks as the girls sparred over hot fudge and whipped cream. Micah watched Haley out of the corner of his eye. Her unguarded, natural laughter was delightful, warming him. Only when she caught him looking directly at her, did the laughter fade to a look of self-consciousness.

"This is how sundaes should be made." Lacey giggled, pointing with her spoon at the mountain of ice cream piled in her dish.

When they could eat no more and finally pushed away from the table, Micah turned to Haley. "Can we sit on the porch?"

"I don't know–" She looked to her sister. Micah thought she was asking for a bailout, but Lacey refused to play along.

"Go ahead, I'll clean up."

"Please, Haley? I'd really like to talk to you."

"All right."

On the wide farmer's porch they rocked on Grandma Clara's ancient love seat, as crickets sang and lightning bugs flickered. "Thanks for the ice cream," she said, twisting and twining her hands together.

~ ☾ ~

Is she as nervous as I am? "You're welcome, but I've been wondering–have I offended you in some way?" he asked. *If only it were that easy...*

"Offended me? No."

"Do you...not like me?" Although he didn't sense aversion coming from her, he'd learned his ultra-sensitive intuition was unreliable, at best, when it came to Haley.

"No," she said it slowly as if she weighed all the options and barely rejected that one.

Is it my Gift, the Terratress, or something else? "Well, then, I must ask—are you keeping your distance through fear?" He was almost sure it was his Gift keeping her at bay. He'd been as helpful and encouraging as he'd ever been and still she remained unmoved. He was nearly out of options, or reasons.

"Why? And why does it matter how I feel about you?"

"Well, I told you we have a future together." He tried not to sound cocky, but his Gift never let him down before.

"You know, not everyone's going to like you in that way, Micah," she said. "I have free will you know."

"Yes, you do." *And wasn't she proving it now? I have totally underrated her.* He'd always thought that when he met The One, she'd be as excited about it as he was. This particular reaction never occurred to him.

"So, is *this* how you get girls? Do you trap them into thinking there's no other choice?" Indignation seeped into her voice, though she managed to keep it low. Obviously, she didn't want to attract attention from inside the house. "Yesterday you tried to beat up Taylor to get to the Terratress and today you show up trying to be my boyfriend. Why not just force me to be what you want and be done with it?"

With that, Micah stiffened, his voice a low growl. "Force you? I would *never* do that. My Gift showed me that you and I have a future together," he repeated. "And I have *never* said those words to anyone else in my life."

"Fine. Listen, I think maybe I should just go inside, before this gets too intense or before we say something we'll regret." She looked toward the door.

"Too late." He rose and without a backward glance, ran

~ ☾ ~

down the stairs and stalked, stiff-legged to his car.

THROUGH THE WINDOW on the other side of the window Lacey addressed Haley. "Well, *that* went well."

"Why are you listening to my conversations?" Haley exploded.

As Lacey pushed the curtain aside, a fat tear rolled down Haley's cheek. In a flash, Lacey was out the door, and Haley was being hugged by her favorite person in the world.

Haley sobbed into her hair. "Sure went downhill fast, didn't it?" She sniffed.

Lacey held her at arm's-length so she could look into her twin's teary eyes. "What were you thinking? He was obviously sincere."

"I don't know. I really like him—"

"And this is how you treat him?" Lacey backed up, hands in the air.

"I just get so nervous when he's around that I say all the wrong things," Haley said as she collapsed on the rocker.

"It started out just fine, then you opened your mouth," Lacey shook her head in exasperation. "What was all that stuff about the future, anyway?"

"I don't know," Haley lied. "Oh, how am I *ever* going to fix this?"

"What do you want, exactly?"

"I want to be friends—" Haley began.

"He was *trying.*"

"No, he wanted more."

"What's wrong with that? He's funny and smart and gorgeous. And I don't know why, but he seems to really like you."

"I guess I'm just scared," Haley admitted and the tears began to flow again.

"But, he's your soul-mate. The Knight of Sticks or Swords or something, right? Remember what the fortune teller said?" Lacey hunched over and crooked her finger. "He vaits for you, dahlink."

In spite of herself, Haley laughed through her tears.

~ ☾ ~

MICAH TURNED THE car off and sat on the edge of Spot Pond, fuming in the darkness. *How could she think such a thing?* He slammed the dashboard with his hand and succeeded in making a small dent. All his previous bad behavior came back to him in a rush. He lied to girls before, misbehaved, done things of which he wasn't proud. But this time, his instincts were right and his intentions pure. Haley questioned him like the others should have, but didn't.

Could his future sight be wrong? He didn't think so. With every fiber of his being, he knew she was The One. He shook his head in disbelief, realizing that he'd been about to pledge his love for her.

He watched the sliver of moon set over the pond and covered his face with his hands, kneading his brow with his fingertips. Because, as sure as the sun would rise over October Mountain tomorrow morning, he knew he loved her. And he always would. He laughed with equal parts frustration and amusement as he started the car and headed for Gisele's. Maybe she could help him make some sense of this crazy situation.

GISELE SAT AT the table while Micah related the whole story, twice, before he let her get a word in. "Maybe it's not Haley you saw."

"It was Haley," he insisted, hunched over his tea.

"Maybe she's just a friend?"

"If you saw my visions, you wouldn't say that." He closed his eyes and smiled.

"Oh, my." She chuckled. "So what do *you* think, Micah?"

"I don't know what to think. I am completely in love with her and I'm going crazy. And she won't tell me why she hates me." He sighed, putting his head in his hands.

"I don't think she hates you, and I'm pretty sure there's no one else..."

Micah gasped. "*That* thought hadn't occurred to me, and it should have. She's so pretty, she must have a boyfriend." He

~ ☾ ~

stared into space contemplating this new, depressing possibility.

Gisele snapped her fingers in front of his face, trying to bring him back to reality. "Micah? Are you in there?"

"Sorry, Aunt Gigi," he used his childhood nickname for her. He scrubbed his face with his hands. "I just want to slam my head against a wall."

"I've never seen you like this," his aunt said, turning to hide her smile from him. *The frustrations of love are often highly amusing to all but those directly involved.*

"Has anyone ever affected you this way before?"

"Never. I'm almost out of my mind with...with...these...*feelings* for her. Ugh!" He bellowed with frustration as he rested his forehead on the table. She let him stew while she made another pot of tea. Soon the calming, healing scents of chamomile and lavender filled the cabin. A large plate of freshly made honey cakes placed in front of his nose dragged a reluctant smile out of him.

"What should I *do*? I love her."

"Don't chase her, Micah. If Haley is meant to be yours, she'll come to you in her own time. It's the best advice I have," she said, remembering herself at sixteen with a boy she desperately wanted but couldn't have. Six decades later, the memory still retained the ability to inflict both sweetness and pain.

"But what if she doesn't?"

She could hear the desperation seeping into his voice. "Don't worry so much. Sometimes I see things in my gazing ball..." She shrugged.

"Like what? Tell me, please, before I go crazy."

"No. You of all people should know that these things need to play themselves out. Have a little trust, a little patience," she finished, rumpling his dark hair as she walked past. "You're my favorite relative, did you know that?"

"That's what you always tell me." He smiled as he ate a honey cake. "I need to clear my head. I'm going home for the weekend. I'll leave in the morning."

"Good idea."

~ ☾ ~

CHAPTER TWENTY-FIVE

"DID EVERYONE HAVE a good weekend?" Gisele asked her young warriors on a bright and sunny Monday morning. Tea, cookies and five specially prepared red pouches graced her tiny kitchen table.

"Yeah, on Friday we went to the movies with Grandma Clara and on Sunday we played mini golf with Dad," Lacey said. Haley hadn't spoken a word, or even made eye contact with anyone. Looking miserable, Micah glanced everywhere but at Haley. With a smug expression on her pretty face, Selena clearly read the tension in the room.

"How's the wand work coming along?" Gisele asked, carefully gauging the energies swirling around her. Her little team was an emotional misadventure.

"We got some practice time in." Averting her eyes, Lacey looked less than candid.

"Any success?"

"I got some blue sparks." Taylor beamed.

"So did I." Lacey brightened a bit.

"Haley?"

"Nothing yet," she admitted. "I'll try harder this week, I promise."

"I know. You'll come here everyday until I can see blue flames from your wand." Gisele's attention riveted on the twins.

"*Every day?*" Lacey asked.

Gisele nodded. "We'll need everyone at top form for these rift healings. There's probably a very good reason you were gifted with wands from the Altar Stone."

Lacey nodded. "What's in the red pouches?"

Gisele took a deep breath. "I filled them last night. They contain a wide variety of protective stones and herbs, created

~ ☾ ~

specifically to shield you during our work in the forest. Understand now, they're created mostly for the lower range entities. The big guys can still get through, so don't get too cocky. The stones are Bloodstone, Black Tourmaline and Red Jasper. And I put in some herbs. A pinch of Dragon's Blood, High John the Conqueror, Mugwort and St. John's Wort." She ticked off the herbs on her fingers. "They are shields, not repellents. You can still be attacked, but carrying the pouch could give you a few extra seconds to find a tool or allow someone to help you." She hoped to heaven they wouldn't be needed, but it made her feel better to be prepared.

"Today we'll return our crystals to the Crystal Cave. We have all but used up their healing energy. We may pass by a rift, but we won't attempt to heal it until we have new, energized crystals. If no one has anything further to add, let's get our gear and head out."

Minutes later, they approached the Altar Stone and found, in addition to Haley's flowered crown, a wide cuff bracelet, fashioned from sparkling crystal. The most surprising tools ever presented also lay on the Altar—five pairs of safety glasses. Haley left last week's dried out and slightly bedraggled crown on the altar.

Selena moved to the Altar Stone, shoved her hand over the bracelet and once again, disappointment showed on her pretty face. Lacey and Gisele tried as well, with the same result. But when Haley approached, the glittering circle flashed iridescent purple, green and pink in the sunlight.

"Guess it's mine," she said. She turned her wrist this way and that, watching the sparkle. "So beautiful and it's making my whole arm tingle."

Gisele's sharp eyes caught the angry glare Selena directed at an oblivious Haley. "Selena," she attempted to redirect the girl's attention and annoyance. "See if these are for you." When she picked up her safety glasses, they glowed in sharp contrast to her curled lip. Everyone but Haley received a set. When Lacey attempted to stow hers in a backpack, Gisele stopped her. "Put them on," she ordered.

"But—"

"We don't know when we'll need them," Gisele said. "Put

~ ☾ ~

them on." Looking at their petulant faces, she relented
somewhat. "All right, at least wear them on *top* of your head.
That way, it'll only take a second to slide them on when
things get crazy."

Accepting her compromise, they moved off into the sun-
kissed forest, green and lush with summer's abundant foliage.
Walking northeast, they checked constantly for any rifts and
line quicksand they might have missed.

"Did you hear? There are strange lights over the swamp at
night. My father says people are getting lost in there," Taylor
said in a hushed tone.

"The Entity is looking for new blood." Gisele replied.
"Once we've healed the rifts, they'll go away. I seem to
remember it happening last time, too. Are they okay?"

"Yeah, they found their way out, but I heard even their cell
phones didn't work."

"That's nothing new. Cell phones have never worked in the
forest. Let's pay attention everyone."

"Rift ahead," Selena announced and soon it was upon
them, a long low mound stretching as far as they could see in
either direction.

"Glasses on, just in case," Gisele directed, lowering her
own.

Lacey pointed at a pile of boulders on her right. "Is that a
Dwarf Closet?"

"Good call." Gisele congratulated her. "Yes, it is. If you're
in trouble, run through the opening, hit the side with your
wand and the door will close behind you. You'll be safe there
until the threat is past."

Soon, the understory foliage cleared out, which made
walking much easier. Old growth trees stood sentinel in the
forest, which was filled with the quietly comforting sounds of
birds, frogs and insects.

And something else...

"Chi, chi, chi, chi...chi, chi, chi, chi!"

"Dragonocepedes! Up a tree! Quick!" Gisele hissed, though
that wasn't exactly possible for *her*.

"What about you?" Lacey climbed a nearby pine tree with
Taylor. Selena scrambled up another with low growing

~ ☽ ~

branches and grumbled when Haley and Micah followed, then passed her.

"I'll be fine," Gisele stood like a stone against her tree. "As long as I stand still, they can't see me. Selena, move up higher in that tree—they can't see above four feet. Micah, help her, please." Micah reached down, hoisting his cousin a few feet higher. Just before the *chi, chi, chi* grew loud enough to terrorize her small group, Gisele looked at her young warriors and, barely breathing, gave them a confident thumbs up.

With dragon-type heads, neck and back, the strange reptilian creatures skimmed the forest floor on thousands of tiny centipede-like legs, which undulated on a flat, foot-wide body. Gisele thought they looked like a dragon attached to a carpet runner as she counted eight of the strange reptilian creatures emerging from the forest, bobbing their scaly, orange dragonheads as they skimmed the forest floor. She almost felt the excitement tinged with fear racing through the band of human spectators as the Dragonocepedes spread out—sniffing, seeking, hunting. With the teens high up in the trees and far out of reach, she remained the only one in danger. And with her body plastered against the far side of a large oak tree, she felt relatively safe. Hopefully, the little monsters couldn't hear her old heart pounding in her chest. Many years past, she'd been forced to watch a dear friend die a painful death from these ugly things and she did not intend for that scenario to repeat itself today. Holding her breath, she observed the creatures from the side of her oak, moving only her eyes to better view their progress, all the while monitoring the silent, wide-eyed kids perched in the trees.

Selena, Haley and Micah perched in the tree closest to the Dragonocepedes, with Lacey and Taylor directly behind them. Most of the pint-sized monsters fanned out to Gisele's right, moving quickly through the clearing. *This is good. They seem to be headed west, whereas the Crystal Cave is northeast. Soon, it'll be safe to travel again.* She began to breathe, to let her guard down, as the last Dragonocepede exited the clearing.

A noise from her left got her attention and before she thought to stop herself, she turned to face a wayward

~ ☾ ~

Dragonocepede, a mere ten feet away. Her eyes widened and her mouth fell open as the little monster opened its mouth, revealing pungent tendrils of saliva hanging in blood-red ropes from its open jaws.

~ ☾ ~

CHAPTER TWENTY-SIX

"ARRGH!" CAME A shriek just before a blue flash decimated the creature about to take Gisele's life. Haley looked up from the smoking, charred hulk whose pungent odor reminded her of rotten eggs and locked eyes with Lacey as her sister slowly lowered her wand.

"Thanks," Gisele breathed.

"Stay still, they're coming back," Lacey hissed. "We'll tell you when you can move."

Five wands trained a semi-circle around Gisele as she tucked her head against the tree, drew a long breath and waited. When Haley saw her wand resting in its sheath on her hip, she hoped Gisele had placed her trust in the team and wouldn't make a move for it.

The remaining Dragonocepedes glided to their fallen comrade, tasting the air, just yards from Gisele's motionless form. With her wand directed at one of the horned creatures, Haley held her breath and watched as the survivors sniffed the blackened corpse, appeared to lose interest and moved on.

"I think it's okay," Lacey said when they could no longer hear the *chi, chi, chi* of the retreating reptilians. Haley watched as Gisele loosened her hold on the oak tree. Wand in hand, Lacey climbed down with Taylor to inspect the dead monster.

Micah beat Haley to the ground and stood waiting to assist her. "I'm fine, thanks," she said, making her own way down. She could sense his disappointment as he dropped his hand and stepped away. *Why do I keep hurting him?*

"Nice job," he said over his shoulder to Lacey.

"Yeah, you were great." Taylor enthusiastically hugged his girl.

~ ☾ ~

"Are you okay?" Haley asked Gisele when they reached her.

"I am, thanks to Lacey," she said as she turned to her defender. "You are officially excused from wand class."

Lacey beamed, but Haley could tell she tried hard to look modest.

The group checked out the carcass. While its long flat body remained intact and recognizable, the badly burned three-foot neck and head looked like lumps of charcoal. "Right between the eyes, huh?" Haley said, admiring her sister's handiwork, while holding her nose.

"Nice shot, Lace," Taylor said, rubbing her shoulder.

"I was afraid they'd stick around for a while," Lacey said. "They were *so close* to you."

"I knew they'd leave," Gisele said. "Any weapon that could kill like that would decimate the whole group. I guess we now know what it takes to slay them."

"Didn't you have wands last time?" Micah asked.

"I can't remember, but I don't think so. It was fifty years ago." She shrugged. "We have a lot to do before this day ends. Let's hurry."

Still checking for line quicksand, they made their uneventful way to the waterfall, walking past the tall evergreens, which stood sentry to the Fairy Ring, a magic circle surrounded by mushrooms where Haley had seen fairies sometimes play. "Do you want us to stay here like last time?" Lacey stood by the pool, but her eyes lit up at the sight of the cave's moss and vine-covered entrance.

"No, I think everyone could use a few minutes in the cavern today." They walked up the mossy steps, behind the waterfall to a small stone-walled, moss-covered chamber, which housed the Blessing Bowl.

After depositing their spent crystals in the Blessing Bowl, they walked carefully to the back of the chamber and down the slippery, mossy steps. Haley took a deep breath and descended to the cavern below, which vibrated with its own healing, pulsing energy. She felt the tension in her body melt away. After spending a few minutes absorbing the spirit and strength of the cave, Gisele sent Taylor up to check the

~ ☾ ~

Blessing Bowl.

"The crystals are here," he called.

Gisele slowly made her way back up the stairs.

"Do you need any help?" Haley said.

"No, thank you. Enjoy the energy of the Cavern while you can," Gisele said.

Haley entered the main Cavern. "This one's my favorite," she said to Lacey as Micah stood a few feet away. She pointed to a huge crystal lying on the floor. About six feet long and three feet wide, it dominated the back of the cavern. The force emanating from the giant stone vibrated with a potent healing energy.

"Mmm," Lacey sighed, laying her hands on it. "It feels great."

"I know. I feel like it would cure any injury that I could possibly have," Haley said, oh-so aware of Micah's presence. Whenever she looked up, she almost always caught him watching her. *Probably hates me, and who'd blame him?*

"We should go," Lacey said. Micah followed a few steps behind.

When they got to the top of the stairs, Haley could see the Blessing Bowl now contained two very different crystals. One rather small piece rested beside another at least six inches long and two inches wide.

"How does it know what size to give us?" Lacey asked.

'This is the Source of the forest's energy. We are given what we require for the job we must perform. No more, no less," Gisele said.

"Are these the same crystals?" Selena asked.

"Oh, I keep forgetting you haven't been here before," Gisele said. "No, when we return our well-used crystals to Source, we place them in the Blessing Bowl where they are reabsorbed by the Crystal Cave. After about two minutes, new crystals appear in the Bowl, fully energized and ready to be of service to the forest."

Lacey rolled her eyes at Selena's ignorance and received a glare in response.

"Whose crystal is this? It's gi-normous," Lacey said.

Haley eyed the sizable gem. She reached her hand toward

~ ☾ ~

the piece, which instantly flooded the tiny alcove with a pulsing electric-blue glow.

"Guess that's yours," once again, Lacey stated the obvious.

"It's bigger than usual," Haley said as she bit her lip.

"Big crystal for a big job, I guess." Gisele held her hand over the smaller glowing crystal. "One more thing. It's a bit strange I know, since it's August, but my gazing ball showed me snow again last night."

Laughter came from all sides.

"I *know*," Gisele agreed with her skeptical students. "But so far, every bit of information I've received from the gazing ball has been correct. I've wracked my brain trying to figure this out and I can't. So, as strange as it seems, we must ready ourselves for snow."

"This is crazy," Lacey said.

"Put your goggles on. Now."

"Maybe we should've worn boots too," Lacey grumbled.

They tramped southwest for about fifteen minutes before a single word from Selena raised goose bumps on Haley's bare arms. "Rift."

~ ☾ ~

CHAPTER TWENTY-SEVEN

MICAH STUDIED HALEY'S face as she stood at the end of the rift, once again wearing her flowered crown. When she raised her hands, her crystal bracelet glittered as it rode high on her forearm and her glorious new crystal splashed her face with an electric-blue brilliance. Watching her sent shivers up and down his spine and he found himself wishing for the opportunity to perform some heroic act for her and simultaneously fearing that necessity.

"Check your goggles, everyone," Gisele warned. "Make sure they're tight."

Accompanied by the calls of hundreds of startled birds taking flight, the requisite sounds of moving earth–the cracking, wrenching, tearing noises that Haley's movements generated could surely be heard halfway across the forest, he thought.

The rest of the tiny group, school children turned warriors, fanned out behind Haley. Wands at the ready, they stood in anticipation, waiting for any number of alarming beasts that could emerge from the rift before them.

The horrifying sounds continued as a few small white moths appeared floating noiselessly over the rift, seemingly unconcerned by the tumult. In a moment they were joined by a few more, then a few more, all hovering mere inches above the fracture. Without warning, the turbulent rift belched a gust of air, pushing the tiny cloud of moths high above the human heads. A second burst of air expelled thousands of the swarming insects. A third torrent spewed millions, which quickly mobilized and began to circle just yards above them. Within seconds the forest grew dark. Without bothering to glance up, Micah realized the thick cloud of white moths nearly blocked out the sun. Then, in the space of a heartbeat,

~ ☾ ~

the cloud thrust itself upon them and all breathable air retreated.

"Cover your mouths!" Gisele gasped. "Micah, call the dragons!"

Got it, he thought while pulling his t-shirt over his mouth and nose to block the noxious invaders. Standing in place, head down to block out any distractions, he sent a thought bubble to Pat and Mike, Gisele's young dragons, named for a bad Irish joke.

Nearly overpowered by the incessant fluttering from all directions, he couldn't be sure if he was even standing upright anymore. He found a tree to lean against for support and stability while his previously reliable wand shot blue fire from its tip to absolutely no effect. And no witnesses either, since with all the mindless swirling, churning and spinning, he could barely make out the tip of his own wand in this blizzard. *Blizzard!* Gisele's snow references came back to him in a hurry. Quaking with anger, Micah growled as his wand emitted puffs of useless blue flame. Occasionally, he would catch a glimpse of a charred wing before it was swept into the maelstrom that surrounded him. He wondered where Haley was, if she'd been hurt, before he realized that as long as he could still hear the unnatural metallic shrieking noises, she remained firmly focused on her task.

He stabbed the air with his ineffective wand, irrationally hoping for a more dramatic result. He hoped, prayed the dragons would come. This situation was irreparable without them. The only thing keeping him from despair was knowing that Haley was fine. Micah sighed as he listened for the dragons. How could he be a hero to Haley if his wand was powerless to thwart their attackers? How could he be her hero, if she was unable to witness his great deeds? Then again, even if she *could* see him, would she care? All day long, he'd been trying to get her attention, trying to help her, only to be ignored, or worse. Frustrated, he swung his wand about, killing dozens of the vile moths among the thousands that swirled around him. *Useless! Where are the dragons?*

~ ☾ ~

THE GROUND RUMBLED as Pat and Mike made their ponderous way to the clearing. A few snorts, a bellow or two, then red-orange dragonfire erupted from their upraised snouts, creating a large hole for sunlight to leak through. Everyone cheered as thousands of marauding moths were reduced to blackened wings littering the forest floor. After the dragons repeated this three more times, decimating millions of the foul invaders, the few surviving moths fled to the tiny, barely accessible gap at the top of the rift.

"Thank you, my friends," Gisele thanked the dragons as they lumbered out of the clearing, nipping each other.

The battle over, Micah pocketed his wand and smiled with relief as he ran, crunching over dead moth wings, to Haley's side. Her job nearly complete, he had to be there to catch her. But just before the rift was healed, an explosion erupted from the tiny hole, showering everything in the vicinity with rocks and debris. Micah jumped in front of Haley, pushing her to the ground and shielding her from the granite shards that rained down on his body. A single pterodactyl-type creature screamed as it roared into the air, where it suddenly wheeled and dropped from the sky. The beast rushed straight for Haley, just as she stood, unaware of the danger, to remove her flowered crown and wipe the sweat from her brow.

Micah grabbed her as the bird-like demon bore down on them from high above and swept her behind his body. With no time to arm himself, Micah stood over her, ready to take the deadly hit. He could see its red eyes, almost smell its vile breath, when in an instant, the creature was irradiated from all sides by four streaks of electric blue flames and two streams of red-orange dragonfire. The carcass landed harmlessly just a few feet from Haley's astonished eyes— followed by its smell, the disgusting odor of burnt, decaying, rancid flesh.

"Yech." Haley wrinkled her nose. "I have to move before I puke." She put her hand down to raise herself off the ground, accidentally hitting a small rock, which shattered her beautiful crystal bracelet. "Oh, no."

"C'mon, let's get you out of here." Micah pulled her to her feet, then gently led her far from the smell, far from the

~ ☾ ~

blackened wings, far from the nightmare.

He guided her to a fallen log, brushed the leaves from her hair and shoulders and breathed a sigh of relief. "Are you all right? Do you hurt anywhere?" he asked as he sat next to her, holding her hand to steady her.

"I'm fine, but you-" she swallowed and, leaning closer, looked into his eyes like she'd never really seen him before– "you saved me." She took both his hands in hers and looked down, frowning and shaking her head as if preparing herself to deliver bad news.

"No, no, you must mean the dragons. They were amazing. And did you see–"

Then her arms looped around his neck and she kissed him. With gusto.

With his eyes wide open, his hands in the air, Micah felt every muscle in his body tense in astonishment. But he recovered quickly. Within seconds, he pulled her closer.

"Haley, are you okay?" Lacey called from across the clearing. A grinning Taylor appeared to be holding her there, possibly to give them some privacy. *Which would never occur to Lacey,* Micah thought.

She pulled back, all wide-eyed and looking just as surprised as he by this amazing turn of events. "Yeah, I'm fine, thanks. I'll be there in a minute."

Afraid she would come to her senses and unwilling to let her go, he leaned against her, forehead to forehead, his heart slamming in his chest. "Haley..." was all he could manage. *My love.*

"You saved my *life*," she said as she nestled against him. "You stood in front of that monster–"

"Of course I did. I said that before–" He shook his head, confused. "You must know I'd protect you from harm, no matter what."

Haley looked into his eyes. "You would have died for me. I mean, really *died,* for me," she said as if just grasping his meaning.

"In all honesty, neither of us would've survived if that thing hadn't been shot out of the sky," he said as he cradled her face in his hands. He closed his eyes and kissed her

~ ☾ ~

forehead before gently peppering her cheeks, chin and jawline with the lightest of kisses. He stood, gently pulling her to her feet. Gathering her into his arms, he thought of all the times he'd wished he could do this. He drew in an uneven breath. Could she possibly guess the depth of his feelings for her?

He gazed at her beautiful face. She slowly opened her eyes and when he looked into them, it was like an electric shock to his system. She knew. He felt like she could see into the private places of his soul. He closed his eyes and with a low moan, he kissed her again.

But this kiss was different.

This, *this* was the long-awaited welcoming of a soul mate, left behind. The relief of a deeply treasured secret, finally shared. The last puzzle piece softly clicking into place.

And for this, all he'd had to do was save her life?

For her love, he'd hold back the Nile, extinguish the fires of Hell or maybe lasso the wind. Saving her life was simply the very least of what he would do for her.

He pulled away, ending the kiss and gazed into her deep green eyes yet again. So many questions: *Is she still afraid of me? Will she ever love me the way I love her? Will she marry me someday?* His burning curiosity raged against his red-hot desire to kiss her again and again.

She licked her lips and swallowed. "Thank you."

"For what?"

"For everything. For coming here this summer, for saving my life, for caring even after I've treated you so badly. Thank you for being you."

Curiosity be damned. Gentleness deserted him as he pressed his lips against hers. When passion overtook him, he embraced her as tightly as he dared. *No one ever felt this way before. That was the best kiss in the history of the world.*

He broke the kiss, then pulled her into a tight hug. "You're very welcome," he breathed into her ear. "I'd do it again in a second." He pulled away to look again into her eyes. "You *know* that, right?"

Nodding, she leaned on his chest, tucking her head under his chin.

~ ☾ ~

"But wait," he leaned back, to address the bigger question. "Does this mean..." He looked away. "I don't know. For so long, you wouldn't speak to me. I thought you hated me." His heart was pounding. In *his* mind, the stakes would never be higher.

She met his eyes, briefly, before looking down. "Hate *you?* Oh, I could *never* hate you. And I'm so sorry about last Thursday—"

"Me, too." He enveloped her in a comfortable embrace. "But how could you see what I did just now? Usually you're sort of zoned out for a few minutes afterwards. This time, it seemed like you witnessed everything..."

"That's true. I saw the bird-thing coming for me and you standing over me and the flames killing it. That was one of the scariest things I've ever seen in my life. I really thought my number was up. I wonder why I saw it this time, since I never did before. My bracelet—"

"Your *bracelet,*" Micah said with sudden understanding. "I think it may have allowed you to see—"

"You protecting me," Haley finished. "Even though Lacey described it to me, I've never really pictured what you do, how you fight the monsters while I'm doing my job. Maybe *this time* I was supposed to see for myself." She leaned on his chest and sighed. "It feels like I've been here with you, all my life."

He tilted her chin up and kissed her as tenderly as he was able. Then, holding his hands clenched into fists at his side, he attempted to contain his passion for her. When he opened his eyes and glanced over her head, he saw the audience he'd been trying to avoid. Across the clearing, they stood in shocked silence, watching. It seemed as though all were delighted at this long-awaited, but inevitable, outcome.

Except one.

Selena, her own hands clenched into fists, strode away—no longer a witness to what was happening. After a few moments, Gisele followed and Micah knew if anyone could help Selena find the shards of her broken heart, it was Gisele. He sighed, but realized his sorrow for Selena's feelings could never, ever match his love for Haley.

~ ☾ ~

HE AND HALEY joined Lacey and Taylor as Gisele, alone now, made her way back to the flattened rift. Blackened wings crunched underfoot as the small group exalted each others' wand work, the dragons' amazing power and a certain newly formed partnership.

"Micah, did you hear me when I yelled for you to call the dragons?" Gisele asked.

"Yeah, I did. I was going to call them as soon as I realized my wand was useless..." he shrugged his shoulders and looked away in distaste. "You know, I thought the dragons left, but wands and dragonfire killed that bird-thing—"

"Pat and Mike waited outside the clearing and let him have it," Taylor said with a smile.

"Why did they leave the clearing, anyway?" Lacey asked.

"The Elementals do not, by nature, associate with each other," Gisele said. "When their service is complete, they defer to the next Elemental warriors, if any. By the way, Micah, that was some stunt."

"Well, you said nothing should happen to Haley. I was only following orders." He shrugged as if heroics were mandated and out of his control.

"You were awesome." Taylor patted Micah's shoulder.

Standing with Micah, Haley agreed. "That thing would've killed me, but he shielded me with his own body. Can you believe it?"

"Neither of us would have survived if you guys hadn't blasted the thing into oblivion. Thanks." His gaze took in the whole group, even Selena, standing a few yards away.

"Where was your wand?" Gisele asked.

"I thought the battle was over and I put it away when I ran to help Haley."

"That's irresponsible. Of all people, *you* should have your wand at the ready every moment we're in the forest." Though Gisele glared at him, he knew it was all a show.

"I'm sorry, but I didn't want Haley to fall. I'm happy the rest of you were prepared to save us," Micah said, suitably contrite.

~ ☾ ~

"Hey, where's your bracelet?" Lacey said.

Haley sighed. "Broken. It—"

"Served its purpose," Micah said.

"Too bad, I was going to ask if I could wear it to the prom this year." Lacey grinned at Taylor. "Hey, did anyone else swallow one of those stupid moths?" she asked, trying to spit out remnants of the offending moth. "It tasted awful—like powdered feathers. Blech!" She tried to remove it by scraping her tongue with her finger.

"Wicked attractive," Haley said, watching her sister dig around in her mouth. "It figures you would swallow one of those things, since you can't seem to keep your mouth shut."

"Oh, be quiet," Lacey said. "You have no idea what it's like out there."

"I think I got a glimpse a little while ago," Haley said. Micah put his arm around her shoulder. After feeding apples to Pat and Mike, they said their goodbyes to the dragons and headed home. Thinking about the many rifts that still needed to be healed, Micah walked hand in hand with Haley, refusing to give into despair at what he knew to be their nominal chances of success.

~ ☾ ~

CHAPTER TWENTY-EIGHT

"SO," GISELE SAID at wand-training class the next morning, "Let's get started on some wand work. I've seen what you can do and I was very impressed."

And I'm the only one who can't manage a wand, Haley thought with a sigh.

"So were we," Micah said, seated next to Haley, his arm slung casually over the back of her chair. "Thanks again, by the way," he nodded to Lacey, Taylor and Gisele for their part in the previous day's life-saving wand work. Selena had opted out of the day's lesson.

"We were happy to oblige," Gisele said. "Although Lacey was excused from today's class, she's chosen to join us today to practice her new skills. We'll start with streaks, short bursts and blaze-blending."

"Blaze-blending?" Haley asked. "What's that?"

"It's when two or three wand streams combine, much as ours did yesterday, for an incredibly strong and powerful streak of flame. You can take down a seemingly invincible foe with blaze-blending in a very short time. Let's begin."

Taylor grinned with excitement.

"Why are you so happy?" Micah asked.

"I feel great. I'm confident. Yesterday when it mattered most, my wand and I came through. So even if today's lesson's a bust, I like my chances in future battles."

They practiced until lunchtime and though Lacey achieved the most success, Taylor sported the biggest smile.

Haley needed the most work. The best she could manage were a few sad little blue puffs. She watched unhappily as Lacey wrote her name in the air and Taylor shot acorns and pinecones out of the tall trees edging Gisele's yard. Their blaze-blending was a thing of beauty, especially next to

~ ☾ ~

Haley's own anemic wand-handling skills.

Micah observed with an amused smile on his handsome face. "I guess you can't do *everything* perfectly."

"What do you mean?"

"Well, you heal rifts better than anyone on earth." He lowered his voice. "You're the best kisser, *ever*, though I think I'll need a few more demonstrations of that—"

"Stop it." She blushed, smacking his arm.

"I'm just sayin'. You can't be perfect at *everything*. Would you like some help?"

"Sure."

He stood behind her. Close, quite close. She drew in a breath as he slid his right arm under hers, closing his hand around hers, barely touching the wand. "Like this," he breathed into her hair, as he lightly flicked the wand. Blue sparks shot out and all but obliterated the plastic bottle she'd set up as a target.

She sighed. *So easy for him.*

"Try it," he urged, kissing the top of her ear.

She attempted a tiny flick. Nothing.

A larger flick. Still nothing.

"Hmmm. Maybe you were meant to heal, not destroy," he said as he stepped back, arms crossed.

"I can live with that," she said. "But then why would the Altar Stone give me a wand?"

~ ☾ ~

CHAPTER TWENTY-NINE

AFTER THEIR LESSON, Micah pulled Haley aside. "Would you like to go with me to Spot Pond tomorrow?"

"I thought we had wand class everyday?"

"Gisele cancelled *daily* wand class. You're the only one who needs the extra practice and I offered to tutor you." He smiled like he had a secret.

She looked into his eyes, eyes she'd been avoiding for the past week and couldn't think of a single reason not to go with him. He never made demands of her, she was no longer afraid of him and just yesterday he saved her life. No, it was more than that. He stood in her place, in the face of certain death. What could possibly be holding her back?

She sighed.

Shyness. Her stupid, crippling, ridiculous shyness.

The very reason she never managed to have a boyfriend before. All her life she found it easy to be a *friend* to boys, but that last step—the kiss—always proved to be just a bit too terrifying.

I kissed *Micah!* She smiled at herself. She still couldn't believe she'd done it...

"Haley?" He waited for an answer.

Decision made, she relaxed her shoulders, turned her most charming smile on him and said, "Sure, what time?"

"Really? Alone?"

"Why not?" He saved her life. What more could he do to prove his feelings for her?

"How's noon sound?" He grinned as she nodded in agreement. Waving to Gisele, he walked her to her bike.

THE NEXT MORNING Grandma Clara called up the

~ ☾ ~

stairs. "Micah's here."

"Coming," Haley answered from her room. Heart thumping, she tossed a few essentials into her beach bag and grabbed a towel. Her grandmother met her on the landing.

"He looks exactly like my first love, Tony," she whispered. "What a dreamboat. I just have to say–you must have inherited your wonderful taste in boys from me."

After a quick hug, Haley grinned. "I couldn't agree with you more." She quickly descended the stairs, slowing halfway down just to look at him. Clad in a pair of cut-offs, tight white t-shirt and boat shoes, he could've been posing for a magazine layout.

"You look great," he said, taking in her yellow bathing suit top and shorts.

"You too," she said, wondering how she'd keep the rest of Bidwell's girls away from him.

AS HE DROVE she looked out the window and gave a little half laugh.

"What?"

"It's just that there's so little here. Drive three miles and there's a cluster of four houses, two more miles, a Grange hall and three houses. Go another mile and a stoplight, a gas station and three houses. It's just so tiny," she said.

Haley looked out the window at a very old three-sided stonewall enclosure with a simple wooden gate, "And what's that thing?"

"That's to collect and hold wandering farm animals," he said.

"Is that a big problem here?" she laughed.

"Not anymore, but in the 1600's, it was."

"So it's an artifact."

"Yeah, I don't think it's used much anymore. And as for Bidwell's unpopulated look, other than Spot Pond, if you check out the lakes, they are almost *over*populated." Although he was driving a few miles an hour over the speed limit, two cars with out-of-state plates passed them. He pointed at them and said, "Now *that's* a problem."

~ ☾ ~

"Why isn't Spot Pond overcrowded?" she asked.

"A few generations ago, my ancestors willed most of it to the town. The rest was parceled off for family use, but must remain unimproved-we can't build on it-and it can't be sold."

"What good is having property if you can't build on it?"

"You'll see." He grinned and turned up the music.

When they got to Spot Pond, she expected him to head to the small parking lot at the Town Beach. Instead, he veered right onto a lightly used dirt road.

"Wait. Where are we going?" she said.

"Spot Pond," he said with a wink and a smirk.

"But the beach is back there," she protested.

"The *Town* Beach is for the rabble." He laughed. "We go elsewhere."

"Hey, that's where *I* go," she frowned.

"Not anymore." He pulled into a narrow rutted lane, hedged in on both sides by trees and bushes. Stray branches slapped and screeched against the sides of his car as he made his way down a gentle grade to a tiny clearing where he parked.

As Haley looked down the hill and through the trees, she saw the sparkling water of the pond. Micah hefted a cooler from the back seat, while she grabbed the blanket and towels.

"Ready?" he asked grinning.

"Sure."

"Good. I'll lead the way."

They followed a footpath, which opened up to a small but well maintained private beach. "This is beautiful!" she said.

"We own about one hundred feet on either side of the beach," he told her, pride evident in his voice.

"It's been *groomed*..." She shook her head. *Who would do that way out here?*

"I came by a few days ago and cleaned up and raked." He looked embarrassed.

He did that for me. Quick, change the subject. "So, no cottage?"

"No. We use tents sometimes or borrow a friend's camper."

"This is paradise," she said, admiring the view.

~ ☾ ~

"It is *now*." He looked at her. "Thirsty?"

"Very," she said, realizing her mouth was parched all of a sudden. She checked out the contents of the cooler, choosing a Diet Sprite while Micah spread his blanket in the sun. He opened a plastic bottle of cream soda and sat on the blanket next to her.

"Do you have sunscreen?" he asked. "You're going to need it."

"Yes." She found it after rummaging in her bag.

"Do your arms or you're gonna cook."

She rubbed her arms, legs and belly then handed him the bottle.

"Can I do your face?" he asked.

"If I can do yours," she said with far more bravery than she actually felt.

"Of course," he squeezed a small amount of lotion onto his fingertips and gently applied it to her cheekbones. At first, she kept her eyes open, watching his concentration, but when her feelings became too intense, she chickened out and closed them. Finally, his hand paused under her chin. Her eyes opened. He lifted her chin, closed his eyes and gently kissed her. He pulled away, tracing her lips with a fingertip.

"There, I think you're done," he said, handing the sunscreen back to her.

Just getting started, she thought as she squeezed lotion onto her hands. Her heart raced as she traced his jawline. Her fingers lightly rubbed over his exquisite cheekbones and lingered on his broad forehead, all the while his eyes never left hers. He watched her every movement and when she sat back, finished, he took her face in his hands and kissed her.

He pulled away, his hands still cupping the sides of her face, hungrily studying her features. With his right hand on her left cheek, he maintained a gentle contact as he lowered her to the blanket. He kissed her softly. "Oh, I think I'm in trouble here," he admitted with a grin as he lay beside her on the blanket, toying with her hair.

"If we keep this up, we'll *both* be in trouble," Haley replied, sighing.

"You're right," he said as he sat up again. "How about

~ ☾ ~

some lunch?"

"Sure," Haley said, taking his offered hand. They selected sandwiches and chips from the cooler and carried them back to the blanket.

"Um, can I ask you a personal question?" she asked while they ate.

"Sure, anything," he said, sipping his soda.

"Have you had a lot of girlfriends?"

He smiled.

"I only ask because you are one heck of a kisser and it seems like you've had lots of practice." She paused, licking her upper lip.

"I have kissed a few girls," he admitted.

"Thought so." She sighed.

"And not one of them has affected me the way you have. And in such a short time." He looked away, shaking his head. "Now, may I ask *you* a question?"

Haley swallowed. "Okay."

"What made you change your mind about me...or, us?"

"Besides the fact that you saved my life, you mean?"

"Technically, Taylor and the dragons saved your life." He looked around. "But I don't see any of them here."

"I never changed my mind about you. I liked you from the first moment we met. Do you remember?" She looked down then, embarrassed.

He nodded. "The earth moved."

"But I never had a boyfriend before and–"

"*Never?*" he asked, surprised. "What's wrong with your friends, your classmates? Are they blind?"

"No...it was my fault. It's always been easy for me to be a friend, but when the boys wanted to get closer I got shy and pushed them away." She looked at him, biting her lower lip. "I'm sorry about that."

"You're *shy? That's* what this was all about?" He laughed. "I thought you hated me, which was crazy–"

"Why is that crazy?" she asked, surprised at his arrogance.

"Because I'm empathic and can feel certain emotions when they're strong–even if someone's trying to mask them–"

"Another Gift? How many do you *have*?" She put a hand

~ ☾ ~

on her hip to indicate her annoyance that yet again, he was in some weird way superior to her.

He chuckled. "That's about it. Anyway, I *thought* I felt attraction from you, but when you continually pushed me away, it caused me to rethink and reexamine that particular Gift. I'm so glad I was right."

She sat back, crossing her arms. "So how many girlfriends have you had?"

"I don't know—thirty or forty?" He laughed, before shrugging as if numbers were unimportant.

Is he serious? She threw her empty plastic soda bottle at his head. "Can you feel my emotions *now*?"

LATER, HALEY STOOD knee deep in the warm water, forced to concede that this was a much better view of Spot Pond. It was amazingly quiet, but for the occasional shrieks from the rabble a half-mile away at the Town Beach. She watched a lone canoeist make his way across the pond before sighing with contentment. Being kissed by Micah was everything she thought it would be, and so much more. *I am the luckiest girl in the world,* she thought.

Micah walked up then and stood close behind her, his hands resting lightly on her shoulders. She felt him bury his face in her hair, inhaling its scent. He sighed. "You are the perfect height to do this. How tall are you anyway?"

"About five-four," she said. "And you?"

"Around five-eleven or so."

As she turned to look up at him, the sun flashed across her eyes. She heard his quick intake of breath, saw his eyes widening.

"What?" she asked.

"Your eyes. I thought they were deep green but..."

"They change."

"But now I can see green and amber and brown, so many colors."

He couldn't stop gazing into her eyes. "Well, I hope you got your fill, I can't keep looking into the sun like that." She turned her head to a more shaded position. But he followed

~ ☾ ~

her.

"You are fascinating." He gripped her in a strong hug and kissed the top of her head.

When she leaned away slightly to look at him, he asked, "Doesn't it bother your neck to bend back just to look at me?"

She smiled. "No. Does it bother you to bend down like that?"

He smiled as he held her face with his hands. "I could do this forever." He kissed her lips softly twice then squeezed her close to him for a final hug before heading back. "I'm toast," he muttered "And I'm not talking about my sunburn."

ONE THE WAY home Micah glanced at her. "Is everything okay? You seem a bit distracted," he said.

"Oh, yes. I had a wonderful day, but I've been keeping a secret from you."

"A secret? Really?"

"Yeah, last Spring Lacey and I went to a carnival and got a Tarot reading."

"At a carnival? How accurate could that be?" He laughed.

"So far she's been spot on," she cleared her throat. "But the part that made me nervous was when she kept repeating, 'one will fall, one will fall, one will fall...'"

"One of us?"

She laughed. "You sound like Lacey and me. She wasn't sure."

"What help is that?"

"Maybe it'll keep us on our guard," she said. "She also said it would be the most dangerous and exciting summer of my life."

"Hmm." He raised his eyebrows and for some reason that seemed to impress him.

Haley bit her lip and brought up a subject she'd been dreading. "I've been thinking...what do you imagine will happen if we fail to heal the rifts?" she said.

Micah blew out a sigh. "Aunt Gisele and I were talking about that the other day. She noticed one of the rifts has grown, gotten longer and thinks...well, she thinks they may

~ ☾ ~

expand outside the forest."

Haley blinked and pulled away. "Outside? To the rest of the world?"

"That's what she thinks. Her gazing ball showed it as well."

She put a hand over her face.

He glanced over at her. "What are you thinking?"

"Huge, green beetles, biting worms, clouds of moths, suicidal bird creatures and holy crap! giant carnivorous frogs..."

"You probably should keep this to yourself."

"That shouldn't be a problem. Nobody deserves the kind of nightmares *I'm* gonna be having."

"I know."

"It was bad enough before, thinking we could lose the forest, but *this*...this is truly horrible." Haley covered her mouth with her hand. The implications were monumental. She imagined The Terrors loose on the world–never mind the rifts. "We can't fail."

"No, we can't."

~ ☾ ~

CHAPTER THIRTY

IT WAS NEARLY five o'clock when he dropped her off at Clara's. "Would you like to stay for supper?" Haley asked, hoping to keep him for another hour or so.

"I'd love to, but Aunt Gisele and I need to discuss strategies," he said while he caressed her cheek. "And you probably need some time with your family. I've been keeping you from them all day."

"That's okay. I don't know about them, but I don't mind," she said, deliberately standing in the middle of the yard so their conversation would remain private.

"Good night," he said, taking a big breath almost as if he were in pain. He kissed her lightly and stroked her face.

"Thanks for a great day." Haley ran up the stairs to the porch. Arms folded, she leaned heavily against the post, and watched him back out of the driveway.

MICAH SHOWED UP to give Haley a ride to Gisele's at eight-thirty the next morning, smiling into her eyes as he started the car. Since they had a little extra time, he took the long way around Spot Pond, stopping at a scenic pull-off for a few minutes. He bit his lower lip and shook his head when he touched the small dent in his dashboard. Hard to believe it'd been just a week since he'd been here, alone and devastated. He closed his eyes briefly, trying to rid himself of that memory.

"You already know all the stuff we're learning today, right? Aren't you going to be bored?" Haley asked.

"Don't worry about me. If I get bored with the material, I'll just enjoy the scenery." His gaze slid down her face.

She blushed again.

~ ☾ ~

THEY PULLED INTO the driveway. "Oops," Haley said, when she realized they'd been outdone by bicycles.

"We'll never hear the end of this," Micah chuckled. "What would you like to do after class?"

"I'm not sure, but I think we should avoid Spot Pond, at least for a little while," she said with a heavy sigh.

"I was thinking the same thing," he said. "Maybe a movie?"

"That sounds good." She cleared her throat, glancing back at the bikes. "Do we want company?"

"Not really, but we should offer," he said, as they walked into Gisele's kitchen holding hands.

"Welcome back," Gisele greeted them. "What took so long? These two have been here for at least ten minutes."

"We took the long way around the pond. It was a nice ride," Micah said.

"I see." Gisele looked over her glasses at him while placing a dainty teapot on the table. "This is another Psychic Stimulation Tea, using century plant in place of mugwort. It doesn't taste that great, so I've added lemon and honey to make it more palatable. *And,* we have Almond Sugar Cookies," she announced as she produced a heaping plate of the freshly baked treats with a flourish.

"Goodie." Lacey softly clapped her hands. "I love sugar cookies."

"So," Gisele began. "I used my gazing ball last night. I wanted to see what we're up against and I can tell you–it's not pretty."

Haley noticed that while Lacey and Taylor hung on her every word, Micah simply gazed out the window. Obviously, Gisele shared this news with him already. *Look at that gorgeous profile. What would our children look like?* she wondered, lost in speculation.

"Haley?"

She snapped to attention. Micah looked at her now, a smile playing across his full lips. Could he imagine what she'd been thinking? It almost looked like he did.

Oh, for heaven's sake. She chided herself and shook her

~ ☾ ~

head. "Sorry."

Gisele looked toward the ceiling and sighed. "Please pay attention. I'll recap, for Haley, the gazing ball showed me that *all* the rifts must be healed by midnight of the next full moon, the Corn Moon, or we're back to square one."

Haley frowned and tipped her head. "What do you mean, square one?"

"If we fail to heal even *one* rift, the forest will descend into darkness and none of what we've done so far, will matter," Gisele said. "It will become uninhabitable, or worse."

"Uninhabitable?"

"Yes, the monsters will take over the forest and destroy the fairies, unicorns, Tinks and every other magical creature."

After exchanging glances with Micah, Haley asked, "What could be worse?"

"I'm afraid that if we don't succeed, the scourge could spread beyond the boundaries of the forest." Gisele paused. "And into the world."

Lacey gasped. "You think The Terrors will be loose? In the rest of the world?"

"Line quicksand, a plague of moths..." Taylor said.

"I saw all that and more—giant carnivorous frogs in Lake Champlain."

"They'll eat Champ, the sea monster," Lacey said.

"Imagine Dragonocepedes headed down Main Street," Haley said, shivering.

"I don't want to," Gisele said. "So we're going to finish this thing. We've only got until the full moon. We have our work cut out for us."

"Why such a short time?" asked Lacey. "That doesn't seem like enough."

"That's the way it is. We got a late start." She shrugged, then turned to Micah. "Would you like to discuss what you and Taylor saw from the pine tree last Monday?"

Haley faced him as well. He seemed embarrassed by his trip up the pine tree, so they never really discussed it. She knew it wasn't his fault, but it still hurt her to think about him racing Taylor up the tree to meet the harpy. *It was magic. A bewitchment that mortals couldn't possibly resist.*

~ ☾ ~

Remembering her near encounter with Pan last summer, she thought she knew how he felt. After almost a year, she still longed for the half-man, half-goat and his sweet flute. *Does Micah think of the Terratress like that?* She decided she didn't want to know.

"When we were up the tree after...well, we saw a number of rifts, angling toward the middle of the forest," Micah said. "They ended somewhere between the Ladyslipper Garden and the Fairy Ring."

"The scariest part was the center." Taylor swallowed. "It was red and glowed like coals. For a second, I thought I saw a long black tongue stick out, but I can't be sure of that." He licked his lips.

"I saw that, too," said Micah.

"We're going to need help," Taylor looked at Gisele and Haley read fear in his eyes. Not since last year's brief encounter with the giant carnivorous frogs had she seen him look so scared. She turned toward Gisele for reassurance.

"We'll continue to call upon The Elementals for assistance. And now that I have this," she touched her leaf pendant from The Greenman. "I'm more confident."

"We can do it, Gisele. We have to," Lacey said.

"Does your gazing ball, um, tell you the final...outcome?" Haley looked into Gisele's weary eyes.

"No, I wish it could."

"Do you think someone will...die?" Haley asked.

"*You* won't," Micah said, with conviction. "I'll always protect you."

Haley smiled and sighed, while her sister's eyes nearly rolled back in her head.

Gisele stared off into space. "No, none of you will die," she said as if trying to convince herself.

So she thinks maybe someone might get hurt, but that no one will actually die. Haley pondered her last statement. *I'm good with that.*

"But as you may have noticed, the creatures of the rifts are getting bigger and progressively nastier. I think this trend will continue. Be prepared for tougher and more brutal fights as we get closer to the center."

~ ☾ ~

"Do we have to close the center, too?" Lacey asked.

"Yes," Gisele poured more tea into her tiny bone china cup. "I think the center will be our last and greatest fight. Everything we do until then prepares us for it. More tea, anyone?"

"No thanks," Lacey said. "Do you really think having The Elementals will help us that much?"

"Absolutely," Gisele said. "Remember Pat and Mike? We definitely needed their assistance, and they came through for us *big time*." She smiled, paused to consider, then seemed to come to a decision. "I feel I must warn you, to finish this we'll need to be in the forest at night. I'm sure you'll remember the last time we were out there in the dark?"

Three grim faces looked at her and Haley recalled her very difficult, painful and terrifying flight through the woods. It was a time she wouldn't soon forget. Micah's glance took in both Taylor and Lacey. "I've heard what happened to Haley, but I understand your experience was a little different?"

"We don't like to talk about it," Taylor said, looking away.

Talking over him, Lacey said. "Worse, much worse. My fault, of course. We were following Haley and Gisele, when I stopped to peek into the Ladyslipper Garden. Taylor told me to hurry, but it was so beautiful, I just wanted to linger for a few minutes." Her eyes went dreamy at the memory. "When we went looking for them, they were gone. We didn't know our way back and it was getting really dark. That's when we remembered the Eclipse. So we made our way into the Ladyslipper Garden and hunkered down."

"How did you know to go there?" Micah asked.

"Last year Gisele explained that it was a safe place to go when in danger and showed us how to get in," Lacey said. "The noises were awful, but the huge yellow eyes in the forest nearly drove me mad. I've never been so scared." Her eyes met Haley's. "Well, maybe *one* other time. Anyway, after about two *days—*"

"More like a half hour," Haley corrected.

"*Seemed* like two days," Lacey said. "Gisele showed up and we levitated back. I have no idea how fast we were going. I covered my eyes the whole trip, but we had cuts and bites on

~ ☾ ~

our arms, legs and backs. Boy, I hope I never see those yellow
eyes ever again." She shivered.

Taylor's nervous laughter seemed loud in the small cabin.
"Gisele's crystal got a real workout *that* day!"

"Which brings us to an important point–" Gisele's eyes
focused on Lacey and Taylor, and there was no smile in her
voice. "We stay *together,* at all times. Is this *very* clear?"

Her students nodded. Micah smiled.

Haley changed the subject. "So I'll need to bring my red
pouch and my crystal. Do I need my opal, too?"

"Bring everything that was gifted to you, even if you
haven't used it yet," Gisele said. "You never know when it will
be needed. Imagine what would have happened to Taylor and
Micah if you didn't have the opal when we met the
Terratress..." Gisele shook her head.

Haley shivered. "Everything. I'll bring *everything* from
now on."

Outside they practiced their wand-work for an hour. Lacey
and Taylor helped and encouraged each other, while Haley
showed little appreciable progress even with her outstanding
tutor.

"Well, I guess that's it for today. Great job, everyone,"
Gisele said, shaking her head at Haley's modest
improvement. "I wish I could go back into the forest sooner
than Monday, but I have a doctor's appointment tomorrow."

"A doctor's appointment on *Saturday?*" Taylor said.
"What kind of doctor works on the weekend?"

"Special ones. Besides, I'm old, my bones hurt and it takes
time for me to rebuild my strength." She sighed. "I'll see you
then. Keep practicing, Haley."

On the walk to the car, Haley asked Lacey if she and Taylor
would like to go to the movies. "Thanks anyway, but I think
we're busy," Lacey said, without bothering to ask a bemused
Taylor for his opinion.

"Okay," Haley smiled. "I'll be back in time for supper."

HALEY AND MICAH walked around the mall, where she
found a gorgeous pair of shoes on sale, before buying tickets

~ ☾ ~

to the first showing. They sat through the movie, a comedy or action flick or something, paying little attention. Mostly, they just held hands, kissed each other and giggled in the darkness. Afterwards, as they walked to his car, Micah asked Haley about her plans for the weekend.

"We spend weekends with my dad. He's actually the reason we're here in Bidwell," Haley said. "My parents got divorced this year."

"Sorry."

"Thanks, but things are better this way. Anyway, he has an apartment in Pittsfield now, and so our weekends are pretty much all Dad, all the time," she said with an apologetic grin.

"You're going to be with your father *all* weekend?" he said, seemingly upset about being away from her for two days.

"Oh, we can't have that!" She laughed, a little pleased that a weekend at Dad's was now an issue when it never was before.

"What *can* we have?" he asked.

"Let's figure out a plan for Sunday, okay?" she suggested. "I'm sure he'll be fine with just one day."

He grinned. "Okay by me. What's the plan?"

"I suppose Spot Pond's out, huh?" she said.

He closed his eyes. "Hmmm...let's talk about *Paradise*. My version would be camping with you, all summer, at Spot Pond."

"You stole mine!"

"How about an amusement park? Six Flags maybe? With Lacey and Taylor? It's not that far from here." He raised an eyebrow persuasively.

She hesitated, instantly regretting her shoe purchase. She didn't want to hit up her father for another advance on her allowance, so she opted for honesty. "It's a little too expensive."

"My treat," he offered.

"No, you can't pay for *everything*."

"Listen, I have a great part-time job and I saved all year for this summer. C'mon, let's have some fun," he urged.

"What do you do?"

"I'm a stable boy for a local racetrack and after mucking

~ ☾ ~

out stalls, I get to exercise the thoroughbreds. What a rush."

"They don't need exercise in the summer?"

"Most are off racing and it's the perfect time for me to take a vacation."

"What a cool job."

"It is and I love it. So what do you think? Six Flags this Sunday?"

"How did I get so lucky?" she said.

"Reading my mind again," he said as he kissed her.

THAT NIGHT SHE discussed the plan with Lacey who quickly agreed after conferring with Taylor. The girls then called their father, begging off for Sunday. For a change, the twins were in accord about how to spend the day.

Micah picked Haley up the next morning and together they drove all over the western part of the state, enjoying the gorgeous scenery, tiny shops and great food along the way. "Another fabulous day," he said, kissing her on the porch after watching the sunset over Spot Pond. "Call me when you get back tomorrow night?"

"If you want me to," she said, almost giddy with happiness at being able to spend so much time alone with him. *I wouldn't trade my life for anybody's right now.*

He pulled her in a tight embrace and kissed the top of her head. "I would *walk* to Pittsfield, if you'd agree to see me." She started to protest. "No, I understand I must share you, but that doesn't make it any easier." He kissed her again. "Take care of yourself. I adore you." He held her hand until he was almost off the porch.

~ ☾ ~

CHAPTER THIRTY-ONE

WHEN SHE CALLED around nine o'clock on Saturday night, Micah asked about her day. "Oh, we played Mini Golf, had pizza and hung around my dad's for a while. Nothing special or exciting."

He blew out a sigh. "What are you doing now?"

"Just sitting on the porch, watching fireflies and feeding mosquitoes," she answered. "Why?"

"Uh...would you like some company for a little while?" he asked, after a slight hesitation. "You don't have to say yes, if you don't want to–"

"I'd love company," she interrupted him.

She could hear the excitement in his voice, "I'll be right over."

MINUTES LATER HE drove up. He ran up the stairs, took her in his arms and before she knew it, he was kissing her. "Missed you," he whispered into her ear.

"I missed you too. Come, sit down." She pulled him back to the ancient rocking loveseat. "I made you some lemonade."

"Good lemonade," he said after taking a drink. "It reminds me of you–sweet, but tart."

"Glad you like it," she laughed and asked a question she'd been wondering. "Why did you really come here, anyway? You know, and give up your whole summer?"

He smiled. "I always show up when Aunt Gisele calls. She's done a lot for me, taught me so much. I just can't refuse her. Besides, the health and safety of the forest is our family's obligation. It's my birthright."

"Birthright?"

"Yes. I stand to inherit a large part of the forest when my

~ ☾ ~

aunt passes. As do my cousins."

"*Everyone* inherits?"

"No, just the oldest from each family. Selena, me and...Trey." His voice dropped.

"Trey? Who's that?"

"My black-sheep cousin. He only shows up when there's something in it for him." Micah scowled and Haley decided she never wanted to see that look aimed at her. "Totally without a conscience. I'm *sure* you'll meet him at Gisele's funeral."

"*Micah*! Don't say those things, ever." She covered her stomach with her hand. Just the thought of Gisele dying made her feel ill.

"I'm sorry, but it's true. I hate him." He took a long drink from his glass.

"What's he *really* like?"

"Oh, he's quite handsome and charming, but he constantly manipulates people to do what he wants and...ugh, let's not talk about him."

"Okay, how about this? Why are the *cousins* in line for the forest and their parents aren't? That seems strange."

"It's complicated, but it's specified in an ancient family will, that the forest will be deeded to one of the oldest in every *other* generation. It's always been like this. The rest of the cousins get small amounts of acreage in surrounding towns, though they rarely settle out here."

"How is it decided then, of the oldest, who gets the forest, and who gets...out?"

"Some sort of weird treasure hunt, is what I've heard. I don't know much about it, but I won't worry about it 'til I need to." He shrugged.

"What would happen if Trey got it, or Selena?"

He shifted in his seat. "If Selena got it, I think things would stay the same and I'd be fine with that, but if Trey takes control"–he ran his hands through his hair–"he'd sell it."

"Sell the forest? How could he?"

"Aunt Gisele's been fighting off real estate agents for years, not only for the building lots the forest could provide, but the

~ ☾ ~

mineral rights as well."

"Mineral rights?"

"The Crystal Cave. We think there are probably more deposits than just the one we know about. Yeah, Trey would sell it all and call us from his yacht in the Caribbean to gloat."

"Now *I'm* worried."

"I'm sorry I brought it up. Can we talk about something else?" Micah's eyes were closed while he rubbed his temple as if trying to force back a haunting of his thoughts.

"Sure. I didn't mean to make you uncomfortable. So,"–she took a breath and went fishing–"besides Gisele and your forest, is there any *other* reason you'd come here?"

"Like what?" he relaxed his shoulders, shrugging off his worries like an old coat. "What other reason could there be?" A small smile played on his lips.

She thought he was teasing now, though she couldn't be sure. "You know.... A feeling, maybe, or a premonition?"

"What sort of premonition?"

"Oh, I don't know. Never mind." She looked away, embarrassed.

He smiled again, reached across and gently drew her chin to face him. "Don't tell my aunt, but I really came here to meet you," he whispered.

"You did?" she matched his whisper with her own.

"Last winter, when I saw the picture of the three of you with your bikes, I *knew*. Even if she hadn't called, I would've found an excuse to be here this summer." He lightly traced her jaw with his fingertips. "And now I can't stand it when you walk into the forest." He shook his head with regret? Amusement? She couldn't tell.

"But, why? You insisted to Gisele that I be allowed to help you." She sat with her head cocked.

"My feelings for you have grown...a lot, since that time and it bothers me to watch you stand before the rifts and not know if you'll be all right at the end," he said, his steady gaze never leaving hers. She found she couldn't breathe and she couldn't look away. She felt like a butterfly in a net.

"I have something for you," he said.

Finally, she tore her eyes away and looked down, biting

~ ☾ ~

her lower lip. "You do?"

"Uh huh." He took a deep breath. "First of all, as I said, I care very much for you."

She nodded, watching his lips, his chin, afraid to meet those dangerous eyes.

"I can barely stand to be away from you."

She swallowed, trying to agree, but unable to form words.

"It's right here." He smiled, leaning toward her to gain access to the left front pocket of his jeans. She inhaled the scent of him, as layers of Irish Spring soap, *(Dad's brand!)* shampoo and clean cotton mingled. Her eyes closed as—

"Haley?" He looked at her now. This was serious. "Because I care for you so much, I don't ever want you to be afraid of me, like you were at the restaurant."

"But I'm not–" she started to protest.

"No." He held his hand up to stop her. "I can't bear to wonder if you're with me because you want to be, or if it's because I'm willing it. Do you see? It has to be your decision, without question."

Brow furrowed, she nodded again as he raised a pendant between them.

"I give you this," he breathed. "It's the ROR Medallion. I received it from my grandfather. My grandmother wore it every day, until the day she died."

"What does it do?" she asked.

"It will allow you to resist my Gift of Suggestion," Micah said, placing the Medallion into her outstretched hand. She held the unusual pendant up by its slender silver chain. The dull silver disc winked in the weak light of the amber porch lamps.

"Your mother doesn't want it?" Haley asked while she studied the small disc.

"My father doesn't have the Gift. When it was discovered that I do, the Medallion was willed to me." He looked steadily into her eyes and swallowed. "For my future wife."

Her eyes widened and she drew in a quick breath when he said 'wife.'

"I'm not going to ask you to marry me right now, but I warn you, one day, that *is* my intention." He gently rubbed

~ ☾ ~

her cheek with the back of his knuckles.

Effectively rendered speechless, Haley opened her mouth, closed, then opened it again. She managed to squeak out a faint "Wow." Then after a moment she asked, "What will your parents say when they discover you've given it to *me*?" Her heart pumped so hard she could barely breathe.

"Congratulations," he said quietly, his eyes still on hers.

"And how did you happen to have it with you this summer?" she asked, stalling for time, trying desperately not to reveal how shocked she was. "It looks valuable."

"I had a feeling I'd be giving it away…" Now he avoided her eyes. "It *is* valuable, but I know you'll take good care of it. By the way, no one can see it on you, unless you point it out to them."

"Wow, all I gave *you* was lemonade."

He smiled. "You've given me so much more."

She blinked. "What does this symbol mean?"

"'ROR means Right of Refusal," he said. "And the chain doesn't look it, but it's very strong. As long as you wear this, you are immune to my Gift. You'll see what I mean in a second." He swept her hair aside as he fastened the clasp at the back of her neck. The Medallion with its unusual markings hung just below the hollow of her throat.

"Stand up," he said. She started to rise, then stopped herself when she realized what he meant. She relaxed on the love seat, drumming her fingers on the armrest.

"I said, stand *up*,'" he repeated, the corners of his mouth lifting slightly. "Haley, I demand that you stand up, *right now.*"

Grinning, she looked away.

"You caught on to that pretty quickly," he said to the back of her head.

She turned back to him. "I thought you were going to teach me how to resist your Gift."

"I would have, if time allowed, but this is faster and…permanent." He cupped her face with his hands and kissed her softly. "You have all the power now. I will do *anything* for you, but I have given you the ability to say no to me."

~ ☾ ~

"I have to admit–you *terrified* me at Freddie's. I kept looking for a phone to call my grandmother and have her pick me up."

"I want you to know that hurt me as much as it scared you." He looked away.

"You could've made me do anything," she said, frowning. "That's what was so scary. I couldn't resist you."

"I know. But then I wondered why you allowed yourself to be alone with me the next day at the Town Common," he said, studying her face. "I'm not complaining, but–"

"I felt it would be okay, as long as we were out in public. After all, what could happen on the Common? Although, I almost insisted on riding my bike there." She paused, thinking about this life-changing conversation. "But, what about Selena? It seems to me that if you used your Gift with her...not that you should bend her will but, um..." she paused. "Things might be ..."

"--a little easier for everybody?"

"Yeah, but for her too. She's hurting. Wouldn't it help her?" Haley didn't want to sound selfish and felt nervous about making the proposal.

"I thought about that of course, but like I said, that Gift doesn't work on family."

"But she's not a close relation," Haley said.

"She's blood. It won't work on her."

She touched her Medallion. "This is a lot to take in."

"But having it helps?"

She nodded. "I love having all the power."

"Kiss me," he coaxed, leaning forward.

"No." Feeling mischievous, she couldn't hold back the grin she felt playing on her lips.

"Haley, I said kiss me," he repeated, his voice low, dangerous.

"Shoot," she said. "Even wearing a magic medallion, I *still* can't resist."

ON HIS WAY back to Gisele's, he stopped at his favorite thinking place, beside Spot Pond. His body trembled with

~ ☾ ~

excitement, terror and love. It was done. His father might burst a vein, but for good or for bad, The Medallion now rested at Haley's throat. Congratulations *might* be offered, but given his father's personality, Micah thought the more likely reaction would be, "It's a valuable family relic and you're too young. Get it back." The skipped generation meant his father could not possibly understand Haley's pull on him. No longer an independent planet, happily orbiting the sun, now he was simply an inconsequential moon, revolving around the beautiful Planet Haley.

He would stand his ground, of course. She was it, The One. He'd known for months. *Let the fighting begin.*

He smiled when his thoughts drifted back to Haley. Unless she asked, he wouldn't tell her that his grandfather and his great-great-grandfather had gifted The Medallion within 24 hours of meeting *their* future wives. He was proud that he'd been able to fight his impulses for all of three weeks.

With her considerable help, of course.

If it weren't for her youthful shyness, he probably wouldn't have lasted a week.

Dad's gonna kill me.

~ ☾ ~

CHAPTER THIRTY-TWO

MIDNIGHT. AND HALEY hadn't slept a wink. She couldn't stop thinking about her incredible evening. *He's going to ask me to marry him one day!* She screamed in her head. *I'm going to be Micah's wife!* She sighed, shivered with happiness and rolled over again.

And again.

"What's going on?" Lacey whispered next to her on the springy bed.

"Mmmm, sorry, Lacewing, I didn't mean to wake you."

"Oh, I never even got to sleep. I've been riding a roller coaster all night," came her dry response. "Can't you just lie still?"

"No, I can't help it. And stop exaggerating."

"Is it Micah?" Lacey asked.

"Who else?" Haley heaved a great sigh.

"Are you worried or in love?"

"In love, without a doubt," Haley said.

"How do you know?"

"I'm so happy when I'm with him, it's actually painful when he leaves."

"Well, I guess you're in love. Kinda fast though, huh?" Lacey asked.

"Not really. I've been waiting to meet him since last month, remember?"

"Yeah, well, Grandma's been asking..."

An intake of breath. "What'd you say?"

"Oh, it's just a summer romance," Lacey said. "I got your back, Hayseed."

"Thanks, Lace."

"He's not just a summer fling, though is he?"

"Definitely not. I think I'm supposed to be with him

~ ☾ ~

forever. Doesn't hurt that he's the cutest guy I've ever met. Mmmm, those *eyes* and he uses Irish Spring soap."

"*Dad's* brand?"

"Yeah, he smells great." Haley laughed, not yet ready to share the biggest secret she'd ever held. She would've said yes tonight, had he actually proposed.

"Yeah. Nice butt, too."

Haley halfheartedly whacked Lacey in the general vicinity of her shoulder. "So listen," Haley said after the giggling stopped. "He's got this Gift."

"Gift?"

"Yeah. He can see people in his future and he says I'm in his future. A lot."

"Great line," Lacey muttered from across the bed.

"*What?*" Haley asked.

"All I'm saying is, it's a great pick-up line," Lacey said. "It could be true, but what are the odds of that?"

"The odds are pretty good. Have you seen what he can do with a wand and a sword? He can call dragons! He's so amazing. There's another Gift..."

"Yes?" Lacey's voice came low through the darkness, more hiss than whisper. Haley recognized it as her 'I-love-gossip' voice.

She'll love this, Haley thought. "He can make people *do* things, even against their will."

"*Make* people do things? What do you mean? *What* did he make you do?" Lacey's body tensed and her voice snarled.

Not the reaction she expected, but she plowed on anyway. "He made me..." she paused, swallowing. "Drop a spoon."

Lacey laughed into her pillow, her body shaking. It sounded to Haley like she was suffocating her stupid self. Maybe she could use some help with that.

"I'll alert the media," Lacey giggled when she finally came up for air. "Film at eleven...wha-ha-ha..."

"Be quiet. You don't know what it was like."

More giggles and a snort. "So explain it to me."

"He kept telling me to drop the spoon. I resisted as long as I could, but after a while, I just couldn't hold on to it anymore."

~ ☾ ~

"Sounds awful!" Lacey said, through muffled laughter. "How will you live with the shame, the disgrace, the dishonor? Will you have to move to another town?"

"Oh, shut up."

Lacey snickered in the darkness. "That's a relief. I thought maybe he made you do something, you know, naughty."

Haley could imagine her sister's raised eyebrows. "No, never. He's not like that. But he could make you hurt someone, even if you didn't want to. He wouldn't, of course, but he could."

"So how are you going to resist him? 'Cause that's what it comes down to, right?""Yeah, he's already come up with a solution." She lifted the Medallion and put one of Lacey's hands on it.

"What is it? A pendant?"

"Yeah, this is how I resist him," Haley said. "As long as I wear it, I have all the power. And he gave it to me so I would feel comfortable with him."

Lacey felt the thin chain. "Is this chain strong enough? It feels no thicker than a hair."

"He told me not to be afraid of breaking it."

"What's the design? It's raised, but I can't make it out."

"It's an R, backwards and forwards, with a diamond-shaped O in the center. It stands for Right of Refusal."

"Hmph, Taylor seems so boring after this guy."

"Taylor's really nice," Haley said.

"Yeah, he is," she paused. "Don't be mad, but I told him about Madam Lola and that 'One vill fall.'"

"I'm not mad. I just told Micah."

"You did? I guess I don't feel so bad." Lacey yawned. "So you think Taylor's cute?"

"Taylor's a great guy."

"Wanna trade?"

"Absolutely not. Go to sleep."

ON MONDAY MORNING Haley sat on the porch drinking tea when Micah arrived to pick her up at eight forty-five. "Six Flags was a blast yesterday," Haley said with a smile as they

~ ☾ ~

walked down the stairs.

"It was lots of fun," he agreed as he drove to Gisele's. "And I can't believe I know someone who loves riding roller coasters as much as I do."

She beamed at the memory. "Lacey and Taylor had a good time, too. We talked about it all night long. Maybe we can go back before the end of the summer..." Looking at him, she sighed, her shoulders slumping and asked the dreaded question. "So, what's going to happen at the end of the summer?"

He looked at her. "You mean, when it's time to go home?"

"Yeah, what happens then?" she asked.

"Well, I was worried about that too, but then I decided, wherever you are, I will find a way to get to you." He pulled over at his favorite look-out point on Spot Pond, took a deep breath and said, "Okay, I'm ready. Where do you live?"

She took a breath. "Auburn," she said, watching his eyes.

He blinked. "Mass.?"

"Yeah, why? Where do *you* live?" she asked.

A slow smile crept over his face and he fell back against his seat. "I should've asked a week ago. I've been putting it off because I didn't want to hear how bad–"

"*Where* do you live?" she demanded.

"Spencer." He grinned.

"Massachusetts? Like twelve miles away?" She shook her head, amazed.

"Our football team kicked your team's butt last year. We're *neighbors*." He sighed, wrapping her in a quick hug. "What a relief."

"It's awesome. I can't believe it." Still smiling, she looked around. "You like this spot."

"I love watching the pond in the morning and at dusk. Heck, sometimes I even come here at night." He rubbed a small dent on his dashboard and smiled at her. "We should be going."

At Gisele's he parked next to her ancient yellow Toyota. They got out of the car and Haley stopped. "Oh, hey, what about Selena? Aren't you supposed to give her a ride?"

"I picked her up earlier. I didn't want to miss any time

~ ☾ ~

with you," he said. She swallowed, suddenly nervous. *I wonder how Selena took it.* They walked into Gisele's cabin holding hands. Haley got a quick look at Selena's angry, murderous face, just before it changed.

"Hey, you guys! You're la-a-a-te!" Selena sang, acting positively charming, leaving Haley unsure she'd even seen that black look.

"Yeah, I guess the time got away from us. Sorry," she said, looking around.

"That's okay," Gisele said. "We're just bringing Selena up to speed on what we talked about last Thursday."

"I guess I should've come after all." Selena pulled a fake pout. "But you grabbed my favorite chauffeur," she said to Haley, as she turned her big eyes on Micah. "And I *really* hate sharing him." She turned her head so only Haley could catch her hateful sneer. "I'll get you for that," she growled before turning her head and laughing lightly as if she were kidding. Haley's mouth went dry. She felt like she was watching a snake preparing to strike.

"Kissing trumps driving anytime, right, Micah?" Taylor said, laughing. Selena's fake smile froze in place. Lacey poked Taylor, who started to protest, then looked around at the silent shocked faces and shut up. Haley swallowed, exchanging glances with Gisele. Micah alone seemed unaffected.

Gisele hastily changed the subject. "Does everyone have their tools? Haley? Opal, crystal, red pouch?"

"Yes," came her quiet reply. She felt Micah watching her and suddenly felt more anxious than ever. Could the others sense something...different, even *ominous* about today's outing?

Gisele finished up her inventory. "Micah, wand, sword, pouch?"

"All set." He smiled. "Time to go, I guess. C'mon." He held his hand out to Haley. They were followed by Lacey, Taylor and Gisele. Haley glanced back in time to see Selena's unguarded hate-filled eyes shoot darts of poison at her.

Trooping out to the Altar Stone, they found two crystals, a crown of flowers and a stone-filled pouch. Gisele waved her

~ ☾ ~

hand above the tools and a crystal glowed as her palm hovered over it. "Just this, I guess."

Selena drew a blank, her beautiful face expressionless as she watched the others. Micah stepped up and the remaining crystal practically jumped into his hand. Shock registered on his handsome face.

Lacey held her hands over the flowered crown. Nope. But the pouch rolled right into her hand. She turned it over in her hand and a few stones spilled out. They glittered like diamonds.

Haley passed her hand over the crown, which positively glowed. She picked it up and looked at Micah. He smiled, took it from her hands and placed it on her head. She heard his sharp intake of breath as he bent at the knees so his face came even with hers. His mouth fell open as he took in her wide-eyed expression. "You look like a bride," he whispered.

"I'm afraid to go in today." She swallowed as she removed last week's crown from her backpack and left it on the Altar Stone.

"We'll protect you, I promise." He kissed her cheek.

She nodded, unconvinced. Aloud, she said, "We're not sacrificing a virgin today, are we?"

"I don't think so," Gisele said with an amused chuckle.

Selena smirked and turned away.

Heading due north this time, Taylor and Gisele checked every step for line quicksand. "There seem to be fewer lines in this part of the forest," Gisele said. "Possibly because the swamps are concentrated in the eastern region." She checked Taylor's map. "All the lines appear to stretch east to west. I wonder if that's significant."

She and Taylor healed a line just outside a beautiful shady meadow and were about to move forward when a scream pierced the air.

~ ☾ ~

CHAPTER THIRTY-THREE

GISELE WATCHED IN horror as Lacey's left leg sunk to the knee at the tail end of an overlooked line. With mounds of sand washing over her, Micah and Taylor reached her in seconds but their attempts to pull her out by her arms met with little success. Each new sand-wave crashing overhead sucked her in a little deeper. Almost like she was being *eaten*. Lacey wriggled, trying to twist away but her knee held fast and now her right leg was in danger of being swallowed as well.

"We're losing her!" Haley screamed and lunged forward to grasp Lacey's waist. Another sand wave exploded overhead, knocking Haley down and covering her face. Micah supported Lacey with one hand and with the other, he and Gisele pulled Haley away from danger. Gisele wiped her face and nose, then fished out the crown, which had fallen from Haley's head, from the mess.

"Do you have her? Is she okay?" Micah yelled to Gisele. He nearly let go of Lacey when he twisted to see Haley.

"I'm fine. Help Lacey." Haley sputtered and coughed.

"Everybody, spit on the mud!" Gisele commanded, then proceeded to do so herself in front of her horrified students. And yet wherever she spat, the mud pulled back, like bubbles chased by a bar of soap. Still holding Lacey, Micah, Taylor and Selena all dove in, spitting as fast as their saliva would allow. Finally the waves of sand slowed then stopped crashing. Micah and Taylor dragged a gasping Lacey back to solid ground where all three collapsed.

"Yuck," she said, shaking her sand-covered hands and feet.

"Well, that was fun," Selena said, wiping spots of sand from her shirt.

"Not to sound too ungrateful, but you spit on my arm,"

~ ☾ ~

Lacey said.

"Guess my aim was off," Selena shrugged. "I don't have much practice spitting."

"And on my cheek!"

"Oops." Selena smiled as she walked away.

Gisele located and passed out small towels from her magic bag while instructing Taylor to find and heal the edges of the newest and most unusual line quicksand. Heaving from exertion, Haley bent from the waist, rinsing her sand-covered hair with bottled water before drying it with one of Gisele's towels.

"Thanks for spitting on me, guys," Lacey said as everyone laughed. "Really. I've never been hawked on by a nicer group of people." She turned to Gisele, "Okay, so why did it work? And how did you know to actually *do* it?"

Gisele smiled. "I've been reading *The Elemental Encyclopedia 5000 Spells,* and came across a passage that said, 'If you spit on a lower level entity, you confuse them and cause them to back down.' So, I tried it and voila!"

"Thanks again. I was going down fast. Man, that was scary," Lacey said.

Taylor hugged her, then quickly pulled back, laughing as the wet sand rubbed off on his shirt. "But wouldn't salt have worked?"

"I was afraid it would solidify with you caught in there, so I opted for saliva."

After studying the area in which Lacey was trapped, Micah said, "Aunt Gisele, did you notice this Line is traveling in a different direction from the others?"

"Yes, I did."

"What does it mean?" Lacey asked, wiping her arms and legs.

"Things are changing." She sighed as she watched Taylor plot the line's course. "Stay in sight," she called to him. "Unlike most lines, this one curves back, toward the south. We can take nothing for granted and we have to be extremely vigilant, watching every step forward and every step sideways. This entity, or whatever it is, is evolving and if we don't watch ourselves, we could lose someone." She

~ ☾ ~

rummaged in her magic bag. "Lacey, could you come here? And Selena?"

The girls walked to her. "Lacey, here's a top and shorts. While we heal this line, you can change behind those bushes." No one even questioned why her magic bag would contain clothes in the right size, Gisele thought to herself with some amusement. "Selena, can you sweep that area and keep her company while she changes? However close, no one should be alone."

"It's okay. I'll be fine," Lacey said, quickly.

A little too *quickly*, Gisele thought. "No, you need to have someone with you. Selena?"

"Well, *sure!*" Selena gushed artificial enthusiasm. "I'd *love* to!" Gisele glanced at Micah for his take on this new attitude, but his eyes were all over Haley.

"I FEEL SO stupid wearing this thing and now it's a mess," Haley said, removing her sodden flowered crown. "No one else has one. Why do I need it?"

"Because," Micah said, replacing the crown on her head, "you are the most beautiful thing in the forest."

"I'm a mess."

"You're beautiful," he tucked a wet tendril behind her ear.

"Have you seen the *fairies*?" she asked, rolling her eyes and wishing she could believe him.

"Why, yes, I have," he said, still adjusting her crown and hair.

"And the unicorns?"

"Uh huh."

"And yet–" She sighed.

"And yet, they pale in comparison to you." He kissed her cheek. "Seriously, keep it on. You never know when things are going to get crazy around here. And it looks beautiful on you." He stroked the side of her face.

His words thrilled her, and his touch made her blush with delight. He was so busy enjoying her company, only she saw Selena pass by at that exact moment. Scowling, she moved quickly away.

A few minutes later, Lacey pulled her aside. "I think she pushed me."

~ ☾ ~

"Pushed you, where? Into the quicksand?"

"Yeah."

"How would she know where it was?" Haley said. "Line quicksand is invisible."

"I don't know, but I was pushed. And she was right next to me."

THEY SAT DOWN for lunch in one of their favorite clearings. Perfectly round and deeply shaded, it was edged with ancient oak trees and filled with softly swaying ferns. The small group paired off to sit on three large, flat boulders. Selena, her back to Haley and Micah, sat with Gisele, while Lacey and Taylor chatted quietly.

Haley whispered to Micah, "Selena's been, well, *polite*."

"I admit I'm a bit concerned," he said.

"Really?" She was shocked and relieved that he finally recognized Selena's hostile feelings for her.

"Yes. She said she'd back off and she has, but her moods have gotten darker. I'm not sure whether that's due to her feelings about our relationship, or just you. I will keep an eye on her," he said, leaning his head on her shoulder. "You smell wonderful, do you know that?"

She giggled. "Thank you, but sit up, okay? We shouldn't flaunt our feelings in front of her, you know? She still likes you a lot." She glanced at Selena, who chose that moment to turn around and glare at them.

"As you wish." He sat up straight and went back to his sandwich, which surprised her and left her feeling a bit disappointed.

After lunch, they hiked another hour before discovering two additional north to south quicksand lines. Almost as soon as they were dispatched, Selena called out, "Rift ahead." The biggest one they'd encountered so far, it stood at least six feet high by eight feet wide, and stretched so far into the forest Haley couldn't see the end of it.

"Is everyone ready?" Gisele asked, looking around. "Haley, you can begin."

~ ☾ ~

CHAPTER THIRTY-FOUR

FROM DEEP WITHIN the earth a small crack appeared high above them. Though the light from the crevice stabbed their eyes, it also drew them forward, inescapably forward. Like a haphazard army, they dragged their useless wings, jerking and skittering toward its unforgiving brilliance. As they drew closer, the narrow passageway around them enlarged, allowing unused wings to expand and flex, lungs to fill and the shrieking to begin. Anxious to escape the scorching heat below, hundreds of winged rats scrabbled for purchase before erupting into the air through a flimsy, fragmented crust of dirt, moss and leaves.

Once in the air, no longer clumsy and graceless, the now synchronized flock swooped and dipped, greasy, leather-like wings barely whispering in the wind. Red eyes glowing, their powerful jaws snapped and long hairless tails whipped from side to side.

The flock had but one target, one goal—The Healer. And each would willingly sacrifice its own insignificant life to reach her. Even now, the rift had begun to close. Time was short.

And then, an attraction so fantastic, so improbable, the original goal was forgotten, lost. Hundreds, thousands of glittering, sparkling diamonds appeared in the sky, challenging and disorienting the collective conscientiousness. Where only moments before, the objective was well defined, now there was but chaos and confusion. Inexplicably, and without warning, the mesmerizing diamonds began to explode, taking out any and all creatures within a six-foot radius. Each hit to the swarm spread anger, panic and shared pain to the individuals of the flock, causing many of those who weren't directly hit to plunge to earth in a sudden death

~ ☾ ~

spiral.

On the ground, those who'd fallen, but somehow managed to stay alive amid the wreckage, dragged broken wings and mangled legs as they jostled through the confusion toward their original goal, she of the crown. The Wretched Healer.

Their Queen.

GISELE WATCHED WITH horror as flying rats exploded in mid-air, spraying the group with a slimy green splatter. Never mind that it melted away in seconds, the sight and acrid smell of it oozing from trees, hair and chins caused at least one stomach to lurch in reaction. Lacey clutched a tree, leaned over and almost lost her breakfast. When Gisele moved toward her, Lacey waved her off and rejoined the fight.

Micah and Selena worked as a team, shooting blue flames from their wands, and picking off the surviving flying rats of Lacey's lethal diamonds while Taylor used his wand to touch and destroy all within reach. Gisele took a breath. "You kids are doing great. Keep it up and we'll be heading home in an hour."

She realized spoke too soon when Taylor slipped on rat guts and fell on a not-quite-dead rat, who took exception and clamped its sharp teeth on his arm. Screaming, Taylor jumped to his feet shaking his arm, in a futile attempt to dislodge the creature.

"Stay still," Micah trained attempted to his wand on his frantically moving friend. "I'll get it for you."

Taylor thrust his arm away from his body, squeezed his eyes shut and looked away while Micah made short work of the foul rodent.

After directing much of the action in the battle and with just a few of the vile creatures left to be eradicated, Gisele watched her young friends vanquish the final three and smiled with relief as she made preparations to clean and heal the injuries.

And then, Round Two.

From the small, unhealed portion of the rift burst forth an

~ ☾ ~

explosion of two dozen six-foot, winged crocodiles. Gisele watched as the monsters circled overhead twice, just long enough for Lacey to toss the rest of her precious diamonds into the sky. But with the sudden shift of the croc flock, Lacey's beautiful diamond exterminators only managed to bring down five of the monsters. Micah took out six more and Selena found her mark with four as the remainder of flying crocs wheeled, screaming through the air. The monsters fell out of the sky thirty feet from Haley, sliding the last ten on scaly bellies, long jaws cracking.

FRANTICALLY SEARCHING THE ground for more diamonds, Lacey looked up just in time to see Selena disappear behind a large pine tree. *Where's she going?* Lacey wondered as she scrabbled around and somehow managed to retrieve ten of her precious stones, hurling them at the backs of the retreating monsters. She winced as Taylor raced ahead, narrowly dodging two exploding crocs, while touching three with his wand. In the lead, Micah charged forward, annihilating three of the four remaining beasts with his wand as he ran.

That left only one. Somehow avoiding wandfire and exploding diamonds, the mutant creature thrust itself upon Haley with a triumphant scream, throwing her to the ground.

~ ☾ ~

CHAPTER THIRTY-FIVE

THE TEAM CONVERGED as one. In the same moment, Taylor touched the beast with his wand tip as Lacey threw her last diamond. Just as Micah pointed his wand to blast it to oblivion, it simply...disappeared.

"Haley." Micah's voice filled with anguish as he knelt beside her unmoving body, still wearing her crown. Ten yards away, the screeching sounds of the closing rift filled the air. Out of the corner of his eye, Micah could see the mound collapsing in on itself, though he spared it barely a glance.

Haley still hadn't stirred.

"Haley, please," Micah whispered, his fingers on her wrist, checking for a pulse. "I can't find a pulse! Haley?"

Gisele knelt beside him and took her wrist. "I got one. It's weak, but she's alive. Lacey, get my bag."

Then Haley took a breath. "Water?"

On his knees beside her, Micah's chin fell to his chest in relief and gratitude. "Oh man, that was a close one." He sighed and stroked her hair.

HALEY OPENED HER eyes surprised to see everyone huddled around her. Usually it was just Micah. And this time, they all looked pretty scared.

"Must've been a good one," she mumbled, closing her eyes again. "Just let me rest for a second." After draining half Gisele's water, she sat up. "How'd it go?"

Her friends stood, open-mouthed, in a circle around her. Lacey whispered, "I can't figure out why you aren't dead, or bleeding at least..."

Haley patted down her arms and legs, checking for injuries. "I'm fine. Why? What the heck happ–"

~ ☾ ~

"Wait a minute. Where's Selena?" Micah rocked back on his heels, looking around.

"She walked away!" Lacey shrieked as if just remembering, "I watched her! They were attacking Haley and she turned around and *walked away!*"

Eyes narrowed, he pointed at his cousin, leaning against a tree on the far side of the clearing. "Is she—checking her nails? Selena!" he bellowed.

"Yeah?" Selena was a model of boredom.

Perhaps where she came from, Haley thought, this sort of thing happened all the freakin' time.

"Where have you been? Why didn't you help?" Micah's face grew darker as his voice got lower. "Haley's chief defender," he spat out.

"I helped. I got four of them." She smiled as she sauntered through the clearing to the small group.

"Where were you just now?" he demanded.

Selena shrugged, her defiant look fading somewhat.

Micah lightly squeezed Haley's shoulder then jumped to his feet. He strode quickly to his cousin, grabbing her arm. "Why did you leave?"

"I did my share. I killed four," she repeated, her eyes narrowing as she jerked her arm away from him.

"Four of twenty-four is your share?" Micah spoke through clenched teeth.

"That's right. One sixth." With her chin jutted out, Selena stood, hands on hips, her back ramrod-straight. "Bagged my limit," she smirked, each word punctuated by a tap on Micah's chest with her wand.

So quick Haley almost missed it, Micah grabbed Selena's wand, snapping it in two over his knee.

"My wand!" Selena shrieked as if in pain. "You broke my wand! I've had it since I was eleven years old!"

"Get out of here, traitor. Leave now before"—he stopped, and shaking his head, threw her ruined wand to the ground— "just get out."

"Without my wand?"

"You won't need it. *Leave now.*" He took a menacing step forward. "The way I feel right now, I could snap your neck as

~ ☽ ~

easily as I snapped your wand."

She backed up in fear. "Alone? In the forest?"

Gisele hurried over. "She can't leave without some kind of protection."

He produced his crystal from the Altar Stone and slapped it into Selena's open hand. "Use this. It's more protection than you gave Haley. Now go."

"Micah." Gisele's tone was stern.

"But it's scary out there—"

"Not half as scary as it would be with me. Get out." He waved vaguely toward the south as she stumbled away, crying. A moment later, the expression on Micah's face changed from one of pure fury to what Haley thought might be troubled.

Gisele went after Selena as Micah walked to Haley, who stood, filled with questions. "You okay?" he asked, brushing her hair from her face. He hugged her a little harder than usual.

"Yeah, fine," she said. "What's the big deal?"

"A six-foot crocodile with wings landed on top of you and she allowed it. That's kind of a big deal," he said. His eyes narrowed as he looked to the south and Haley recognized the effort it took to keep his temper contained.

"On *top* of me?" she asked. "No, I just collapsed, like I always do. Nobody caught me this time, though. What's up with that?"

"The creature plowed into you. You should be dead," he said, pulling leaves and twigs off her arms. "I'm glad you're okay, but what happened?" he looked to Gisele who had just rejoined them.

Eyebrows raised, Gisele said, "A shield. I think the crown must be a shield. Heavy-duty protection from all kinds of danger. But somehow it attracts them..."

Standing next to Haley, Micah nodded in agreement. "They sure seemed to zero in on you, didn't they?" His voice hitched a bit, like he was close to tears. "You never even saw them though, did you?"

"No, I was too busy. When I came to, you were all looking at me." She shrugged, unconcerned and drank more water.

~ ☾ ~

"Why did that thing just disappear?" Lacey said. "Where did it go?"

"It's getting late," Gisele said, looking at the sky. "We'll talk about that next time we meet."

"Is Selena okay?" Haley said.

"Who cares?" Micah frowned.

"I do." Haley turned to Gisele. "Can she get back okay?"

"She'll be fine. I programmed the crystal to take her back to the cabin. It will protect her and she only has to follow the blue line through the forest."

"What about the line quicksand?" Haley said.

Micah looked up in the air and sighed.

"It will follow our tracks over the healed lines and get her back safely." Gisele looked at her. "I must say I'm impressed at how you're taking this, Haley."

"I don't think this is her fault. I think the Entity made her do it."

"That's an intriguing idea, Haley." Gisele nodded, picking up her bag. "Come on, everyone, we should get going."

Micah stepped back a bit, studying her face. "Are you ready to travel?"

"Sure."

"Let's go," Micah said. "Maybe we can catch up to Selena and push her into the quicksand." Although he smiled when he said it, Haley didn't think he was kidding.

"AUNT GISELE WOULD you drive Selena back to her aunt's house this afternoon?" Micah asked as they hiked back. "I can't. I'm afraid of what I would do or say." Haley watched him shake his head in exasperation.

"I understand and of course I will give her a ride, but you know she did this for *you*, right?" she said.

"You think this was *my* fault? Because I rejected her?" He stopped walking.

"Well..." Haley watched Gisele's eyebrows practically disappear into her hairline.

"Oh my god, it's all because of me. You were almost killed, because of me."

~ ☾ ~

"Maybe you could have been kinder–" Gisele said.

"I don't believe this." He turned to her. "I put you in danger. I did this."

"You couldn't have known."

"But I did. I knew she was a bit, um"–he paused– "unbalanced, and I felt something dark from her, but I didn't care." He sighed. "I should have paid more attention to her, let her down easier, but I didn't." He turned to Haley. "All I could think about was you. And when she said she was fine, I thought...well she *seemed* like she was doing okay."

"She was not okay. She was *never* okay. Highly obvious to everyone but you, Micah," Gisele said. "Since you're an Adept, I hope and expect you to work on becoming more aware of other peoples' feelings, especially strong ones, like Selena's."

"Maybe I blocked most of it out," he said. "But I can't help that. I don't feel the same way about her. Never did."

"You and I will discuss this later," she said. "When we get back to the cabin, you should leave right away. Oh, and we're sticking to our schedule—we'll return to the forest on Monday."

"But we'll be one short–" Lacey said. And they all looked at her. "I mean, if she doesn't come back."

"What else can we do? Can't be helped." Gisele looked away and mumbled, "I hate being right all the time."

~ ☾ ~

CHAPTER THIRTY-SIX

SELENA WAITED AT the picnic table next to the cabin. Though Micah glared at her, he in fact reserved most of his anger for himself. The others passed her wordlessly on their way to their bikes, but Gisele stopped and invited her inside for tea. "Haley, I'm sorry," Selena called. Her apology hung in the air, unacknowledged, except for a small nod from Haley.

Micah bristled at her words and struggled to control his anger toward his traitorous cousin and himself. *How could she do such a thing?* He wondered as he started his car. *Never mind that now. I'll deal with it later.* "Are you okay?"

"Yeah, I'm great," Haley said.

"You really are, aren't you?" Micah marveled. "I guess it doesn't affect you the way it did the rest of us."

Haley shrugged.

"After I drop you off, I'm coming back. If Selena is still here, we'll have it out then. If I miss her, Gisele and I still have a lot to discuss." He closed his eyes and sighed, thinking how close he had come to losing her. "Are you busy tomorrow?"

"No, I think my calendar's clear," she said. "What did you have in mind?"

"Well, we could go to the mall in Pittsfield, back to Spot Pond, or hiking in the State Forest."

"Let's skip the State Forest, okay?" she said. "I get enough hiking these days, I think."

"Okay, the Mall or Spot Pond."

"If we go to the Mall, we'll have to bring Lacey," she considered, wrinkling her nose. "Spot Pond, I guess."

"We could go someplace else, you know," he offered.

"No, I love your beach."

"Spot Pond it is, then. It's my first choice as well," he said,

~ ☾ ~

wrapping her up in a powerful hug and breathing in her warm fragrance. He knew then that if he lived to be a hundred years old, he would never feel love more deeply than he did for this beautiful girl.

WHEN MICAH ARRIVED the next morning, he found the twins outside reading The Splinter Chronicles, a popular Young Adult fantasy-adventure. "You like that stuff?" he asked with a smirk.

"Yeah, they're fun to read. Don't you like them?" Lacey asked with a glance at her sister. "Haley *loves* these books."

"I prefer the real thing."

"Well, the real thing is a little scary sometimes," Lacey said.

"Speaking of scary, why don't you tell me about the giant carnivorous frogs?" Micah said.

Haley laughed. "Don't ask about them in front of Taylor."

"Why not?" he said, preparing himself for another one of their wild stories.

"He hates them! They attacked him last year and he barely escaped with his life."

"Start at the beginning," he said. "What happened?"

"We went into the forest to collect herbs," she said. "Gisele needed Water Hemlock which is only found on the edge of the swamp. She and Taylor went to the end of the muddy peninsula jutting into the swamp and just as she was reaching for the Hemlock, a giant frog the size of a Volkswagen jumped up at her. Taylor pulled her out of its way just in time and they fell on their butts in the mud."

"Then the frogs attacked each other!" Lacey said.

"I guess I'm with Taylor on this one," Micah chuckled.

"We don't speak of them often," Haley said. "And never in front of Taylor."

"So where are you two going today?" Lacey asked.

"Spot Pond," Micah said, his eyes on Haley.

"Oh, Taylor and I are going there too," Lacey said. "If you wait 'til noon, we'll go with you."

Micah exchanged the briefest of glances with his girl.

~ ☾ ~

"Thanks for the offer, but I think we'd like to go early. Ready?" he asked Haley.

"Yes." She grabbed her bag.

"See you there," Lacey called.

"Okay." Haley replied over her shoulder.

As they walked to his car, Micah laughed at their private joke. Lacey would never see them, no one would.

ELEVEN A.M., AND it was already hot when they spread out the blanket.

"I'll do your back if you'll do mine," Micah offered, jiggling the suntan lotion in front of her face.

"Okay," she said, propping her chin on her hands as she lay on her belly. "Can you *believe* what Selena did? I'm still kinda shocked about what happened."

"Please don't remind me. I still feel horrible about the whole thing." He scowled.

"Did see her after you dropped me off?"

He sighed. "No, they were gone by the time I got back. Oh, and you'll be happy to know that Gisele is thinking you might be right. She thinks maybe Selena was being controlled by the Entity." *There was more to that conversation, lots more—but I'm not sharing how she yelled at me.*

"Really?"

"Yeah, she thinks Selena's jealousy and negativity weakened her and made her a good target for the Entity's influence."

"The Entity wants me out?" Haley turned to look at him, her beautiful eyes wide.

"Of course. You're the only one who can do what you do. You're the biggest threat to the evil in the forest." He scowled, still furious at his cousin, even if it wasn't all her fault. *At least she's gone now.* "Selena sure gave me and my Gift a run for my money. I didn't realize how strong her feelings were until yesterday," he said "I should have known."

"Even *we* could see that—" Haley shrugged.

"*Who* could see that?"

"Lacey and I," Haley said. "We talked about it a few times.

~ ☾ ~

Selena's feelings for you are completely out in the open. Even someone *without* your special powers could see that."

"I guess I wasn't paying attention." His gaze never left her face.

"Some Gift," she said with a trace of sarcasm.

"What do you mean?" he asked.

"That's two people whose feelings you misinterpreted." She smiled. "Hers *and* mine. Maybe you're losing your touch."

"Maybe it doesn't matter any more. Nice suit," he gazed at her one-piece with its plunging back line.

"Thanks. Hey, when's your birthday?" she said.

"Halloween."

"Cool."

"I'm a natural sorcerer."

"I never asked, and now I feel silly, but what's your last name?" she said while he rubbed the lotion on her back.

"I guess last names never came up in conversation before." He laughed. "Fuller."

"Favorite color?"

"Do I get a chance to ask questions too?"

"Mmmm...hmmm."

"Feel good?"

"Mmm hmm."

"I could do this all day, but I think I'm rubbing it *off* you now." He laughed. "So I guess it's my turn," he said as he laid down beside her on the blanket.

"Okay." Haley grabbed the lotion and began applying it to his back.

Resting his chin on his hands, he looked out at the pond.

"Have you always been so pretty?"

She giggled. "I was cuter as a baby."

"Impossible. When's your birthday?"

"August twenty six," she said.

"The day after Christmas, in August."

Her hand stopped abruptly. "Why'd you say that?"

He leaned on one elbow, turning around to see her shocked expression.

"What do you mean?"

~ ☽ ~

"Just tell me why you said that," she demanded.

"I don't know. It just came to me." He frowned. "Did I say something wrong?"

"No. That's what we always say," she said. "It helps people to remember our birthday."

"I won't forget now." He laughed, rolling back onto his stomach. "What's *your* last name?" Though he'd known since January, it might seem strange if he didn't ask.

"Miller, like my grandmother."

"Hmm. Miller and Fuller."

"Shall we start a law firm or sell vacuum cleaners?" she said.

He smiled. "It'll be an easy transition for you, Haley Miller to Haley Fuller..."

Again she stopped rubbing the oil. "How sure are you about this? We've only known each other a short time, you know."

"Very sure," he said, never more confident in his Gifts. "I have future vision, *and* you're wearing my Medallion." He licked his upper lip. "How about if we try something different today?"

"Okay, I guess."

"Good. Lie on your belly." He squeezed out another large drop of sunscreen, and rubbed it on her back. "How about this–I'll write something on your back, and you try to figure out the letters and the message?"

"Okay, sounds like fun," she agreed as she flopped down on her belly again. "Umm, 'M'?" she guessed, giggling.

"Yes."

"'F?'"

"Yes. You're good at this."

"Plus?"

"Correct."

She smiled. "H and M."

"That's right. I was going to spell the next one out, but it takes too long, so I'll just say it."

"Yes?" she said.

"I heart u."

She drew in a long breath and rolled on her side, meeting

~ ☾ ~

his eyes. "I heart you, too."

He lay down facing her. "I heart you more than you can imagine." And then he kissed her and it seemed he couldn't get close enough. When he pulled back and opened his eyes, Haley's eyes filled with tears.

Using his thumb, he gently wiped her cheek. "What's the matter, my love? Did I say something wrong?" His eyes searched her face.

"Don't worry." She sniffed, swiping her cheek with the back of her hand. "They're happy tears. I just can't believe you feel the same way I do."

He looked deep into her eyes. "I love you. I knew it the moment I saw your picture. I've waited months to be with you, to do this..." He kissed her again. He looked into her wide, surprised eyes and another wave of love washed over him, threatening to drown him with emotion. Time to change the subject.

"So, like I said, you're wearing my Medallion–" he began.

"Always."

"Are you *that* afraid of me?" he asked, looking at the pond, suddenly aware of his own heartbeat.

"Afraid? No, of course not. I wear it because it's from you. If you'd given me a rusty old nail instead, I'd be wearing that right now," she said, a shy smile playing on her lips.

He looked away shaking his head. Medallion or not, Micah realized he was going to have to watch himself. It would be too easy to get carried away by their feelings for each other. But he knew one thing–if his life ended this very minute, he would have no regrets.

~ ☾ ~

CHAPTER THIRTY-SEVEN

WHEN MICAH DROPPED her off later, he asked about her weekend plans.

Haley noticed the living room curtains twitching. Big-Nose Lacey, spying on her again. "We have to spend our weekend with my dad, remember?"

"Oh, yeah," he said. "I should meet him soon."

"Really?"

"Shouldn't he meet his future son-in-law?" he said, winking.

"Stop it. When you talk like that, I get goose bumps." She laughed, rubbing her forearms.

"Get used to living with goose bumps." He smiled. "So, how about this weekend?"

"You wouldn't tell him that, would you? He'd freak."

"Not yet." He gave her a dazzling smile.

"Let's ease him into it, okay? Lacey broke ground for me, but you're as different from Taylor as a shark from a goldfish."

"And *I'm* the shark, right? Okay, but *soon*." He bent down and kissed her goodbye then hugged her fiercely. "Can I call you tomorrow night?"

"Of course. Good night."

She walked up the stairs and was practically attacked at the door.

"Where have you *been*?" Lacey demanded.

"Oh, lay off, buzzkill." Through the window, Haley watched until Micah's taillights disappeared into the night and sighed. So this was love. *Wow*.

"You *lied* to me!" Lacey fluttered around her, indignant. "We went to Spot Pond and you weren't there."

"I didn't lie. We went to Spot Pond." Haley smiled at the

~ ☾ ~

thought, deciding to share *none* of her euphoria with her toady twin.

"His car wasn't there *all day*," Lacey hissed.

"There's more to Spot Pond than the Town Beach," Haley said.

That stopped her. "What do you mean?"

"I mean, we went to his private beach."

"He doesn't have a private beach."

Haley nodded. "Yes, he does."

"Yeah, so what did you do there?"

"Went skinny-dipping," Haley said with a smirk. *This was fun. Lacey's so gullible.*

"You *what?*" she shrieked. "You saw him *naked*?"

"Uh-huh. He's beautiful." Haley closed her eyes, trying to hold back laughter.

"Describe him, *right now* or Grandma's going to be part of this conversation," Lacey growled. Then realization hit. "Wait a minute? *You* were naked, *too?*"

"Of course," Haley laughed.

"So it's like he saw *me* naked? *Eww!*" Lacey put her hands over her eyes.

"Not really, I have way more curves than you. I don't think he'll even make the connection," Haley said, looking her twin up and down with what she hoped was a condescending sneer on her face.

Lacey immediately launched herself at her sister, claws out.

When Haley sidestepped at the last second, Lacey tripped over Grandma Clara's knitting bag and went down. Haley sat on her sister's back, laughing. "Oh, for heavens sake, I was just kidding, dufus."

"No you weren't. Let me up!" Lacey struggled to extricate herself.

"Look, I have tan lines," she moved her strap so Lacey could see the pure whiteness of her shoulder. "See? *Idiot.*"

Lacey stopped fighting and sighed, exhausted. "So, you *didn't* go skinny-dipping?"

"No."

"And you *didn't* see him naked?"

~ ☾ ~

"Nope."

Heavy sigh. "You really got me going, you know?"

"I know, but I'm sure you'll return the favor at some point." Haley stood up. "Where's Grandma?"

"At the store. She'll be right back."

"So *you* lied? You brat." Haley gave her sister a half-hearted smack on the shoulder, knowing Lacey's lie in no way cancelled out her own.

The kitchen door closed with a slam. "Girls, I'm home," Grandma Clara called. "Can I get some help with the groceries?"

"Does he even *have* a private beach?" Lacey asked as she followed her sister into the kitchen.

~ ☾ ~

CHAPTER THIRTY-EIGHT

AS THEY SAT in Gisele's kitchen the following Monday morning, Lacey said, "Gisele, why did those rats and"–she shuddered–"alligators just *disappear* after they were killed?"

"Yeah, I thought there would be dead bodies everywhere," Taylor said, "but they exploded and were gone."

Gisele smiled. The question was not unexpected. Her young warriors sat around the table. Haley seemed interested, but not grossed out like Lacey and Taylor. Micah sat nursing his tea, a slight nod told her he probably already figured this out.

"The creatures expelled from the rifts are basically just energy," she said. "The Entity wants to terrify us and make us leave. But because you've been so brave..."

"Wait a minute. I saw them–I got *bitten*," Lacey protested.

"We all did," Gisele explained. "But those were magical injuries. Painful, of course, but easily healed by our crystals. The monsters disappear after they're killed off and that's part of being a magical forest Entity. Their magic expires at their destruction, but then it ramps up the power on the remaining creatures. That's why the last ones exiting the rifts seem stronger and harder to defeat. But the forest is helping us. And that's why you almost always figure out a way to battle back, to defeat the creatures with the tools you were gifted. When you believe your tools will work, you will be successful."

"Can we really be hurt? " Taylor asked.

"Absolutely." She nodded, "Fifty years ago we had many injuries and one of my friends was killed by the Dragonocepedes. The dangers are very real. We've all been hurt and be aware that it could be worse if we're not very careful."

~ ☾ ~

"So, where do they go again?" Lacey said, frowning.

"The dead creatures and their energy, are reabsorbed by the Entity," Gisele said. "This is a magical battle and so far, amazingly, unbelievably, we're winning, or at least holding our own. You are all doing far better than I could've imagined." She laughed. "A crazy old lady, leading a band of teenagers against an angry supernatural Entity–who'da thought? Which reminds me. Micah, why on earth do my own relatives think I'm exaggerating all of this?"

Micah bit his lip before he spoke. "They said they'd helped you with a cleansing like this before."

"Cleansing?"

"Right. And the cleansing was permanent. It shouldn't have to be done again." He sighed. "They think either you invited it, brought it all on yourself, you're *imagining* it, or..." he swallowed.

"Or?" Gisele prompted with a steely-eyed glare.

"You're senile..." He held her gaze.

"Senile?" Haley put her fist to her lips, like she could prevent the vile word from escaping.

"Hmph," Gisele said, taking care not to allow her fury to spill out. "My *own* relatives? So, my friends, am I *imagining* things? Am I *senile*?" she asked, a sarcastic tone in her voice. "Does anyone think I brought this on *myself*?"

"No." The kids were adamant, shaking their heads, rolling their eyes.

"But what happened last time?" Lacey asked. "Were things as bad as now?"

"Actually, they weren't." Gisele took a deep breath and felt calmer than she would've thought possible after hearing such rubbish. "There was an earthquake then, as well, but quite mild. We had some unexplained disappearances though, and lights over the swamp. A few of us went in to investigate. Micah's parents came, a couple of aunts, my mother, three magical friends and a cousin."

"Quite a crowd," Micah said, eyebrows raised.

"You're right. Most came in for the fun of it. No one thought anyone would be hurt, of course. These were *our woods*, you understand. We were in and out of them all the

~ ☾ ~

time. But on this particular day, we were met by shrieks and howls...in the middle of the day. We left quickly, thinking we would come back the next day, and with our incantations and spells, we'd take care of the problem. They didn't work, but on the way out, we stumbled upon the Altar Stone and were gifted with crystals. We did most of our healing with just those crystals, and now that I think of it, I seem to remember one of the aunts got a wand. We were traveling to the Crystal Cave to get new crystals when we first came upon the Dragonocepedes."

Gisele covered her eyes, but continued to talk. They needed to hear this. "We were able to climb up a tree, all except for one person, a good friend of mine named Gina, who was distantly related to your grandmother. A city girl who never learned how to climb trees, she panicked, tried to run and was killed by those little monsters. At that point, we didn't know how to destroy them and we were devastated by her loss. We healed the three or four rifts–there weren't very many–and pronounced the forest cleansed, as your parents put it."

"So was Gina an...*offering* to the Entity?" Haley asked.

"No, of course not," Gisele quickly dismissed the idea before thinking it through. "Though, after she died, healing the remaining rifts seemed all too easy..." She frowned, sifting through murky and fading fifty-year-old memories.

"But, she was a relative of *ours*?" Lacey asked.

"Well, yes, I guess she was," Gisele said. She would've been a third or fourth cousin to you, I think."

"What did you tell the authorities about how she died?" Taylor, ever the cops kid, asked.

"She had absolutely no marks on her, and we certainly couldn't tell the truth about what had happened. Who would've believed us? So we said she took a nap in the sun and never woke up. Clara wasn't speaking to me at that point, so she never really knew what happened. Fifty years later, it still hurts to speak of it."

"Will you tell her now?" Haley asked.

"Do you want to see this through to the end?"

"Yes," she and Lacey said at once.

~ ☾ ~

"Then I think you answered your own question," Gisele said. "After a half century, I see no reason to dig up old ghosts."

"The Dragonocepedes don't come out of the rifts though, do they?" Lacey asked.

"No, they seem to just wander around looking for trouble and the only time I've ever seen them is right after an earthquake." Gisele said, "I put them in the same category as the line quicksand, the Terratress and the swamp lights."

"So, did monsters come out of the rifts back then?" Taylor asked.

"We had some big beetles, lava flow, and some small lizards. Nothing that compares to what you've faced this summer," Gisele said. "When you go back, Micah, you have my permission to tell our caring relatives that I am supremely disappointed in their lack of concern for the welfare of the forest. And for me, as well." Though she'd wondered about it for the last month, she found herself wishing she never asked the question that started this conversation.

"I have every intention of doing just that, when this is over," Micah assured her with a smile. "They *should* have been here all along."

"Why don't you call them now?" Lacey said.

"This might sound selfish, but I don't want to share this experience with anyone except for the people sitting here right now," Micah said. "Aunt Gisele, if you ever need help again, please call me first."

"Me, too," Haley and Lacey chimed in together, with Taylor nodding in agreement.

"With the four of you behind me, why would I need anyone else?" She laughed. "For a rag-tag little group, I think we're doing just fine. Loyalty, luck and natural talent–that's what we have."

"Plus youth and experience," Micah said, raising his teacup. The others clinked their cups in a magical-tea-toast.

"Youth and experience," Gisele said.

"Is everything we fight going to be as bad as...well, flying alligators?" Taylor said.

"I'm not sure," Gisele said. "Things are changing, whether

~ ☾ ~

that's good or bad, I can't say. I think it's good, though. I think we've got them on the run. They're pulling out all the stops, but we just keep on winning."

The twins exchanged high fives.

"Don't get too cocky, you two. Each time we go in, it's going to be more perilous than the last time," she warned. "The monsters are getting progressively larger and more dangerous. We can't afford to let our guard down, even for an instant."

"I miss last year," Lacey pouted. "We met fairies and dragons and unicorns and Tinky-tinks. We gathered herbs and had *fun*."

"I don't." Haley glanced at Micah. "Compared to *this* year, last year was just plain boring."

"I'm with you," Micah said with a wink.

"So...what's the deal with Selena? Is she coming back?" Lacey said.

Micah and Haley exchanged glances, while Taylor looked at the floor. "Selena has left for the summer," Gisele said.

"Good riddance," Micah muttered, looking away.

"But, why? Why did she abandon us the way she did?" Lacey asked. "Haley could have *died*."

"I know," Gisele said. "Selena, as I'm sure you all know, has quite a thing for Micah." He rolled his eyes in exasperation. "When we talked before she left, she told me she thought this summer they would rekindle whatever romance they began two years ago."

"But there's nothing to restart," Micah protested. "We've been over this *three times*–"

"Doesn't matter," Gisele said. "She has deep feelings for you. But I think Haley was right. I think the Entity preyed on her weaknesses and urged her to walk away during the battle. The Selena I knew would never do such a thing."

"I was so mean to her the last time," he said, shaking his head. "Just to get the point across."

"The rest of us could see how she felt about you," Lacey said.

"I don't know what else I could have done." Micah, his hands falling flat on the table, a pained expression on his face

~ ☾ ~

said, "I never led her on..." as he looked at Gisele.

"You are her first crush and her first heartbreak," Gisele said. "It's a hard lesson to learn. I know—I've been there."

"Did she have a plan of some sort?" Taylor asked.

"Just before she left, she told me her plan was to let something, anything disable Haley, then she would take her place as the rift healer and save the day. She thought this would so impress Micah, he would have to fall *back* in love with her." With eyes closed, Micah began to massage his temples. "With Haley out of the picture, Selena would become his main focus."

Micah snorted. "Get *out*." Gisele smiled sadly. *Even with a spirit so old, he is still so young.* "True love can be difficult. Unrequited love, love that is not returned, is devastating. She couldn't deal with the rejection. Simple as that."

Lacey shook her head and looked down. "She told you all this? Wasn't she embarrassed?"

"A bit. But toward the end, she seemed anxious to confess, to get it off her chest,"

Gisele said. "Haley, Selena didn't want you *dead,* just temporarily out of the way. That's all. But as it stands, she's too unreliable and too dangerous to bring into the forest. We must be able to trust each other with our lives. I knew she was a bit of a gamble, so I never gave her anything too important—"

"You made her Haley's *chief protector*," Micah almost exploded. "That's been bothering me all *week.*"

"I had to give her a job—"

"But protecting *Haley?*" he interrupted again.

"Was *your* job," she said. "Never anyone else's. Selena was *your* back-up, not the other way around."

"You might have told me that," he said, equal parts placated and exasperated.

"Use your common sense, Micah. I knew Haley would always be your first priority. That really goes without saying, don't you think?" Gisele said as he looked away. "I also hoped that if she acted as Haley's protector, a bond would form, which would benefit our team. But it never happened."

"So, she's really not coming back?" Haley asked.

~ ☾ ~

"Not this summer. I asked her to stay away and she agreed. We will miss her strength, though," Gisele said. "If everyone's ready, we should get going."

~ ☾ ~

CHAPTER THIRTY-NINE

A BEAUTIFUL NEW flower-bedecked crown replaced the very wilted, sand-covered one she left on the Altar Stone. Resigned to wearing the crown, Haley didn't even argue when Micah positioned it on her head, sweeping errant strands of hair from her face.

"More beautiful everyday," he whispered so only she could hear just before they headed into the forest. Traveling north, they reached their favorite lunch spot, in an area previously cleared by Gisele and Taylor.

"I didn't want to say this and I'm a little embarrassed to admit it, but I'm glad Selena's gone," Haley said while they cleaned up from lunch. "I feel lighter somehow. Like a load's been lifted."

"I know what you mean," Lacey said. "I tried to like her, but—" She shrugged her shoulders.

"This is a perfect example of how the forest magnifies energy," Gisele said. "That girl was a fountain of negative energy—we talked about it a few times—but her feelings for Micah were so strong, she simply couldn't contain or control it. But she's a smart girl. I hope she can get over this and move on."

"Why couldn't *I* see it?" Micah asked.

"You might have, if your head wasn't elsewhere," Gisele said, glancing at Haley.

"Hmm..." He followed her gaze.

"Oh, so now it's *my* fault," Haley said, hands on hips, feeling both embarrassed and flattered at the same time.

"Get used to it," he said to her. "Guys will always love you and girls will always envy you."

"On that note," Gisele said, eyes skyward. "Let's move out."

~ ☾ ~

HEADING WESTWARD THEY checked for line quicksand which Gisele thought, seemed to be absent this far from the swamps. "Keep checking, Taylor, we can't be too careful," Gisele said, as she poked and prodded the rich earth. They continued to walk for a few minutes.

"Rift ahead," Lacey's quiet voice broke the silence. With no rift in sight, the group stopped as one. All heads turned in her direction. "Did I say that?" she whispered.

"Uh huh." Haley's eyes were wide with shock. "And how do you know this?"

"I don't know. The words just popped out of my mouth." Lacey grinned.

"Well, isn't this a nice surprise?" Gisele smiled. "Everyone ready? Let's go find Lacey's rift."

They walked another fifty feet and in the center of a small clearing, near a giant boulder, the predicted mound appeared. Lacey beamed.

"You go, girl." Haley patted her sister on the head as if she were a well-behaved puppy.

"Let's get ready," Gisele said, quietly removing her wand and crystal from her bag. "Wands up." *This* time they would be prepared. "Are you ready, Haley?"

Haley nodded once and walked to the rift. Her arms raised, crystal in her right hand. Gisele watched as she took a deep breath. The fun started as Haley exhaled.

Rocks the size of pumpkins blew out of the rift and began crashing down on the small group. Blue streaks flashing from Gisele and Micah's wands, bouncing harmlessly off the falling boulders. "Take cover behind the trees!" Gisele shouted.

"Haley!" Micah yelled, about to make a run for her.

"Her shield's holding." Gisele grabbed his arm. "See? She's protected." The stones fell around Haley, glancing and rolling off an invisible bubble, which seemed to stretch about two feet on all sides of her. She stood alone, seemingly unfazed by the turmoil around her.

"But for how long?"

"Long enough. Summon the Tinks," she ordered.

"These aren't energy—they're real!" Taylor yelled as he touched his useless wand to one of the rocks. Nothing

~ ☾ ~

happened.

Of course, Gisele thought, *There's nothing magical about granite boulders.* She held her maple leaf pendant, kissed it once and summoned The Greenman, speaking as quickly as she dared. When finished, she put it back on and prayed. Within seconds, unusual, but welcome sounds could be heard in the clearing.

Tink! Tink! The audible drip of water falling on a metal barrel.

"Yay!" Lacey peeked out from behind a big oak tree while boulders crashed all around.

Tink! Tink! Tink! Pieces of leaves, pine needles and dirt puffing two feet into the air from various places around the clearing announced the arrival of an army of foot-tall creatures. Gisele smiled at their comically pointed ears and fur covered padded feet. *Phew-phew* rang out as the Tinky-tinks sent bright orange charges from their absurdly long fingers into the air. The ground grew thick with rubble. Shards flew everywhere. The humans ducked their heads to avoid being hit by flying wreckage.

Gisele's attention was drawn by a sudden movement of branches from the other side of the clearing. The Greenman materialized with a beautiful woman, clad in vines, leaves and flowers. Stones falling on or near them somehow glanced away harmlessly. Together they approached a huge boulder twenty feet from the rift. They looked into each other's eyes, nodded slightly and turned to the boulder. Before her amazed eyes, they bent down in unison and heaved the tank-sized granite rock onto the center of the rift, sealing it.

The rending crack that followed signaled another healed rift.

Tink! Tink! Tink! Orange flashes continued as the Tinks reduced boulders to stones, then gravel and finally to sand. A smiling Greenman nodded to Micah, who bolted across the clearing to Haley, just as her knees buckled.

~ ☾ ~

CHAPTER FORTY

HALEY COLLAPSED IN MICAH'S arms while Gisele quickly checked her for injuries. "She seems okay," she said, holding Haley's hand and wondering how many more rifts the girl could heal.

"This was the worst rift yet," Micah muttered as he held her.

"Water, please," Haley breathed, eyes closed.

"Right here, sweetheart," Micah said, placing the bottle in her hand. "How are you feeling?"

"Like I was hit by a garbage truck. What happened anyway?" She finally opened her eyes. "Where'd all this sand come from? Ooh, and why do I have a headache?" she asked after drinking from his water bottle.

"Your Queen is ill?" The Greenman asked.

"Queen?" Micah looked up, startled.

"That's what the Entity called her," The Greenman said, tilting his head toward Haley. "From deep in the rift, as I arrived, I heard, 'Kill the Queen, kill the Queen, kill the Queen'..."

"We wondered," Gisele said then second-guessed herself. "She's been targeted ever since she put on that crown... Maybe she shouldn't?"

"Although the circlet identifies you as their quarry"–The Greenman faced Haley as she recovered on the ground–"you should continue to don it as it confers astonishing protection, making you nearly invincible to our foe." He lightly touched her forehead.

"Ahh, my headache's gone," she said in wonder, looking up at The Greenman, who nodded once.

"She'll wear it, I promise," Micah said, helping Haley to her feet.

~ ☾ ~

"This is your mate, then, young warrior?" The Greenman asked Micah, who nodded. "Well chosen. Let me introduce you to mine, The Lady of the Green Wood." He held his hand out while the vision in green drifted to his side as if gliding on a carpet of air, accompanied by the scent of wild flowers and untamed places. Gisele watched the ends of her long blonde hair floating lazily around her shoulders as though she drifted underwater, and was as mesmerized. Lacey and Taylor stood with their mouths open.

"The Lord and I wish to thank you for your heroic efforts to protect our forest." Unlike The Greenman's graveled voice, His Lady's was musical, like birdsong. "If we can be of further assistance, please do not hesitate to summon us forth." She smiled and linked hands with her Lord.

Lacey shook her head and stepped forward. "I have a question. Why aren't *you* healing the forest? You are so much more powerful than us. It seems as though you could do this better and faster than we ever could."

"Lacey!" Gisele said, her voice and eyebrows raised in indignation.

"An excellent question, little one," she answered in her beautiful voice. "This scourge was created by mortals and can only be healed by mortals. We are here to provide physical assistance to our human warriors and even close the rift ourselves when deemed necessary."

"Man-made?" Gisele said. "I had no idea..."

"No one's ever asked us before," The Lord of the Forest said. "And we are unable to reveal many of the specifics to you. However, I can tell you this: not only do the five of you possess the necessary abilities to heal the rifts, but some may also be instrumental in healing our forest forever."

"Aren't we doing that now? Healing the forest?" Haley said.

"You are healing the rifts, but as Gisele has probably told you, this happened before." He looked to Gisele who nodded. "I am speaking of a Generational Curse which has reoccurred every fifty to seventy years for the last three centuries. By healing the *forest*, a more difficult task, the Curse will be banished forever."

~ ☾ ~

"Can we do that *this* summer?" Lacey asked.

"Alas, no. And before you ask," The Greenman said as Lacey opened her mouth to form another question, "I am unable to impart further information in that regard. But know this: should you succeed in healing the rifts this summer, it will then be possible for the forest to be healed of its curse forever."

"And the Great Wrong shall be made right by the one who is pure in heart, mind and body," His Lady said.

"But will we–" Lacey began.

"I regret I may say no more. Good day and blessings of the forest to you all." The Greenman nodded to the group and with His Lady, stepped back, disappearing into the thicket so quickly that Gisele was left wondering if the unearthly visit actually occurred. Though when she turned, the proof was there for all to see–the rearranging of boulders left a gaping hole in the earth. Of a supernatural visitation, there could be no doubt.

"Three century curse?"

"The Great Wrong which shall be made right?" Lacey said. "I feel like for every question they answer, they leave us with five more to wonder and worry about."

Micah brushed aside Haley's bangs to kiss her forehead. "Our Queen," he said.

Lacey laughed and curtsied. "Your Highness." Haley waved her away.

"Is everyone all right?" Gisele asked. "I see bumps, bruises and scrapes from the falling rocks, but nothing serious." Since none of the injuries were magical, bandages replaced the healing crystal.

"So who's The One?" Lacey asked while Gisele tended her. "Is it me, do you think, or Haley?"

Micah glanced at Haley. "The Greenman said *some* of us will be involved in healing the forest. Righting the Great Wrong."

"Maybe it's you, Taylor and Gisele," Haley said to him. "Our best and smartest."

"Or maybe you and me," Lacey winked at Taylor, who shrugged. "Or Haley and Micah."

~ ☾ ~

"Sounds even more dangerous than what we're doing now," Haley said, her eyes half closed. "If so, you can do it, Lacey. I'm all set."

Gisele offered no opinion beyond her raised eyebrows, as she moved to assist Haley. Though she showed no outward injuries, she obviously fared the worst. Her vitality seemed weakened, diminished since The Greenman's exit. Gisele produced a dark stone egg from her pocket. Using a circular motion, she lightly rubbed the stone down Haley's arms and back. Within minutes, the girl's breathing grew deeper and stronger. Gisele could almost see her essence strengthening, as her sparkle returned.

"What *is* that?" Haley asked, flexing and stretching as if shaking off the trappings of a dreamless sleep.

"This is a Rainbow Obsidian, the Stone of Pleasure," Gisele replied. "Also used to develop and repair your etheric and physical body. I've been using it all summer. Let's just say, it's exactly what you need."

"It is," Haley said, still stretching. "Can we go now?"

"Sure. Would you carry this back?" Gisele handed her the egg.

"With pleasure," Haley replied, then paused as her brow furrowed. "Unless *you* need it?"

"I'll be fine," she assured her, then watched as Haley pressed the stone against her sore left shoulder for the long walk back. Gisele's headache returned, but she could tolerate it until they reached her cabin.

They hiked out of the forest, quiet for once—each lost in their thoughts.

Gisele watched her tiny band of school children turned warriors with interest. For the second time, the group found themselves unable to defeat the Entity without help from The Elementals and she could feel their confidence sinking. Even Micah all but abandoned his assertive swagger. *Maybe this was the best thing for him,* she thought. *He'd been a bit too cocky before this incident, too sure magic could solve any problem.* If she hadn't been so seasoned, it may have done the same to her. But she'd lived a long time and knew it was better to ask for help than to go down with the ship. *Micah's*

~ ☾ ~

young, he'll learn, she smiled to herself.

Time for his big lesson.

"Micah," she said, looking back. "Don't make any plans for tomorrow."

Haley looked up in obvious surprise. Gisele would bet that's exactly what she'd been doing. Too bad.

"Why not?" he asked.

"I have a lesson planned for you and it's going to take a while."

"What lesson?" Haley asked.

Micah shook his head as he barely held back a laugh.

"None of your business," came her quick retort. "It's between Micah and me."

Lacey giggled and Haley's eyes widened from the reprimand.

Micah smiled and lifted her hand to kiss the tips of her fingers as she blushed. Lacey pointed a finger at her mouth, making gagging sounds, using the exact motions of her twin, almost one year ago.

When they reached her cabin, Gisele announced that their Thursday lesson was cancelled. Haley smiled until Gisele told them Micah would be her *only* student—*all* week long.

~ ☾ ~

CHAPTER FORTY-ONE

"THE TIME HAS COME, young man," Gisele said to her nephew over tea the next morning.

"For what?"

"Levitation Training," she announced.

"*Finally.*" He grinned. "I'm old enough then?"

"Not by a long shot, but we're attempting it anyway. My gazing ball"–she waved a hand at her glowing eight-inch, clear crystal ball resting on an ornate pewter stand–"showed me you'll need this skill–soon. So I guess, ready or not, it's your turn."

"I'm ready. I've been waiting *years.*" He sighed and leaned back, arms crossed over his chest.

"I know. Let's get started." She led him in a brief meditation with some creative visualization tossed in for good measure. Then, drawing upon her own lessons from the past seventy years, she began.

WHEN THE PHONE rang that evening, Haley pounced on it like a cat on a moth.

"Hello?" she said.

"Hello, sweet thing. Did the phone even ring?"

"Of course it rang." She laughed. "You think I'm psychic?"

"Maybe. Hey, are you busy? Can I come over?"

"Absolutely. I missed you today."

"Good, I'll be right there."

Haley ran upstairs, changed her shirt, and brushed her teeth. The doorbell rang just as she finished putting on mascara, a new addition this summer. She opened the door, only to be swept into his arms.

He pulled away. "How about ice cream at Freddie's?"

~ ☾ ~

"Sure, I'll be hungry sometime tonight, or tomorrow," she teased. Their legendary slow service would never be a problem as long as she could stare into those eyes.

THEY WERE SEATED at a booth soon after arriving. "So how was your lesson, if I'm allowed to know?" she asked after they ordered sundaes.

"It was okay," he said without enthusiasm. "I thought I'd do better, but I guess it's a process, like everything."

"What was it about? Can you tell me?" she asked, not wishing to appear nosy, but intensely curious just the same.

"Levitation." He grinned.

"*Whoa,* you get to *levitate?*" she said. "I'd *love* to learn how to do that. Will she teach me, do you think?"

"Nope," he said. "You're way too young."

"Hey!" She crossed her arms and pulled a fake pout.

"Sorry, but that's the way it is." He smiled and she melted.

"Maybe someday," Haley sighed. "So, have you managed to do it?"

"Once, for about a foot." The very picture of disappointment, Micah sat with his shoulders slouching, eyes downcast.

"That's great," she said after their drinks were brought to the table.

"No it's not. I tried for *hours,* and that was the best I could do." He sighed.

"I'm sure it takes lots of practice," she said. "If it was easy, everyone one would do it. I know *I* would."

"I know, I know. But I'm used to mastering Skills, especially magical Skills more quickly than this. It's very discouraging." He sipped his water. "Gisele said it took her three lessons to master it."

"But you've already done it."

"One foot doesn't really count." He laughed. "When I can zip across a room and stop when I want to, 'cause that's a problem too, then I'll consider myself a Levitator." He raised an eyebrow at the term.

"Oooh, I will be so impressed when I can call you a

~ ☾ ~

Levitator," she said.

He shrugged. The sundaes came and they dug in.

"So, you expected to get the hang of it in *one* lesson?" she asked.

"Actually, yes. I was hoping it would only take one lesson." He smiled. "I was impatient to be elsewhere and I messed up a few times. Gisele knew it, too."

"Elsewhere?"

"Yes, anywhere with you."

She smiled, her cheeks reddening with pleasure. *He loves me.*

"I have to try again tomorrow."

"Really?" she sighed, and her own slumping shoulders matched his, though she tried hard not to let her disappointment show.

"Uh huh, and Friday, too, if I don't catch on. Gisele saw something in her gazing ball and I need to be able to do this. Flawlessly."

"What did she see?"

"She wouldn't tell me," he said. "Which makes me think you're involved."

She swallowed. "Study hard."

"Gisele's worried, I think. She's not sleeping."

"How do you know?"

"She paces the floor half the night. The rifts are getting harder to beat and so unpredictable." He took a bite of his pistachio ice cream. "But she wouldn't tell me any more than that."

"Only two more weeks until the full moon."

"I know." He nodded. "Stupid Selena."

"What? Why?" *How could he blame this on her?*

"It's just that it's going to be so much harder without her. She's an awesome fighter. We were a good team–"

"Oh?"

"Yeah, we had each other's back. We knew each others' strengths and weaknesses..."

"Hmm. So, what's your weakness?"

"You," he stated simply, licking the hot fudge off his spoon. "That's why I have to master levitation. You will never

~ ☾ ~

be harmed while I live."

"I don't know if you can make that promise."

He grabbed her free hand across the table. The abrupt movement caused her to gasp. "If you weren't so damned important to this effort," he said in a low voice, "I would insist you be left at the cabin. Unfortunately, we can't seem to do our job without you. I *will not* let harm come to you. That is my promise. If I think I can't protect you, you're not going in."

She sat up straight and just as abruptly yanked her hand back. "I appreciate your concern and your protection," she said with an edge to her voice that made him wince. "But I can make up my own mind. Of all of us, I seem to get the most help from the forest. *I* will be *fine*."

He looked stricken. "I just meant—"

"I know what you meant. And thank you, but this *is* the twenty-first century. We girls can take care of ourselves." She paused a moment to let her message sink in, then willingly took his hand again. "So. What's your strength?"

"That's easy. You." He found his smile again.

ON THURSDAY WITH Micah busy with his lessons, Haley only saw him for the briefest time after supper. On Friday afternoon, as the weekend loomed, she got a surprising phone call from her father. Seems Grandma Clara had informed him of her new beau and he was anxious to meet the young man.

Because of his connection to Gisele, Haley assumed he'd sail through the half-hour interrogation that Taylor endured the previous year.

Apparently, not the case.

Although Micah was officially *invited* to spend the afternoon with the girls and Dad, Haley thought *summoned* a more appropriate term. Although Saturday's visit with Dad began a bit awkwardly at first, with *lots* of questions, by afternoon the two were sharing Red Sox stats, comparing Patriots' picks and generally ignoring the girls. Toward the end of the visit, her dad took Micah aside for a few words.

~ ☾ ~

They shook hands and parted amicably.

When she asked about the conversation later, Micah would only say he had agreed to act like a gentleman with her. He smiled. "It was an easy promise to make. With you, how could I be anything else?"

"WHAT DID YOU do yesterday?" Micah asked when he picked her up on Monday.

"Went to lunch, then a couple of bookstores with my dad, came back to my grandmother's, missed you...what did you do?" She smiled and took hold of his hand.

"I went home, called a couple of friends, visited with my family, thought about you..."

"Tell me about your family," she said.

"Mom's a psychic. She reads cards at a new age shop in town called Some Enchanted Evening. My dad's a professor at WPI."

"Why didn't they come to help, again? If your mother's a psychic, couldn't she tell what would happen?" Haley didn't want to insult his mother's abilities, but–

"When she read the cards for Gisele, they said she overstated the danger. At the same time, Mom saw this was going to be the best summer of my life, so she let me come." The finger he ran down her jaw left it tingling.

"Gisele overstated *this*?"

"She was a bit hysterical when she called..." He shrugged. "So, anyway, when I told them some of what we've been doing, they freaked and tried to keep me home. Imagine *me* abandoning *you*? Not to mention Gisele and the forest–*our* forest! I don't know what they're thinking."

"They love you."

"I know, but they're going against everything they taught me, everything they stood for."

"Did they offer to help?" she asked.

"Not really. My father just had knee surgery and my mother can't leave him."

"How did you leave it with them?" she asked.

"They're mad at me." He laughed without humor. "I have

~ ☾ ~

to check in everyday at five o'clock."

"It's just because–"

"I know–they love me. Let's go in." He parked next to Gisele's Toyota and turned off the car.

"Hey, how's the Levitation going? Are you doing better?" she asked.

"I'm getting better, but I'm not quite there yet. Sometimes I feel like I'm doing it by accident. C'mon, lets go. I can't wait to get started today." He grinned as they got out of his car.

"GOOD MORNING YOU two. How was your visit home, Micah?" Gisele asked as they walked in.

"Okay, I guess," he said before his gaze darted to her. "Why? Did they call?"

"About a half hour ago. To apologize. You must've put up quite a fight in order to come back here."

He looked down at the floor. "Well, I couldn't just *leave* you like this."

"How much did you tell them?" she asked, her arms crossed as if to brace herself.

"Not even half of what's happened." He shrugged his shoulders. "I told them if they really wanted to know, they should come here and see for themselves."

"That's quite a challenge. They're not coming though, are they?" she asked.

"No," he said. "My dad just had surgery."

"Well, for better or worse, it'll all be over in two weeks," Gisele said, as Taylor and Lacey walked in. "We're going northeast this time, which will bring us close to the swamp. I was thinking I might harvest some Water Hemlock–"

"No," Taylor said. Lacey and Haley echoed the sentiment quickly in a first-ever veto of her plans.

Micah stood back, arms folded, looking amused.

"Stupid Water Hemlock," Taylor spat out. "We're *not going.*"

"All *right,* Taylor," Gisele said. "We can skip it this year. I still have some left from last year anyway. Fortunately, it survived the quake." But Haley noticed a few minutes later

~ ☾ ~

that she secretly tucked her collection basket into her magic bag when she thought no one was looking. *That's Gisele, willing to risk her life for an herb.*

"Let's get going. We have a long hike in front of us today." Gisele hoisted her bag. "Micah, I'd like you and Taylor to climb one of the pine trees again and check our progress. Oh, and we'll be traveling on the eastern edge of the forest where most of the line quicksand seems to be, so we must be extra alert against falling victim to it. Everyone should find a walking stick. Taylor, you're up front with me."

AT THE ALTAR STONE, a new flower crown awaited Haley, who put it on without prompting. Three crystals glowed for her, Gisele and Micah as well. Gisele left the spent crystals with a word of thanks. They hiked into the forest, everyone checking, testing, ever alert for line quicksand. After identifying and dispatching one line, they stopped for a quick lunch. With only two weeks left to rid the forest of this menace, Haley knew everyone wanted to get down to business. Gisele directed Micah and Taylor to climb a huge pine tree just north of the stone wall to scout out remaining rifts.

"Check for line quicksand, if you can," she said as they clambered up the tree. Haley watched, hardly breathing, as the guys crawled around the tree branches about sixty feet off the ground, pointing out various features and details below. Finally, to her relief, they descended, and in high spirits. The news was good.

"There are only three rifts left," Micah said, "including today's."

"Which should be a piece of cake," Taylor interrupted. "It's the lowest, smallest mound we've ever seen. We'll be home in an hour."

The girls smiled and clapped, giddy with relief.

"I think I'd hold off celebrating for the time being," Gisele suggested. "The Entity would never be that cooperative..."

"The mound is right—" Taylor turned to point.

"Wait! Don't tell me," Lacey interrupted. "I want to see if I

~ ☾ ~

can find it."

"Fine." Taylor feigned exasperation.

"Did you see any quicksand?" Gisele asked.

"No, we couldn't locate any obvious signs on the forest floor," Micah said. "Sorry, but I think they're too well concealed."

"That's okay," Gisele said. "We'll just have to be careful. Which way, Lacey?"

"North," she said, beaming.

"Follow Lacey, everyone," Gisele said as she pulled Micah aside. "Is this the right way?" Haley heard her whisper.

Smiling, he nodded.

Just after they passed a swamp and Taylor gave an involuntary shudder, Lacey called out, "Rift ahead."

~ ☾ ~

CHAPTER FORTY-TWO

WHEN THE MOUND appeared about a hundred feet away, Gisele smiled when Haley gave her sister a good-natured smack on the shoulder. "Nice going, kid."

"Can't let you get *all* the glory." Lacey grinned.

"Let's get set up. Quickly now." Gisele took a deep breath while brandishing her wand in her left hand and her crystal in her right. One to attack, the other to heal.

Haley stood at the front edge with Micah on her right, Gisele behind. Taylor and Lacey stood wands up, ready on her left flank. When Haley raised her arms to begin the process, Gisele watched as the rift opened and tiny white lights, no bigger than the sparks of a campfire, shot out in wave upon wave, forming a small dense cloud of lights hanging about eight feet over the forest floor.

When Micah attempted to swipe at the lights with his wand, she saw that the cloud simply folded away from him. After staring at the cloud for a few moments, he and the others dropped their arms to their sides and watched the mesmerizing light show as the glittering cluster rose high above them. The cloud swirled and twisted like a school of fish in formation. And still, tiny glittery sparks continued to spew from the rift, all joining the ever-growing cloud as it swirled and danced overhead.

Millions, it seemed, then tens of millions, hundreds of millions.

Suddenly the rift appeared to close, the grating, cracking, screeching sounds at odds with the surreal beauty wheeling silently overhead.

The tiny group, clutching their useless wands, watched entranced, each swaying side-to-side, seemingly unaware of any danger. A final turn and the descent of the multitude was

~ ☾ ~

upon them.

TAYLOR WAS STRUCK first. His wand, which fell unneeded to the ground, would have been of little use against the strange, glittering cloud.

Shaking her head to clear her mind, Gisele raised her crystal high overhead, protecting herself and Micah, who stood entranced, in a strong translucent bubble. "Call the fairies!" she said, over Taylor's screams. "Quickly!"

"But, Haley—" he began, blinking.

"She's fine! The others are unprotected!"

She watched as he closed his eyes and used his Gift to summon the fairies. Together she and Micah rushed to Lacey, curled in a fetal position and covered by a sparkling cloud. Like water on a flash fire, their bubble immediately snuffed out any white lights they happened upon. Micah picked Lacey up and as a group, they moved to Taylor, now completely engulfed. As they stood over him, the rest of the swarm circled the four, seeking a way into their protective envelope.

"Your crystal?" Gisele concentrated on strengthening her bubble.

"Right here," he said, carefully placing a weeping Lacey on the ground next to Taylor. He removed the crystal from his pocket.

"Taylor first."

Crouching down, Micah waved the crystal over his friend's face, arms and legs. Taylor slowly began to regain consciousness. Micah then switched to Lacey, who responded more quickly since the swarm spent less time with her. Gisele looked through the thinning swarm and saw globes of soft pastel colors fluttering through the sparkles. "The fairies have arrived," she sighed.

Lacey was on her feet. "Haley?" she whimpered, looking across the clearing to where her sister stood.

"She'll be fine," Gisele assured her as dozens of pulsing pastel spheres swelled to the size of basketballs, each attracting thousands of glittering lights around them and away from Gisele and her team.

~ ☾ ~

"Is everyone okay?" Taylor asked with a voice now as rough as The Greenman's.

"We're fine. How are you doing?" Gisele looked into his clear, gray eyes.

"Better now. It felt like a thousand bee stings." He rubbed the welts on his arms.

"The lights. They were so bright and pretty I couldn't look away."

Micah nodded. "I know what you mean. Aunt Gisele, what's happening out there?

The fairies have arrived, but I still can't see Haley." He peered through the throng.

"You'll have to trust me when I say your girl is still alive," Gisele said, but he still trembled with fear for her.

Outside their sheltered bubble, the fairies began to swirl and twist into a cylindrical column nearly fifty feet high, causing the stinging points of light to undertake a similar movement. The fairies elongated their cylinder and, quite suddenly, shot to the north. The sparkling cloud surged to keep up, still swirling and rotating through the air.

And then they were gone. Gisele released her bubble just as the smallest of the mounds flattened, healing the latest portion of the rift.

AND WHEN HALEY'S knees finally crumpled, Micah raced across the clearing, leaping stones, roots and fallen logs to get to her in time to prevent her from crashing to the forest floor. She opened her eyes, smiled at him, and he felt her melt into his embrace. This would be his job, he decided as he lowered her to the ground. He would always and forever be there to catch her. He would live his life to be her hero when in all honesty, she was his.

~ ☾ ~

CHAPTER FORTY-THREE

AFTER A QUICK walk back, during which Micah refused to relinquish Haley's hand, however briefly, the group sat around Gisele's table. Exhausted and bone-weary, they were more than ready for a cup of tea and a chat.

"Since you all seem to still be in shock, I guess I'll start." Gisele sipped her tea. "First of all, how is everybody? Any cuts, scrapes, anything that needs to be treated? No? Good. So, today was a little unusual, huh?" She looked around the table, "We were hypnotized."

"Hypnotized?" Haley folded her arms. "By what?"

"A huge swarm of tiny points of stinging lights," Gisele said. "First time I've ever seen anything like that."

"Stinging lights?" Haley said. "How did they hypnotize you?"

"At first, they seemed kind of pretty, like holiday lights, almost," Micah said, "but then they started to swirl around and around overhead and I nearly lost myself. If Aunt Gisele hadn't been there protecting me with her crystal, I think I would have watched them until they flew down and landed on me."

"Thanks for coming to my rescue," Lacey said.

"Yeah, me too," Taylor said, "I'm not sure I could've lasted much longer."

"What happened to you?" Haley asked Taylor.

"I was in a daze until the first few stings. Then it hurt so much, I curled up into a ball. It felt like I was on fire."

"You looked like a glittery rock. You couldn't tell there was a person under there. Oh, and the wands didn't work again," Micah muttered, frowning.

"Remember, I said this was going to get harder," Gisele said. "But the universe provides and we all had our crystals.

~ ☾ ~

Fortunately, today that's all we needed."

"Besides that run-of-the-mill ability to call fairies," Haley said, looking at Micah.

"Those balls of light? Those were fairies? They were *huge*," Lacey asked.

"Yes, Micah called them," Gisele said, nodding her head. "It's a good thing, too. We had nothing available to defeat that swarm of lights."

"No weapons." Micah's bitterness was undisguised. "We had nothing to fight them with."

"Yes, we did," Gisele said. "We had *you*. Only you could have called the fairies to lead the swarm away.

"Where did they go?" Haley asked.

"From what I got telepathically, the fairies led the swarm to the lake," Gisele said. "I'm not sure exactly how it happened, but in my mind I saw the fairies, when they left the clearing, were huge—basketball size, by the time they got to the lake, they got smaller and smaller, creating an optical illusion, as they lured the swarm into the water and to its ultimate destruction."

"Wow," Lacey whispered. "But the fairies are okay, right?"

"Perfectly fine," Gisele said.

Micah folded his arms and sighed, clearly unhappy.

"Micah, we were given the tools we needed to destroy that piece of the Entity. I'm sorry they weren't the tools you prefer to use, but it's not up to us to decide. There are many lessons here, and *this* may be *yours*," she said.

Micah met her gaze and shifted uncomfortably. "You're probably right. I'm sorry. I just feel I should be the muscle, the warrior. I hate feeling so helpless out there."

"Our fight is mental as well as physical. It exists on all levels. Do not limit yourself. And we must be present spiritually as well," she said.

He nodded. "I understand. Still unhappy, but I think I'm finally understanding."

"You will have your chance, I promise," she said. "This fight is about to get very physical. And one of us may fall..."

Her words hung in the air. The twins stared at each other.

"Fall, as in...die?" Taylor asked. Haley bit her lip. *This is*

~ ☾ ~

too weird.

Gisele shrugged. "I don't know. The vision remains unclear."

"Male? Female?" Micah asked, gripping Haley's hand.

"Again, unclear, but you know, if we stick together and do our best, I think we can beat this "One will fall" prophesy. I'm really very proud of all of you. For weeks, I've been angry that all I got was a bunch of kids to help me. And now, I seriously doubt a group of adults could've done any better."

The kids smiled at her.

"Micah, another lesson tomorrow?" Gisele said before sipping her tea.

He blew out a long sigh. *More time away from Haley.* "Sure."

~ ☾ ~

CHAPTER FORTY-FOUR

WHILE FOLDING LAUNDRY, Haley thought about a conversation from the previous day. "When Gisele said one may fall, did you remember where you heard that before?"

Lacey nodded. "The fortune-teller, Draculola."

"Wasn't that *weird?* That Gisele should say it, too?"

"Yeah," Lacey agreed. "And when we asked about specifics and Gisele said, very unclear, she sounded like Draculola without the accent."

"Hey, are you scared, I mean, about the full moon and everything?" Haley asked, as she folded her favorite jeans. "I'm a little nervous about Gisele. I'm sure she's not as strong as she appears."

"She can protect herself, can't she?" Lacey asked.

"Yeah, but I think she'd go down defending one of us."

"It's going to be okay. Remember what The Greenman said? We have the skills to do this," Lacey said.

"You're probably right." Haley grabbed her folded clothes and headed upstairs. "Hey, I need some chocolate. Wanna go to the Bread & Bud with me?"

"Love to, but we're going to Spot Pond for a quick dip," Lacey said with an apologetic shrug. "Taylor's on his way."

Haley grabbed a couple of dollars, got on her bike and headed for the Bread & Bud by herself. On her way, the turn-off to Gisele's beckoned. *I could drop by to see how the lesson was going.* She bit her lip. *No, that would be rude. Tempting, but rude.* Anyway, the chocolate was so close. She pedaled on. Butterfingers called and she had to listen.

Haley paid for two candy bars, one for her and one for Lacey, when a noisy group of kids hurled themselves through the screen door. Catching a glimpse of the tallest, she turned away as fast as she could without giving herself whiplash.

~ ☾ ~

Tim Russell, the troublemaker from last year!

He and two friends tried to get her into trouble with the police when they forced her to commit vandalism against Gisele. Ironically, it could be said that *they* were the ones who introduced her to the herbalist. Haley kept her head down as the noisy group passed her on their way to the soda cases, all the while filling the air with rude comments about the clerk, other customers and each other. With luck, she could be out the door and away from there without being recognized.

Less than a yard from the door, she heard "Hey!" just past her right shoulder. She automatically turned in that direction. Two aisles away, Tim held up a bag of chips, yelling at the clerk for a price. Their eyes locked for an instant and she was through the door, racing for her bike, heart pounding. She heard yelling and crashing displays behind her as she jumped on her bike. *Gimme two seconds! That's all I need to get out of here,* she thought as she pushed off, jamming her right foot down on the pedal. Her bike lurched forward. *Almost there!*

She cried out when she felt the back of her bike rise into the air. Haley whipped her head around and saw Tim lifting her seat and back wheel, halting her forward momentum.

"Where ya going, Haley?" A wicked smile played on his lips.

"Let go," she demanded, as his four creepy friends slithered out the door.

"Who's this?" a chubby boy asked in a scary sing-song voice.

"Boys," Tim said, "this is Haley, the nice girl who sent me to Juvie last year, for the *whole* summer."

"You did that to yourself," she said. "Now let me *go*." She yanked her bike away and pushed it. With his long legs, it took Tim only two steps to reach Haley, grab her by the back of her shirt, and pull her off the bike. Caught off-balance, she twisted around, almost falling. "Let go of me!" she screamed, the noise of her crashing bike masked the sound of a car driving up. Tim grabbed her right hand, let go of her shirt, then latched on hard to her left arm.

"So *nice* to see you again, Haley." He sneered as he squeezed her forearms, forcing her to face him.

~ ☾ ~

"I said let go of me," Haley snarled, twisting to loosen his grasp on her.

"That's not gonna happ-*HEY!*" he yelled. So fast it was almost a blur, a muscular arm reached over Haley and shot to Tim's throat, grabbing the front of his dirty t-shirt. Haley felt pure relief when Tim released her and turned to confront the stranger.

Micah!

Surprised and delighted by the turn of events, Haley willingly stepped aside as Micah shoved Tim easily and relentlessly, creating a path through the punk's greasy friends. In less than a second, Tim was propped up against the brick wall of the Bread & Bud. His slow-witted and cowardly friends, just now realizing they had numbers in their favor, suddenly began yelling as they advanced on Micah.

"Sit down," he ordered. To Haley's astonishment, all of their knees buckled, including Tim's. Micah released his grip, Tim slid down the wall and within seconds he and his goons began yelling from the sidewalk.

"Shut up, all of you," Micah commanded.

Blessed silence. The nitwits' futile attempts to open their mouths and speak were punctuated by sounds like of a litter of puppies. Haley almost laughed out loud.

"She told you to let go of her," Micah growled at Tim, now sprawled on the ground against the wall. "You need to learn some manners. Talk."

"*I* should learn manners from *you?*" gushed out, as if he'd been holding his breath.

"If no one else shows up. Haley, are you all right?" Micah asked without looking at her.

She realized he hadn't once taken his eyes off the idiot in front of him. "Yeah, I'm fine," she said, rubbing her arms when Tim's grumblings suddenly got louder and profane.

"Quiet," Micah said. "Haley, please wait for me in the car."

"My bike—"

"I'll take care of it, as soon as I'm finished with this."

~ ☾ ~

WHEN HE KNEW she was safe, Micah grabbed Tim by the front of his shirt. "Stand up," he said. Micah was beefier and half a head taller than Tim, whose knees finally locked in place. He pushed Tim against the wall again. With one finger, Micah found the very sensitive area under the jaw and pushed.

The thug's eyes crossed.

"Speak."

"Let me *go!*" Tim squeaked.

"Why should I? You wouldn't let *her* go." Micah jerked his head toward the car and Haley.

"I'm sorry," Tim whimpered.

"She can't hear you. Say it louder."

"I'm sorry, Haley!" he yelled.

"You *know* her?" Micah's mouth fell open.

"Yeah, she was my girlfriend last year. Who are you?"

"None of your business. Sit down and shut up," Micah said. After releasing him, the punk fell flat against the wall. "Stay there!" he said over his shoulder and walked to his car where Haley sat. "Did he hurt you? Let me see." He leaned forward to examine the red marks on her arms.

"I'm fine. Can we go?"

"You *know* him?" He asked in a flat voice.

Haley's shoulders slumped. "Yeah." She looked miserable.

He didn't look at her as he stowed her bike in the back seat. "Let's get out of here. I'm not sure how long they'll continue to be cooperative," Micah said, glancing at his wriggling, whimpering captives.

He drove about a mile in silence, before pulling his car to the side of the road. *Let's get this over with.* "So, how are you, really?" he asked.

"I think my heartbeat has slowed to around two hundred beats a minute, or so," she said, looking out the window.

"Hey, look at me."

She turned to face him and sighed.

"So, what happened back there? Who was that guy?" *And do you* like *him?*

"His name is Tim and I met him last year. He sort of introduced me to Gisele." She swallowed. "I don't know *those*

~ ☾ ~

guys, but last year he hung out with a couple of losers–and one was a girl my age. They tricked me into stealing one of Gisele's sunflowers and she caught me."

"You *stole* from Gisele?"

"I didn't want to, but they said if I didn't, they would tell the cops I was causing all the trouble in town. Afterwards I helped Gisele weed her gardens and she offered to teach Lacey, Taylor and me about herbs and potions. We've been friends ever since. I guess I owe him." She shrugged.

"He said you were his girlfriend..."

"Hah! Our friendship lasted about an hour."

"Anything else I need to know about?"

"I don't think so." She turned away.

He reached for her chin and gently drew it toward him. "Hey, this doesn't change anything."

"You sure?" She blinked several times.

"Positive. We've all done things we're ashamed of. I could tell you stories."

"Tell me."

"Another time."

"How'd you know to find me there?"

"Lacey told me where you were." He grinned. "I thought I'd come by and surprise you."

"And you did." She rubbed her temples. "You scared the crap out of them as well."

"Imagine what I could've done if I had my wand!"

LATER AT A little shack called The Silver Grille, they found a picnic table with a view of the reservoir and Micah ordered their barbequed hot dogs. He turned to smile at her and a surge of love washed over him. *Life doesn't get much better than this,* he thought.

"It was—interesting watching your Gift in action today," she said after popping the top of her Diet Sprite.

"Yeah, it comes in handy sometimes," he agreed, biting into his hot dog.

"Have you always had it?"

"Ever since I can remember, but I didn't realize how

~ ☾ ~

strong it was until I was about ten years old."

"What happened?" she asked, watching a family of ducks making their way across the lake.

"I made a friend throw a snowball at a neighbor." He laughed with a trace of embarrassment. "He got her good, too."

"Oh?" she said.

"Back of the head. Knocked her ugly hat off." He bit back a grin. "Boy, did we get in trouble."

"Both of you?"

"Yeah, he said I made him do it. I was laughing so hard, she believed him." He smirked. "I really caught it at home. My Gift was identified at an early age and I'd been warned never to do stuff like that." He smiled at the memory. "My father was furious. Grandpa, however, was delighted and willed the Medallion to me shortly after. He talked to me about using his Gift to find my grandmother and how in all their years they'd been together, his love never wavered, never lessened."

Haley swallowed and smiled. "But that's a different Gift, right?"

"Yes, but if you have one, you almost always have the other. My magical training began that summer."

"You said it doesn't work on your parents, right?"

"No, tragically. Somehow, family is immune." He shrugged.

"That's only fair," she said. "Ever use it to get a date?"

"Yes, but–" he paused. Now he really was embarrassed.

"But, what?"

"I didn't enjoy myself. It felt forced, which of course it was. She had no choice. I never did it again." He looked away, hoping this disclosure wouldn't make her think any less of him. "Basically an experiment, it happened over a year ago."

"Too unsporting? Too easy?" she said.

"I guess," he watched the ducks swim in the reservoir. "But mostly it was just ...rude. I won't do it again. Not for something like that."

"So, the Gift where you see important people in your future. How does that work?"

~ ☾ ~

"Sometimes I see quick pictures of a particular person at different ages, in different situations, that sort of thing," he said.

"What did you see with me?"

"I don't want to talk about it," he said, instantly regretting the direction of this conversation.

"Why not?" Her brow furrowed with either fear or dread. "What did you see?"

He sighed in frustration. *Scared for all the wrong reasons.* "Because we have free will. *You* have free will." He looked at her, willing her to understand. He saw a future with her that he desperately wanted, but wouldn't push on her. "What if I told you that I saw you in bed, beside me, at eighty years old—"

"Did you?" she asked with the trace of a smile.

"It's just an example. So, we're in bed at eighty, but in reality, after ten years with me, you want out. What then? Do you stick around, hating me because you think it's the only future you can have? Or leave, and wonder if it would've gotten better? I care about you too much to mess around with your free will. It's the same reason I gave you that Medallion. I don't want you to do—or *not* do—anything just because it's been suggested or foretold."

"Can you tell me just *one*?" she pleaded. "It's my future. Don't I have a right to know?"

"Fine," he said in exasperation. "I'll give you the perfect example. I've seen you, sometime during your twenties, holding a newborn baby. It could be your baby, or Lacey's. It could be *my* baby"—he paused and lowered his voice—"or your husband's. I have no way of knowing. All I know for sure, is that you're important to me now and you will continue to be in the future."

And the baby's name will be Gisele.

She smiled. "I've never met anyone I'd rather share my future with more than you."

"Well, you say that *now*..." He smirked and ate the last of his hot dog.

~ ☾ ~

CHAPTER FORTY-FIVE

"I WAS AWAKE most of the night," Micah blurted out the next morning at the front door instead of saying hello. "Levitating from one side of the cabin to the other. Once you get it, you don't want to stop!" He stepped into the front hall.

"You can do it? Yay!" She hugged him. "I'm so proud of you."

"Yeah, it was so great." He couldn't stop smiling. *Boy, she looks good today. Even better than usual.*

She stepped back. "Do it!" she said, her face alight with excitement.

"Here? In the hallway?"

"Yes, just a few steps." She flattened her body against the wall.

"Okay." He closed his eyes, raised up on his toes and hovered before shooting forward. He made it down the twenty-foot hallway in less than two seconds before colliding with the closed kitchen door.

"Micah!" Haley yelled. He heard rapid footsteps on the other side of the door and when Grandma Clara opened it, he slumped into the kitchen.

Haley helped him to his feet. "What happened?" she whispered.

"Control issues."

Grandma Clara and Lacey squawked and clucked in the doorway. "Hey, what's going on? What was that? Micah?"

Haley said, "He tripped, you guys, that's all." She lowered her voice. "You'll be fine, right?"

He nodded, grinning. "Let's get going."

AS SHE BACKED out of the driveway, Haley looked at

~ ☾ ~

Micah. "That was exciting."

"It's a lot more impressive when I don't body-slam doors."

"Has that happened before?"

"No, at Gisele's everything went perfectly. But in the hallway for some reason, I couldn't slow down." He rubbed his forehead.

"So, you'll teach me?" The question he expected.

"Seriously? After that demonstration?"

"Yes, until the last second, it looked like a blast." She giggled.

"I told you before–you're too young," he said completely unsympathetic, as he looked her up and down.

"But–"

"Besides, Gisele put a Binding spell on me so I can't share my knowledge. Even *I'm* too young to do it, but Gisele is sure I'm going to need this skill and soon. You know, she was already *twenty* when she learned to levitate." He lowered his voice. "I was still awake at two o'clock this morning. I wanted to levitate here and kidnap you." His wicked grin matched his intent. *And do naughty things to you.*

"I'm kinda glad I'm wearing my Medallion." Haley pulled it out of her shirt to display it with a nervous laugh. "You're so *bad.*"

"Yes, yes, I am," he said. "After class, let's go to the *Town Beach*, okay?"

"The Town Beach? You want me to swim with the rabble and the riff-raff?"

"Yeah, as much as I'd like to be alone with you, I think we should be out in public today."

"Okay, but why the sudden change of attitude?" Haley asked.

"Because you are so incredibly ravishing and I do not trust myself," he said. *What is going on here?*

"What did Gisele *do* to you?" she wondered aloud.

"I plan to ask her the same question myself," he said, kissing her hand.

GISELE WELCOMED HER students. "This is more of an

~ ☾ ~

organizational class to discuss logistics for Monday night, so there will be no practice and you're free to leave early. Oh, and in case you didn't know, Micah learned to levitate late last night. In this very room." She beamed.

Micah felt himself reddening slightly. Although proud of his accomplishment, its after-effects were becoming embarrassing.

Gisele continued. "He's had a hard time keeping his feet on the ground ever since. In our family, this is a very special rite of passage, almost like a graduation. Well done."

Lacey's head whipped around, eyes slitted.

Micah looked at his feet while his friends and teacher applauded him. "Oh, and Micah, I forgot to tell you, the farther from the forest you are, the less command you'll have over your ability."

Haley laughed and coughed until her face was red.

"For a few days, some of your feelings or emotions may be amplified. Have you noticed?"

He merely nodded his head. He clenched his hands tightly at his side and avoided looking at Haley.

"You should be back to normal by Sunday, at the latest."

"Whew," he blew out a lungful of air in relief. "Good."

"Why?" Gisele asked, her curiosity piqued. "How is the magic manifesting itself in *you*?"

"Oh, it's not important," he lied, once again avoiding Haley's eyes.

"Very well. You know, after my Levitation Training, I experienced extreme sensitivity to animal thoughts and feelings," Gisele said. "I could feel everything, from their hunger, to their need to burrow, to their fear as they were hunted. I sat in the forest and absorbed it all for three incredible days. I'll never forget it. Enjoy the magic in you, Micah."

"In regards to Monday night's midnight trip into the forest, I don't suppose any of you, with the exception of Micah of course, will be allowed to show up at ten o'clock on Monday night?"

"Hmmm..." Taylor said. "As a cop's kid, I know how important a good cover story has to be. Trouble is, I don't have one."

The girls looked at each other, shrugging their shoulders. "No help here." Haley accidentally brushed Micah's leg and he gasped. "You okay?" she asked in a low tone.

"Fine."

"That's what I thought. So how about a camp-out?" Gisele suggested. "You can bring sleeping bags and tents. We'll sit in front of the fire pit and tell spooky stories."

"Do you *know* any spooky stories?" Lacey asked.

Gisele brought a hand to her mouth. "Never mind. After midnight, you'll have plenty of your own. I'll be the chaperone and if your parents have questions, they can call here." She looked from one to the other. "If there's any tent-trading, I'll know, though I don't think there will be."

"Why not?" Lacey asked after tossing a flirtatious wink in Taylor's direction.

"I have a feeling everyone will be so exhausted, you'll fall asleep in seconds," Gisele said with a smug look.

"My dad and uncle have sleeping bags at Grandma's. They need to be aired out," Haley said. "A lot."

"We have a couple too. I'll bring one for Micah," Taylor said, smiling. "This'll be fun."

"Naturally, Micah, you have the option of sleeping on the couch."

He smiled. "I look forward to the camp-out." This time he did not avoid Haley's eyes.

"Good, then on Tuesday morning, we'll have a celebratory breakfast. How's that sound?" Gisele said.

"Excellent. Pancakes?" Taylor asked.

"Sure, French toast and sausage, too," Gisele said. "A breakfast banquet for the triumphant warriors."

"Sounds wonderful, but I'll just be happy to walk in the forest without worrying about quicksand," Lacey said.

"Yeah, remember when we used to see *nice* things, magical things in the forest?" Haley said. "I can't wait to do that again."

"We will. After Monday, things will go back to normal again," Gisele said. "I promise."

~ ☾ ~

CHAPTER FORTY-SIX

THEY ATE LUNCH at Grandma Clara's and to Haley's great surprise, Lacey and Taylor agreed to accompany them to the Town Beach.

Once on their blanket, Haley and Micah applied suntan lotion to each other. Then Micah, citing concerns for her fair skin, re-applied more lotion to Haley a little later, he re-re-applied until Lacey said to her, "You look like a basted Thanksgiving turkey. All we need is some cranberry sauce."

For her part, Haley thoroughly enjoyed herself, basking in Micah's adoring attention. She'd never felt so desired. She knew it was leftover magic, but she didn't care as she tested him. "Wow, look at *that* bikini!" she said. His loving eyes never left her face.

"YOU'RE *SURE* THIS is okay with Gisele?" Grandma Clara asked them again on Monday morning as they packed for their overnight expedition.

"Yes, Grandma," Lacey said, again. "Didn't she call you?"

"She did, but I wanted to make sure you didn't nag her 'til she said yes–"

"Gram, it's a sleep-over with a campfire and spooky stories," Haley said with a sigh. *Oh, and we're also going to save the world, did we mention that?*

"Didn't you ever camp out?" Lacey asked. "Isn't this what normal kids do on a summer night?"

"Well, yes, but–"

"So it's not a big deal, right?" Haley said, tag-teaming her poor grandmother.

"No, I guess not."

"Good, we have to get the sleeping bags from the

~ ☾ ~

clothesline, find the Coleman lantern and pack our overnight bags," Haley continued. "Micah will be here at noon–"

"Noon?"

"Yeah, we're all going swimming, then to Gisele's," Lacey said. "We're meeting Taylor at Spot Pond."

"Wait a minute, two *boys* and two *girls,* sleeping out, *unchaperoned?* I don't know about this. I've seen the way Micah looks at you," Grandma Clara said to Haley, who could barely contain a grin. *So, other people notice, too?*

"Grandma, we'll be at Gisele's. She's going to do bed checks all night," Haley said. *But if there's a way...*

"I'm calling her," she said to their exasperated eye-rolls. "Just making sure."

They dragged a small, fully packed duffel bag downstairs and left it by the door.

"Nervous?" Haley asked her sister.

"A little, I guess," Lacey said.

"Got butterflies, or *moths* in your stomach?" Haley giggled, thinking about the one her sister swallowed.

"Ha, ha, ha." Lacey poked her with an elbow.

A soft knock at the door spurred the girls into action.

"I'll get it," Haley said.

"No, *I'll* get it." Her twin giggled.

"I've *got* it," Haley said through gritted teeth. "He's *my* boyfriend. Back off."

Feeling Lacey's dark look on her back, she walked to the door and opened it slowly.

"Hey," she said smiling.

"Hey," Micah said, reaching for her with both arms. She stepped into his hug. "Ready?"

"Of course." She looked down at the duffel bag. They bent at the same time to retrieve it, finding their noses only an inch apart. He grinned at her in a way that suggested he knew something about her that even she didn't know herself. Caught in each other's gaze, they straightened slowly and as Micah picked up the bag, he gave her a provocative smile.

Grandma appeared at the door. "You kids behave yourselves, understand?" she said, her gaze traveled from Haley to Micah to Lacey to include all three in her warning.

~ ☾ ~

"We will," the twins said, as Lacey kissed her right cheek and Haley kissed her left. Micah promised nothing.

"We're invited for breakfast at Gisele's tomorrow morning, don't forget," Lacey said on the way out.

"Okay, have fun and don't cause any trouble." Clara's final warning made Haley laugh.

"If she only knew," she said as the three got into Micah's car.

"You mean that we're about to save the world?" Micah asked.

"Something like that," Haley said. "Hey, let's not talk about it anymore until we get to Gisele's, okay? I just want to have fun today."

"Deal."

AT SPOT POND, they met up with a grinning Taylor, who looked like a vagabond with his every worldly possession stowed on his bike.

"Oh, I forgot you were bringing the tent," Micah said. "We could've picked you up at home."

"That's okay," Taylor said, laughing. "It became a challenge to see if I could get everything on the bike, and still ride it."

"Let's go to my campsite," Micah said.

"Sure, but why?" Lacey asked.

"One word—shade," he said. "If we're going to be here 'til five o'clock, we'll be sunburned, in pain and useless tonight."

"I've been dying to see this private beach Haley's always talking about," Lacey said.

"Let's go." Taylor followed astride his one-man peddler's cart.

"ARE YOU GLAD you came?" Micah asked Haley as they sat on the blanket while the others cooled off in the water.

"Sure, I love your beach," Haley said. *And your eyes and your hair and your smile...*

"No. Are you glad you came this *summer?*" He touched her

~ ☾ ~

cheek. "I think I know the answer, but I need to hear it from you."

She smiled at him. "Best summer of my life."

"Mine too, as predicted." He sighed.

"What's the matter?"

He looked away. "I still wish you weren't a part of this. I'm so worried about you tonight—"

"I don't understand. This is my job and you knew last winter I was coming here."

"My feelings for you then were *not* what they are now." He shook his head.

"You fought for me to do this."

"Let me see if I can explain. Last winter, you were in my mind—all *over* my mind, but that's as far as you got. Now, you're in my heart and I'm in about as deep as a guy can get." He kissed her then, lightly at first, but then deeper and she felt his longing, a longing that matched her own.

Nothing will happen to you while there's breath left in my body.

And then she stiffened in his embrace.

He pulled back. Her eyes wide open, she gasped in surprise.

"What?" he asked. "Is something wrong?"

"I'm not sure." She blinked several times. "But I think...I just heard your thoughts."

Now it was his turn to look shocked. "What?" He laughed, sort of.

"Did you just think nothing would happen to me as long as there was a breath left in your body?" she asked.

"Yes," he swallowed. "You *heard* that?"

"Yes."

"This is...strange. And unusual."

"Are you going to stop kissing me?" She heard the flutter in her voice.

"No, I couldn't do that." He grabbed her shoulders and kissed her.

He leaned back, waiting.

She frowned. "*Pink* elephants?"

"Yep. Hmm. Does this work on everyone, or just me, I

~ ☾ ~

wonder?" He looked at her, then out at the water and sighed. "Who can you kiss that I won't have to kill? I can't believe I'm saying this, but Taylor. You have to kiss Taylor."

"What? No! *Ew.* I'm *not* kissing Taylor. It would be like kissing my brother."

"Haley, this is really unusual. Don't you think we should to do a little research?"

"You'd really want me to do that?"

"No, I don't. I hate the thought, but we should see if it happens with others or if it's just confined to me. Just once and *never* again."

She looked down, not wanting to meet his eyes. She was surprised. Shocked really, at the intensity of his feelings for her. They were easily as strong as her own. *He loves me,* she thought. *And I'm going to call his bluff.* "Okay," she turned and took one step toward the beach before he caught her arm.

"Never mind. I'd like to know, but not that badly."

She laughed. "Lacey would never allow it anyway." *I'm not kissing Taylor. I'll never kiss anyone else.*

"Do you get anything from this?" he said, kissing her forehead. He looked at her, eyebrows raised in question.

"Fruit. *Peaches*, I think, but it was muted," she said, shaking her head.

He grinned. "I was thinking your skin is like peaches and cream."

"This is weird."

"I agree. What about *this*?" He looked down at their linked hands.

She paused, closing her eyes. "No, your thoughts are safe. You know, I think I've been doing this for a little while. I just didn't realize it."

"Why do you think that?"

"Because before, when we were kissing, random words began to pop into my head, for no reason."

"How long?"

"A week or so, I guess," she said, tipping her head as she thought back.

"Do you get pictures in your mind, or..."

"It's usually an aimless word or two"–she paused–"but

~ ☽ ~

this time, I heard, or felt, a whole sentence."

"Either you're getting better at this or we're becoming more in tune with each other," he said.

"Are you nervous?"

"A little," he said. "But I'll live with it," he kissed her again.

"Yes, let's." She stood up.

He raised a questioning eyebrow.

"You just thought, *let's get wet*, right?" She stood, and then winked at him over her shoulder as she walked to the beach.

~ ☾ ~

CHAPTER FORTY-SEVEN

THEY ARRIVED AT Gisele's at around five o'clock, with Taylor chugging in about ten minutes later.

"Micah, would you and Taylor set up the tents, while the girls and I make salads and get the grill going?" Gisele asked.

"Sure." The boys got cracking, pulling out tent stakes, poles and ropes.

During supper the conversation centered on the Red Sox, music, the weather—nothing scary or too controversial. Light fare to complement their burgers and salad. Haley's new ability was not mentioned. Earlier, she told Micah that instead of celebrating her new Gift, what she really craved was a little privacy.

"WE'LL LEAVE AROUND seven o'clock," Gisele said as the five sat at her picnic table, roughing out their strategy. Haley smiled when Micah took her hand under the table. "According to my almanac," Gisele continued. "This month, the moon goes full at one minute past twelve and we must challenge the last rift at that exact moment. I've actually synchronized my watch to match the National Timepiece."

"There's a National Timepiece?" Lacey said.

"Yes, it's called the Atomic Clock in Boulder, Colorado. Anyway, we're synchronized with it so we don't miss our window of opportunity." Gisele said.

"You said, 'this month.' Doesn't it always go full at the same time?" Haley said.

"No, the moon can go full anytime during the day or evening," Gisele said. "And it's only considered full for a short time, then it starts to wane, so timing is critical."

"Wait. Why go in so early if we don't have to be there 'til

~ ☾ ~

midnight?" Lacey frowned. "Are we really going to spend *five hours* hanging around in the forest?"

"Yes. Remember our old friends The Terrors? Do you honestly want to meet them again?" Gisele asked. Her three students responded in the negative with a quick shake of their heads. "It's settled then," she said, and Haley knew there'd never been a choice. "We'll go in at seven–before dark–and check the Altar Stone for tools. We'll need to walk quickly so that we don't have to deal with The Terrors on the way in. Then we'll rest in our safe place until just before midnight–"

"But *five hours*?" Haley said. It seemed like such a long time to sit and wait.

"Afraid of being bored?" Micah asked, raising a playful eyebrow.

Her mouth snapped shut. "No, never."

"*Anyway*," Gisele began again, trying to recapture their attention. "It will take us about an hour and a half to get there. I don't want to walk in full dark, so we need to leave with plenty of time to arrive safely. Expect this to be the most difficult battle of all," she said. "Please be aware of each other as well as whatever exits the rift. Use every tool you were given..."

Haley flinched at her words. '*Use every tool you were given.*' *Where had she heard those exact words before?* Then she saw the look of panic on Lacey's face.

Draculola. She shivered.

"Remember, if we don't succeed tonight, everything–all our efforts, all our fighting, will have been for nothing," Gisele said. "At the very least, Evil and darkness will overtake the forest and maybe more. The stakes have never been higher." They all exchanged looks. "You've all done a marvelous job this summer. You've each brought unique skills, talents and determination to assist in this process and I couldn't have asked for a better team. Do you have any questions?"

"Does this mean we won't get back until one thirty in the morning?" Haley asked.

"Closer to two thirty, I'm guessing. But don't worry. You

~ ☾ ~

can sleep until noon." Gisele smiled to herself.

"Where are we staying until midnight?" Lacey asked.

"In the Dwarf Closet," Gisele said. "It's safe and quiet enough in there to get some sleep. Now, if there are no other questions, you should start loading your backpacks with provisions for tonight. It's almost time to leave."

AT SEVEN O'CLOCK, they stood before the Altar Stone. Haley was gifted with a pouch containing four crystals, one each: red, blue, yellow and green. As she left her old crown and reached for the new one, she brushed against the most unusual crystal Gisele ever saw. A notched five-inch long crystal began to glow, shooting tiny rainbows onto the Altar, their faces, and nearly every tree in the immediate area.

When Haley picked it up she said, "I feel vibrations from my forehead down to my toes."

"Look at that," Taylor said. "It's got a hole down through the center."

The unusual crystal ceased its light show when anyone else touched it but when Haley slid it onto her little finger, Gisele noticed the colors became brilliant, almost blinding.

"Unfortunately, I don't have any more pouches," Gisele said, frowning after a prolonged search through her magic bag. "Can you store it with the new crystals?"

"It's too big for that pouch. I'll put it in with my wand." After Haley stowed it, a steady band of brilliant colors escaped through a tiny hole at the top of the bag and disappeared high into the trees.

"Wow. What do we need a rainbow for?" Lacey asked as they stared at Haley's dazzling multi-colored shaft of light.

"I assume we'll find out tonight but until then, tie that bag closed or we'll advertise our presence to every evil creature in the forest," Gisele said with a chuckle.

Haley retrieved her crown from the Altar Stone while Lacey and Taylor picked up a bag of faceted salt chunks.

"Cool," Taylor said of the giant crystals. "Did you bring your water gun?"

"It's in my bag." Lacey patted her knapsack while she

~ ☾ ~

stashed her salt.

"Waste of time," Haley said. Lacey and Taylor exchanged looks.

Gisele and Micah each accepted a blue-white pulsing crystal. A bewildered Lacey claimed a small pouch containing dozens of tiny round mirrors, while Taylor took possession of a small glowing sword with a gleeful grin. Micah nodded at him.

Chuckling, Gisele claimed an empty mayonnaise jar, which she cheerfully stowed in her magic bag. Her laughter died abruptly and her shoulders slumped when she scooped up two tiny jars filled with a glittery pink liquid.

"What are those?" Lacey asked. "They look like—"

"Never mind. Micah and Haley, leave your spent crystals," Gisele said, digging her own from its pouch. "Return to Source," she whispered to them, before placing the weakly pulsing crystals reverently on the Altar. Taking a deep breath, Gisele gazed at the Altar Stone, empty save for the three spent crystals and Haley's wilted crown. "I hope we've been given everything we'll need to win this last fight. Let's go." *One will fall, one will fall, one will fall,* reverberated in her brain with every step she took. With the addition of those tiny jars, Gisele now felt she knew *who* would fall.

And more importantly, how she could help.

STOPPING ABOUT HALFWAY for a quick break near the stonewall, Gisele asked Micah, "Did the magic work its way out of your system?"

"Mostly, I guess. But I don't think it'll ever be completely gone." He glanced at Haley.

"I for one, will miss it, if that ever happens," Haley said, locking eyes with him.

He leaned forward. "As long as you're here, there will *always* be magic in my system."

Haley tipped her head and smiled. Lacey pointed a finger at her mouth and pretended to gag.

After a long, humid walk, they finally reached the Dwarf Closet, an imposing collection of boulders. *And not a minute*

~ ☾ ~

too soon, Gisele thought. In the forest, night skittered in quickly. Already she could hear whisperings from the forest edges. Soon whispers would give way to growls, then shrieks. "Last bathroom break of the night, folks. Boys to the left, girls to the right," she announced. "Make it quick."

They met back at the opening of the Closet. "Everyone in the center now, and wands up," Gisele said, tapping the doorway.

Emanating from the bowels of the earth came a low, growling rumbling noise as huge boulders shifted and moved toward the center. Lit only by the wands' tiny light, the movement seemed perilous and unstoppable. Gradually, the clear night sky with its twinkling stars and huge full moon disappeared as the rocks reshaped themselves into a rugged ceiling. After a few bumps and lurches, the small doorway merged with the wall. Gisele tapped her wand twice on the ceiling and the group was instantly bathed in lamp-like brightness.

"Everyone, spread out your blankets. Nice and cool in here, isn't it?"

At about ten feet across by seven feet high, the inside area somehow remained blessedly free of mosquitoes and other creepy-crawlies.

"I've set the alarm. Let's all take a nice long nap," Gisele said. "And I'll *know* if there's any funny business."

Micah lay on his side behind Haley, burying his face in her hair at the back of her neck. Taylor and Lacey lay on their backs, holding hands. With a flick, Gisele adjusted her wand to a soothing night-light glow. The darkness did its work. Within minutes, soft, deep breathing was the only sound.

AFTER WHAT FELT like seconds later, Gisele's alarm went off and the game was on. By wand-light, blankets were folded, stowed and wands, crystals, and other tools were readied. Haley stuffed her backpack, trying to steady her trembling hands.

"Before we leave, everyone please hold hands while I ask for the Blessings of the Universe," Gisele said. The kids

~ ☾ ~

exchanged looks, but did as they were asked. Haley looked down, closed her eyes and asked for guidance. Amazingly, when she opened her eyes, thanks to a powerful vision, which included a volcanic type explosion, she knew exactly how and when to use her new crystals, as well as one highly important, very underutilized tool.

JUST BEFORE MIDNIGHT, as protection against The Terrors, Gisele directed that all crystals be brought out, and wands at the ready. "Out there, my crystal will work to protect Lacey and myself. Micah, yours will shield Taylor. Haley has her own, as well as her crown. We move as a unit to the last remaining rift. If you forget everything I told you, remember this—Haley is the key and she must be protected." She tapped the door of the Dwarf's Closet with her wand and grinding began as the huge granite boulders parted, revealing the darkened forest.

This time, though, along with the low crunching, gravelly noises came the high-pitched shrieking, snarling, screaming pandemonium known as The Terrors. Gisele remembered the day the police came to her door asking for permission to search the forest after noise complaints. No one was really sure what made up the cacophony of sounds heard in the forest by night, but its ugliness and raucousness never failed to persuade visitors to leave.

Clinging to each other for support and protection, the small group made their way to the rift, from whose crevasse red-hot sparks spewed into the air like fireworks. As they watched, the red molten coloring darkened to black, then glowed red, before darkening again, giving the impression that the rift breathed.

"What now?" Lacey shouted over the din.

"Are you ready, Haley?" Gisele asked, just as loudly. The girl nodded.

"Then we should begin. Stand well back." Her voice was almost lost as the noises around them swelled. "And Haley"– she locked eyes with her young rift healer, knowing that there wasn't a lot she could do if it all went bad–"be very careful.

~ ☾ ~

We'll be watching." She stepped back, terrified for all her charges, but especially for Haley.

Micah suddenly leaned forward and hugged Haley fiercely as the rest stood around them. He looked at her, his love and concern for her safety obvious. She smiled. "I love you, too."

Gisele checked her watch, then tapped her shoulder. "It's time. *Now*, Haley."

The girl nodded her head as she stepped toward the rift and dropped her pack to the ground. She opened her blue pouch and her red crystal glowed as if it were on fire.

"Stand with me, Lacey," Gisele said as loudly as she could. "Taylor, go with Micah." The bedlam from The Terrors was increasing with every passing second. She wondered how well she'd been heard. Still, everyone took their places. Hopefully, Haley's crown would deflect whatever mythical nightmare snuck by them.

Haley held out her red crystal and the healing began. The cracking, bending metallic noises caused by melding the rift were all but drowned out by the higher-pitched screeching clamor of The Terrors. At the moment she lifted her crystal, a bolt of fire spewed from the rift, sending lines of flame rolling down the mound toward the forest floor.

"Water guns!" Gisele yelled. "Call the dragons!" Her shout burst forth during the briefest pause of ear-splitting shrieks. Lacey and Taylor attempted to answer the command, squirting water at the fiery columns bearing down on them. The water guns weren't just ineffective, a fireman's hose would have been ineffective, the water guns were laughable.

And now the lines of fire were pulsing toward Haley.

Gisele glanced at Micah. "Stay where you are," he ordered.

As the flames began to lick the forest floor, the ground beneath them shuddered and Gisele was never so happy to see those two hell-raising dragons in her life. Pat nudged her, and with his brother, Mike blew a towering blast of flame toward the mound.

Fight fire with fire, she thought with undisguised satisfaction. The dragons' super-heated walls of flame appeared to chase the lines of fire back to the top of the rift. At that point, the dragons' flame curled over the summit,

~ ☾ ~

disappearing within. The shrieking forest noises abated slightly, enough for Gisele to hear a wildly premature celebration from Taylor.

She shot a look his way to quiet him just as three huge black and green beaded salamanders belly-crawled out of the slightly smaller opening in the rift, crests raised, black tongues twitching, testing the air. Blue fire from three wands hit their marks, but served only to enrage the armored beasts, which now focused their attentions solely on Haley, her red crystal a beacon. The bellowing six-foot monsters picked up steam with every second, their heavy bodies undulating as they raced toward her.

"Fire with fire," Gisele breathed, and an instant later, thanks to her dragons, the salamanders were incinerated. Consumed by dragonfire.

Haley then stepped forward, tossing her spent red crystal into the super-heated red-orange molten gulf, which bubbled up and radiated in fiery waves. *How does she know what do?* Gisele wondered.

FIRE SHOT OUT of the rift, fifty feet into the sky and Haley blinked twice, aware of her surroundings for the first time. Afraid but determined, she took a deep breath and reached into her blue pouch. Intuitively she grabbed the small green crystal, which pulsed rhythmically, matching the glowing red to black to red, changes of the rift. The usual grinding noises associated with the healing began anew, as the forest noises ratcheted down a notch. She could barely hear herself think and almost wished that she was unaware of what was happening to her and around her.

Haley watched the dragons, plumes of smoke billowing from their nostrils and felt the earth move with each footstep as they drifted toward the east before fading into the woodland, their service complete. She hoped they would stay, but knew the clearing was too small to hold them and any other Elementals who might be summoned to help.

Her green crystal pulsed in her hand igniting a vibration, a thrumming that reached to her very core. Her senses

~ ☾ ~

heightened, she could smell and taste sulfuric smoke gusting from the rift, hear the muted, guttural mutterings from beings below ground and see every blade of grass circling the rift as it rippled in the crevice's foul wind. Her new awareness felt strange and overwhelming, wondrous and horrible all at once. She raised her hands.

AS GISELE WATCHED, Haley put up her hands to challenge the rift, a short volley of boulders burst forth and were met by the ice-cold, fiery blue blasts from Taylor and Micah's highly charged swords. Out of the corner of her eye, she glimpsed tiny shards of granite showering the group in tribute to their fine marksmanship. *Why hadn't they thought of* swords *last time?* She wondered during the boys' impressive demonstration.

Taylor and Micah were still high-fiving each other when the first troll hauled himself out of the rift, axe in hand. It seemed to her that rather than concentrating on the rift, Haley became somehow distracted when the troll turned, grinning, to face to her.

Gisele had a moment to wonder *is she awake?* before screaming, "Send for the Tinks!"

The troll growled, displaying his yellowed and missing teeth. Standing about four feet tall and barrel-chested, he was possibly the ugliest thing Gisele had ever seen. She stood in shock, gazing at the hairy, filthy creature with revulsion, willing the rift to close. It was one thing to battle monsters, but this brute looked human. He brandished his cruel axe as another joined him, equally as repulsive, the new one laughing and pointing as if amused by these pathetic kids. When he swung his broadsword, it cleaved through the air with a *whoosh.*

They were joined by another, and another. More trolls climbed out of the rift until they were outnumbered four-to-one.

Glancing over her shoulder, Gisele watched Taylor's mouth fall open in shock, his new sword held loosely at his side, glinting in the moonlight. *He's in so over his head,* she

~ ☾ ~

thought.

Gisele and Lacey stood their ground, wands raised. "Don't move, Micah," she yelled at Micah who appeared ready to run to Haley's aid.

"Do they take prisoners?" Lacey asked during a short lull. "It doesn't matter, I'll die first." She took a warrior's stance, bravely aiming her wand as the monstrous horde scrambled, caterwauling down the rift, lending their voices to the pandemonium.

UNAWARE OF HALEY'S protective bubble, several of the savage brutes charged directly at her. Quaking in fear, she stood her ground, crystal pointed at the rift, while the vile monsters wasted time attempting to penetrate her defenses. Using their axes and broadswords, the revolting ogres whacked and hammered against her transparent barrier. Alarmed, she wondered how long it could possibly hold. Still pointed at the rift, her crystal wavered with her fear.

She heard Gisele yell at Micah and struggled to contain her terror. *When will this stop?* She thought as the trolls continued to batter her. Each strike of an axe or sword felt like the one that could take her down and she knew the trolls could read the fear on her face as easily as she could see the triumph on theirs. The light from her crystal dimmed with her cowardice before she closed her eyes and once again threw herself into the healing. She heard a loud boom from the area around the rift that all but drowned out the guttural yells and shouts of the ogres trying to kill her. When she heard the welcome sounds, *phew! phew! phew!* she opened her eyes.

To her intense relief, the Tinky-tinks, whose arrival was heralded by puffs of leaves and tiny flashes of orange light across the clearing, overwhelmed the mob of trolls battering her defenses. The Tinks' mini missiles found their marks and exploded, swiftly transporting the vile ogres to the netherworld and she sighed with relief.

Then a strange rumble that began in her feet and raced through her body came to rest inside her head, forcing her

~ ☾ ~

eyes closed, stopping her breath and in a silky whisper, said, "You'll never win." When it was over, Haley drew in an uneven breath and swiped away a few anxious tears running down her face so the others wouldn't see how unheroic their rift healer actually was.

GISELE AND LACEY backed up Micah and Taylor who were each engaged in a swordfight. At one point, Gisele watched with admiration as Lacey ran sideways and with her wand, tapped and disabled a troll creeping up behind Micah. Then with a deadly shot from her wand, she destroyed another ghastly brute before tripping on a large piece of granite.

As Lacey picked herself up, Gisele thought of the prophesy: *One will fall, one will FALL!*

A giant *Boom!* sounded and Gisele looked up in time to see a portion of the rift cave in on itself, swiftly transporting several screaming trolls underground. Gisele watched with satisfaction as, with his gleaming new sword, Taylor fought and exterminated three of the ugly ogres and Micah vanquished four. She and Lacey managed to vaporized two each. The rest of the trolls were dispatched, due in large measure to the quick work of the platoon of Tinky-tinks.

Haley tossed the weakly glowing green crystal into the still bubbling maelstrom. Flames shot into the air as the token was consumed. For the third time, Gisele saw her dig into her pouch. On this occasion, she extracted a yellow crystal, which shot a steady stream of golden light into the rift.

"Wands up!" Gisele called through the crackling, grating din. Once again, her students faced the mound, bracing themselves for whatever maladjusted horror it chose to serve up. They weren't kept waiting. In deep shadow, nine dark shapes exploded from the rift, widening the chasm as pieces of rock and debris sprayed the ground. Nine bird-like silhouettes screamed across the full corn moon before turning on their tiny human adversaries. Nine black missiles thrust toward earth.

"Call the fairies!" Gisele screamed.

~ ☾ ~

"Blaze-Blending!" Micah yelled, while aiming at the attacking throng. Taylor combined his wand's stream, which together with Micah's, condemned four of the beasts to a fiery hell.

Lacey did not join them, but bent over her backpack. When she finally straightened, it was to toss dozens of small round mirrors into the night.

Gisele watched, open-mouthed, as the flying monsters veered away, crashing into each other. Confused and confounded by the glittery discs, the beasts fell to the ground in a greasy, tangled heap of broken wings, claws and beaks.

At that moment, hundreds of glowing pastel orbs filled the clearing. The remaining earthbound, birdlike creatures staggered about, black as death, awkwardly propelling themselves on bat-like wings, shrieking and snapping their long yellow beaks at anything that moved, spectral orbs included. Gisele watched as the orbs distracted the beasts, giving the humans a viable target.

"Blaze-Blending," Micah called again. This time, with an impressive complement of three blazing wands, four more of the ancient bird-things were destroyed.

AFTER THE LAST spectacular volley of Blaze-Blending, Haley saw Micah, Lacey and Taylor congratulating each other when an unholy shriek split the air. The largest of the pointy-headed, bat-winged beasts, she realized that it had remained hidden on the other side of the mound. The foul creature advanced upon her, its wings raised and beak open. She looked up toward the rift's opening, now blocked by the monster's oily, leather-covered body, leaned to the left in an effort to get past it and was horrified when the monster mimicked her movements. When she then leaned right it screamed and blocked her again, leaving her unable to toss the gold crystal into the rift, the only thing that could end this round of horror. Screaming, the creature pivoted and extended its bat-like wings, clipping her shoulder and knocking her to the ground.

Fear clutched at her heart. Her useless wand was deep in

~ ☾ ~

her bag and her clueless friends were celebrating a victory as the monster advanced on her. She beat back her fear and darted away, just managing to avoid its thrashing wings. Scrambling to her feet, she tripped on a root and her crown, her protection, fell off and twirled out of reach. The monster's head dipped down at her and gouged out a chunk of dirt with its beak as she rolled to her side. Screaming, it raised its beak to the sky before trying again and as she shrank from it in terror, she wondered...was the prophesy for me?

One will fall.
One will fall.
One will fa-
A loud crack!

Over Haley's head, a brilliant flash of light signaled the beginning of a welcome round of Blaze-Blending. She attempted to scurry up the rift, but found herself sliding back down on a raft of loose stones and dirt. Behind her, the creature roared in pain from the direct hit, but though badly wounded, it simply refused to die. Charging after her as she crawled to the rift's opening, the creature thrust its lower beak under her body.

Unable to move, Haley squeezed her eyes shut, waiting for her doom.

Then just before its beak closed, a second turn of Blaze-Blending ended monster's life, with Haley still in its mouth. After a long, shuddering breath, she pushed the beast's upper beak away from her body and with Micah's help, pulled herself out of the its maw.

"Are you all right?" he asked, his voice heavy with anxiety. The rest of the team raced to join them, filled with questions.

"I'm fine." She assured them. "Thank you so much for killing that thing. I thought I was a goner. But I'm so thirsty. Do you have any water?"

"Of course. Here you go, my love," Micah handed her a bottle of water. She took a long drink and wiped her brow. She stepped over the rancid smoldering wreckage, retrieved her crown and tossed the spent gold crystal into the rift.

"Better?"

"Much. Is everyone okay?" she asked. *You can never win.*

~ ☾ ~

"We're doing fine," Lacey said. "But why do you think we're getting a break between opponents?"

"I can feel the brain as it keeps changing appearances to catch us off-guard," Haley said. "And I think it must take lots of energy to manifest new creatures."

"This is a different kind of battle with multiple foes and different rules," Gisele said. "How are you so—awake?"

"I've been trying to zone out while I'm healing, but for some reason I'm as awake and aware as you."

"Every time?" Gisele looked worried.

"Yeah, the battle with the trolls was...interesting." She swallowed, "I was aware the entire time."

"Even when they—?" Micah began.

"Even when they attacked me. I was terrified and what a *smell!* The bubble doesn't protect me from that."

"I'm so sorry I wasn't here to help you," he said.

"It's okay, you were doing your job."

"You're a mess," he brushed off her shoulders, dusty from rolling on the ground and sticky from monster spit. "Eww."

"Yeah, I know. Try wearing it," she said, glancing at the rift, while pulling leaves from her hair. "The hole is a lot smaller now. Our job is almost done, I think."

"Yeah, and you're doing great. How do you know what to do?"

She shrugged. "It came to me in a vision just before we started tonight."

"You're amazing." He kissed her lightly. "Are you ready to finish this thing?"

You'll never win. She nodded and held up her pouch. "Only one left."

"Let's end this. I'll be right there." He pointed to an area twenty feet away, then kissed her forehead. "For luck."

Haley glanced at the others, exhausted, but smiling. She took a deep breath, held up a blue crystal, blinking in the darkness and directed it at the mound's ever shrinking chasm. For the last time, clashing, crashing metallic clamor filled the air. Everyone waited and watched to see what hellish nightmare the Entity had reserved for their final challenge in 'the battle that seems without end.'

~ ☾ ~

CHAPTER FORTY-EIGHT

INTERSPERSED WITHIN THE din, Gisele heard loud clicking noises. She swallowed as huge black claws appeared over the crevasse. The rest of the monster quickly followed, a giant scorpion whose slick, black carapace was at least a yard long. The massive front claws clicked and snapped as an overgrown red stinger bounced over its back. Several more of the black-shelled creatures followed, pausing on top of the mound, clicking furiously as if choosing an unlucky contestant in a game show from the bowels of Hell.

"Call the Undines," Gisele said. *Could these desert devils be conquered by simple water sprites?* The last to be called to service, her tiny water sprites had appeared in her gazing ball opposing the scorpions.

The electric blue fire, which shot out from three wands, proved ineffective against the scorpions' hard shells. The monsters, with six of them now on the forest floor with more exiting the rift, skittered closer, their many eyes focused on the young warriors, whose unproductive wands were now sheathed. Micah and Taylor brandished their swords, reflecting the full moon's dazzling white light back at the menacing scorpions, forcing them to recoil.

Though blinded by the swords' radiance, one of the beasts charged forward. The boys slashed off its claws and stinger, rending it powerless and twitching at the base of the mound. But like mindless zombies, the scorpions continually moved forward, each taking a fallen comrade's place in line. Taylor and Micah stood back to back, readying themselves for the onslaught.

Gisele was delighted to witness the Undines descending through the trees. Overhead, the softly transparent, mint-green, lake-creatures sprinkled the company with water. Less

~ ☾ ~

than a foot long, the delicate water sprites undulated through the air with movements similar to jellyfish, although with their large, clear bodies and long, feathery legs, they were more reminiscent of a fluffy octopus.

Gisele let out a nervous sigh. They already tried water tonight—it didn't stop their previous rivals. But then she observed the scorpions' agitation as the water pelted their hard shells. They began to writhe and thrash about and in their confusion and distress, they set upon each other.

"The salt," Lacey said. "I think it'll finish them off."

With a smile, Taylor pulled a few of the beautiful faceted crystals from his pouch and threw them into the melee at the same time as Lacey tossed hers. The reaction was immediate and devastating. As the scorpions' bodies twisted, buckled and contorted, they quickly entangled themselves into a massive, greasy, snapping ball of melting horror. The warriors carefully approached the mass and were witness to the grim crunching, scratching noises that emanated from within, though thankfully, Gisele thought, the unearthly clicking had finally ceased.

Taylor sighed and turned his back on the disgusting, quivering sight. "We won," he said wearily to the rest. "It's finally over!"

And yet, in that sweet moment of victory, it wasn't.

An errant stinger, protruding from the mass, suffered a last unconscious spasm, and struck Taylor in the middle of his back. Too late to shout a warning, Gisele watched in horror as he fell face-down onto the forest floor.

"Taylor!" Lacey screamed, while Micah dragged him away from further danger. Gisele hurried over, crystal in hand.

One will fall.

One will fall.

One will fall. Though no one said it out loud, Gisele knew it was the common thought. Checking Taylor's injuries, she wondered how she could have been so wrong about the type of injury and who would sustain it.

Out of the corner of her eye she saw Haley toss the spent blue crystal into what remained of the last rift. As Gisele waved her own crystal over Taylor's wound. Lacey sobbed

~ ☾ ~

and wrung her hands. "Hush," she said. "Taylor?"

Almost immediately Taylor stirred. Everyone looked down, ready to welcome him back to the living. And that's when Gisele glanced at Haley and watched with a terror so intense she couldn't even form words. Thick, black serpentine tongues, rose silently, appallingly, into the air before descending the mound in search of retaliation. Haley, her back to the rift, stowed her flowered crown, the one object that could have protected her in this last scrap of nightmare.

FOLLOWING GISELE'S STRICKEN look, Micah turned to Haley just as a thick, black tongue wrapped around her. Haley shook her head in what might have been an attempt to clear it, when the screaming began.

Wand out, and yelling for all she was worth, Selena burst into the clearing, the blue flame from her wand streaking, arcing in Haley's direction.

Micah roared as he stood to confront his murderous cousin. In the time it took to process the attack, Micah had drawn his wand, aimed at Selena and readied to fire, only to have Lacey knock his arm away and spoil his shot.

"What are you doing?" he screamed as he fought for control of his wand.

"Helping her save Haley!" Lacey pulled her wand and began slicing up black slithering tongues, littering the forest floor.

Once Micah realized Selena wasn't attacking Haley, but in fact protecting her, he used his wand to savagely hack the nightmarish slices. Selena and Lacey worked side by side, slashing the monstrous embodiment of evil into pieces. He ran toward Haley.

"Don't touch her or those black things!" Gisele yelled, forced to abandon a semi-recovered Taylor. "The tongues are poisonous."

Micah sheathed his wand and pulled out his sword, a much better tool for slicing through the fragments, while screaming his rage. Self propelled, the severed shards continued to make their inelegant way toward Haley. He

~ ☾ ~

hacked a path closer to her side while avoiding the long pieces of slimy black tongue that rolled awkwardly around the clearing, the largest still wrapped around Haley, lying unconscious on the ground.

"Can I touch her *now*?" he pleaded with Gisele. Most were in the process of dissipating, including the one around Haley.

After spending a long moment surveying the area, Gisele said, "Yes, it's safe. They're gone."

"Haley, can you hear me?" Micah said in an anguished voice he would hardly recognize as his own as he crouched beside her. The random pieces of rubbery tongues were now nothing more than ash spots scattered about the clearing. Micah rolled his girl over. There were burns across her back and midsection. "Haley, wake up," he begged. Her eyes fluttered as she started to breathe again.

Gisele said, "Lacey, go check on Taylor." Sniffling, she ran to her boyfriend, still lying on his side twenty feet away.

"I can't believe she's still alive," his great-aunt whispered. Then she pointed to the stone still clutched in the girl's hand. "Ahh, there's the answer," she said, looking into Micah's eyes. "She carried the protection of that powerful opal. I've never heard of anyone surviving a brush with Devil's Tongue."

"But–"

"Later. You can ask your questions later. She's been envenomated and needs serious magical healing, *immediately*. Pick her up, Micah–"

"Bring me to the rift," Haley mumbled after he picked her up.

"Why?"

"*Now*, Micah, then I can be healed." Her voice was weak, but firm.

He looked at Gisele, who gestured to the rift. "Hurry!"

"After I toss this in, step back," she said. He held her three feet from the tiny hole left in the rift. She looked at the fissure for several seconds.

"Hurry!" Gisele said again.

Haley took a deep breath, then with amazing accuracy, she lobbed her priceless fiery opal into it. "Back up, *back up!*" she said, tucking her face into his chest and plugging her ears

~ ☾ ~

with her fingers.

He withdrew quickly as the area around the rift first heaved, then dropped slightly. Standing next to the mound at that moment felt like trying to stay upright on a rolling log. The earth beneath them buckled and pitched. The noise was deafening, similar to what he imagined would be the sound of icebergs colliding, though he noticed the rift failed to flatten. Still carrying Haley, Micah quickly returned to Gisele's side as the rift noises subsided and the entire clearing began to glow. From the north side, a strangely glowing greenish moss crept, a low luminescent carpet, which grew inch by relentless inch, stretching toward the south where the group stood rapt.

"Okay, I'm done," Haley sighed and her head lolled to one side, in exhaustion or pain, he couldn't tell. At the moment he realized he could hear her, Micah also sensed a lessening in the overall noise level until it finally dropped off. It then appeared to him that The Terrors were being kept at bay somehow, no longer trying to get into his crystal-reinforced shield.

Gisele looked up and said, "This is new. We seem to be surrounded by a bubble of protection. I don't know why, but The Terrors can't get in. Haley, are you able to sit?" Gisele asked, patting a log.

"I think so. I'm so sore." She leaned her head against Micah's chest, grabbing fistfuls of his shirt as she took in shallow breaths. After a few moments, she leaned forward and moaned, "Oooh, my belly hurts."

Micah looked over as a fresh onslaught of screeching, grinding noises thundered from the rift. *It should be flattening shortly*, he thought. He was sure he never heard anything so loud.

"Haley, drink the fairy fizz from this little vial," Gisele said. Micah watched Haley's dazed expression with concern.

"It will turn you, temporarily, into a fairy and Micah will transport you to the Crystal Cave. There you'll regain your strength. It's the only way; otherwise, you won't last very long. Now that the opal's gone, you'll continue to get weaker every second until...well, never mind. Do you understand?"

Her nod this time came with a moan. Though Micah could

hardly hear her, he saw the effort it took for her to respond to Gisele's questions.

"Drink this." Gisele handed her the vial. "Stay a fairy for no more than an hour. This is important. Micah will give you the antidote."

Haley drank the fizz, shrinking and glowing, shrinking and glowing until she was but a tiny pink orb, pulsing weakly in the moonlight.

"The rest is up to you, Micah," Gisele pulled him close to speak in his ear. "Remember, you must whisper to her or you'll hurt her ears."

Micah looked up at the protective bubble, surrounded by The Terrors and thought, *it's almost tomb-like in here, compared to earlier.*

She scooped Haley into her hand and whispered, "I'm putting you in this jar for your own protection. We'll see you soon." She carefully placed Haley, the fairy, into the mayonnaise jar and screwed the cap on. Biting her nails, Lacey paced nervously while Taylor sat on a log and Selena watched with her hands shoved in her pockets.

To Micah, she said, "You'll need to levitate. Go as fast as you can. Take her clothes and here's the antidote. *Don't* drop it! There may still be Terrors out there, so shield yourself with your crystal. Remember, don't speak above a whisper while she's a fairy. We'll wait here for you. Check your watch—you have one hour. Now *go.*"

Micah flew out of the clearing, faster than he'd ever run or levitated, faster than he thought humanly possible. He glanced down repeatedly, distressed at how quickly Haley's glow seemed to fade. While The Terrors screamed at his back, the wind blew his hair into his eyes, blinding him, but it didn't matter. His crystal led the way, heading home, Micah merely a conveyance, the means to an end. Nearly there with the full moon lighting his path, he refused to let himself speculate about whether or not this would work.

It had to. *Haley could not die,* he thought, pressing his lips together in determination.

When he finally reached the pool, he raced behind the waterfall and left his crystal in the Blessing Bowl with a brief

~ ☾ ~

thanks. He fled down the mossy steps nearly dropping the jar, in his haste to reach the crystal alcove and the giant crystal lying on its side. Haley's favorite.

"C'mon out, my love," he said softly as he placed Haley, a flickering pink orb, on the huge healing crystal. "Time to get better." He arranged her clothes next to the vial filled with the antidote and sat on the floor to wait.

~ ☾ ~

CHAPTER FORTY-NINE

FROM THE CLEARING, Gisele and the others watched Micah streak away, holding the jar with Haley to his chest.

"Is she going to be okay?" Lacey said, just before glancing north and pointing her wand at the ground.

"I think so." Gisele squinted. "Is that moss?" She pointed at the luminescent lime-green carpet advancing toward them, an inch at a time.

Lacey, whose wand was trained on the fast approaching moss, turned back to Gisele in consternation. "What should I do?"

"Nothing."

"But, Taylor!" Lacey ran to where Taylor lay on the ground and tried frantically to pull him away from the suddenly encroaching moss, which now crawled against him. "I think I'm too tired to care," Taylor said, rubbing his back as she dragged him, until...

"Hey! It's under me!" he yelled, trying to brush it away with his hands. "It's und–" he twisted, fell back, closed his eyes and smiled.

"Taylor...Gisele, help Taylor! It's attacking him!" Lacey said.

"Calm down, it's on our side," Gisele said.

"What do you mean? It's coming..." Lacey said. The moss swept under their feet and as one, they said, "Ahhhh."

"What's happening?" Selena asked when the mossy matt stopped spreading upon reaching the southern edge of the clearing. "Why does it feel so good?"

"We don't need the crystals' protection anymore." Gisele put her crystal in her pocket.

"Why not?" Lacey's wand hung limp at her side. "And when did it get so quiet?"

~ ☾ ~

Gisele smiled and took a deep breath as another wave of calm spread through her. "This is Peace Moss, which brings with it a feeling of calm and relaxation as well as certain protections. The Terrors cannot breach this barrier." She pointed overhead at the throngs of black beating wings against an invisible bubble.

A few minutes later, Gisele found herself staring at Selena, who was, frankly, a mess. She had cuts and scratches on her arms, hands and legs and her hair looked worse than she'd ever seen it. Even with that, she looked better than 95% of the human population, but...

"So what are *you* doing here?" Lacey asked, eyebrows raised.

"Saving your sister's butt and you're welcome." Selena's arms folded across her chest, her hand tightly grasping her wand.

"And welcome back," Gisele said. "You came at *just* the right time."

"Well, that's more like it," Selena groused. "I can always trust *Gisele* to say the right thing."

"Thank you," Lacey said. "I meant to say that first. Thank you for saving Haley's life. I can't even tell you how much I appreciate what you did"–she paused–"but...what are you doing here, anyway?"

"Well, I felt really bad about the way things...ended, and I knew tonight would be the big fight. I thought maybe you could use a little...muscle." Selena shrugged her thin shoulders.

"But you're so late," Lacey said.

"Yeah, it was tough going through the forest with The Terrors all over me. The Altar Stone left me a crystal so I had a shield to protect me on the way here, but it was so scary even with it. The noises, the wings–it was horrible. I...I even thought about turning back."

"Maybe *that's* why The Terrors weren't as bad as usual," Gisele said. "I'll bet *you* kept some of them busy during the worst part of the battle."

"And you *came*. That's the best part," Taylor said, grimacing.

~ ☾ ~

"What happened to you?" Selena asked. "You look worse than me."

"Stung by a giant scorpion," Taylor forced out through gritted teeth. "Gisele's been working on me with her crystal, but it's awful. I ache like an old man."

"Huh." She turned from him.

Gisele laughed to herself and continued to work on Taylor while Selena spared him as much sympathy as if he'd stubbed a toe.

"I've missed the forest and the battles and *even you guys*, so much," she continued.

Gisele smiled, ignoring the obvious slight.

"But your wand! I saw Micah break it," Taylor gasped in agony.

"The Altar Stone." She hefted her new wand. "This one is stronger and better. No one will ever have to take it from me," she promised. "So, tell me what I missed."

~ ☾ ~

CHAPTER FIFTY

IN THE CAVERN, Haley's light glowed brighter and steadier as she grew in strength. Micah allowed himself to hope everything would be fine as he checked his watch. Only fifteen minutes to go before she must drink the antidote, healed or not. He knew that if she didn't take it before the hour was up, the antidote wouldn't work. Unable to change back to her human form, she would continue her existence as a fairy for about a week. Shortly after that, her light would flicker and go out, both as a fairy and as a human. Timing was critical.

With just ten minutes to go, he was gratified to see her light pulsing, her life force increasing. He leaned against the immense crystal, drawing some of its strength into his tired, aching, bruised body. What a night. It would be another two hours at least before he could get some sleep. If he closed his eyes for a moment..."

They flew open as he grabbed for his watch.

Thirty seconds! She had only *thirty seconds* to take the antidote or be lost to him forever.

"Haley," he whispered, his voice edged with hysteria. "Drink. Drink *now*. Hurry, my love, there's no time to waste."

She drifted slowly to the tiny bottle, hovering over it as if considering what she should do.

"Now, *please*."

She flitted around the cavern, landing on various crystals before returning to the vial. "Haley?"

She drank or inhaled, or whatever fairies do. When the bottle was empty, she drifted to her clothes, brightening and getting larger.

He exhaled and laughed. Her pulsing seemed to be getting stronger and her glow began to expand. "I'll wait upstairs

~ ☾ ~

while you get dressed," he whispered, sighing in relief as he slogged his way up the mossy steps. He looked at the empty stone Blessing Bowl, breathing deeply as his heart slowed to only double its normal pace. If he hadn't wakened when he did, would Haley have taken the antidote in time? He didn't think so.

So she would've died. And all because of him. He *had* to do better for her.

Minutes later, he heard her call.

"WHY IS THE rift still here?" Lacey asked. "It hasn't flattened out like the rest."

"I was just wondering that myself," Gisele replied, frowning with concentration. "Maybe there's something else we need to do here."

"We're not done yet?" Lacey whined. "But it's late and I'm so tired. I could easily sleep right here on the ground."

"I'm not sure, but it doesn't look finished to me either," Taylor said, trying to massage his back one-handed. "What should we do?"

"We'll wait for Haley and Micah to come back before we make any decisions," Gisele said. "I don't want to leave a single thing unfinished here." Watching Taylor turn so slowly and painfully forced her to realize the inadequacy of her healing crystal. Something else would have to be done for him.

"It's not as big as before she threw in the opal," Selena said.

"But it's still not flattened to the ground like the other rifts." Gisele checked her watch. An hour and a half since they'd left. "They should be back soon."

MICAH'S FIRST LOOK at Haley made him gasp. Her face was radiant, almost glowing, though her dirt-smudged clothes hung in tatters and he could see burns on her stomach.

"How are you?" he whispered.

~ ☾ ~

"You don't have to whisper anymore."

"I can't help it. You're glowing and uh–" He knew his mouth was hanging open, but he couldn't seem to close it. He feared any second now he'd begin to drool.

She smiled in understanding. "Oh, that's just Fairy-face, silly."

"Fairy-face?" He scrutinized her and found he couldn't stop looking. His girlfriend was suddenly the most gorgeous creature on the planet.

"It's a glamour, not real, and there's a certain...softness to my face, right?"

"Yeah," he breathed, hungry to take in every unbelievable feature of her amazing face, from her brow to her chin and back again.

"Enjoy it," she laughed.

Even that was sweet!

"It only lasts for a day or two."

"How do you know that?" he asked, still drinking in her stunning appearance.

"Last year, we drank fairy fizz and became fairies for an hour. We looked pretty good for a while."

He licked his lips and nodded. "And how are you feeling? Any pain?" His gaze lingered on her face, her body. She looked so...delicious.

"In here, with all this energy, I feel great. Once we get outside though, I'll need a healing with Gisele's crystal," she said, leaning against him. "Wonder how Taylor's doing."

"Better, I hope. You know when he got stung, all I could think was, it's not Haley, it's not Haley, it's not Haley...and I hated myself for feeling that way." She snuggled closer. He moaned before collecting himself and pulling back to look down at her. "I *really* need to kiss you," he said. "May I?"

"Of course," she closed her eyes and tilted her head back. After a long, lovely kiss, Haley smiled. "Oh yes, that reminds me...about your little nap–"

"What? Oh." He dropped his eyes, ashamed. "I'm so sorry. If I hadn't woken up in time–"

"Don't worry, I forgive you. By the way, I knew how much time I had left."

~ ☾ ~

"You did? But why didn't you drink when I first told you?" He was incredulous, but any anger he might have for what she did, melted away when he looked into her eyes.

"I was teasing you." She grinned and dipped her chin in a playful gesture.

"*What?* I was so worried."

"No need," she said. "We, uh *they,* the fairies, don't require watches. You just *know* when time is up. I would've played all the way until the last second, if you hadn't gone into hysterics."

"Ugh, Well...I...you..."

"Thank you for your concern though." She smiled at him from under thick lashes.

"Thank heavens the magic is mostly out of my system," he said.

"Why?" She slowly licked her upper lip and his control slipped a notch.

Oh, the things he wanted to do to her. "I might not be able to restrain myself," he said, almost drowning in her Fairy-face.

"Who says I want you to?" she asked, clearly unaware of her power over him.

"You do not know what you're saying." He closed his eyes, willing his heartbeat and breathing to slow down. "I'm glad you're only going to look like this for a short time. I know appearance shouldn't make a bit of difference between us, but the way you look right now"–he shook his head before looking at her–"I'd never be able to refuse you anything, *ever!*" He slowly unclenched his fists, fighting to master his impulses.

"Now you know how the rest of us feel about *you,*" she said. "I don't want to leave. I'm sooo not ready, but it's time." She took a deep breath and climbed. Halfway up, her breathing became labored and she stopped briefly to rest.

"Can I help you?" he asked, a little more worried than before.

"Thanks, but I just need to rest for moment. I'll be okay." She resumed climbing and heaved a sigh at the top.

Upstairs, in the cavern's alcove, one large crystal, meant

~ ☾ ~

for Micah, rested in the Blessing Bowl.

"Nothing for me," Haley said. "Good."

Outside near the pool, Micah realized from her expression, that her injuries were becoming more painful. "Would you like a ride?" he offered.

"Yes, but I'm going to have a hard time holding on," she said, lightly rubbing her stomach.

"Don't worry about that." He leaned over and scooped her up like a new bride. "Close your eyes and rest, sweet thing. We'll be there in a minute." He kissed her forehead.

"I love you too," she murmured in answer to his kiss. "To the moon and back."

~ ☾ ~

CHAPTER FIFTY-ONE

"HERE WE GO," he said. No conversation was possible as they tore through the forest, The Terrors shrieking, screaming and beating their wings against his crystal's fragile barrier. They levitated to the clearing, which Haley noticed had a completely new look, with a strange glowing green moss carpeting the forest floor. She saw Gisele waiting just outside, using her crystal to shield her from the brunt of The Terrors' painful attacks. Once inside the now quiet clearing, Micah gently released her to walk, hobble was more like it, to a log where she could rest and see the others waiting for them.

She looked over her head, watching the black shapes batting against the invisible barrier high overhead, "No Terrors? I can actually hear you." After rubbing her hand on the blanket of moss, she took a deep breath. "Ahhh, what *is* this and how did it happen?"

After a brief explanation, "Isn't it cool? It just showed up!" Lacey welcomed her back with a gentle enthusiasm. "And here's your backpack."

"Thanks," Haley faced Selena. "Thank you so much for returning to save me. I don't know what would have happened if you hadn't come back." She shuddered. "I owe you my life."

"I'm so sorry I failed you the first time. Please accept my apology," Selena said.

"I forgive you. And I don't blame you for what you did." Haley glanced at Micah, hoping he would go easy on Selena.

"Micah, I know what I did was horrible and you may never forgive me, but I wanted you to know that I am truly sorry," Selena apologized.

"I hate what you did and I'll never forget it," he glared at

~ ☾ ~

her. Haley put her hand on his arm. "But you saved Haley's life. I won't forget that either."

"Haley, show me where it hurts." Gisele waved her crystal over the area affected on Haley's stomach.

Feeling a little better, Haley stood up. "Why didn't the rift collapse?"

"I don't know. I don't think we're finished," Gisele said.

"Maybe we should ask The Greenman," Micah suggested. "I don't think we should leave it like this."

"Good idea." Again, Gisele used her maple leaf pendant to call upon the Lord of the Forest. And within minutes, he stepped smoothly away from a nearby thicket. "Greetings, my friends. Congratulations, you have fought well. Once more, we of the forest thank you for your efforts," he said before studying the small group of warriors. "But your young ones sustained injuries," he said to Gisele.

"Yes, they fought hard and have incurred wounds, which have proven difficult to heal, even with my crystal."

"Ah, scorpions," The Greenman noted as he looked at Taylor's pallid face. "Come forward, young warrior." He beckoned with a leaf-covered hand.

Wincing, Taylor stood up, the knuckles of his right hand jammed against his back.

"Be well," The Lord of the Forest held his hand over the boy's head.

Taylor took a deep breath in and out before sighing with relief. "No more pain—thank you!" Haley watched miserably while he experimentally flexed different muscles and practically skipped back to his place on the log. "I feel wonderful!"

"And you, little one." He motioned to Haley. She stood awkwardly as he moved toward her. "Devil's Tongue," he said sadly. "Impossible to fully cure..."

Haley gasped and turned to see Lacey look stricken and Micah covering his face with his hands. Even Selena appeared unnerved. Only Gisele smiled.

"..except, of course, by Yours Truly," he smiled and touched her forehead.

She sighed heavily as her entire body relaxed, the muscles

~ ☾ ~

no longer tight with pain. "Nothing hurts."

Completely healed, she gave him her prettiest smile.

"Touched by fairies, I see," he said. "If you wish, I have the power to make that change permanent."

Her breath caught, and again she looked at Micah and Lacey. "Thank you so much, but I think I should stay as I am. For now, at least."

"As you wish. You've done an exceptional job, young healer. And you are almost finished."

"Almost?" she asked, her surprise mirroring that of her friends.

"Yes, you have but one final task before leaving tonight, or should I say, this morning? Due to your nearly fatal injury, the rift's healing was incomplete. Would you be so kind as to accompany me to the mound with your crystal and your wand?" he asked. "You brought your wand, did you not?"

Her shoulders sagged. *Wand-work? There's no one worse at that than me.* "Of course," she answered, rifling through her pack, struggling to locate her wand.

Her beautiful, stubborn, uncooperative wand.

This is going to be a disaster.

"How are your wand-working skills, my little rift healer?" he inquired.

"Not very good," she said. *Horrible.*

"I think your mate was right," he said, eyeing Micah, who smiled with pride at the title. "You were always meant to heal, not destroy. Did you notice that your newest crystal was formed with a hole through its center from top to bottom?"

She nodded.

"Slide it down the length of your wand and it will stop near the base, creating a handle."

She followed his directions and her beautiful wand came to life, shooting rainbow colored sparks from its tip and creating quite the light show when she pointed it at the full moon.

"Wow," Lacey breathed.

"Your wand was incomplete without its crystal partner, thus could not do your bidding," The Greenman said.

She grimaced, remembering the many fruitless hours

~ ☾ ~

spent trying to coax sparks from it. "It worked for Micah," she protested.

"Micah is a supremely talented warrior, even able to create a weapon from an acorn or a blade of grass. But *you* are a Healer. Come forward, please."

They walked to the front of what was left of the final rift, a mound about three feet high, ten feet wide and at least fifty feet long. "And now, my dear, hold your wand, close your eyes and think *heal*," he said. She did as asked and immediately a glowing white luminescent stream of light shot from her wand. When her eyes snapped open, she found herself surrounded by narrow bands of swirling light, which made it appear as though she stood in the center of her own personal rainbow. She was forced backward slightly with the strength of the magic before recovering her balance. The Greenman stepped into her colorful orb to guide her unpracticed hand back and forth over the mound. "Think of it like a sewing machine," he said, green eyes twinkling.

She turned her head and gaped at him.

"Does that make sense to you?" he asked.

Still in shock, she nodded, playing her wand from one side of the rift to the other, listening to the quiet rumble beneath the earth. Her white rope-like ray followed the mound with hardly any direction from her, as if being guided by an unseen force. The rumbling continued even after the mound was completely wrapped in a veneer of light, except for a small fissure. There was a *whoosh,* a long line of raucous screeching black winged creatures were sucked into the gap. The ground beneath her trembled for a few seconds, seemingly from the weight of the light, before the mound collapsed and sunk into the earth. She breathed a sigh of relief as, for the first time in months, it appeared as though she was standing in a typical New England forest under the pale, spectral light of a glorious full moon.

And it was quiet. No rumbling, no shrieking, no Terrors. Just a few crickets and cicadas broke the stillness of the night.

Haley grinned and exhaled. "Is it over? Really over?"

"It is, little one," he answered, before turning to the rest.

~ ☾ ~

"You have fought well, distinguished yourselves and are weary."

No one argued with him.

"And now, I think, you'd like to rest?"

Their heads nodded, eyes half closed. "It's gotta be four o'clock in the morning," Lacey yawned.

"Actually, it's about twelve ten a.m., in human terms," he said.

"*What?*"

"Manners, Lacey," Gisele said.

"Sorry, uh...what, *sir*?"

"Time, as you know it, stopped when the rift was first challenged tonight. It only resumed with this last healing," he finished. "And now, as your reward–"

"Reward?" Taylor asked, his eyes blinking open.

"The denizens of the forest would like to thank our brave human warriors for their successful efforts in eradicating the evil intruders," The Greenman stated as if reading from a proclamation. "Tomorrow, at two o'clock p.m., human time, a Ceremony of Gratitude will be held, in your honor, at the clearing where you partake of nourishment."

Ceremony of Gratitude? Rewards? Haley looked around. They were wide awake now.

"Will you be in attendance?" he asked and smiled as all heads nodded. "Wonderful. I look forward to the presentation. Blessed eventide to you then," he said, motioning to the forest behind them. "You'll notice my phosphorescent moss stretches toward the south. Follow it to the herbalist's cabin and at least for tonight, you will be unfettered by the pests known as The Terrors. Again, you have our thanks. You've far surpassed our highest hopes."

"Are The Terrors gone forever?" Taylor asked, yawning.

"Alas, their confinement is only temporary. Someday, perhaps." The Greenman smiled and bowed his head. "Well done, my friends." He stepped back into the trees and disappeared.

"Wow, let's go before I fall down," Lacey said, yawning and stretching.

"One more thing," Gisele lightly touched each forehead

~ ☾ ~

with her crystal. "One little bump of energy should invigorate us for the long walk home."

She was right. The walk back on the eerily glowing phosphorescent moss was easy, celebratory and merry."And, look." Taylor pointed to the East. "No more lights over the swamp."

By the time they reached Gisele's cabin, their extra energy had waned and everyone was ready to hit the sack. Quick kisses were exchanged as the boys headed for one tent and the girls another. Selena slept on Gisele's hastily made-up couch.

Finally on this, the longest night in the history of the world, Haley was able to relax and fall asleep untroubled by nightmares, visions or even dreams.

~ ☾ ~

CHAPTER FIFTY-TWO

THE FIRST SLEEPY head to hit the bathroom the next morning was Lacey. Bleary-eyed, hair tousled, she spent quite a while in there, finally emerging for breakfast sporting mascara and lip-gloss. Haley, who'd been banging on the door for five minutes, emerged in similar fashion, though with Fairy-face, she knew she looked as pretty as she ever would. Naturally gorgeous, Selena required almost no time at all.

The girls helped Gisele prepare the breakfast feast, the largest spread Haley had ever seen outside the Breakfast Buffet at Jumpin' Juniper's back home. Gisele served ham, bacon, sausage, eggs, French toast, pancakes, muffins, juice, coffee and tea all laid out on a tablecloth-covered picnic table in the clear August sunshine. It was nearly eleven o'clock by the time the boys, clearly enticed by the tantalizing aromas, dragged themselves out of their sleeping bags just in time to sit down and eat.

"That's men for you," Gisele said, laughing. "Eat up, there's plenty."

And eat they did. Except for the sound of cutlery on plates, and the occasional, "This is *so* good!" they ate, refueled actually, in near silence.

Finally, when they could eat no more, Gisele began, "How's everyone feeling this morning? Tired? Happy? Sore?"

"All of those," Haley said. "But mostly relieved." The others nodded in agreement, sipping tea or orange juice.

"Not me," Taylor said, standing and stretching. "I am miraculously free of pain. I think I could run a mile. They should bottle The Greenman cure."

"I've said it before, but it bears repeating—I am so very proud of you," Gisele said, her eyes lingering on Selena.

~ ☾ ~

"Every one of you. The bravery you showed in the forest was extraordinary. Selena, for instance. You stood up to The Terrors—alone, at night, armed with only a wand and a crystal to guide you. Few people would have had the courage to do such a thing. And how about Haley, our incredible rift healer? She was hurt so badly by the Devil's Tongue yet, she still insisted on throwing the opal in to heal the rift. You were so brave."

"Not really," Haley shrugged and looked away. She didn't feel so brave. "*Micah's* brave, and strong. He fought all night, and then when everyone else was resting, he carted me all the way to the Crystal Cave, fighting off The Terrors, waited around for an hour, then carried me back."

"And I'd do it again in a second. But did you see Taylor with his new sword? Totally untrained, yet he fought like a soldier, destroying giant scorpions and trolls. You're a natural, buddy. I can't wait to teach you even more techniques." He and Taylor fist-bumped, laughing.

"*He* was brave too," Haley said with a short sigh. "But, how about Lacey? She was everywhere. She did some incredible Blaze-Blending, tossed the mirrors at just the right time to confuse those ugly birds, and knew exactly when to throw the salt that killed the scorpions." She smiled, "Of course, we would've been lost without you, Gisele. You brought us where we needed to be, directed our movements and knew exactly which Elementals to call. You're the best."

"Thank you, thank you all," Gisele said. "How about a toast?"

They raised their juice glasses. "To age, wisdom, youth and *now*, experience!"

"And I'm so thankful that *this* experience is behind us," Haley said. They clinked their glasses and drank deeply.

"I'm going to clear the dishes away. No, sit," Gisele insisted when the kids rose to help her. "Talk about last night, relive it all you want. Because remember, outside of this little group, you cannot talk about this—either your summer or your experiences here, ever."

Lacey gasped. "To no one?"

"That's right. I'm so sorry, but no outsiders can ever know

~ ☾ ~

how wonderful, how strong and how brave you all are," Gisele said, a sad smile playing on her lips as she stacked the dirty dishes. "That's the price we pay for magic."

"So, I guess Madame Lola's out of luck, huh?" Lacey snickered.

Gisele whirled, banging the dishes on the table, "Madam *who?*"

When Lacey appeared to be too startled to speak, Haley answered for her. "Madame Lola. She read my cards last month at the carnival. She told us to come back next year, tell her about our summer and we'd get another reading for half-price. Why?"

"What did she look like?" Gisele's voice was low, dangerous. Her mood did not seem to improve after Haley's description of the fortune teller. "That was my *cousin*," she spat. "'Much too bee-say,'" Gisele perfectly mimicked her accent, though Haley thought her voice seemed a little shrill. "She already knew what was going to happen."

"That accent! We could barely understand her–" Lacey began.

"She's Romanian, a Gypsy," Gisele fumed. "So, how was the reading?"

Haley shook her head in wonder. "She nailed it, got everything right. Well, almost. She said 'one will fall.'"

"I heard that line, over and over again, when I consulted my gazing ball. It was very unusual because I've never heard sounds or smells like I did last month," Gisele said. "But I think the important part is that we've proven ourselves better than the prophesy. We overcame it and didn't let it define us or our experience."

Haley nodded. "Madame Lola also told us we would have the most dangerous and exciting summer of our lives and"– she glanced at Micah, then Lacey before averting her eyes– "and a few other things."

When she looked back at him, his slow smile made her blush. He leaned close and whispered. "Just try and hide it, my love." In her ear, his light laughter gave her goose bumps. "I have *forever* to get it out of you."

~ ☽ ~

FOR THE NEXT hour, they compared war wounds (Haley had a fading black line across her belly, sides and back, Taylor had a faint red mark on his back, and everyone else showed off spectacular bumps and bruises). Reliving last night's fantastic adventure, everyone had a slightly different point of view, which they related and commented upon.

"Did you know the fairy fizz was meant for me?" Haley asked, knowing she would have been part of the adventure, no matter what.

"I had a good idea," Gisele admitted. "It was so hard to let you go in, but I knew we couldn't possibly accomplish the healing without you. That's why I watched you so closely. It wasn't until the end–"

"I *hated* myself for not being with you at the very end," Micah interrupted.

"Then you would've died," Gisele said. "She only survived with the help of her opal."

"How did you know the fairy fizz was for *her* though and not me?" Lacey asked.

"Last year, when you changed into fairies, you were lavender, Taylor was blue and Haley was pink. It stood to reason, *pink* fairy fizz would be meant for Haley," Gisele sighed. "I tried not to dwell on it, since the presence of fairy fizz meant you could be saved, although... it *did* indicate a fairly serious injury."

"*Taylor* was a *fairy*?" Micah's grin could not be contained. "A *blue* fairy?"

"Shut up," Taylor said to gales of laughter.

"I'm so glad we were able to accomplish our goal. But in hindsight, I exposed you kids to far too much danger. I'll never do that again," she said.

"You can say what you want, but we would have gone in on our own, just so you know," Haley said, fairly secure that she wouldn't have to do it again. Taylor and Lacey nodded in agreement. "Being with you was definitely safer."

"Thank you. It's twelve thirty. Ready to go back in?" Gisele asked to smiles and nods all around. "Excellent. Grab your wands, crystals and water bottles, then we're off."

Haley grinned. "No more crowns for me."

~ ☾ ~

CHAPTER FIFTY-THREE

GISELE SMILED, FEELING pure happiness as they entered her forest. Her calm, peaceful, tranquil forest. "First stop, Altar Stone."

And that's where they found...*six* crowns.

The two circlets decorated with oak leaves, acorns and ivy went to Taylor and Micah, who looked quite mythic. "All you need are a couple of togas," Gisele said with a wry grin.

"You look so handsome, my lord." Haley said. Gisele sighed as Haley arranged Micah's crown, then accepted a pink flowered crown, which Micah, of course, insisted upon adjusting, knees bent, eye to eye. "My fairy lady."

Lacey looked skyward and muttered, "Oh, please."

Selena's crown held yellow flowers. Lavender flowers covered Lacey's, while Gisele's was created with maroon flowers and foliage. Crowns in place, they hiked through a much changed, much more welcoming forest than they had in weeks.

Gisele smiled with relief. This was the forest of her fondest memories, alive with butterflies and birdcalls. She breathed in the pungent scents of fern, cedar and leaf mold.

With the troublesome line quicksand eradicated, their walk was swifter and far more relaxed. Sooner than expected, the little group reached their favorite clearing.

Which was empty.

"Are we early?" Lacey asked.

"No, we're right on time," Gisele said, her head cocked toward the west.

"Where are they?" Taylor looked around the beautiful sun-dappled glade.

"They're here. Have a seat everyone." Gisele pointed to the stump and logs that ringed the clearing.

~ ☾ ~

Tink! Tink!

They exchanged glances, their lips rounded in surprised, silent O's. The earth shook slightly, heralding the arrival of two very large dragons. Pat and Mike snorted, nipped and chaffed each other from outside the clearing. A flurry of pastel orbs floated down from the sky, hovering slightly over their heads, a silent ethereal light show. Clustered around the treetops, water sprites bobbed and floated on the air currents.

Tink! Tink! Tink!

Gisele sighed watching Micah rub Haley's shoulders. Still so captivated by the girl's Fairy-face, he could look nowhere else. So she couldn't keep them apart, so what? From where she sat, it looked more likely that Haley would be the heartbreaker, instead of Micah. *But if they*—Gisele's musings were cut short by the trembling of a large bush at the edge of the glade. Without preamble or fanfare, The Greenman stepped forward.

"Welcome, my friends and thank you for coming," he said in his seldom-used voice. "On behalf of the citizens of the forest I am pleased to offer tokens of gratitude and appreciation to each of you, for your part in the victorious campaign against the curse, which would certainly have destroyed our home. Selena, would you step forward?"

Her eyes wide, Selena stood, took a deep breath and walked to the center of the clearing. "Although banished from the forest, you returned, enduring the vermin known as The Terrors. You did this in order to fight for our forest and in doing so, you saved the life of Haley, the young rift healer." He reached into a small gold pouch, removing two tiny vials filled with a glittery golden liquid. The two bottles were immediately surrounded by a galaxy of softly colored orbs, bouncing and cavorting.

"The fairies would be honored if you would agree to frolic and flutter among them, in their form, for the next hour," he said, holding the vials in front of her.

Selena visibly relaxed. "It's my most secret wish. I would love to."

"Wonderful. Please hold these until everyone has received their rewards," he said, handing her the vials.

~ ☾ ~

"Of course." Smiling, she returned to her place on the log. "Lacey?"

Lacey licked her lips and rose, joining The Greenman in the clearing's center.

"You have learned and improved much in the past few weeks. We of the forest are so moved by your new level of maturity, your confidence and your ability to think on your feet. Under extreme pressure, you riddled out exactly which actions were necessary to achieve victory."

I can't believe how much she's matured, Gisele thought.

"And now, I bestow upon you a most personal gift: the ability to become invisible, to blend with your surroundings, to journey as I do, throughout the forest in seconds. You'll enjoy the freedom of the forest to go wherever you wish, unchallenged and unfettered, for the span of one hour.

"You and you alone, will be witness to all other rewards as they are being experienced in our fields, woodlands and skies. Do you accept this reward?"

"Abso*lute*ly," she said.

"I am honored that you approve. Please be seated." He smiled. "Taylor, please advance."

Taylor strode forward.

"My young friend, in a few short weeks, you have become a superb warrior and swordsman with the instincts of a gladiator. You have impressed your friends and the inhabitants of this forest with your moral courage and your will of iron.

"The dragons would like to extend an offer of friendship and a ride through the forest and the skies this afternoon. Is this compensation agreeable to you?"

"Wow! Yes, of course." Taylor's freckled face was ruddy with excitement.

"Excellent. Please be seated." The Greenman handed him a pair of asbestos gloves. As he turned away, Taylor's grin stretched from ear to ear.

"Micah, please come forward." Gisele's favorite nephew released Haley's hand and stood, squaring his shoulders as he stepped into the clearing to face The Greenman.

"Micah, your fierceness, daring and gallantry in battle will

~ ☾ ~

be legend in our world. You fought with the ease, patience and valor worthy of King Arthur's court. You are a Knight, in all but name. Within your world, there are none who could best you." Tears of pride and joy filled Gisele's eyes as The Greenman's words echoed her own thoughts.

"The dragons' offer of friendship and an afternoon ride has been extended to you as well. Do you approve, young warrior?"

"I do, sir, with pleasure." Micah's smile lit his face as he too, accepted a pair of asbestos gloves before returning to his seat.

"Haley?"

Pausing as if unsure she should be there, she finally stepped forward.

"Haley, our little rift healer. Rarely has someone so outshined our expectations. You are extraordinarily brave."

"I'm not brave," she said, head bowed. "I don't deserve your thanks or gratitude. I shouldn't even be here with them." She nodded to her friends who sat with shock written on their faces. "I could never battle monsters like they did. I'm a coward." Her voice wavered.

"A coward could not have faced what you did, day after day. Without your heroic spunk, stoicism and lion-hearted tenacity, we would be having an entirely different conversation."

"Most of the time I was hardly even conscious," her lower lip quivered. "Then I heard things, terrible things. I wanted to turn and run."

Gisele half rose from her seat and noticed Micah doing the same. When The Greenman motioned with his hand, they sat down again. "But you didn't run," he said. "You stayed and finished your job. No one knew how scared you were. No one knew the Entity spoke to you."

"What?"

"It spoke to you?"

"Why didn't you tell us?"

"It told me I was doomed, that I could never win. It told me it would kill all of you." She turned and Gisele saw tears slide down her cheek. "Half of me was afraid it had spoken to

~ ☾ ~

me and the other half was afraid it didn't," she said. "Just
before I threw the opal into the rift, it pleaded with me not to
and I almost didn't. After I tossed it in, I heard screaming and
shrieks of pain coming from the middle of the earth. Even
when I plugged up my ears, the noise was horrible."

"No one here doubts your courage," The Greenman said. "I
remember your first healing–"

"You were there...Sir?" she interrupted, her eyes wide. "I'm
sorry, Lord."

He smiled. "Little one, except for one brief moment, I have
never left your side."

"But when did you leave?"

"Can you not guess?"

She nodded her head. "Devil's Tongue."

"I, too, let my guard down at a critical moment. I
apologize, Healer."

Haley shrugged her shoulders and smiled. "Forgiven."

"As I was saying, during your first healing, when the
beetles attacked you, it was I who whispered *water gun* in
Lacey's ear," The Greenman said.

Lacey's mouth fell open. "I thought I was going crazy," she
whispered.

"Not at all. The Entity isn't the only one who can whisper
in someone's ear." The Greenman smiled and turned to her,
"You were all so young, so courageous, so willing to fight, yet
completely untrained. It was then *I* chose to whisper in
Micah's ear."

Micah blinked, then sat up straight.

"Does this sound familiar?" The Greenman asked. "Fight
for her, fight for her, *fight* for her..."

Micah's face paled even as he shivered in the August
warmth.

"Do not be dismayed, my young warrior. I did not change
or amplify your emotions when it came to Haley. The love
you feel for her is true and yours alone," The Greenman said.
"I merely convinced you to change Gisele's mind about
allowing Haley to assist in the forest." He faced her. "You
were not up to such an exhausting and difficult task."

Gisele sighed. "I knew that and it terrified me."

~ ☾ ~

"So I sent my unicorn to entice our young ones back into the forest, to test their courage, cleverness and Haley's untapped skills," he said to their shocked young faces. "Lacey also found my opal..." he said and her mouth fell open, "...after I nudged her to look deeply into the pool at the Crystal Cavern. In fact, you were all somewhat manipulated and again, I apologize, but you were needed desperately and it was for the greater good."

"My bracelet?" Haley asked in a low voice.

"Did its job. It enabled you to witness the lengths to which this young warrior"– The Greenman inclined his head toward Micah–"would go to ensure your safety. As he indicated in the past, he is willing to sacrifice his own life to save yours. It was important for you to know that."

The Greenman smiled at Haley. "You have an extraordinary future ahead of you and I hope you will never forget this place. May you know that we will never forget you. Your reward was the most difficult to obtain, but will certainly be worth it. Our benevolent unicorn mare has agreed to something unprecedented in our history. She will permit you to touch her golden horn. This is a rare honor and will enable you to see the world as the unicorns see it, know some of their secrets and feel a bit of their magic. As far as I know, they have never, ever felt the touch of a human. Is this reward acceptable to you?"

"Absolutely. It is far more than I deserve," she said.

"Young healer, I assure you, it is far *less*," his rough voice was serious.

~ ☾ ~

CHAPTER FIFTY-FOUR

"GISELE?"

She sighed as she rose to her feet.

"Ah, Gisele, our teacher. I remember you as a small child, a silly rambunctious, spirited child, always questing, always learning. And then as an adult through your sorrow, you continued to learn and teach. You have always been a friend of the forest. What reward shall we bestow upon you, then?"

"Oh, nothing," Gisele waved her hand. "I've had many adventures and now I'm content to simply watch the young ones enjoy theirs."

"Immortality?" he said. "It is within my realm to offer this to you as I did last evening to Haley. You could live a fairy's life..."

The offer hung in the air.

"Thank you, my Lord," she said. "But I too must decline."

He took her arm, and led her to the far side of the clearing and lowered his voice so only she could hear. "We have been blessed that your remaining months on this plane have been spent in our service. Can I do nothing for you?"

"Do you have a cure for me?" she teased, her voice softer than a breath on the wind.

"Alas, I can change your shape, but not your human fate," he answered, his leaf-green eyes sad.

"Very well, may I keep the Leaf Medallion?" she asked. "That I may call upon you, if needed?"

"Of course."

"That's really all I ask then," she said. "But I am anxious to witness their rewards." She nodded her head toward her students sitting yards away.

"As you wish."

They walked back to where the kids sat, excitement on

~ ☾ ~

their young faces.

"Micah and Taylor, Gisele's dragons would love to give you a walking tour at fifteen feet above the forest floor and a flying tour at about one hundred feet. Hang on tight and enjoy yourselves."

The boys excitedly donned their fire-retardant gloves. The dragons ducked their heads, allowing the teens to clamber up their necks to a natural perch where they sat, ready for their adventure to begin.

"Bye. Have fun," the girls called, waving.

"I'd wave, but I'm too afraid to let go." Taylor laughed as the dragons lurched to their feet and sped into the forest. Pat and Mike shook the earth, knocking over trees and shrubs in their haste to get into the air.

"Selena, you may drink your fairy fizz now," The Lord of the Forest said, positioning an hourglass on the log next to the antidote. "You must drink the antidote *before* your hour is up. Do you understand?"

The girl nodded, shivering with excitement. She tossed down the concoction and shrank to a pinpoint of amber light before joining a few dozen new friends whirling around the clearing. As the only fairy with golden coloring, Selena was easily spotted amid the growing throng. The cluster of fairies made a couple of test passes, seemingly readying her for the trip, then they were off, cavorting wildly through the trees, spinning and swirling–a softly colored, ever-changing work of art in flight.

Those remaining in the clearing watched until they frolicked out of sight.

"Haley, your reward lies just a few yards away. The unicorns are highly protective of their privacy and prefer to meet with you in the western glade." He gestured to his left. She smiled, nodded her thanks and walked in the direction he indicated.

"Lacey, it's your turn," The Greenman said, handing her a small bronze disc on a thick chain. "As soon as you put this on, you'll begin to feel *changed*..."

She slipped the chain over her head. "I'm hum-m-m-ming and vibraaaating. Thh...iiii...s-s-s...iiizz...w...ee...ir...d," she

~ ☾ ~

stammered.

"Speaking will improve with practice," he said. "However, you have but one hour and I wouldn't waste it trying to speak when there are so many wonderful things to see. By the way, your eyesight and hearing are many times more acute than you are accustomed to. Keep your distance from the dragons. If you are near them when they roar, you won't be able to hear for a week."

Lacey grinned, looking around the clearing.

The Greenman continued, "For invisibility, just imagine, *I have all the features of these leaves, that rock or this brook,* and you will. No one, not even I, will discern a difference. When you want to appear somewhere in the forest, concentrate on a feature, such as the waterfall at the Crystal Cave or the birches at the Ladyslipper Garden and you'll be transported there. Lastly, remember this stump when it's time to return, else you'll suffer a long walk back. Off you go now. Enjoy your reward."

Gisele watched Lacey grin as she leaned back into the foliage lining the clearing. For a few seconds, only her eyes and smile were visible. Then even they were gone.

"May I broach the question that preys on my mind?" The Greenman said while he sat alone with Gisele in the clearing.

"Of course, Lord," she said, though she thought she knew what would come next.

"Why will you not accept my offer of immortality?"

"I don't know," she began. "Maybe because I'm so tired–"

"As a new fairy, fatigue is virtually unknown," he said.

She smiled. "Or maybe, just maybe, I cannot wait to see my Tony again."

"Ahh, the young man of your adolescence," he said. "The scoundrel."

"Yes, I've learned nothing in sixty years."

"Well, you're *only* human," his voice rasped. "But we will miss you."

"How much time do I have left, do you know?" she asked, her voice a study in nonchalance.

"I do know, but I'm not at liberty to share that information with you or any other human. But if–" He sighed. "I'm sorry.

~ ☾ ~

I'm needed elsewhere. I'll return presently."

"Is there a problem?" Gisele asked, on alert for trouble.

"Not really. Lacey's stuck in the waterfall. Humans, especially human *children* are so predictable." A raspy laugh sounded in the air next to her, and then he was gone.

~ ☽ ~

CHAPTER FIFTY-FIVE

HALEY WALKED IN a westerly direction for a few minutes to a sunny spot awash with soft green grasses bending and swirling in a light breeze. She saw, glistening in the sunshine, in grass up to her hocks, the mythical unicorn mare, her horn sparkling as she tossed her beautiful head.

Haley approached slowly, watching the unicorn paw the ground. She stopped ten feet away, waiting for the mare to become more acclimated to her presence. The luminous white creature snorted several times, ducked her regal head and moved forward, stopping at Haley's side.

Mindful of the mare's nervousness, she gently rubbed the soft snowy shoulder. After a moment, when this seemed acceptable, she maneuvered her hand closer to the animal's muzzle, inviting a sniff. Instead, the mare nodded her head, actually placing her horn upon Haley's outstretched hand.

Immediately, magical images flooded her brain. She now perceived the forest and its foliage in a completely different way. Colors appeared richer, more varied, the life essence of each stalk or branch obvious as it pulsed with its own vital energy. Each leaf or blade of grass stood outlined in a kind of glitter, which raced, flickering and sparkling, up one side and down the other. The unicorns, she discovered, lived in a truly magical world. As she maintained contact with the horn, she felt a gentle pulling, a teasing of her own mind and memories.

The unicorn was reading *her*, too. A varied collection of her thoughts and feelings from this extraordinary summer reintroduced themselves—love, fear, elation, betrayal...

Haley felt as though she'd never known another creature so well. She absorbed the mare's emotions, her own fears, devotion to her mate and their foal, even her annoyance with the Tinks, as if that irritation were Haley's own. She decided

~ ☾ ~

she'd never look at the Tinky-tinks the same way again. *Little buggers.*

The swirling, dancing colors of the sky seemed like a fiction of the mind. She could actually *see* ultraviolet light streaming through the clouds, re-coloring the forest. And then, a memory: Gisele surrounded by a glittery purple aura. Lacey sported a pale lavender with a blue tint, while Taylor's blue aura was edged with lavender. *Is that why they're so well matched? Because of their compatible and blended essences?*

In this memory, Selena's aura was yellow. Standing next to Micah, everything about her including her essence, attempted to blend with his, a beautiful twinkling teal. In a moment of blazing clarity, Haley realized that *she, herself* became the spoiler as her own aura mingled perfectly, harmoniously with Micah's in exactly the same shade of shimmering teal.

Soul-mates.

In that one, sparkling moment, she saw that for all Selena's beauty and talent, she could never compete with the unwavering life connection shared by Haley and Micah.

Micah was right.

The *fortune teller* was right.

They belonged together. She laughed softly when she realized that it only took the memories of a *unicorn* to reinforce all she knew about Micah's feelings for her.

Best reward, ever.

A quick gust of wind stirred pinwheels of color through the grassland. She dropped her hand, which broke the connection and instantly transported her back to the familiar glade, while still beautiful, was no longer extraordinary.

"Thank you," she whispered. The mare bowed her snowy head, turned and trotted into the forest. As the foliage closed behind her long silky tail, the high whinny of her foal reached Haley's ears, making her smile.

A blissful, radiant and forever-changed Haley rejoined Gisele in the clearing.

"Did you enjoy yourself?"

"Oh, yes. It was amazing," Haley said, closing her eyes as she relived the experience. "Did you know the unicorns see

~ ☾ ~

you with an amazing purple aura? It's really quite beautiful."

"No, I didn't. Thank you for sharing that with me." Gisele sighed.

"You sound sad. Is everything okay?"

"I'm fine. Just contemplating the benefits of a peaceful forest."

Without warning, the clearing filled with hundreds of tiny softly colored orbs swooping, dipping and whirling, a frenzied iridescent kaleidoscope of nature. A single golden orb separated itself from the rest, lighting on a pile of clothes next to Gisele. With just a few grains left in the hourglass, the orb ingested the contents of the tiny bottle. The change happened quickly. In seconds, Selena grew into her clothes, laughing, exhilarated...healed?

Haley couldn't stop looking at the devastatingly gorgeous girl. Fairy-face turned the already beautiful Selena into Miss Universe. Micah would be back soon. Soul-mate or not, would he be enticed by this beautiful temptress? To make conversation, she asked, "Did you have fun?" though the answer was obvious.

"Mmmm, oh, yes. And I learned a lot, too," Selena responded, glowing. Haley felt positively *dowdy* next to this vision.

"Really? What did you learn?" Gisele asked.

"I discovered that I have yet to meet *my* true love, but it will happen soon," Selena replied and looked at Haley. "And that Micah was never meant for *me*. You know, fairies are smart and fun. But mostly they just laugh and giggle. I could not have chosen a better reward. It was just what I needed." She sighed and closed her eyes.

Haley sighed, too, with relief. "That's how I felt, too."

"Are you feeling better?" Selena said.

"Yes, thanks."

"None of us thinks you're a coward, you know. Even me." Selena smiled.

"That means a lot," Haley said. "Thanks."

At that point, the leaves of the nearby foliage began to quiver. As they watched, Lacey and The Greenman materialized, stepping away from the bushes.

~ ☾ ~

Lacey grinned sheepishly. "Screwed up again."

The ground rumbled as the dragons broke through the trees and into the clearing. "The boys are back," Lacey said. Micah and Taylor dismounted with the easy grace of those who'd spent their lives around magical creatures. Laughing and flushed with pleasure, they patted and hugged the dragons, who reciprocated by dipping their massive heads to their new friends.

"Whoa," Taylor said as he waved to the retreating dragons. "That was a blast."

Grinning, Micah strode through the clearing. "Hello, Fairy-face." He walked past Selena, eyes trained on Haley. He grabbed her hands, pulled her to a standing position and kissed her gently. "I saw you with the unicorn," he whispered. "Did you have fun?"

"Yes, it was wonderful," she said, hugging him. "I wish you had been there to share it with me. I'll tell you all about it later." They sat down, holding hands. Smiling, Haley happily imagined their auras merging.

"Welcome back, my friends," The Greenman said. "I trust you enjoyed a fun and informative reward?"

They nodded enthusiastically.

"Summer's end is upon us and most of you will be returning home. We pray you will revisit us soon and grace our woodlands. Until then, I must take my leave. Many thanks for your heroic work this summer and many blessings. You have our everlasting appreciation for what you've accomplished here." He bowed his noble head, stepped back and once again, disappeared into the forest.

"Did you have a good time, boys?" Gisele asked her grinning students.

"Amazing, incredible, fantastic," Taylor said. "We saw the ponds, the waterfall, the Ladyslipper Garden, Haley and the unicorn. All from a hundred feet in the air."

Lacey let out a long sigh. "Best summer, ever."

"You said that last year," Haley teased. "I agreed with you then, too."

"It's probably time we all got back," Gisele said. "Before they send the posse out looking for you."

~ ☾ ~

"Yeah, I guess you're right," Taylor agreed reluctantly. "We've probably been gone from home for about thirty hours."

Haley nodded in agreement while strapping on her backpack as they exited the clearing, the place where so many of their wild exploits began. "What was your reward like, Lacey?" she asked as they walked.

"Two words: in-credible," her twin said. "When I was a tree, I felt the sap running through my arms and legs. What a sensation! Then, I was one of the crystals in the Crystal Cave. The energy was *phenomenal*. I saw you for a few seconds as I was zipping through the trees in the glade. I *caused* that breeze, by the way—"

"That was *you*?"

"Yeah, how cool is that? I watched as you touched the unicorn's shoulder. What a powerful moment." Lacey turned to Taylor. "I could go everywhere and I could see *everything!* It was amazing. I saw the unicorns from a half mile away, I saw Tinky-tinks on practically every surface. I even went underwater with the giant carnivorous frogs—*that* was a little scary—"

"You did *what?*" Taylor said. "You went *near* those horrible things? Ugh. Please don't do that again. *Promise* me you won't go near them again. I *hate* those things." He shuddered.

"You fight trolls and scorpions, but giant frogs creep you out?" Lacey giggled.

"Never mind. Promise you'll stay away from them?" He looked quite serious.

"No problem," she laughed. "Did you know there are, like, dozens of Tinky-tinks hidden throughout the clearing? And why have we never seen those tiny translucent tree frogs clinging to the undersides of the jewelweed? I screwed up, though. I got into the waterfall and couldn't get out. The Greenman had to rescue me," she said with an embarrassed grin. "I never had so much fun in my life. So, how was yours, Hayseed?"

"Pretty wonderful. The unicorns see auras around everything, even plants. She showed me yours. It's lavender."

~ ☾ ~

"I love lavender."

"That's probably why you like it so much. Their world is so beautiful. I can still see it if I close my eyes..."

"What color is *your* aura?" Micah asked, his lips close to her ear.

"A glittery teal," she replied, looked away, then came to a decision. "Exactly the same color as yours."

"Really? A combination then, of blue and green?" he asked, staring at her. "One of my favorite colors." He smiled.

"Mine, too. How was your ride? It looked like a blast."

"Really wonderful," he said. "It was fun, inspiring, exhilarating and so much more. I wish you could've joined us. Did you know there are mermaids in the lake? The view from a hundred feet is so different than from down here."

"Was it hard to stay on, with all the wind?" she asked, quickly moving the subject from mermaids. She wished she'd been flying with him. Oh, but she needed her reward. Even now, the mare's sweet thoughts came back to her...

"No, it was easy, comfortable. I'd love to do it again," he said.

"Maybe you can go up again after the *next* crisis," she said laughing.

"Don't even *suggest* such a thing!"

The pungent scents of sweet fern and juniper filled Haley's nostrils. The forest was back once again. A fragrant and welcoming sanctuary.

THEY REACHED GISELE'S clearing and she blew out a sigh as she sat down at her picnic table. "Home, sweet home. My young friends, I'm dead tired. Can you break camp and head out on your own? I need a shower and a long nap."

"Of course, Gisele." Haley was by her side in a moment. "Do you need help?" The others crowded around her now, concern evident on their faces.

Their energy is still high, Gisele thought as she breathed it in. During times like this, she thought she might breathe her last...but no, her strength was returning.

A gift from the kids.

~ ☾ ~

"Please don't worry about me. I just need a rest." She waved them off. Still, Micah and Haley walked her to the cabin and made her a cup of tea. She checked her messages and found one for Taylor. "Micah, would you get Taylor for me? He needs to call his father."

"Sure," he said and returned minutes later with Taylor who assured his father everyone was fine and he'd be home a little later.

Gisele sat at the picnic table, hearing snatches of conversation as they packed their belongings. Normal teenage kids, sharing fantastic adventures. What would it be like when they returned home to homework and laundry? Would this thin ribbon of intense experiences be enough to bind them together throughout their years? Would they remember and keep this in their hearts and minds all their lives like she did? Or would they cast them away, burying the memories like her cousin and former comrades did? And would they, *could* they stay in touch with each other? She hoped so, but she'd be long gone by then. That was the *only* thing she could guarantee.

~ ☾ ~

CHAPTER FIFTY-SIX

HALEY AND MICAH stowed most of the equipment in his backseat. Micah pulled Taylor aside. "We'll drop off the tents and stuff at your house, then the sleeping bags at Mrs. Miller's. After that, you and Lacey are on your own. I need a little alone time with my girl." He looked at Haley sitting in the car, his eyes softening.

"We've got plans as well." Taylor glanced at Lacey by the picnic table. "She's going to be gone soon and I can't miss a moment with her."

"What is it with these Miller girls? I can't think of anything else."

Taylor shook his head. "I know what you mean. I always assumed I'd go to Pittsfield State. But last week I decided—it's Worcester State or nothing. I can't stand to be away from her and last year was pure hell. I haven't told her yet, but I've saved up almost enough for a car."

"Congratulations, man." Micah clapped him on the shoulder and shook his hand. "You've been a great partner in all this and no one deserves it more. Oh, and you have amazing taste in women, too." He looked toward the car. "I'm in about as deep as a guy can get."

"I know what you mean." He paused. "Micah, I just wanted to thank you for this summer. I knew nothing, but not only did you let me stay and help, you taught me everything I know. There's real magic in this forest, even a down-to-earth guy like me can feel it. I wouldn't trade this summer for anything."

"SO, TOMORROW'S YOUR birthday. Big fifteen. Do you have any plans?" Micah asked after they spread their blanket

~ ☾ ~

at his small beach.

"Just with you."

"Oh, they won't let me keep you all to myself for the whole day, will they?" Though he tried to sound playful, he was quite serious.

"No, I guess not," she sighed.

"I want to be with you as much as I can, whatever I'm allowed," he said. "From now on, I want to share as many of your special moments as I can."

"Same here."

"Do you mind getting your birthday present a day early? It requires explanation and I'd rather we were alone."

Her eyes grew wide. "Uh, I don't mind."

From his pocket, he pulled a gold ring. A stunning, light-green faceted stone sparkled, flanked on either side by a gold oak leaf. In the center of each leaf, rested a small blue stone. Reaching for her right hand, he said, "This is a Peridot, your birthstone. I got the darkest one to match your eyes, but it still isn't nearly as beautiful."

She swallowed hard. "And the other stones?"

"Blue Topaz. The clerk said they match *my* eyes." He looked at her.

"She was right."

"This is not an engagement ring," he said. "It would be foolish to propose marriage to a fourteen year old girl." He paused, tilting his head slightly as if reconsidering. "'Course, a *fifteen* year old might know what she wants. But still, shall we call this a friendship ring?"

She opened and closed her mouth, twice, before nodding in agreement.

"The deepest, most profound friendship with the bravest girl I've ever met," he continued, slipping it over the knuckle of her right ring finger. "Do you like it?"

She smiled with love and gratitude. "It's incredible. When did you get it?"

He sighed. "On one of those weekends you were kidnapped by your father, I was at the Pittsfield Mall killing time until I could see you again. I stopped at a jewelry store hosting a 'Design Your Own Ring' Promotion. Since your

~ ☾ ~

birthstone is a Peridot–did you know that, by the way?"–she shook her head–"and since I'm so fascinated by your eyes, I thought it would be a nice choice. The clerk suggested the Topaz. Bigger commission for her I guess..."

She moved her hand in the sun, watching the facets sparkle. "The leaves?"

"Represent the forest you rescued."

"*We* rescued," she corrected.

He shrugged. "Does it fit okay? It was just a guess on the size."

"It *is* a little loose," she said, as the top-heavy ring slid sideways on her finger.

"We can have it sized, no problem," he said. "But let's try something–for now." He removed the ring, then placed it on her left ring finger.

"Perfect fit," he breathed.

She nodded her head. "Perfect."

He leaned down and kissed her before wrapping her in a tight hug. His breathing quickened to almost panting with his desire for her.

She's only fourteen, Micah 'the gentleman,' thought with longing.

*But fifteen tomorrow...*the 'pleasure-seeking, hormone-filled rogue' responded.

No, he decided with a wistful sigh. *I will forever aspire to find in myself the honorable man she deserves.*

~ ☾ ~

CHAPTER FIFTY-SEVEN

ON THEIR BIRTHDAY, Haley woke Lacey and they stumbled down the stairs in their old bathrobes, unwashed, half-asleep, lured by the scent of their favorite breakfast-- pancakes topped with strawberries and whipped cream.

Only to see two special guests.

Micah and Taylor sat, grinning, at the kitchen table. As one, the girls turned and raced back upstairs, more than a little annoyed by Clara's birthday trickery.

Their grandmother's laughing comment followed them up the stairs. "I just thought they'd like to see what you *really* look like in the morning."

Fifteen minutes later, faces scrubbed, hair arranged and *dressed*, for heaven's sake, they returned to their impromptu birthday party to accept birthday wishes. Their gifts were worth the wait and most of the embarrassment, Haley thought.

Clara gave her granddaughters each a $100 Gift Card to the Mall. "Buy whatever makes you happy," she said, waving her hand. "I never know what teenagers want."

From Gisele, ("Sleeping in today," Clara informed them) a huge assortment of home-crafted teas and a half-dozen herbs to plant in their garden at home.

From Taylor, a crystal heart necklace. Lacey blushed as he helped her put it on.

From the group, came an 8"x10" photo featuring Gisele, Clara and the two boys. They would celebrate again, Haley knew, with her parents the following weekend.

Not a bad haul.

LACEY LOOKED UP from her beautiful pendant to Micah,

~ ☾ ~

expectantly.

"Forgot about it, huh?" Taylor laughed, lightly punching Micah's shoulder.

"Um, no," came the curt reply.

Knowing Micah would enjoy releasing the air from this particular balloon, Haley smiled and uncovered her right ring finger.

Lacey and Grandma Clara gasped.

Taylor's face fell three stories.

"That's *gorgeous!*" Lacey exclaimed, grabbing her sister's hand for a closer look.

Grandma's reaction was pure Mom. "What kind of ring is that?"

Eyebrows up, Haley responded. "It's a friendship ring, of course."

"Not *engagement?*"

"Not even pre-engagement, Mrs. Miller," Micah assured her, his arm around Haley's shoulders. "She's only four"–he smiled, correcting himself–"fifteen years old."

"Why green and blue?" Lacey asked.

"Our favorite colors," Micah said quickly, a hint of a smile for Haley.

AN HOUR LATER, Haley and Micah stopped in to see Gisele, who greeted them warmly, her cabin smelling of fresh-baked maple sugar cookies and orange spice tea. After Haley thanked her for the birthday gifts, they reminisced about their day of rewards, The Greenman and this, their most dangerous and exciting summer.

"I understand there's a ring?" Gisele asked Micah, her eyebrows raised in mock anger.

"Word travels fast," Micah said.

Haley held out her hand. "It's a friendship ring."

"Uh huh." Gisele looked over her glasses perched on her nose. "It's beautiful. Peridot is a wonderful stone. It promotes openness and acceptance in the matters of love and relationships. And Blue Topaz is known to be a stone for true love and success in all endeavors. Lovely choices, Micah."

~ ☾ ~

"I know I wasn't your first choice for Haley—"

Haley's startled gaze went from Micah to Gisele and back again.

"I was afraid you'd hurt her."

"Never. I promise."

FROM THE CAR, Haley watched Gisele waving good-bye from her tiny porch and said, "Darn, I forgot my sunglasses." Jamming them in her pocket, she jumped out. "I'll be right back." *Just one more hug, then I can leave.*

"Did you forget something?" Gisele asked when Haley brushed by her. Her old teacher stepped inside, eyebrows raised in question.

"I just wanted you to know." Blinking back tears, Haley held onto one of Gisele's ladderback chairs as she paused to collect her thoughts. "You mean so much to me—please take care of yourself. I don't know what I'd do if anything happened to you." It all came out in a rush as she tearfully hugged her friend and mentor.

The old woman laughed and pulled away to look her in the eyes. "No one lives forever, child. My time on this plane is winding down, just as yours is beginning."

"No."

"You still have much to do here, most of it without—"

"Haley, do you need help finding your sunglasses?" Micah called from beside his car.

"She's coming, Micah," Gisele called.

Haley sniffed back a few tears and smiled, "Best summer, ever. I'll remember it for the rest of my life."

Gisele nodded. "So will I."

Haley pulled her sunglasses out of her pocket. "*Please* take care of yourself."

"You should go now." Gisele looked toward the door. "Your life together is just beginning. He vaits for you."

THE END

~ ☾ ~

Diane Haynes

Diane Haynes' dreams have always been rich in imagery and storyline.

She grew up drawing, painting and sculpting. Writing was relegated to the occasional short story or reports written while working with disabled adults. But on the morning of her brother's birthday, seven months after his passing, when she woke with the incredible fantasy of a girl turning—temporarily—into a fairy, she knew she had to get it down on paper.

A few days later, dissatisfied with a mere twelve-page short story, she set on a mission to expand it, creating the tale that would lead to her climactic dream. Years later, she considers RIFT HEALER to be a 'spirit-gift' from her brother.

Diane lives in Central, Massachusetts, where she and her husband care for their special needs friend, Richard. Their home also includes two rescued Basset Hounds, Basil and Ruby, whose sad pasts do nothing to diminish their spirit, or their willingness to be naughty.

Acknowledgements

I had lots of support when writing this book, starting with my friend and mentor, best selling author Annette Blair. She helped me to understand the rules of writing while guiding me to refine my writing technique and find my voice. When I felt like giving up, she became my cheerleader, full of encouragement while generously sharing her time and talent. She's a wonderful person who deserves every bit of success she achieves.

Deepest appreciation goes to the folks at Crescent Moon Press. To acquisitions Editor Donna O'Brien, who read my manuscript and saw its potential. To Ty Johnston, who found its mistakes. To editor Kathryn Steves who rode in on her white horse to save the day. Marlene Castricato proved she could work her own magic when things get scary. Finally to publisher Steph Murray, who brought a talented staff together.

Artist Taria A. Reed's Cover rendition of a dark and mysterious forest fit in perfectly with what I imagined.

Astute comments came from my readers: Gabbie Savage, Crystal Clarke, Tammy Van Wart, Sue Snow ("It is good, you are a writer"), J. Barry Winter, Tracey Simpson, Trish Herholz, Kimberly Farina, Lisa Rossetti and Teri Jessen, all of whom repeatedly assured me the book was not crap.

Karen Snow, Jamie Desmarais & John Desmarais also read, typed and provided technical support. In addition, Gabby helped with the website, book trailer and my many computer questions as well as talking me through my attempts to e-mail queries, manuscripts, edits and attachments. Computers remain a mystery to me to this day, though admittedly it's a bit easier now that I have a Mac.

Thanks to my friends, Medium Gary McKinstry for his invaluable advice on wand-work, levitation and certain types of glowing moss and to Melissa Nelson for her expertise with the Tarot.

My "Plot Princesses," Serena Smith and Jamie Desmarais deserve a mention here. They came up with wildly implausible situations that, when shaken up and stirred somehow managed to sound adventurous and fun.

Thanks to my friends and customers at Some Enchanted Evening who patiently waited "just a moment" while I finished writing a line, and those who kindly offered to listen while I read them a new one. Many of these added their names to the list of those wishing to buy the book. I love you guys!

To my parents, Dick Desrosiers and Claire Burack, thanks for telling me I could do anything. This book is my 'anything.'

Thanks to Atty. Phillip Stoddard who generously lent his legal expertise and for Sharon, super efficient and always cheerful.

Last of all, thanks to my husband, Kevin, with whom I could finally be myself. You held down the fort during the years of writing and editing, often making dinner while I was immersed in my story. You did good, Sweetheart. Tonight, *I'll* cook.

CPSIA information can be obtained at www.ICGtesting.com
Printed in the USA
BVOW082105301112

306853BV00001B/2/P